DADDY

JERÉ ANTHONY

Cover Designer: QAMBER Designs & Media, www.qamberdesignsmedia.com

Editor: Jovana Shirley, Unforeseen Editing, www.unforseenediting.com

Developmental Editor: Heidi Shoham

ISBN-13: 978-1-7368195-9-3
978-1-7368195-8-6 (ebook)

For all the brats out there searching for a book daddy
to put them in their place...
I've got you, babes

AUTHOR'S NOTE

Please be advised...

While *Don't Call Me Daddy* is a fun, hilarious, and spicy romcom, **grief and loss** are a reoccurring theme throughout this story.

Though, there are no specific details, brief mentions of losing a loved one from **cancer** , as well as **parental mental health issues**, are present in this story.

I'd also like to note that I tried to be as transparent as possible in the marketing and branding ... So if you don't enjoy the nicknames **Daddy or Baby Girl...** or a **Daddy Dom/Brat Dynamic** this probably isn't going to be the book for you.

Remember, it's 2024, we don't kink shame.

With that being said, I hope you love this story as much as I loved writing it!

XOXO
   Jeré

FERN & (IVY'S) ~~BUCKET~~ FUCK IT! LIST

- [ ] TAKE A CROSS COUNTRY ROAD TRIP
- [ ] GO CAMPING IN THE APPALACHIAN MOUNTAINS
- [ ] LEARN TO FISH
- [ ] JUMP OFF A WATERFALL
- [ ] ENTER A WET T-SHIRT CONTEST
- [ ] PARTY IN VEGAS FOR OUR 21ST BIRTHDAY
- [ ] MAKE OUT WITH SOMEONE RICH AND FAMOUS
- [ ] KISS IN THE RAIN
- [ ] TALK TO STRANGERS
- [ ] MAKE MISTAKES AND LEARN FROM THEM
- [ ] SAY (YES!) WHEN ADVENTURE CALLS
- [ ] HAVE A FLING WITH A (BOSS)
- [ ] TRUST THE UNIVERSE AND TAKE CHANCES
- [ ] MAKE FRIENDS EVERYWHERE YOU GO
- [ ] VISIT THE HOME OF THE ASHFORD FALLS PHANTOM
- [ ] DO SOMETHING THAT TERRIFIES YOU
- [ ] MAKE SOMETHING BETTER THAN IT WAS [BEFORE]
- [ ] VISIT DRACULA'S CASTLE IN TRANSYLVANIA!!!
- [ ] CHANGE SOMEONE'S LIFE FOR THE BETTER
- [ ] FALL IN LOVE. (THE REAL KIND YOU READ ABOUT IN ROMANCE NOVELS!!!)

PROLOGUE

Ivy

Seven Years Earlier

"Ahem. Are you ready?" My twin sister clears her throat and stands up on her bed, waiting for my full attention. She's only two minutes older than me, but she takes her big-sister role very seriously, especially when it comes to planning things.

One thing about Fern is, the girl loves a list more than anyone I've ever known. We look identical, apart from our eyes. Fern's are a cloudy gray while mine are a warm amber. It's like our souls chose the most distinguishing feature possible to express our differing personalities.

She's meticulously organized, focused, determined, and she has a plan for everything while I'm more of a ... free-spirited, go-with-the-flow kind of person.

Honestly, she's probably the only reason I'm passing any of my classes since I've always had a tendency to daydream. I don't know what I'd do without her bossing me around, telling me what to do next. Probably fail out of school and need to get myself a sugar daddy or something.

"Hello? Earth to Ivy?" She waves a hand to get my attention. "Jeez, sis, am I that boring?"

I blow my fallen bangs out of my face. "I told you, I'm listening. Just because I'm not making direct eye contact doesn't mean I can't hear you." I lean back on my arms and cross my outstretched feet in front of me. "What's so important about this list anyway?"

"It's not just a list, Ivy. It's a road map of how I'm going to live the most incredible life possible." She rolls her eyes and holds up the list as she begins to read. *"Visit the home of the Ashford Falls Phantom ..."*

"Not this again." I laugh. "Why are you so obsessed with this one? Is it the daddy issues? Because I think maybe you just need a real-life boyfriend to help you get over this monster obsession."

She bounces on her knees on the edge of the bed. "This is *my* list we're talking about, so don't start shaming me just because you don't understand him."

"He's a cryptid, no different from Bigfoot or the Lochness Monster. He's not real." I grab a book from the pile of monster romance novels from her side table and wave it in front of her. "None of them are, and even if they were, I'm pretty sure we wouldn't be able to fuck them."

"You wouldn't know real if it walked in this room, Miss Head in the Clouds." She snatches the book away and clenches it to her chest.

Ever since she stumbled upon the monster romance section in our public library two summers ago, my sister has been obsessed, and it looks like the Ashford Falls Phantom is her latest monster du jour.

"Okay, so you want to visit Ashford Falls, West Virginia," I say to appease her. "What else?"

She narrows her eyes. "Are you actually going to let me finish or just tell me how stupid you think it is?"

I hold out my pinkie, and she loops her thin finger in mine. "I promise I won't interrupt you again."

She smooths her hand over the notebook. "First, I'll take a cross-country road trip. I'll visit ghost towns, go on cemetery tours, stop at every interesting attraction that catches my eye along the way—"

"Like those weird monster festivals people are obsessed with," I add.

She rolls her eyes. "Obviously. Now, do you want to hear the rest of the list or not?"

I hold my hands up apologetically. "Sorry. Please continue."

"Then, I'll do all the adventurous stuff we never got to do growing up because Dad was too busy chasing women half his age and Mom was too depressed to even notice."

"Such as?" I ask, trying to bring the conversation in a more productive direction. The last thing we need is to deep-dive into our fucked-up family life right now. I'd rather think about the things that are actually in our control.

She shrugs. "I could go camping in the Appalachian Mountains. Learn how to fish. Jump off a waterfall—"

"Jeez, Fern, are you trying to live a full life or a short one?"

She drops the list just enough to glare at me. "It's about experiencing everything life has to offer, dear sister. And doing things that scare me pushes me out of my comfort zone, thus making me better as a result."

"If you say so." I laugh.

"I do say so. Now, stop interrupting." She clears her throat again, then reads, *"Enter a wet T-shirt contest. Party in Vegas for my twenty-first birthday. Make out with someone rich and famous. Kiss in the rain. Talk to strangers—as long as they're not creepy. Make mistakes and learn from them. Say yes when adventure calls. Have a fling with a boss."*

"Fern!"

"Shush, I'm not done." She holds her finger over her mouth. *"Trust the universe and take chances. Make friends everywhere I go. Do something that terrifies me. Make something better than it was before."*

"Those seem reasonable—"

"Visit Dracula's Castle in Transylvania ..."

"And we're back to the monster obsession," I say with a laugh. "Honestly, sis, where do you come up with this stuff?"

She taps her lip like she's thinking. "I don't know. I guess if I had to pinpoint it back to a specific event, I'd have to say when I was three and watched *Beauty and the Beast* for the first time and the utter disappointment I felt as soon as the Beast transformed into a human ... but I can't be sure."

I twist my lips and nod my head, considering ... because she's got me there. I sure as hell didn't expect her to actually have a good reason, but alas, Fern never ceases to amaze me with her ability to sell even the most absurd of ideas with confidence.

"And how exactly do you plan on doing these things?"

"I have no idea, but I trust the universe to make a way for me. I want it; therefore, it wants me too."

"I don't know what that means, but you know what? Somehow, I believe you anyway." I shake my head and laugh. "Anything else?"

She wipes a hand over the paper, as if smoothing out the wrinkles, and starts reading, "Change someone's life ∴ for the better. And last but not least, fall in love—not the kind of love that Mom and Dad had, but the real kind—"

"Like in your romance novels?" I tease.

Her grin widens. "Exactly. The real kind. But not right away. I want to be sure of it, and I can only do that if I've lived a full enough life—so I know what to compare it to. Which is why I need to do all these things—so I'll be ready."

I nod in agreement because if she's going to be delusional, at least she's being as logical as possible.

"Your imagination is somewhat concerning—you know that?" I throw a pillow at her, and she ducks out of the way, then curtsies before jumping down to lie on the floor beside me.

With our heads resting on our open palms, we stare up at the glow-in-the-dark stars that she made me help her stick on when we were ten. It almost feels like we're camping with only the dim glow of the sunset filtering in through her large bay window.

"When do you think you're going to have time to do all that stuff?" I turn on my side to face her, propping my head on my hand. "And sleeping with your boss ... that's one way of getting fired."

She waves my question away like it's no big deal. "I don't know. Maybe I'll take a year off before I go to college and knock out most of it. That's what they do in Europe, isn't it?

I'm not worried about the timeline. I'll have my whole life to work on it."

"And then what? What happens when you finish the list? Are you just done, or do you get some kind of prize or—"

"The adventure *is* the list, Ivy." She turns to face me now, like what she's about to say is something profound. "Finishing the list will just mean that I did all the things I'd always wanted to do. That I tried a lot of new things. Failed a lot. And hopefully learned a ton along the way." She sucks in a breath and smiles. "Finishing the list is just the beginning. I hope to have ten more lists created by the time it's all said and done. I never want to be complacent, you know? I always want to have an experience to look forward to. That's what makes life so fun."

In other words, she doesn't want to be complacent like Mom. That makes two of us. If I've learned anything from my parents' rocky marriage, it's that it's easy to lose yourself when you're with the wrong person. We've watched our mother slowly lose herself over the last few years, eventually receiving disability benefits for her crippling depression. It finally got so bad that Dad left, which makes things a little easier now that we don't have to pretend he's not running around on her.

Lucky for me, Fern's always been the one to keep the household running and take care of things. I can't help but dream of the day where we only have to worry about ourselves ... but then I feel guilty.

I know Fern does, too, but she's stronger than me. She doesn't let it get to her as much ... or she doesn't show it anyway.

"Why are you so weird?" I ruffle her long hair, and she moves to tickle me as we both launch into a fit of giggles.

With a sigh, we fall back on our backs in the same position we started in.

"You know what would be, like, the funnest thing ever?" Her voice comes out in an excited squeak ... and I already think I know where this is going.

"What would be the funnest thing ever?" I humor her.

"What if we did it together?" She flips on her stomach and kicks her feet behind her. "It can be our sister trip after we graduate. We can take off a year before college and check as many things off as we can. And we can document the whole thing and write a book about our adventures. Then, when we're old and we can't remember anything, we can read it and experience it all over again!" She squeals the last part out, her voice trailing higher and higher, like hearing her idea out loud was just as much of a surprise to her as it was to me.

I can't help but laugh and agree because no one can tell my sister no when she's excited about something. "Fine, Ferny, I'll do it. But only if you promise you'll hold my hand for all the crazy stuff."

She grabs my hand and interlocks our fingers. "Don't worry, Ivy. I've got you. I promise I won't let go until you tell me to."

She kisses our clasped hands, and then we lie back down, staring at the plastic stars in silence until we both fall asleep. And just like she promised, she doesn't let go of my hand all night.

CHAPTER ONE

Ivy

Cloudy days always remind me of my sister, so I guess the weather suits the occasion. I've been driving nonstop for two days with no specific destination in mind, just a general direction of what feels the most right.

Right.

Nothing about anything in my life feels right, but maybe that's what I'm trying to find out here.

Fern's list weighs heavy in the front pocket of my damp overalls, like a tether keeping me from floating away. It's a burden and a comfort all the same, one I've promised to fulfill, no matter how long it takes.

She should be here for this. She should be holding her ridiculous checklist and navigating us through this spectacular mountain range she was always so obsessed with. She should be driving while I sit with my feet propped on the dash, controlling the playlist.

That's the way it should be happening, but lung cancer

doesn't care about any of that stuff. It doesn't care about Fern's dreams or the countless lists she made to catch them. It doesn't care about any of our plans—or lack thereof—and it certainly doesn't care about what any of us wanted. Otherwise, I wouldn't be lost, somewhere in the mountains of West Virginia, with my twin sister's ashes riding shotgun in my passenger seat.

It's awfully poetic in a morbid way that I have to fulfill that damn list by myself, with only my sister's ghost to guide me. But I can't help but think Fern's enjoying watching me try to figure it out, how I'll manage to accomplish this ridiculous list without her careful planning. How I'll Ivy my way through it, just like I always do—in the least graceful way possible.

I used to hate how Fern made everything look so easy and seamless while I bulldozed my way through life, leaving a trail of destruction and chaos in my path. But after everything I've lost, I can't seem to make myself care what anyone thinks anymore.

I tighten my sweaty palms around the steering wheel as I maneuver my old Volkswagen Cabriolet around the tight, hairpin turns of the Appalachian Mountains.

I've got the legs of my overalls rolled up to my knees as the soppy, wet fabric clings to my skin like glue. So much for my attempt to hike to the waterfall.

I was two miles into the hike when I slipped and fell into the ice-cold stream I was attempting to cross.

Luckily, the stream was shallow enough that my overall pocket stayed dry. I wish I could say the same for my cell phone.

I glance at my phone in the comically large bag of rice,

strapped in with a seat belt next to my sister's urn. It's not a combo you see every day, and the absurdity of it all gives me an odd sense of peace.

Sure, having a working navigation system would be nice, but there's nothing I can do about that now, so I might as well enjoy the ride. There are certainly worse places to get lost. At least I've got the gorgeous mountain views to distract me, right?

Fun fact about me: I could get lost in my own neighborhood. In fact, I have. I have quite possibly the worst sense of direction ever known to man, so I'm not sure what I was thinking, trying to Lewis-and-Clark my way to the waterfall.

Lesson learned. Mother Nature—1. Ivy—0.

Another fact about me: My life is an absolute mess. After my mother's little accident that resulted in losing my childhood home in a housefire, she finally agreed to move into the long-term care facility I'd been suggesting for over a year. The depression episodes had become so debilitating that I couldn't trust to leave her unattended, which didn't exactly make for the carefree college experience most people my age get to have.

I was barely passing my classes as it was, commuting back and forth multiple times a week to check on her. After she fell asleep with a lit candle and the whole house went up in flames, I couldn't take it anymore.

I helped move her into the facility, and I dropped out of school the next day.

I cashed out the last bit of my savings—the money I'd worked for every summer since I was fifteen to save and pay for college and whatever happened after that—and booked a one-way plane ticket to Transylvania, just like my sister had always dreamed of. Only I won't just be visiting. In order to make it work, I had to get creative. One drunken night spent wallowing in my dorm room after my childhood home and all that was left of my sister's possessions were destroyed, I came across an ad for international hospitality jobs in tourism. A few clicks later, and I was filling out an application to work on-site in Dracula's Castle. The pay is shit, but dormitories are provided for all staff members who sign a one-year contract.

I'd almost forgotten all about it, but the day my mother moved into her long-term living facility, I received an email that I'd been accepted for the position. I could hardly believe it, but took it as a sign. Fern always dreamed of doing this, and now, I was going to make her dreams come true for the both of us.

So, I signed the contract. Dropped out of school. Booked the flight. And now, I'm here, driving around through the Appalachian Mountains with the only objective of finding somewhere to sprinkle Fern's ashes and to check off as many items on her list as I can before I start my next adventure in Transylvania next month.

I might be low on cash, but I've only got to stretch it for about a month. So what if I have to live out of my car? I love my car, and it's the only reason I had Minute Rice on hand to save my phone—see, I'm making lemonade here.

It's getting late and harder to see with only my dim headlights illuminating the road. I try to avoid driving at night because it's not exactly safe, considering my car's over twenty years old and seen better days. But surely, I should be getting close to some sort of civilization soon ... right? I've been driving all day, and I'm so exhausted that everything seems to be running together.

I come around a sharp turn, and I wipe my dry, sleepy eyes when a dark figure appears in the road.

Everything happens so fast.

My heart skips a beat, and my stomach drops as my reflexes take control.

It's there one second, and then it's gone.

Only it's too late.

I grip the steering wheel to brace myself as I slam my foot on the brakes. The smell of burned rubber, the high-pitched shriek of tires. I crank the wheel to the right, and my car rolls off the road and down a hill, narrowly missing a large tree before finally rolling to a stop.

Heart racing in my chest, I cough several times, trying to catch my breath as my airway starts to restrict. Thankfully, I've still got an emergency inhaler stowed in my glove box from when Fern first bought this car. She insisted I keep one in here just in case ... even though I haven't had an asthma attack in years.

I take a couple of puffs, feeling my breathing return to normal, and sag against my seat. Even from the grave, my sister's still watching out for me. That sounds exactly like her.

I don't know how I've managed to survive all on my own these past five years, but I can't rely on my sister's forward thinking to save me anymore, no matter how much I wish she would just appear to me and tell me what to do next.

That's why I'm here.

I tried to do things my way. I even went to college and did all the things I was supposed to do, but no matter how much I pushed myself, I somehow still felt empty. It was like I was walking around with a giant hole in my chest, only feeling things halfway ... like the other piece of me was missing.

Maybe I'll never feel whole without my sister, but I've got to try. I'm desperate for something to make me feel alive again, so desperate that I dropped out of school with only one semester left and sold all my belongings—not that there was much left.

I needed a change and figured, *What the hell do I have to lose?*

So, I packed up the few belongings that could fit in my car, donated everything else, and set out to have an epic adventure with my sister's list as my only guide.

Maybe not the most responsible idea I've ever had, but that's what desperation will do to a person. Besides, I never claimed to be responsible. That was all Fern. I'm more of the fun, impulsive twin.

And now, it seems I'm getting to deal with the consequences of my own actions.

I twist the key in the ignition, but rather than rumbling to life, there's a hiss coming from underneath the hood. I try again, and hear a clicking sound, but the car doesn't start.

"Are you serious right now?" I shout to no one.

With an annoyed huff, I grab the bag of rice containing my phone and step out into the dark, eerie forest.

I narrow my eyes, trying to make sense of where I am. If I can just find the road, maybe I can flag someone down for help.

A bead of sweat drips down my spine, the damp, muggy air not doing me any favors. I tighten my grip on the plastic bag of rice to keep from dropping it as my feet come to a stop.

Was it left or right? I'm so turned around from the car

spinning out of control that I don't know which way I came from. I spin around as if the change of direction will suddenly spark my memory, but it's no use.

I'm lost.

I suppose I have a fifty-fifty shot of picking the right way, so I might as well get going.

What was that thing in the road anyway? It was huge and gone just as quickly as it had appeared. An eerie feeling creeps up my spine, and I shiver at the thought of it.

Now is not the time to remember Fern's creepy bedtime stories.

As if on cue, her words play in the back of my mind ...

"Whatever you do, don't look in the trees. If you don't see them, then you're safe, but once you see them ..."

I dart my eyes down and cup my hand, shielding my eyes as an extra precaution as my heart races and my imagination goes wild.

Just don't think about it.

They can sense fear.

Stop being scared.

Whatever you do, don't run.

Stop it, Ivy. This is so stupid.

Monsters aren't real. Especially the fuckable monsters written about in romance stories.

None of this is real. You're just freaking yourself out for no reason.

I suck in a calming breath and toss the bag of rice over my shoulder as I continue moving.

It was probably just a bear or something ...

Somehow, that thought doesn't make me feel any better. Because bears are real. Bears can actually kill me.

I pick up my pace, my whole body on high alert as I scan the tops of the tall, dense trees for any hint of light.

There's a sharp crack in the distance, and I freeze.

I hear what sounds like crunching leaves beneath footsteps... the snap of a twig.

My stomach drops as panic races through my veins.

And then the forest goes completely silent.

I don't wait to find out why.

"Nope. Nope. Nope."

All logical thought leaves me as my fight-or-flight response kicks in, and I bolt, putting as much distance between me and whatever might or might not be chasing me, Fern's warning be damned.

If something really is out there, trying to kill me, I'm at least going to make the fucker work for it.

I sprint as fast as I can, zigzagging through the overgrown, tangled forest to throw whatever's chasing me off my trail. Hanging limbs and tall weeds smack against my skin as if the forest itself were trying to swallow me whole.

"Wait!" The voice comes out like a whisper in my ear, but I don't stop as my heart nearly beats out of my chest.

They'll try to trick you, throwing their voice. Whatever you do, don't fall for it. It's a trap.

I cover my ears with my hands, the rice bag slapping me in the face as I run and gasp for air, chest heaving and pulse racing. My muscles scream in pain as I weave through the forest, jumping over tree stumps like hurdles until my foot connects with something hard, and then, I'm falling.

Down. Down. Down.

My body beats against the rocky earth, and I clench the bag of rice to my chest as I take hit after hit. The only solace I have is that the faster I tumble down this hill, the more distance there is between me and whatever's chasing me.

When I eventually stop tumbling, I let out a groan of pain and roll to my back, staring up at the bright stars shining through the treetops.

It's a remarkable view. I really wish I weren't running for my life so I could enjoy it.

Everything hurts, but I think I'm okay; nothing feels broken. I pat myself, checking for injuries, and am relieved to have only suffered some minor cuts and bruises.

My overalls are caked in mud, and there's a big gash on my knee that's bleeding. I wince as I push myself to a seated position, brushing the little rocks and dirt off my arms when a shadow figure towers over me.

"Hey, are you—"

I let out a bloodcurdling scream, then use the only weapon I have available to me. Grabbing a fistful of rice, I hurl it straight at its face.

"Ow, fuck!"

I squint my eyes as the dark figure comes into view, and I realize it's not a scary monster—at least, it doesn't look like one—but a man. It's hard to see him fully, but it looks like he's wearing a light-blue button-up shirt and black dress pants.

"Is that ... rice?" he says as he bends over and wipes at his eyes.

"What do you want from me?" I answer his question with one of my own.

I might be relieved that he isn't a monster trying to eat me, but that doesn't mean this guy isn't going to try to kill me either. I've seen enough true crime documentaries to know that you don't just trust every random man who sneaks up on you in the woods at night.

"What are you talking about? I was driving, and I saw your car run off the road. I thought you were hurt, but then you weren't in your car, so I came looking for you. I called after you, but then you took off running and fell down the hill." His voice comes out a little breathless, and I realize he must've been running to catch up to me.

I tilt my head, considering him. That actually makes sense, and he doesn't look like a bad guy. He's clean-shaven, and he looks like he's showered recently ... and he's wearing a tie. Would a murderer go through the trouble of tying a tie to impress their prey? I wouldn't think so but ...

My endless loop of thoughts comes to a halt when I get a better look at him.

Holy shit, this guy is hot. Dark, wavy hair; strong jaw; big, broad chest, and he's easily over six feet tall. There's an expensive-looking gold watch around his wrist, and he's got his sleeves rolled up over his forearms. His body looks like something out of a Marvel movie, and suddenly, I find myself more curious than afraid.

What the hell? If I'm going to be murdered, at least I'll enjoy my view.

I hold out my hand, and he pulls me up, steadying me as my legs forget how to stand up properly.

"Whoa, you sure you're okay? That was a nasty tumble."

"Oh, yeah, I'm fine." I bend attempting to brush the dirt from my overalls and almost fall over.

He grabs my arm to help stabilize me, and this time, my knees go weak for a different reason entirely. Maybe it's his cologne?

I take advantage of his close proximity and lean into him, feigning weak knees again, and suck in a long sniff. My eyes nearly roll back in my head in pleasure, and I wonder if he's wearing one of those pheromone enhancers. Maybe that's how he captures his victims—by luring them in with his amazing scent?

I don't have the energy to be suspicious anymore. I'm much more curious anyhow. I sway to the side and bump back into him, and he wraps a hard, muscled arm around me. And there it is again—that tingly feeling shooting straight through me. Weird.

Maybe I need to revisit this little scenario in the future. Who knew being chased through the woods could get me so worked up?

"Come on. I'll give you a ride to town. My car's just over here."

He leads me back up the hill—the very one I just tumbled down—and we're both out of breath by the time we reach the top.

There's a small two-door black car parked on the side of the road, and I follow him on shaky legs.

He opens the passenger door and motions for me to get in. "Uh, you dropped this," he says as he hands me the heavy, tattered bag before closing the door.

I can't imagine what he must be thinking right now ... and yet he's still helping me.

His door closes with a thwack. "So, where are you headed?"

My eyes drift over his face, and he's even handsomer than I realized. His sharp jaw is clenched, like he's trying to keep from saying something.

"Do you do this often? Chase down women in the woods and convince them to go home with you, I mean. Or am I just lucky?" It's hardly an appropriate time to flirt with the guy, but the words fly out of my mouth before I can stop myself. Maybe I hit my head harder than I realized.

He clears his throat, keeping his eyes trained on the road. "I, uh ... that's not what—"

Oh my God, is he nervous? That's actually adorable.

"I'm just fucking with you."

I place my hand on his forearm, and his body goes stiff, like I frightened him. When I pull away, his shoulders sag in relief. Interesting. I can't tell if he's afraid of me ... or disgusted.

I look down at my tattered overalls, caked in dirt and blood. I don't even want to think about what my hair looks like, much less my face.

He clears his throat again, breaking the silence. "So, what's with the rice?"

"Oh, I accidentally dropped my phone in a stream earlier when I was trying to hike to the waterfall," I say with a shrug.

A flash of confusion crosses his face. "And you were walking in the woods at night without a working phone because ..."

"An animal or something—it was big, whatever it was—ran in front of me. I ran off the road to avoid it." I gesture behind us with my thumb. "Way back there. I don't know where because I sort of got turned around when I freaked out and started running. I was walking to find a pay phone or somewhere I could make a phone call." I shrug again, not knowing how much this stranger really wants to know.

His lips press together in a flat line, and his jaw tics again, like he's holding back from saying what he really wants to say. But then he surprises me. "Do you have any idea how dangerous that is? You'd have been better off waiting for someone to pass by than walk through Phantom's Reach alone at night."

It's not his words but his tone that's laced with annoyance that has me taken aback. I won't be lectured by a complete stranger—handsome or not.

"How was I supposed to know how far away the next town was?" I pull my legs up, crisscrossing them, and I swear I see him give me the side-eye.

This prick thinks he's better than me.

"Because you didn't have a phone," he answers, and I roll my eyes. "What do you think would've happened if I hadn't stopped—"

"Statistically, or is this a creative exercise? Because, truly, I think the possibilities are endless. I could've broken my neck falling down the hill, or knocked myself unconscious at the very least—"

"You know what I meant—"

I pretend I didn't hear him. "Or a bear could've eaten me while I was unconscious, or I could've stumbled upon a pack of wolves—"

"All right, all right. Enough with the sarcasm. You've made your point."

The muscle in his jaw twitches, and that little involuntary response fills me with a deep satisfaction that I should definitely speak to a therapist about.

"Why do you care so much? It's not like you know me," I say, suddenly feeling curious.

This guy doesn't seem to be the least bit charmed by me;

in fact, he seems annoyed to have to deal with me at all. So, why stop to help me?

"I care because you're ... you're a young woman, walking around a notoriously dangerous area at night ... alone ... looking like that." He nods in my direction.

"Ew. Don't call me a young woman." My lip curls in disgust. "And what do you mean, *looking like that*? What's wrong with how I look?"

"You know exactly what I mean by that," he scoffs. "You're not even wearing a shirt."

I look down at my cropped tank beneath my overalls. Is this guy serious? "It's a crop top, and with the overalls covering the middle, it's barely noticeable." I narrow my eyes. "Unless you're a perv. Is that what this is about?"

"What? No. That's, like, the opposite of what I meant." He scrubs a hand down his face in frustration, then turns to look at me. "I'm the one who's helping you—"

"And judging me," I add. "What do my clothes have to do with anything?"

"God, you're irritating," he says through gritted teeth. "I'm just saying, it's not the smartest thing for a"—he pauses, as if to consider his phrasing—"*female* to be wandering around the woods alone at night."

I blow out a breath and fold my arms back over my chest. "Well, thank you."

"Thank you? Thank you for what?"

"Clearly, you find me attractive, though you have a really odd way of showing it, and I am choosing to accept your judgmental comments as a compliment," I say as I prop my feet up on the dash.

They barely make contact before he swipes them down. "Don't do that. It's dangerous."

Interesting. Not the reaction I was expecting.

He lifts the center console, pulling out a bottle of medication, and tosses a couple back. "Do you have any idea where you left your car?"

I just look at him because I think we both know the answer to that question.

He lets out a frustrated sigh and massages his temples. "Of course you don't know where it is."

"Because I'm so irresponsible," I say in a deep voice, mimicking him.

He rolls his eyes, but his voice comes out surprisingly calm. "Look, it's getting late. I think it's safer to look for your car in the morning. Are you hungry? Do you need somewhere to stay?"

"Yes."

"Yes? Yes what?" he huffs. "I asked you two different questions."

"And the answer to both of them is yes."

"You're really annoying—do you know that?"

"So I've been told ... mostly by old people though." I have to bite my cheek to hold back my grin as I watch his face fight to hide a scowl. I don't miss the way his hands tighten around the steering wheel, and I know I struck a nerve.

Serves him right. I hope he thinks twice before pointing out the truth to complete strangers again.

* * *

Thirty minutes later, I'm happily chomping down on my Taco Bell peace offering—I even splurged and got nacho fries since it was his treat.

He pulls into a parking spot in front of a sign that simply reads *Inn*. After a quick glance I notice the business next to it says Bakery... and then Restaurant catches my attention.

Before I can ask if this place is real or if he's brought me to a movie set, he's handing me a wad of cash. "Make sure to ask for a room upstairs. Sometimes, old man Melvin sleepwalks, and he's been known to be somewhat of a surprise snuggler."

I open my mouth to speak, but he holds up his hand and continues, "Auto Shop is just off the square. It's an easy walk, but they won't really open until nine even though the sign says eight. You might want to wait until ten just to be safe. Dan can take you to get your car in the morning and get you all fixed up." He bites the inside of his cheek, then points to the bag of rice in my lap. "There's enough cash here to replace your phone and put you up for the night. Market's a few blocks away, but you can probably ask Dan to make a pit stop on the way to get your car. He loves shit like that." He snaps his lips closed, signifying he's done.

"Oh, well, thank you ..." I pause for him to tell me his name.

"Doesn't matter. We'll never see each other again anyway."

"Right. Well, I guess I'll be going then." I flip through the wad of cash, and my eyes go wide. "Are you sure about this? You gave me, like, five hundred dollars."

He pushes the cash back toward me. "It's no big deal. Maybe invest in a waterproof phone case next time."

"Yeah, I'll think about it." I look down as I shove the cash in my overall pocket. "What are you, a millionaire or something?"

"Or something," he says, and when I look back up, he's staring at me with a look I don't quite recognize.

Concern? Worry? Regret?

"Please take care of yourself. No more wandering around in the woods at night alone, okay?"

My head nods on its own. "Yeah, um ... I'm Ivy, by the way. Ivy Lane. Thanks for your help tonight."

CHAPTER TWO

Leo

"Dude, what the fuck's wrong with your eye? Why do you keep winking at me?"

I swipe at my eye, rubbing tears away. "I'm not fucking winking at you, Roman. I just scratched it or something."

I don't think I could explain what really happened to my eye if I tried.

Fucking bag of rice. Who throws rice anyway?

Apparently, hot blondes who throw caution to the wind regarding their safety—that's who. I still can't believe she was just out there, walking alone, with no phone. I don't know what would've happened if I hadn't shown up, but my imagination is doing a pretty good job of filling in the blanks.

It's not like our small town isn't safe. Hell, I think my family and I know everyone who lives here on a first-name basis, but there's something eerie about those woods.

It's not that I actually believe in the infamous Phantom our small town's known for—no one in their right mind believes something like that—but anything could be out there. She was lucky she didn't stumble upon a pack of wolves or trip and bust her head open on a rock. The forest is a dangerous place, and call me paranoid, but I don't fuck with things I can't see.

Not anymore.

A full-body shiver runs up my spine, and I shake my head to rid the thoughts.

The important thing is, she's safe, and she hopefully learned her lesson to not be so negligent in the future.

I think it's best to suppress that memory as deep as I can get it. I don't have time for the rabbit hole that would take me down. No, I'm too busy working on more important things, like healing our planet and creating a safe work environment for our company's one thousand-plus staff members. I've devoted everything to this company; for better or worse, it's my purpose for living, and I can't let any distractions prevent me from that, no matter how beautiful they might be.

Ivy Lane.

I've had to stop myself from looking her up about ten times already this morning, not that I think I'll find anything. Maybe a minor criminal record. She seems like the kind of woman who's not afraid of breaking a rule or two, hence her fearless walk through Phantom's Reach last night.

Worry pinches in my chest, which only annoys me more. It's ridiculous to be worried about a stranger, especially one who's clearly not concerned about her own safety.

I've known the woman for what, two hours? And I spent most of that time seething with irritation from her smart mouth and careless attitude. In another life, I would have taken great joy in showing her a few manners ... but that's not who I am anymore. Besides, she's got to be at least a decade younger than me, which could never work.

What am I thinking? This whole fantasy is ridiculous. Clearly, I'm more sleep-deprived than I thought. I should be paying attention while Carl talks about import taxes and whatever else he's been going on about for the last ten minutes.

It's just annoying how comfortable she seemed, sitting there with me, asking me questions and talking like I wasn't a complete stranger. I don't think I've ever met someone so ... authentically themself ... straight out of the gate. It's fascinating and infuriating, all at the same time.

I bite my cheek, suddenly itching to get out of this stiff office chair and pace ... or run. Hell, I just need to exert some of this energy before I snap or say something I don't mean to someone who doesn't deserve it.

I take a cautious sip of my steaming hot coffee, willing the caffeine to work a miracle and somehow pull me out of this foul mood.

I've never been much of a morning person, but between the sleep deprivation from working late over the last three months and last night's escapades, I'm barely hanging on by a thread.

Carl finishes his presentation, and my brother, Roman, takes the floor.

It's our quarterly meeting, so I should really be paying more attention, but it's not like they're saying anything I don't already know. I make it my mission to know everything that goes on even if it means I work holidays and weekends.

Roman clicks open his first slide, and a picture of our

town square comes into view, that damn Phantom statue front and center.

Goddamn it. Not this again.

I have to force myself not to sag in my seat like a toddler because of all the shit I've got on my plate; the fucking Phantom Festival is the last thing I need to be worrying about.

We're literally trying to save the planet with our sustainable, eco-friendly product line. Call me crazy, but I feel like our time is best spent doing our actual jobs. No one likes when I point that out though.

It's ridiculous and my least favorite thing about living in the Appalachians. But nobody asked me, and no amount of bitching is going to change the annual Phantom Fest the town throws every year to commemorate our founding members—my ancestors actually.

"As you are all aware by now, this year is the one hundredth anniversary of the first sighting of the Phantom, and this year's festival has the potential to be bigger than ever.

"For many people, he's just a tall tale, but at Kingsley Industries, we believe he represents something so much more than a spooky story passed down for generations. As the story goes, my great-grandmother, Arlene Ashford, experienced the very first encounter with the Phantom, where he not so kindly warned her about the pollution the town was creating with their coal mines and processing factories.

"The people were sick. The land was barren. The town was all but deserted, as families were forced to move away for any chance at finding work. The men who stayed worked dangerous jobs, many of who lost their lives that horrible day."

The room falls silent as we remember the tragic past that led Ashford Falls to where we are today.

"Every year, we honor the message the Phantom brought my great-grandmother, and by doing so, our home has flourished with rich job opportunities, a booming economy, and clean air with pollution levels at an all-time low."

I join in as the table erupts in applause. I might not like the festival, but I am proud of the changes we've made for our community's health.

"So, in honor of the one hundredth anniversary, I'd like to put together a task force and planning committee to lead and take full ownership of the festival." He pauses for an uncomfortable moment as awkward tension fills the air.

"Anyone at all? Come on. Surely, someone's eager to offer a helping hand to put on the town's favorite event of the year. Remember, your workload will be temporarily assigned to another team so you can focus on your festival planning duties. It could be a fun way to mix things up." He pauses once more, and the room goes so quiet that you could hear a pin drop.

He tries again. "It's an important part of our company culture as well as this great town's heritage, not to mention all the charities we're able to help with the proceeds every year. Maybe this year, someone *new* will feel called to give back. Someone who hasn't done it for the last five years in a row."

I fake a cough to cover my laugh at the desperation of his plea, which only draws more attention to me as heads turn in my direction. My father's gaze finds me, and I quickly look away.

Who in their right mind would be okay with a group helping to take on their workload?

I, for one, am far too much of a perfectionist for that … not to mention my mile-long list of trust issues.

"Of course, everyone will receive fair compensation for their time," Roman adds.

"I'd like us to get a head start on the planning. So, if that's something you're interested in helping with, I'd love to get the ball rolling." He looks around the room, and my eyes conveniently fall to my computer screen, where I finish typing out an email.

After a moment of complete silence, my dad clears his throat. "Good idea to get on top of things, Roman. Maybe we can send out an email at the end of next week and ask for volunteers, give everyone some time to come up with their ideas."

We all know whoever's appointed to the committee will have to be volun-*told* because no one has time for planning a festival on top of everything else they have to do.

"That brings us to our next topic of discussion." My dad fidgets with his pen as he waits for everyone's attention.

I sit up a little straighter, and my pulse kicks up a notch. My dad only fidgets when he's got something important to say or he's nervous. And I think I know just what this is about.

"As you know, Leo's been working on the Thompson Brothers deal diligently over the last year, and I'm pleased to inform you, they signed a contract to partner with Kingsley Industries and carry all our brands as generics in all two thousand stores across North America."

The table erupts in applause with people whooping and

hollering and slapping my back to congratulate me. My chest swells with pride, and in that moment, all the stress and long hours feel worth it. I'm beaming, and it feels incredible to hit such a gigantic goal.

When my father started this company twenty-five years ago, he didn't cut any corners. We've been able to reduce our carbon footprint by thirty-eight percent, and that doesn't even account for the extra steps we've taken to utilize sustainable energy in all our factories. This partnership will allow us to serve thirty percent more of the low-income families in rural America, thus eliminating further pollution and providing safe, chemical-free, biodegradable products to the people who need them most.

It's a big fucking deal, and I feel honored to have contributed to that.

My dad stands from the far end of the conference table, and everyone's chatter settles down.

"As you all know, I'm not getting any younger ..."

I suck in a breath. Is he really doing this today?

I straighten my tie and wipe nonexistent wrinkles from my pants. I can't believe this is happening. Everything I've been working so hard for is all about to come true ...

"I've been giving a lot of thought to retiring—what it would mean for this company and the people of Ashford Falls. When I started Kingsley Industries, I had a great idea, sure, but it was just a seed. It was my beautiful wife, Mary, who insisted we rebuild this place she grew up into its former glory ... and then some. But it's the people here, that are the fertile soil which enabled it to grow. Ashford Falls wouldn't be what it is today without Kingsley Industries ... but we wouldn't be who we are without this town either." He weaves his fingers together to demonstrate. "So, after much deliberation and persistent nudges from my lovely wife, I've decided to retire on my sixtieth birthday, which just so happens to fall on the same day as this year's Phantom Fest."

You could hear a pin drop; the room is so quiet. My dad's always had a way of commanding attention, but this is perhaps the biggest news this company's seen since we went public ten years ago.

"Which brings me to my next announcement." He pauses until he has everyone's complete attention. "I've decided my replacement will be ..."

I wipe my sweaty palms on my pants legs as I steady my breathing.

"Carl Manchester."

My heart drops to my stomach, and I nearly fall out of my seat. A high-pitched ringing fills my ears from the sudden change in my blood pressure.

Did I just hear that right?

Did my father just name Carl as his replacement over me, his oldest son?

I shake my head, trying to make it make sense. I thought for sure I was a shoo-in.

I mean, I landed the Thompson deal; he was just congratulating me two minutes ago over it. I've worked my ass off for this company, never taken a vacation, only called in sick once when I had the flu and they forced me not to come in—and still, I worked from home until I was cleared to come back.

How? How is this happening?

Is this about the incident? Who am I kidding? Of course it is.

I meet my dad's gaze, and his eyes are rimmed with tears. He looks disappointed, and my gut sinks with that all-too-familiar feeling of shame.

If it takes me the rest of my life to atone for my mistake, then I'm prepared for that, but I know my impact will go further if I'm the one calling the shots. I can only control so much from my current position.

But now's not the time to dig up the past. People are watching me, and I need to put on a professional face.

I congratulate Carl and shake his hand, pretend like I'm excited even. Honestly, it's nothing against Carl. The guy is fantastic—hence why my dad chose him—but he's in his late fifties, and he doesn't exactly have the freshest ideas for growth. Nothing like how I'd lead.

"With that said, that's a wrap for Q2. Now, who's up for tacos? There's a food truck parked outside and a bar set up with margaritas in the cafeteria. Carl, yours is on the house." Dad wraps an arm around Carl, then calls over his shoulder, "Just kidding. It's all on the house."

As if we all didn't know that already.

My dad might be a savvy businessman, but he will always find room in the budget to celebrate his people. It's the foundation of our entire work culture and everything our family stands for.

Soft chatter fills the room as everyone gathers their things, then follows my dad downstairs to the cafeteria like he's the Pied Piper.

I sag back in my seat with a grunt and stare up at the ceiling. The last thing I want to do is make small talk over shared tacos right now.

"So ... that's kind of a bummer," Roman says, and I squint my eyes open to see him standing over me.

"Do you need something or—"

He holds his hands over his chest and looks offended. "Can I not commiserate in your misery, big brother?"

"Sure. But I'd like to be miserable in silence." I close my eyes again, doing my best to ignore him.

"I know now's not really the best time to bring this up ... but since it looks like you're already kind of having a shitty day, I just thought I'd warn you that Bartholomew's birthday party is this weekend." He snaps his fingers and then claps. "Obviously, we need you to be there for the group photo."

I sit up in a rush, making my head spin. "Are you fucking with me right now?"

"No. Why would I joke about something like this? You know how Mom is—"

"He's a cat, Rome. Mom found him in a trash can. She has no idea how old he is, much less when his birthday is—"

"You know as well as I do that the pet psychic told Mom his birthday—"

"Do you hear yourself right now? I don't know if I've ever heard so many words in a sentence that don't go together." I grip the arms of the chair and spin in a circle as I stare up at the ceiling.

How is this what I have to deal with after receiving that soul-crushing news?

"Anyway"—he winces—"that's not all." He shoves his hands in his pockets and puffs out his cheeks.

"Oh, for fuck's sake, just spit it out."

"Mom's planning a surprise blind date for you at the party.

She's going to ambush you with an errand or something, so you'll be stuck with one of her knitting group friend's daughters ..." He lets out a heavy exhale like he's relieved to get that off his chest.

Roman is the sweet brother, which means my mom feels comfortable telling him her wild plans ... which also makes him the family snitch. I don't envy him for it, but I guess that's what happens when you're the middle child of five boys.

I groan and press the burning ache in my chest. This stress is giving me indigestion. In fact, I can't remember the last time I didn't have indigestion ... maybe the last time I was stress-free? So, when I was twelve?

"Why does she keep doing this? I told her I'm not interested—"

"Maybe if you actually got out of this office and dated, she wouldn't feel the need to *help* you," Roman offers.

"Gee, thanks, Einstein. But you have no idea about my dating life. You don't know what I do when I leave. Just because I don't galivant my private life all over town doesn't mean I'm not dating." The wheels in my head begin to spin as the lie starts to take root.

"Whatever, dude. You're so full of shit—"

"I'm serious. Just because you haven't met her doesn't mean I'm not seeing someone," I lie.

"Really? Where did you meet?"

"We, uh ... we met at a charity event last summer. She spent the whole night busting my balls, and I couldn't get enough of her. I'd never met anyone so ... vibrant and magnetic. I don't think I could've stayed away from her if I tried. At the end of the night, I gave her a ride home, and we ended up spending the whole weekend together."

A little truth sprinkled in with the lie makes for a believable story.

Not too bad for being off the top of my head.

"We hit it off, and we've been doing the long-distance thing ever since."

I give him my best convincing grin, but he narrows his eyes like he doesn't believe me. Not that I blame him. All I do *is* work.

"A year, huh? So, I guess it's pretty serious?"

Okay, maybe a year was a bit generous, but I'm committed now.

"Oh, yeah. Very serious. She's incredible—"

"What's her name?" he fires off, and I'm taken aback by the abrupt question.

"Her name? It's, uh ..." I answer with the first name that comes to my head. "Ivy. Her name's Ivy Lane."

A slow smile breaks across his face as he pulls out his phone and types something. Instantly, I feel the buzz of a message notification in my pocket.

"Cool. I guess if she's real, you don't mind me telling everyone. I mean, since it's been a year, it kind of feels like it's time for us to meet her, don't you think?"

He backs away, wearing a sly grin, and I have to force myself to not throw the phone—which is now blowing up with text messages—right at his cocky face.

"See you at the party this weekend. I can't wait to meet Ivy," he singsongs before turning to leave.

"Fuck me," I sigh as I pull out my phone to assess the damage. It's worse than I imagined.

ROMAN

Guess what Leo just told me

Apparently, he's got a secret girlfriend he's been hiding… for a YEAR!

GUY

Why are you interrupting me in the middle of the day to tell me this?

MOM

SHUT UP!!!

Are you serious, Roman?

Is this a prank?

Because you know I hate being pranked.

ROMAN

It's not a prank, Mom. He just told me about her.

MOM

Oh my goodness. Miracles do come true! I'm going to knit her something.

Leo, what's her shirt size? How large are her breasts? I want to make sure it's comfortable.

LUKA

Whoa, Mom, you can't just ask how big her tits are first thing…

Seriously though, how big are they?

LEO

I don't know. They're normal. Why do you need to know?

GUY

Normal? Really, Leo? Wait... has she not shown you?

Tell me she's not one of those wait-for-marriage girls???

LUKA

IDK. I think it could be hot...

LEO

I don't think she needs a sweater. She's got plenty of clothes.

MOM

Who said anything about a sweater? I'm making a halter top. I can show you mine so you can see.

LEO

I'd really rather not.

GUY

And now, my weiner's sucked inside my body.

MOM

It's doing that again? It always used to do that when you were a baby. The doctor said it was because you were so fat, but maybe you can ask Dr. Stone to look at it next time you see him?

GUY

I WAS JOKING, MOM!

LUKA

Ha-ha, Guy's got an innie weenie.

MOM

There's nothing to be ashamed of. It's a medical condition.

JETT

I thought I unsubscribed from this text thread…

ROMAN

You can't escape us that easily. I added you back.

JETT KINGSLEY HAS LEFT THE GROUP MESSAGE.

LEO

Okay, I'm putting my phone away now. Some of us have work to do.

I pocket my phone and make my way down the hall into my office. As soon as I open my email, my phone buzzes again. This time, it's just from my dad, and it's sent directly to me.

DAD

That's fantastic news, Leo. I assume you're bringing her? I can't wait to hear all about the woman who finally broke down that hard shell of yours. She must be something special. Let's talk this weekend. —Dad

"Fuck," I mutter as I bang my head against my desk. What am I going to do now?

CHAPTER THREE

Ivy

"That oughta do it for you, Miss Ivy. We've got you all fixed up with a brand-new tire, and I was even able to get most of that dent out of your front bumper," Big Dan, the owner of Auto Shop, says as he wipes his greasy hands on a towel.

"Thank you so much. I don't know what I would've done without your help."

He brushes me off. "Oh, no, I should say the same to you. I can't wait to surprise Susan with that dress you helped me pick out for our anniversary tonight."

"Remember to call and make the reservation. Women love it when their partners take initiative. It's the little things that'll get you laid," I say with a wink.

Dan throws his head back, letting out a roar of laughter, which makes me smile that much wider.

I took my grumpy hero's advice and showed up at ten this morning with a warm pastry and a hot cup of coffee from

Bakery. That was just about all the convincing Big Dan needed to push my car up to the top priority of his morning.

We were on our way to find my car when he got a call to pull old lady Marion's car out of a ditch—apparently, it's the third time this year. Dan thinks she's got someone on the inside at the DMV helping her pass her driving tests, and after meeting her, I have to agree.

Then, he mentioned that tonight was his wedding anniversary, and one thing led to another, and I was helping him pick out a dress to surprise her with. Dan had recently picked up a few of her romance novels she'd left lying around and wanted to put some of his new *knowledge* to good use. I could only hope if I ever settled down with someone that he'd still be trying to woo me forty years later. Of course, that'll never happen since I don't plan on ever settling down.

I yank at the neck of my T-shirt and shiver, just thinking about it.

Me and commitment go together just about as well as baptizing a cat, and I don't have any plans of changing my mind. I've seen what happens when people stay together for the kids, and I've experienced enough loss to last me a lifetime. It's easier to be detached because if losing my sister taught me anything, it's that everything comes to an end eventually.

So, why put yourself in a position to be hurt to begin with?

"Thanks for tagging along with me this morning. I enjoyed having the company, not to mention all those great date night ideas." He taps his temple and gives me a wink.

"Anytime, Dan." I pull out my wallet and reach for my credit card. "How much do I owe you—"

He waves a hand and shakes his head. "That won't be necessary, Miss Ivy."

I narrow my eyes. "Why not? I don't expect you to do me any favors. Let me pay you—"

"It's already been taken care of. There's nothing to pay," he says like it's the end of the discussion.

"By who?"

Dan just flashes me a shit-eating grin and motions like he's zipping his lips shut. "I've been sworn to secrecy, but I reckon it can't be too hard to narrow down, considering you just got to town last night. You must've made a good impression on someone." He shrugs, then hands me my keys.

"Yeah, well, *someone* has a weird way of showing it." I take my keys and tuck them into my pocket as I turn to leave.

"See ya around, Ivy! And please don't go on any more nighttime hikes. I wouldn't want the Phantom to get you!" Dan playfully calls from behind the counter.

"Maybe that's just the kind of trouble I'm looking for!"

"Why do I not doubt that in the slightest? You're trouble, Miss Ivy, and I think we could all use a little more trouble around here. Some of us more than others ..."

I wave goodbye and thank him again as I turn the corner onto Main Street and take in the quaint little downtown before me.

Who knew an old coal mining town in West Virginia could be so ... cute?

According to Dan, Ashford Falls was completely barren up until thirty years ago, when some bigwig billionaire family swooped in and bought the whole town. Frank Kingsley and his wife, Mary Ashford—whose family was founding members—and their five sons came in and started an international eco-friendly company, and set Ashford Falls as their home campus.

Since then, the company's grown, and so has the town. They've personally subsidized everything from the roads to the schools and local businesses. As Dan said, they breathed life back into this little town. It's an odd thing to think people that rich could care about other people enough to bring back local jobs, much less the environment, but if what Dan says is true, then maybe there's hope for us yet.

Rows of colorful Victorian-style shops line the streets, and it feels like I've taken a step back in time or been transported somewhere else entirely. Everything here seems to be preserved to its original state but somehow better with an eclectic mix of old and new infrastructure.

I laugh to myself as I read the shop names, all in the same font and style—Bakery, Market, Bookstore, Boutique, and Auto Shop, where I met Dan this morning.

Whoever's in charge of the city commerce either has a dry personality with no time for frills and fluff or they're committed to the bit because this is hysterical. Fern would have absolutely loved it.

Across the street, on the corner, there's Inn, and along the next corner, a large black building—the only black among the sea of bright colors—sits Restaurant.

It's got ornamental stained-glass windows and a steep-pitched roof. It looks like it used to be an old church that was converted into a restaurant, and I can't help but think that of all the buildings in this little town, this one would've been Fern's favorite. With the juxtaposition of timeless and modern, it captures the essence of this town perfectly.

I notice my stomach growling, just thinking about it, and

I make a mental note to visit ... after I take a better look at my bank account.

I cross the cobblestone street, taking in the elaborate displays set in deep bay windows, and even though it's still very much summertime, a cool breeze blows my hair out of my face, giving me the slightest preview of fall.

It's not hard to imagine the streets lined with pumpkins and sugared-up children running around in Halloween costumes.

If I were ever going to start a family, I'd raise my children someplace like this. Cozy, small, safe, and charming to boot, but with just enough of an edge to keep things current and fresh.

Maybe in another life.

I press my hand over the list I keep tucked in my overall pocket and take a deep breath.

"Okay, Ferny, you got me here. Now what?"

I don't have to hear my sister's voice to know what I need to do next because with Fern, the next right thing was always ... ice cream. And what do you know? There just so happens to be an ice cream truck parked across the street, next to a line of food trucks.

She might not be much help in how to get from point A to B, but at least I know she's still watching out for me, sending me ice cream trucks and hot, rich grumps to help me out when I need it.

What more does a girl need than that anyway?

* * *

Melted chocolate ice cream drips down my arm as I race to finish the triple-scoop cone before the sun melts it all over me.

I crunch the last bite of cone between my teeth and attempt to wipe my sticky arms in the soft grass. It doesn't help. In fact, I just manage to make a bigger mess, sticky *and* covered in grass. Great.

I'm sitting under a large oak tree, people-watching—my favorite pastime—as birds chirp all around me.

Days like today make me nostalgic about my childhood. Back when my biggest decisions were what color friendship bracelets to make and if I could still beat Ferny in a foot race —spoiler alert: I always did.

Now, I've got much bigger worries, but I promised myself I'd only start thinking about them after I finished this ice cream cone.

My stomach churns in a tight knot, and no matter how hard I try to reframe it, there's no shaking the panic gnawing at my stomach.

I'm broke.

It's so much worse than I thought.

After I treated myself to an ice cream, I sat down with my new phone—thanks to my grumpy guardian angel last night— and nearly choked when I saw the balance.

Every time I look, there's new charges from my mom's facility—random fees or expenses I didn't anticipate.

At this rate, I'll be bankrupt before the end of the summer, and the worst part is, I was the one who encouraged her to go through with it. I assured her we could make it work and I'd be able to catch whatever expenses fell through the cracks.

I swallow a gulp and set a ten-minute timer to worry. It's something Fern's therapist taught her to help cope with her illness, and after she realized how stressed I was, she started making me do it too.

Sometimes, I think I'm too good at compartmentalizing my stress. I'll do just about anything to distract myself from it.

Even dropping out of college and signing a one-year contract to work in Dracula's Castle with barely enough money to get me through the next month. All while trying to cross off as many things on this list as I can. I'm living out of my car, and what little I have left in savings is rapidly deteriorating as my mother's living expenses steadily accrue. I really should've read the fine lines before agreeing to cosign for her expenses, but attention to detail was never my strong suit.

Fern would've planned for this for years—hell, in a lot of ways she already did by making this list. But that's how we were different. She was the planner, and I was the doer. It never failed that she'd have to bail me out of trouble, but we'd always walk away with a hell of a story to tell. That was what she always told me to make me feel better anyway.

I don't know what I'm going to do. It's not like I have a home I can crawl back to, and I've already dropped out of school, lost what little scholarships I had, and used my savings to buy a nonrefundable plane ticket to Romania. It was Fern's biggest dream, so I just need to figure out how to patch enough odd jobs together for the next thirty days, and then I'll have the fresh start that I desperately need.

I twirl Fern's plain silver ring as I try to think of a plan. Her fingers were thinner than mine, so I have to wear it on my ring finger. She was such a little weirdo, and I miss her so much, it hurts. As much as I want to live out all her dreams, the thought of not knowing what she'd do next eats at me more than I'd like to admit.

When I think of what I'm really here to do—find somewhere to sprinkle her ashes—it makes my throat tighten up and sends a cold chill up my spine. I'm not ready to say goodbye, but maybe finishing the list will help me to be.

There's also the pressure of choosing the perfect resting place, and she certainly didn't help me by asking me to do it before she died.

"You'll know where to sprinkle me, Ivy. I trust you to find the perfect place."

No pressure, right, sis?

I scoff a laugh at the absurdity of it all just as my timer alerts me that my worry session has come to an end.

So much for coming up with a plan. I guess I'll just wing it, like I always do. I'll keep my eyes open, and something will come along. It always does. It's not like I'm afraid of getting my hands dirty with a little hard work, and I'm not above doing whatever it takes to make ends meet.

I've done just about any odd job you could imagine— from dog walking to food delivery to selling pictures of my feet to creepy guys online. For the right price, I'd be willing to try just about anything once. The important thing is flexibility with the freedom to pivot when I get bored, which makes short-term jobs ideal for my chaotic lifestyle.

"Okay, Ferny. You want me to check off this list for you? Then, I'm going to need you to help me find a job. Okay?"

No sooner do the words leave my mouth than I hear that deep, familiar voice that played through my dreams all night long.

I sit up in a rush, and immediately, my eyes land on his pristine white button-up shirt, stretched over his thick, broad shoulders. My stomach pirouettes, and I swallow a gulp.

I'm already walking toward him before I can even figure out what to say. Somehow, *Thanks for the new tires, 'kay, bye,* doesn't feel like enough, but my mind's drawing a big fat blank.

Since when am I, of all people, at a loss for words?

He's talking on the phone, sitting on a park bench, eating a bowl of noodles. I pause when I get close enough to hear his conversation.

"No, Roman. I told you, you can tell Mom I will not be wearing the bow tie she crocheted for family portraits."

Consider my interest piqued. I move a little closer.

"No, he's not my brother. Do I seem like someone who knows where to find a last-minute Siegfried and Roy impersonator for a cat's birthday party? Listen, I'm trying to eat my lunch in peace. Can we talk about this later? Fine. Bye." He hangs up the phone and shakes his head.

Have my prayers been answered? So soon?

Feeling a renewed sense of hope, I step behind him, tapping him on the shoulder. "Excuse me, I don't mean to bother you ..."

His eyes widen in recognition, and he chokes on his bite of noodles.

"Sorry, I didn't mean to sneak up on you." I give his back a little pat as he coughs into his elbow. "I don't know if you remember me, but I couldn't help but overhear your conversation and—"

He wipes his mouth with a napkin, then coughs some more before nodding his head. "You nearly blinded me with a fistful of rice. That's not exactly a first impression one easily forgets."

It's then I notice his left eye is red and swollen. I purse my lips, feeling awkward. "Sorry about that. If it helps, you can only tell if you're looking at it."

"Great. Just what I was hoping for." He dabs his forehead with his napkin and coughs again. "Is there something you need, or did you just want to come by and insult me?" He rakes a glance up my body like he's taking inventory of every detail.

I don't know why, but heat pools in my belly, and I have to squeeze my legs together to distract myself from the physical effect his gaze has on me.

What the hell is with this guy?

I wipe my sticky, grass-covered hands against my shorts, suddenly feeling insecure about my dishevelment. I knew he was hot last night, but seeing his striking features in broad daylight is something else entirely.

His jaw is sharp and peppered in the faintest day-old stubble, like he was too tired to shave when he got up for work this morning, and his wavy brown hair is styled to perfection. He's got his white button-up shirt rolled up to his elbows, revealing thick, corded forearms that are almost too indecent to be waving around without any warning. The faintest dusting of chest hair peeks out where he's loosened his tie and the top button of his dress shirt, and my fingers itch to touch it.

I consider myself to be a fairly confident woman, but I've never felt more out of my league than standing next to this extremely *grown* man.

He's got to be at least ten years older than me, and

judging by his fancy car and tailored clothing, he's clearly got his life together—unlike me.

I shake my head to clear my thoughts. What did I come over here for again?

Oh yeah, the birthday-party gig ...

"So ... I couldn't help but overhear that you're in need of a performer for a birthday party?" My voice pitches up an octave making it come out more like a question.

Why does this guy make me so nervous? Probably the suit or the scowl, or maybe it's the glare he's shooting in my direction with his one good eye.

"You're a magician?" He quirks a brow, then takes another bite of his noodles.

"Well, no. More like an opportunist," I say with my best charming smile. "I'm in need of work, and I have a large enough skill set to do just about anything decently enough."

He shakes his head and almost smiles. "Why am I not surprised by that?" He goes back to eating his lunch, then pauses. "Sorry, but I don't think you're what my brother has in mind. Maybe check out the job boards posted around town, or better yet, keep driving east until you hit some bigger cities."

I nervously twirl my sister's ring around my finger, my eyes falling in defeat.

Silence spans between us, and when I look up, I expect to find him wearing a look of sympathy or even concern. Instead, his face is flushed bright red and sweaty.

He coughs several times into the crook of his elbow.

"Uh ... are you okay? Do you need some water or something?"

He waves me away and holds up his water bottle, but

continues coughing. When he pulls away, I notice the bright red stain of blood on his pressed white dress shirt.

My eyes go wide. "Are you sure? Because it doesn't look like it," I say as I point out the blood.

He jerks back in surprise and goes into another coughing fit, groaning and holding his stomach. The noodles drop to the ground, and I look around in panic, but there's no one here but me.

"Call ... 9 ... 1 ... 1 ..." he croaks out.

Oh shit. Okay. I can do this.

I look around to assess my surroundings and see my car parallel parked just a few feet away.

"Come on. My car's right here. I can get you to the hospital faster than an ambulance anyway."

I tug him up, but he pulls away and shakes his head.

"No way. I've seen the way you drive. Just call an ambulance." He shrugs me off, then groans again as he doubles over, a streak of blood at the corner of his mouth.

"Stop being such a baby and come on. I promise I'll drive safely, but you're wasting time here." I pull him up again, and this time, he relents.

I lead us to my car, and it's only when I'm opening his door that I remember all the shit I've got stowed in here. This guy's got to be at least six-three, maybe even six-four.

I shove the passenger seat back as far as possible, tossing piles of books and a box of my bathroom things loosely in the back seat, carefully unbuckling Fern's ashes and moving them to the box.

"Sorry about the mess." I help him into the seat, bending his legs before tucking them inside.

It's almost comical the way his knees stick up like he's

completely folded in half. If this wasn't a medical emergency, I'm sure we'd both laugh at the absurdity of how crammed he looks right now—well, maybe not him, but I sure would.

I run around to my side and slam the door behind me, throwing the car in drive. My tires squeal as I peel out, the smell of burned rubber filling the air. So much for my new tires.

We fly down the narrow city street. Luckily, the hospital is close enough to see from here, and thanks to Dan's tour this morning, I've gotten well enough acquainted with the town.

Adrenaline floods through my system as I maneuver my little car through the town's two-lane streets. When we come to a Stop sign, I turn left on a one-way in the wrong direction.

"You're going the wrong way!" he yells before gripping the oh-shit handle with a white-knuckled grip.

"Just for a sec." I turn into an alleyway, weaving around dumpsters and piles of crates like a street racer fleeing from the police. My heart kicks up a beat as panic rises in my chest.

"Let me out! You're going to get us killed." He braces himself before going into another coughing fit and wincing.

"Just hang on. We're almost there." I whip the car left across two lanes of traffic and straighten out just as someone behind me lays on their horn. I wave an apology.

"What the fuck is wrong with you? Are you trying to kill me?"

I ignore him as I ramp over a speed bump and fly into the hospital parking lot, straight into one of the several empty handicapped spots right by the front door.

"You can't park here. This is a handicapped spot," he says, shaking his head.

I shrug. "There are plenty of them. Besides, this is an emergency. I'm sure they'll understand. Now, let's go."

He starts to protest, but another wave of coughing has him too winded to argue. I don't know what's going on with this guy, but I know one thing: I can't sit back and not help him.

Especially after what he did for me.

I hate hospitals. I hate the overly sterile smell. I hate the way it makes my throat burn. I hate the fluorescent lights that illuminate the stark white hallways and make you feel dizzy. I hate the noises of machines beeping and Velcro from blood pressure cuffs. I hate the palpable mixture of fear and hope mingling in the air as people wait to find out the answer to the very same question—*Will they be all right?*

I hate the cracked plastic seat cushions that pinch my legs as I squirm, watching the minutes on the clock tick by.

And I especially hate the way time seems to slow down and the way I haven't been able to take a full breath since I walked through those sliding glass doors.

So, why am I still sitting here, six hours later, waiting to hear about a stranger I hardly know?

I wish I knew myself.

But I don't know if I could leave if I tried, it's like I'm frozen in place by a magnet.

It's pathetic really ... or maybe it's a trauma response left over from all the times I did this exact same thing when my sister got sick.

All I know is, I haven't been that afraid in a very long time.

After Fern died, I didn't think it was possible to be afraid. Living through your worst nightmare does that to you. You realize there's nothing else that can be taken away.

I certainly don't plan on tempting fate again. It's why I don't do relationships and I'm not afraid of change. I don't stay in the same place very long or even the same job. I don't have close friends. I'm the most extroverted loner to ever live, and that's exactly the way I like it.

The sliding doors open, sending a gush of hot air swirling around the too-cold waiting room. The warm air soothes my chill-bump-covered skin like a soft blanket straight out of the dryer. I look up to see a group of people walking in, all wearing the familiar look of worry.

My eyes land on the only woman in the group. She's old enough to be my mother, maybe even my grandmother, not that she looks it. Rather, her platinum-white hair is cut into a stylish bob, and she's dressed cooler than any older woman I've ever seen with wide-legged trouser pants and a denim sleeveless top tucked into it.

She's cute, and there's something about her vibe that makes me instantly like her—not that she needs my approval but, hey, I'm bored. What else am I supposed to be doing while I wait to hear if my grumpy stranger is okay?

My eyes catch on the book she's holding, and a strange sense of recognition comes over me. Then, it clicks. It's been a long time, but I remember that book. Fern used to be obsessed with it.

What are the chances that more than one person shares my sister's obsession with this Phantom creature?

Maybe it's the triggering hospital noises, but suddenly, I feel like I need to talk to her, to tell her that my sister also loved those books. I don't know why, but I need to tell this kind-looking woman about my sister.

I walk up to her and clear my throat.

"Excuse me. I'm so sorry. I hate to bother you, but are you ... I noticed the book you were reading and thought, *What a coincidence*. My sister used to love that series—"

She spins to face me, and I'm struck by her mysterious forest-green eyes, the beautiful smile lines that frame them, and the familiar shape of her sharp nose. She's beautiful and somehow so familiar ...

Her lips curve into a warm smile. "Oh, I just love hearing that. You know, the author's a local. Word around here is, she writes under a secret pen name." She nudges me with her shoulder. "Isn't that exciting? I suppose I could be talking to her right now and not even know it!"

It's rare, meeting anyone as obnoxiously enthusiastic as me. I want to be best friends with this lady, and I've only just met her.

I laugh and shake my head. "Trust me, I'm no secret monster romance author, just a regular hot-mess express, trying to figure out my life as it comes."

Is it weird that I'm having a full-blown conversation with this complete stranger in the middle of a hospital room waiting room? Absolutely. But stranger things have happened.

"I'm so sorry. I didn't mean to disturb you while you're waiting. I guess I just felt like I needed to meet you," I say with a smile, feeling embarrassed all of a sudden.

She extends her hand in greeting, sandwiching mine with her other palm. "Well, it was very nice to meet you ..."

"Ivy," I offer, shaking her hand.

Her eyes widen, and she shakes her head. "Did you say Ivy?" Her voice hitches.

She looks at the older man beside her, and they share a glance.

"Yes?" I ask, feeling like I'm missing something.

"Oh my God. I'm Mary. It's so good to finally meet you." She opens her arms wide before pulling me into a firm hug and smashing my face against her cheek. "Frank, did you hear that?! She's real! And so ... *young*."

My whole body goes limp with confusion, letting her squeeze me.

She's real?

I don't know what I was expecting from a beautiful stranger with kind eyes, but consider me pleasantly surprised. Though I don't know why. Everyone I've met in this town has been kind and welcoming. Apart from the grumpy guy I'm still here for, but I think I have enough evidence to prove he's the exception.

"Would you look at that? No wonder he waited so long to tell us about you—probably knew he'd never hear the end of our teasing," the man says, clapping me on the shoulder. "It's nice to finally meet you, Ivy. I'm Frank." He points to the three other men in their group. "That's Roman, and Luka, and the tall, ginger on the end is Guy. I'm sure Leo's told you all about his brothers—"

My ears perk up, and my brain does acrobatics, trying to make sense of all this new information.

"Holy shit. I could've sworn he was lying," Roman says before shaking my hand.

"He must've wanted to surprise us for Bartholomew's birthday party!" Mary claps her hands in front of her face, her green eyes filling up with tears.

And that's when the final puzzle piece clicks into place.

This kind-looking woman is none other than my grumpy stranger's mother ... and for some crazy reason ... it seems like she knows me.

Just then, a nurse comes through the mechanical double doors, holding a clipboard. "Leo's in the recovery room. I can take immediate family members to go back and see him now."

"Oh, wonderful!" Mary hoists her purse strap on her shoulder and tucks her arm around mine.

She moves to pull me forward, but I stop.

"Uh, you go ahead. I'm not ... I'm not family."

"Of course you are, dear. Did you think I wouldn't notice that ring on your finger? You're as much family as any of us now."

I swallow a gulp and grit my teeth and follow her into the sterile hospital room.

What the hell is going on?

CHAPTER FOUR

Leo

"Not only did you keep your girlfriend a secret from me, but you also neglected to share that you were *engaged!*" My mother's voice pulls what's left of the anesthesia right out of me, and I sit up with a grunt, realizing I'm still chained to an assortment of beeping machines.

"Mom, what are you talking about?" I rub my eyes and blink, and a roomful of blurry people come into focus.

My family—everyone apart from my brother, Jett—all stand in a half circle around the foot of my bed, but when my eyes land on her, I have to lie back down.

What the fuck is she doing here?

Suddenly, my conversation with Roman—and the family group text—comes blaring like a freight train back into my mind.

Shit. This is bad.

The machine monitoring my vitals begins beeping as my blood pressure cuff tightens around my arm.

Great, nothing like having my utter panic broadcasted to my entire family in real time.

I force a deep inhale through my nose to calm my spiking blood pressure just as a nurse rushes in to check on me.

"Whoa there, that's a little higher than I'd like to see. You feeling okay, Leo? Need me to ask everyone to leave?" she asks, but I wave her off.

"No, but thank you. I think I just got a little overstimulated for a second. I'll be fine though."

"Okay, well, don't be shy." She places the call button in my hand before leaving.

When she moves out of view, I find my mother—her arm around Ivy like she's afraid if she lets the girl go, she'll disappear—wearing a confused look on her face.

My mother might seem ditzy on the surface, but she's perceptive as shit, and I don't think there's any detail she doesn't notice, no matter how small. And right now, she's watching my every reaction like a hawk.

If I have any hope of this not blowing up in my face, I'll need to keep my cool and pray that Ivy doesn't give me away before I can think of an explanation.

"Are you okay, honey? I'm sorry. I didn't mean to startle you." She squeezes Ivy in another side hug. "I was just excited. I can't believe you'd go through all this trouble to surprise us for Bart's party."

My dad moves to my side and places a hand over mine, his face etched with concern. "I told you you've been pushing yourself too hard. Arthur called us and said you've got a nasty stomach ulcer; he said you're lucky it didn't rupture."

He scrubs a hand down his face and takes a seat in the chair by my bed, and then my mother rushes to me.

She gnaws on her cheek, looking between my dad and me uncomfortably. "Leo, you told me you were going to start taking better care of yourself. You promised me at Easter. Do you think maybe it's time to take a step down and let someone else do the heavy lifting for a while?"

I hold up my hand. "No, Mom, it's not like that." I grab her hand, keeping her from biting her thumbnail, and hold it in mine. "This isn't a big deal. I swear. And I'm already making more time for myself ..."

I gesture to Ivy, who's standing awkwardly behind her. How or why this woman hasn't already run for the hills is beyond me.

My mom's worried face pulls into a warm smile, and I can see the immediate sense of relief wash over her at the mention of Ivy. I notice my dad's shoulders relax as he looks between us.

Okay, it looks like they're buying it. I just need to keep it going until I can figure out a way to get myself out of this hole.

Roman starts on about remembering one of the nurses from high school, which sparks a whole family argument over which one of my three younger brothers she dated.

I take the opportunity to try to get Ivy's attention, folding my lips in a flat line and holding my hands together like I'm praying, silently begging her to stay quiet. If she can just keep her mouth shut and let me do the talking, maybe I can salvage some of this horrendous misunderstanding.

She furrows her eyebrows and mouths something, but I can't understand her because her lips are moving too fast. When the room falls silent, I realize they're all watching our failed attempts at ESP.

So much for subtlety.

"Who'd have thought that Leo—the town recluse—would be the first of us to settle down?" Roman shakes his head and laughs. "Better you than me, brother. Though I cannot wait to hear more details about how you two met ..."

"Yeah, like, did you know that you didn't have to date our brother?" Guy adds under his breath.

"Now, let's not scare her off already. I'm sure they'll be happy to tell us all about it at Bart's party tomorrow night," my mom says with a proud grin.

"Actually, I—" Ivy starts, but I interrupt her.

"I was just catching her up on all the festivities, and she can't wait!" I say for her, my voice sounding not at all like my own.

Please just go with it. I give my best attempt at telepathy, but this time, she nods like she understands, and a small smirk pulls at the corner of her lip.

And it doesn't take a rocket scientist to know that the smirk means trouble.

"Yes, Leo was telling me all about the party ... tomorrow? Tomorrow night?" she answers, reading my head nod as encouragement. "He's so excited about it actually. Said he couldn't wait to wear the matching crochet bow tie you made him for the photos."

My mother's eyes light up as she hangs on Ivy's every word. "You should see how cute they look together. I think I'm going to put it on this year's Christmas card."

Ivy places a hand on my mom's shoulder. "You should. It'd be iconic."

My mother beams and audibly gasps. "We could all match!" She pulls Ivy closer and not so quietly whispers,

"Now, tell me, would you say you're a B cup? I don't want to assume—"

The nurse call button slides out of my hand, landing on the tiled floor with a sharp thwack, and all their heads snap to look at me.

"Jesus, Mom, can you not—"

But she just brushes me off. "Oh, stop eavesdropping. We're having a little girl talk over here."

She tugs the end of Ivy's long braid, to which Ivy just laughs. They're talking like they've known each other for years rather than ten minutes.

"I'm usually a B, but it depends on the bra. Half the time, I don't wear one because I don't like to be restricted," Ivy answers pushing her breasts together.

I nearly fall out of the bed.

"Hell yeah," Luka says as he and Guy dab knuckles.

I snap my fingers at my two youngest brothers and point. "Hey, fuckwads. That's enough!"

"Leo, you can't scream *fuckwads* in the hospital. There could be children on the other side of this wall!" my mom hisses, as if *that's* what's inappropriate right now.

I snap my mouth closed and grind my teeth as all three of my brothers try to hide their snickers.

"You have lovely breasts, dear. I know my son likely agrees," Mom says. "I think you'll love the top I'm crocheting for you. I only started on it this morning—since I didn't know you existed before then—but I'm nearly finished. I was just waiting for your cup size, but it doesn't look like it'll take more than a few rows."

"Knock, knock," Dr. Stone announces as he walks in the room. "Am I interrupting?"

"Not at all!" I practically yell, thankful for the interruption.

He greets both of my parents, who are more than delighted to catch him up on all the happenings of the last ten minutes—which is admittedly a lot.

"Well, Leo, it seems you've been busier than anyone realized."

"It appears so," I agree because that's all I *can* say right about now.

"It's nice to meet you, Ivy. I'm Dr. Stone, resident doctor of Ashford Falls and Leo's godfather. I've known your fiancée his whole life, so if you ever need blackmail on him, please know you can always come to me. I'm more than prepared and happy to help."

Ivy shakes his hand and laughs. "You know, I might just have to take you up on that."

"So, Arthur, do you have any updates on what you said on the phone? How were his tests?" my dad asks.

Dr. Stone clicks his pen and scribbles something on his clipboard. "After taking a better look, it's easy to see that you've probably had this for quite some time, but luckily, you got here before it ruptured. We'd be having a whole other conversation if that were the case."

He shoots me a glare over his reading glasses. "I wish you had said something sooner. I could've saved you a lot of pain."

"Well, he wouldn't be Leo if he did things the easy way, now would he?" my dad says, his tone laced with frustration.

Dr. Stone laughs and shakes his head like he knows exactly what my dad is talking about. "No, he wouldn't." He nods his head toward Ivy and then back to me. "You're going to have to keep him in line if you want him to get better. Lots of rest. Maybe even taking some time off work if you're in the miracle business."

To my utter shock, Ivy moves toward me and tucks her small hand in mine like she's not going anywhere, and fuck if that doesn't knock me right off my axis.

I don't know how I got so lucky—or utterly fucked, depending on how you look at it— that she saved my ass, but I'm in way over my head here. And I'll do whatever I need to do to keep from disappointing everyone in this room with the pathetic truth.

I'm a boring, workaholic coward, and I can't even handle the job I have. How the hell did I think I was cut out to be CEO?

And soon enough, everyone else will realize it too.

"These things are always exacerbated by stress," I hear Dr. Stone say, but all I can do is stare down at our conjoined hands as a multitude of emotions battle against each other in my chest.

"You're going to be just fine. With a little rest and a few lifestyle changes, you'll be feeling froggy in no time." He gives me a wink, and I choke on my saliva at his slight insinuation.

The last thing I need in my head right now is to be thinking about feeling froggy around this dangerous woman, who is way too young and exciting for me.

"Thank you, Arthur." Dad shakes his hand.

My mom pulls him into a hug. "Thank you so much for all you've done today. Will I see you and Evelyn tomorrow night at Bartholomew's party?"

"I wouldn't miss it for the world. I'll get started on those discharge orders now. Ivy, you keep him in line, okay? You've got to keep your eye on him at all times," he says, gesturing from his eyes to me. "He's been known to sneak away to work, even when he's been advised against it."

Ivy smiles and gives Dr. Stone a salute. "You got it, Doc."

Roman goes into a story about the time I came to work with the flu and got the whole executive team sick, and my parents jump in, adding their own details. I watch Ivy wipe a tear from her eye in laughter, asking questions that only prompt my family to reveal more embarrassing stories.

She looks so natural, standing there with them, like she isn't someone I found wandering alone in the woods less than twenty-four hours ago.

Not only is she not scared off by my mother's inappropriate questions, but she also actually looks like she's enjoying herself.

Where did this woman come from, and why am I finding myself growing more curious about her by the minute?

A reckless, negligent, idiotic idea starts to churn in my mind ...

Maybe this could work?

It's a dangerous plan, one that could backfire in my face if anyone found out ... but it just might be worth a shot.

"Hey, uh ... do you guys think you could give us a moment alone?"

"Sure, honey. Your dad and I still have some errands to run to get ready for the party anyway." My mom kisses her two fingers and touches my cheek. "Feel better and please let me know when you're home and settled."

"We'll talk more about lightening your workload tomorrow," Dad warns, then whispers something to Ivy before leaving.

Roman, Luka, and Guy wave silent goodbyes, but as soon as they're through the doorway, I hear them whooping and hollering like idiots over how hot their future sister-in-law is.

When it's finally just the two of us, Ivy crosses her arms over her chest and tilts her head. "Care to explain why your family knew my name and thinks we're engaged?"

Suddenly, I'm keenly aware that I'm in nothing but a hospital gown, which only makes this conversation more embarrassing. "I, uh ... I might have told Roman a little white lie this morning that was completely blown out of proportion." I point to the silver ring on her left hand. "But the engagement? That's all on you."

I push my hair back from my face, realizing how little I actually know about this woman. "I'm sorry ... I ... I didn't think to ask you before, but ... are you married? Because if you are, I didn't mean to—"

"No. Don't worry about that. I'm as single as a Pringle. I don't really do relationships, much less marriage." Her smile falls a little, and she spins her ring again like she's nervous. "It's my sister's ring. It only fits on this finger ..." Her words trail off, and I don't pry further even though that explanation seemed to bring up more questions than it answered.

The important thing is that she isn't attached, so I won't have some angry husband to worry about.

She props her hand on her hip, but doesn't say anything, so I pick back up with my explanation.

"My mom was trying to set me up on this blind date ... like she always does ... and Rome was giving me a hard time about working too much ... and I just found out my dad's naming Carl as his replacement when he retires."

"I missed the part where this has anything to do with me."

I massage my aching temples and sigh. "My mom's throwing this party tomorrow—"

"Bartholomew's twenty-first birthday party," she clarifies.

"Yes, that. And I mentioned to Roman that I'd secretly been seeing someone and it was pretty serious. Then, he asked me on the spot what her name was, and yours was the first name to pop in my head." I point at my still-swollen eye. "Probably because this was still fresh. Anyway, that's how it happened. I never in a million years dreamed I'd see you again, much less that you'd drive me to the hospital and still be waiting hours later. Why were you still here again?" The last part comes out a little more accusatory than I intended.

She adjusts her arms around herself a little tighter. "Don't you dare act like I'm the creepy one in this scenario! I didn't have anywhere else to be, so I thought I'd wait to make sure you were okay. Then, I saw your mom holding my sister's favorite book—it's not a book you see every day—and I felt like I needed to tell her—never mind why—but we got to talking, and I introduced myself, and suddenly, it was like they all knew me. Like they were expecting me ..."

"I'm really sorry about that. Like I said, it wasn't the smartest thing on my end, but how was I supposed to know that I'd run into you again? I thought you said you were just passing through?"

She shrugs. "Well, maybe I told you that so you wouldn't try to stalk me. It's not exactly smart to tell some grumpy stranger all your plans just because he's cute and helps you."

The word *cute* hangs in the air between us, and I really

wish my heart didn't skip a beat from her admitting that, but I try to ignore it.

I pick at the thin, scratchy blanket in my lap. "Listen, I understand if you're freaked out by everything. And I understand if you want to run out of here and never speak to me again ... but at the risk of already sounding insane ... I was wondering if maybe you'd be willing to keep this going with me for a little while longer?"

She sucks in a small breath, and just when I think she's about to call me a psycho, proving all her suspicions right, she asks, "What do you have in mind?"

I perk up at the question, feeling relieved that she isn't running for the hills. "I, uh ... I don't really know. I haven't given it much thought, but do you think you could stick around until the Phantom Festival at the end of the summer? That's when my dad will officially step down as CEO. I think this might be the only shot I have at changing his mind and convincing him I should be the one leading the company."

"So, what is that, thirty days?"

"Yeah, unless you have somewhere to get back to?" I can't help but ask, feeling like I need to know everything there is to know about what's she's doing here and why. But I know it's not my business.

Rather than answering my question, she responds with one of her own. "So, you think if you have a fake fiancée, your dad will make you CEO?"

"No, maybe not. It's dumb, but I have this thing about letting people down. It started out as an innocent lie to dodge another setup attempt from my mother, but after seeing their faces this evening, how happy they were to meet you ... I don't want to crush them. And selfishly, I know I could kiss any hope of my dad reconsidering goodbye."

"So, you *do* want him to change his mind?"

"Well, yes." I flatten my lips. "But that's just because I want what's best for the company, and right now, I believe that's me."

She looks down, biting her lip. "I don't know, Leo. Your family is so nice. I don't know if I could lie to them—"

"I just need your help convincing my dad that I'm capable of handling more responsibility, that I'm not as stressed out as I seem to be. That's all I'm asking."

"This job must be a really big deal if you're willing to lie to your family because of it. So, what is it anyway? Anything I've heard of?"

I tell her all about our brand, how my dad founded the company with the mission to change the world, starting with our patented one-hundred percent biodegradable plastic, and things quickly grew from there. But it doesn't take much explaining for her to catch on.

"Wait. You're Leo Kingsley? Of Kingsley Industries? As in the billionaire family who owns this town?"

"Yes ... did you not know that? I thought that's why you stuck around."

"How would I have known that? Everyone knew you by your first name when we got here. Are you telling me that I've been shooting the shit with a roomful of billionaires for the last half hour?"

I let out a laugh. "Yes. Technically."

"Huh. No wonder you just handed over five hundred dollars like it was nothing. Do you use dollar bills as toilet paper? I've always wondered ..."

"Seriously? That's what you're worried about right now?" I quirk a brow.

She holds up her hands defensively. "You're right; it wouldn't be very environmentally friendly. Bidet?"

I sigh and roll my eyes. Clearly, she's not going to drop this. "Yes. I have a bidet in every bathroom. Now, can we please get back on track here?"

"You really seem to care about this stuff, don't you?"

"It's all I care about."

She pops her lips and rocks back on her feet like she's deliberating.

"Look, I'm not asking for charity. I'm happy to compensate you for your time. You seemed eager for the opportunity to do that Siegfried and Roy gig ... no one wants to do something like that unless they need money."

She twists her lips to the side and looks up as she thinks. "So ... like a sugar daddy/sugar baby arrangement?"

I jerk my head back and blink several times. "What? No. Nothing like that."

"I'm just saying, that's what it sounds like. Paying someone younger to hang out with you or pretend to be engaged with you or whatever."

She rolls her eyes and picks at her yellow fingernail polish, complete with smiley faces drawn on top. It's such a small detail, but it only reinforces all the assumptions I've already made about her. This girl is all sunshine and adventure while I'm more like storm clouds and canceled plans.

I shake my head. "That's not what this is. Anyway, what do you think?"

She narrows her eyes. "What's in it for me?"

"Name your price."

"Do you expect me to have sex with you?"

"Would you?" The question rolls off my lips before I can stop it, and I quickly correct myself. "I'm sorry. I didn't mean to say that. Of course not. I just need you to show up to family dinners and sometimes a work event with me. Stuff like that."

"So, no sex. Do you want me to do anything weird while you watch?"

"What? No. Will you get your head out of the gutter? What do you think I am?"

"It would behoove me to know exactly what I'm agreeing to."

"Behoove you?"

"What? I'm just practicing for mingling with rich people."

"Nobody says behoove. Is that a yes?"

"Fifty thousand dollars."

"Done. Anything else?"

She blinks several times like she can't believe it. "Seriously? I was just fucking with you. That's too much—"

I hold up a hand to stop her. "Ivy, I'm asking you to help me lie to my family ... and I'm rich. I have no intentions of taking advantage of you. You're doing me the favor, remember?" I pull out my phone and type out a quick email to my assistant. "Why don't we make it an even hundred just to be safe?"

Her mouth drops, and she lets out a little gasp, then snaps it shut, nodding her head vigorously.

I can't help but smile at how cute she looks.

I don't know her story or what she's running from—

because she's no doubt running from something—but it's hard to ignore the warm, tingling sensation that spreads through my chest at the thought of helping her.

Down boy.

This is not anything like that.

"So, now what? What do we do next?"

I blow out a sigh. "It would probably be more believable if you stayed at my place. You'll have your own room, of course. Is that something you're comfortable with?"

A slow, mischievous smile spreads across her face, and I already know by the way my heart skips a beat that I'm going to regret this.

"Looks like you've got yourself a sugar baby."

I bury my face in my hands. "Please stop saying that."

CHAPTER FIVE

Leo

"Here we are." The nurse locks the brakes of the wheelchair just as Ivy's dingy red death mobile comes into view.

She honks three times, then rolls down the window. "Hey there, pookie bear. Are you ready to go home?"

I grit my teeth. I can't believe *this* was my solution.

Of all the plans I could've come up with, I chose to hand over all my hopes and desires, everything I'd worked my entire life for, to this woman of all people.

I blame the anesthesia for my temporary lapse in judgment and my delusional proposition back there.

It's too late now. I can either admit that I lied about being in a relationship—which is only made worse, considering everyone already met her—or I can go through with this obscene plan and hope that she can help me sell it as believable ... or at the very least not exacerbate things to the point of destruction.

I don't have the mental energy to consider how badly this

could end right now, but I figure what I've been doing wasn't working anyway. Maybe shaking things up and doing the opposite of what I normally do is worth a try.

"Everything okay?" the nurse asks as she looks between me and Ivy, who's now walking toward me.

"Fine. Just a little groggy still."

Perhaps I should be more concerned with my own acting.

"What's wrong, snookums? Do you need help getting in the car?" Ivy offers me a hand, but I swat it away, grunting as I stand.

"No, that won't be necessary."

"Okay, Grandpa, whatever you say," she says as she runs to the passenger door and opens it, then swipes the parking ticket out from under the windshield wiper and tosses it amid the chaos in her back seat.

I force myself to take a deep breath as I mentally count to ten.

Of course she's going to push my buttons and take things to the extreme.

I know her type. I am very familiar with her type, and I'd be lying if I said that little spark of brattiness isn't what piqued my interest in her from the start, but that's not what this is about right now.

The shadow inside of me doesn't care about my rules or what's best for my career. No, the selfish bastard caught a taste of something he liked, and I already know I'm going to be working double time to keep his thirst at bay.

I force myself to remember the pain, playing that tender memory in the back of my mind on repeat, and just like I knew it would, the thoughts fizzle out, and I'm the one who's back in control.

Good. Now, I just need to keep the reminder front and center. I'm nothing if not an expert at self-torment, so this should be easy enough.

Here's to hoping anyway.

I clench my jaw as I lower myself into the tight space, my knees painfully pressed into the dash. There is no way this is safe.

She closes her door and puts the car in drive. "All right, where to?"

"Drop me off up here at the bank. I'm going to have my driver pick me up there, and you can follow us." I pull out my phone to send my location to my driver.

"Now, why would I do that when we're both going to the same place?" She spins to face me and furrows her brows.

I see disappointment flash across her face, but she quickly masks it with a half smile, and all at once, I feel a heaviness in my chest.

How is it that I've hardly known this woman for twenty-four hours and I'm already familiar with her facial expressions?

She needs the money—that much is obvious—and if I were a better man, I'd just give it to her, no strings attached. But I wouldn't need her help if I wasn't desperate, and selfishly, I can't ignore the rush I get from this little power exchange we've agreed to. So, I'll bite my tongue and play along, if only for curiosity's sake.

I shove my phone in my pocket. "Just forget it. Can you just drive a little safer this time? Use your blinkers and go the speed limit?"

She sucks in a gasp. "You think I'm a bad driver? I was rushing on purpose because I didn't want you to die, but don't worry; this time, I promise to obey all traffic laws. I'll even slow down at yellow lights if you want."

"It's not *if I want*; that's what you're supposed to do." I yank my seat belt across my chest.

She narrows her eyes. "I think it's more of a situational judgment call."

"No, it's not. It's literally the law—"

"What's your address?" she interrupts, swiping open her navigation app.

I suppress the urge to scold her for cutting me off and tell her the address.

I also hold back from commenting on the conditions of her dirty, bug-splattered windshield, clamping my jaw shut and gripping the door handle as she pulls onto the highway.

And to my surprise, she actually uses her blinker before pulling out across two lanes of traffic.

In the short drive from the hospital, I've learned a few things about this woman.

The background check I ran on her came back squeaky clean ... apart from a few outstanding parking tickets and a small lapse in insurance coverage.

1. She prefers riding with the top down to using the air conditioner—though that might be because her air conditioner doesn't work. I don't have enough evidence to support this theory.

2. She can't listen to an entire song all the way through before switching it, and her playlists are more chaotic than

the current state of her back seat ... which is really saying a lot.

3. She appears to be fearless—at least behind the wheel of a vehicle, going ten miles over the speed limit, driving like Evel Knievel.

4. She's only twenty-two.

Yeah, not exactly the best look to be romantically involved with a woman thirteen years my junior—I can't imagine what people with think about that—but it's not like we're really engaged. I don't have any intentions of sleeping with her, so maybe we'll be able to sweep that minor detail under the rug.

Who am I kidding? In this town? I think I have a better chance of getting struck by lightning than something like that going unnoticed.

Even if I did have the time and energy to devote to being in a relationship—which I absolutely do not—she couldn't be more wrong for me. She's too young, too bubbly, and way too much of a mess to fit into my carefully curated life.

A woman like that needs attention ... and as much fun as it might seem to be, I'm already stretched too thin. Hell, I can't even handle the job I have without landing myself in the emergency room from stress.

I learned a long time ago that I can't have it all, that there's pain in showing people the real me. I've made my fair share of mistakes, mistakes I'll spend the rest of my life paying for, and I'm not naive enough to believe it can be any other way. Not anymore.

Instead, I've spent the last decade unattached and focused on creating safety systems so nothing like a manual error can ever cause such devastation ever again. My cause is so much bigger than my desire for love—or whatever the fuck people get from relationships.

Besides, to say that I'm not good with balance is the understatement of the century. I'm not interested in a watered-down vanilla relationship, no matter how badly I wish I were.

So, I'd rather spend my time and energy working toward my goal of becoming CEO because it's the only way I'll be able to have complete control. It's not that I don't trust other people to take care of our employees—I'm sure Carl would do a fine job—but there's not a single person who cares as much as me. Probably because they don't have the blood of sixty-three men on their hands.

There's nothing that fuels you quite like that, trust me.

That's why I've got to find a way to change my father's mind. It's the only way I'll ever know peace and my only chance at having a halfway-fulfilling life.

Which is why I don't have time for any distractions.

No matter how beautiful or tempting they might be.

This can never happen, if only for her sake. I might be a selfish bastard, but I won't make the same mistakes twice.

That much I am absolutely certain of.

So, maybe this is a good thing?

Besides, at thirty-five, I'm sure I'm way too old for her to find me attractive. Hell, she's already calling me *Grandpa*. All I've got to do is keep my eyes down and remember the bigger picture. That's easy enough, right?

The thought alone gives me indigestion, but what else is new?

"Wait. This is your house?" Ivy's mouth drops open as she pulls up to the ornate wrought iron security gate.

"Yes. This is my home. Can you press the call button? I don't have my key."

She reaches out and presses the call button, buzzing it several times, making a jingle.

I lean over and grab her arm to stop her, and she sucks in a breath. The clean scent of citrus from her shampoo sends a wave of heat up my spine.

"Once is plenty," I say, retreating back to my seat.

A moment later, the gate swings open, and I'm greeted by my security officer over the intercom. "Welcome home, Mr. Kingsley."

"Fancy," Ivy says as she eases the car up the winding driveway. Her eyes grow wider and wider as she takes in everything on the property. "You live here? Like, this is your *house*?" she asks as she parks in the small parking lot outside the front door.

"Yes." I climb out of the death mobile, my shoulders sagging in relief to finally be home after this grueling day, and make my way into the house.

Ivy follows closely on my tail, peppering me with her endless burning questions.

"But ... why?"

"Why what?" I say as I open the door, kicking off my shoes and making a beeline to the fridge.

"Why is your house so massive?"

I open my beer and take a long pull, and the ice-cold liquid takes a bit of the edge off my nerves. "Because I'm rich."

"So, all of this"—she gestures in a circle around her—"is just for you? One person? No one else lives here?" She raises an eyebrow.

"Yes. It's just me."

I move past her and make my way to the living room, where I plop down on my leather sofa. I take another sip of my beer, and when I look up, she's across the living room, inspecting pictures on my bookshelves.

"What are you doing?"

She sniffs the candle in her hand, then pulls away, wearing a look of disgust. "I'm making sure you're not a murderer, luring me here to kill me ... obviously," she says as she places the candle down on the wrong shelf.

"And you're going to find that out by digging through my bookshelves and rearranging my stuff?"

Her spine stiffens, and she turns around, crossing her arms over her chest. "Yes, actually. It was a test."

"What was a test? Did I pass?" I ask, feeling even more confused.

She walks toward me and takes a seat on the opposite end of the sofa, then props her dirty white Converse sneakers on my three-thousand-dollar coffee table. "Can I have a beer?"

My eyes catch on the wings she's doodled on the side of each sneaker in black marker, and I can't help but wonder what that could mean. I'm slowly collecting little clues that has me forming a better idea about her, whether I mean to or not.

Hell, I certainly don't want her to scrutinize minor details about me, so it's best to drop it. It's none of my business anyway.

I push myself up with a grunt and head to the kitchen. "IPA, milk stout, pilsner ..."

"Oh, do you have anything that tastes like apple juice?"

She snaps her fingers as she tries to think of the name. "What's it called—"

"Cider," I answer as I place the cold mug in her hand, having already predicted what she'd ask for, which earns me a massive grin of approval.

She crosses her legs on top of each other and gingerly sips her drink, making a loud slurping noise. "Ooh, this is good. It doesn't taste like alcohol at all—"

"Exactly. That's why it's your only one," I snap before she can argue.

"Well, somebody's stingy, aren't they?"

I grit my teeth, growing more irritated. "Not stingy. *Responsible* ... which seems to be a novel concept to you. Now, get your dirty sneakers off my sofa. Were you raised in a barn?"

"So sorry, Grandpa. I didn't realize we were supposed to treat our homes like a museum." She kicks off her shoes and delicately tucks them under the table.

"I'm not the odd one here for wanting to take care of my stuff. Now, I think we need to establish some ground rules if you're going to stay here."

I catch sight of her mismatched socks—an ankle and a crew—and I get a wave of full-body shivers. Seriously, how can she stand the feeling of two entirely different-length socks all day? In fact, I don't know how she functions at all.

"Okay, rules. What do you have in mind?" She taps her finger to her lip and glances around the massive, open space. "Oh, I know this one! I can go everywhere in the castle, except for the west wing—that's your beastly lair and completely off-limits."

"Are you done?" I shoot her an annoyed look, to which she just shrugs.

"Anything the light touches is our kingdom?"

"Fuck me." I shake my head and drain the rest of my beer.

She holds out her arms, crossing her fingers in an X. "Uh-uh. You said sex was off the table. If you want to throw in physical stuff, then I'm going to need to adjust my pricing—"

I tighten my grip on my pint glass as a fresh wave of irritation boils under my skin. I don't know how, but she seems to know exactly what to say to press my buttons.

My nostrils flare as I exhale long and slow, willing my blood pressure to come back down.

She's looking for a reaction, and I need to tread carefully before I show her all my cards, or this little game has the potential to get out of hand—and quickly.

"For Christ's sake," I grunt, trying to play it off like I'm unbothered. "You know that's not what I meant. Will you stop talking about prostitution so casually? I don't like the idea of you even joking about that."

The faintest bit of pink tints her cheeks, and she holds up her hands. "Touchy. Okay, fine. I'll stop."

I don't miss her reaction to my little reprimand, and it certainly isn't helping my cause.

"I just think we need some ground rules to make sure we're meeting each of our *expectations*," I continue, trying to get my mind back on track.

"Calm down. I know what you meant. I'm just giving you a hard time. Maybe I like making you squirm. Do you have a notebook or something? I'll write down the rules, so we can make this official."

I point her in the direction of my briefcase, and she skips off to retrieve pen and paper. Am I making a terrible mistake, going through with this? My better judgment tells me I shouldn't be signing a contract or making any life-altering decisions after everything I've been through today. But when I feel the couch dip beside me and look up to meet those brilliant amber eyes, full of enthusiasm and wonder, all my hesitation and worries go right out the window.

There's something about her energy that's magnetic, it's like nothing I've ever felt before. When I look into her eyes, I see hope, and for some reason I don't understand, it makes me feel a little lighter too. Even though it doesn't make sense, I feel like if there's anyone who can help me convince my family that I'm enjoying my life and I can handle juggling it all, it's her.

You can do this, Leo. It's not like you haven't been practicing for the last decade.

Leo and Ivy's Relationship Rules, she scribbles at the top of the page.

"*Rule number one, no sex or sexual exchanges ... or expectations of sexual favors from either party,*" she says as she writes, then looks up, waiting for me to chime in.

I shuffle in my seat and scratch my now-days' worth of stubble. "We should include an end date." I think for a moment. "How about September 20? That's the day of the Phantom Festival, when my dad will officially name his replacement. That should give us enough time to make things feel real. Does that time frame work for you?"

"I'm leaving the country that day, but my flight isn't until the evening, so it works out perfect. Now, I won't have to fill in the gaps and find somewhere else to stay before I leave."

She scribbles something on the page, and then without looking up, she reads, *"Thirty days to convince your family that you're not a robot and you do in fact have work-life balance."*

I resist the urge to press her for more information, reminding myself that her personal life is none of my business ... no matter how badly I'm starting to wish it were.

With a shake of my head, I bring my attention back to the contract. "Great. You are welcome to stay here until then, but I'll need you to be available for work and social events. And you'll need to play the part that we're engaged, really make them believe I'm happy and ready to settle down."

"The sugar daddy will pay the sugar baby to be available at his every beck and call," she says as she writes, and I let out a frustrated groan. "What? What else am I supposed to call you?"

"I don't know. Maybe Leo? Or you seem to be quite fond of Grandpa ..." I grab her empty cider glass and take it to the kitchen, feeling the sudden need to busy myself so I don't talk myself out of this.

"It's just a name. You're the one who gives it power. Stop being such a prude, *Leo*." She draws out my name with extra emphasis. "I think for clarity purposes, we should keep the language as correct as possible." She draws a line where the amount should be and looks up in question. "Are you sure you're okay with paying me one hundred thousand dollars? It feels like highway robbery for what you're asking of me, even for a billionaire."

I clench my jaw to suppress the urge to scold her for questioning her worth and finally say, "It's not your concern whether I'm getting a good deal or not, Ivy. Now, just write the damn number."

"Fine." She sets her jaw and meets my eyes. "Anything else?"

I have to sit on my hand to keep from tracing my thumb over her stubborn mouth.

"I think if we're going to convince my family, coworkers, and everyone else who could be peeping around town, we should be careful. We need to look like a couple when we go out. So, no dating other people during our agreement. I don't want to go through all this trouble and have a photo getting leaked, only for all this to blow up in my face."

No dating, she writes. "That isn't a problem for me." She lifts a brow in challenge. "Does that apply to you too or—"

"Of course it does. I obviously wouldn't be asking you for help like this if it didn't." My retort comes out a little too harshly.

She holds up her hands. "Hey, I was just asking, no need to be so sensitive."

"I'm not being sensitive. I'm just annoyed by pointless questions." I look down at her list and tap my finger on the paper, then grab the pen and add, *House rules: both parties should be fully dressed at home.*

"What about in the shower?"

I blow a breath through my nose, gritting my teeth. "Obviously apart from the shower—"

"What about in my bedroom? I enjoy sleeping in the nude. Are you planning on sneaking in my room to spy on me?"

"No, Ivy. I have no intentions of watching you sleep or

spying on you," I say, pinning her with a stern glare, to which she innocently bats her eyes.

Great. As if I needed any more temptation, now, she's giving me something to visualize. Fucking hell, this is going to be harder than I thought, and I can already see she's not going to make this easy for me. No wonder I was so drawn to her ...

I bite my cheek and continue, "Quiet hours are between ten p.m. and seven a.m."

To my surprise, she scribbles down the rule without protest.

"And I shouldn't have to say this, but I've got a hunch you'll only follow what's written on this list and nothing more. Clean up after yourself and don't go snooping around."

She quirks a brow. "You hiding something illegal around here that you don't want me snitching about?"

I shake my head with a laugh. "No. Nothing illegal. Believe me, my life couldn't get any more *vanilla* ... I just don't want you digging around, getting your sticky fingers all over my nice things. Got it?"

Her eyes widen a little, but she doesn't argue, just nods her head slowly and draws two lines at the bottom of the page. She signs her name on the first in big, bubbly letters before handing me the pen.

I quickly scribble my signature and tear the paper out of the notebook. "Come on. Let me show you your room."

I might be a fool for thinking of this idiotic scheme, but there's a part of me that's excited by the challenge. I know trouble when I see it, and Ivy Lane is the most dangerous kind of all.

My favorite kind, if I'm being honest ...

CHAPTER SIX

Ivy

"I've actually never been to a cat's birthday party. Are you sure I look the part?" I tug on the hem of my hot-pink micro dress, shimmying it over my nearly exposed ass.

I might have been a little too ambitious with the micro dress, but, hey, how many chances will I get to attend a billionaire cat's twenty-first birthday party? And I am nothing if not committed to a theme.

His eyes flash over me for the briefest moment before darting back to the road. "They didn't have anything a little more *decent*? You look like a stripper." He tightens his grip on the steering wheel, and his jaw tenses like he's biting his tongue from saying anything else.

He's not wrong. I was pressed for time, and when I came across Adult Store, conveniently located among the conventional shops downtown, I knew that I couldn't get more Vegas-themed than that. I was hoping it'd make him squirm, and by the way he keeps adjusting himself, I'd say my evil plan is working.

Besides, if I'm doing this for the plot, I might as well have all the fun I can, right?

Ignoring his rude comment, I pull down the visor mirror and fluff my wavy, teased hair before applying my new bright pink lip gloss I also picked up today. "You know, it's funny; I'm almost the same age as your family cat. I never went out for my twenty-first birthday, so this is sort of my first big hurrah too."

"For Christ's sake, Ivy, please do not repeat that sentence to anyone here tonight." He scrubs his hand over his face before massaging his temple. "I already feel enough like a creep; let's not point out the numbers and have everyone doing the math."

"Oh, come on. Lots of girls my age find older guys hot. There's no need to feel insecure about it—"

"I said, drop it, okay?" His words come out clipped and commanding, eliciting the strangest tingle of excitement deep in my belly.

What the hell was that?

I sit up a little straighter, pressing my thighs together, where the evidence of my confusion pools in my panties.

Rolling my eyes, I snap the visor shut. "Fine. I won't go out of my way to point out our thirteen-year age gap. Anything else, Daddy?"

My body jolts forward for only a moment before the hard barrier of my seat belt snaps me back against my seat when Leo slams on the brakes. My chest heaves for air from the shock, but when I turn to look at Leo, I find him glaring at me. His green eyes are laced with darkness as his jaw clenches so hard that his muscles spasm.

"What was that about? Did you almost hit something?" I ask through panicked heaves as I try to calm my wheezing before it gets any worse.

A moment of silence passes as his fingers tighten around the steering wheel. "Do *not* call me that again. Ever," he says with a growl.

My eyes scan his guarded frame as I try to understand his reaction. He's so rigid and tight, like every muscle in his body is tense and wound in a hard knot. But then I notice the tips of his ears tinted pink and his own heavy breathing.

If I didn't know better, I'd say that Leo Kingsley has a sneaky little secret kink, and I just hit the nail on the head.

Oh shit, this is going to be even more fun than I thought.

A small smirk pulls at my lips, but I quickly cover it with my hand before he notices. "Sure thing. Freudian slip, I guess. It won't happen again."

I dart my eyes away from him and busy myself with another layer of body glitter, and this time, he doesn't chastise me, even when I accidentally spill some on the seat.

We finally pull through the iron gates of his family home, if you can even call it that. An ornate Victorian-style home is lit up with cozy twinkling lights as the soft rumble of music vibrates around us. There's a huge wraparound porch with a basketball hoop just off the side and a large circle driveway, where I suspect the family parks. I can imagine his parents sitting on the front porch, drinking coffee as they watch their gaggle of teenage boys out in the yard, throwing a football or playing a game of basketball together. I don't have to know Leo's brothers to know they have to be competitive.

If I were to ever settle down and start a family, I don't think I could dream of a more perfect picture than this. It's beautiful, and it feels like home the moment we pull into the drive.

A knot forms in my throat, and I cough to clear it away. What is with these weird bodily reactions today? First, I got aroused by Leo scolding me for dressing too sexy, and now, I'm getting emotional over a house.

Go home, hormones. You're drunk.

Leo clears his throat, breaking the silence, and I'm thankful to be pulled from my thought spiral.

"You remember the script, right?"

I nod.

"Okay, because there will be a lot of important people here tonight, and if we blow this, then I'm afraid I might be worse off than I was to begin with." He clears his throat again. "I'm sorry about ... back there. I ... I just don't want anyone to get the wrong idea. You're a beautiful young woman with your whole life ahead of you, but I could see how people could think ..." His voice trails off, and I place my hand on his arm to stop him.

"It's no one's business anyway."

My eyes meet his, and I catch a flash of something that looks like hope, but then he looks away.

"Relax. People love me." I grab his bow tie and straighten it, daring him to look back at me, but he doesn't.

"I mean it, Ivy. This is important to me. I don't know

what I'd do if all this blew up in my face. Promise me you won't go rogue, that you'll stick to the plan."

I roll my eyes. "I promise to be a very good girl tonight."

He grumbles something under his breath and walks around to open my door. But I don't miss the way his heated neck burns brightly under his black collared shirt or the fire burning behind his jade-green eyes when I step out of the car. Leo Kingsley might be the strictest of rule followers, but I think I just made it my newfound mission to push him until he breaks.

You know, for health reasons. All that pent-up stress needs to come out somehow, doesn't it?

I tuck my hand in the crook of his elbow as he leads me up the cobblestone path to the entrance.

"Where did we meet?"

"At a charity event last summer. We bonded over a deep conversation about climate change, spent the whole weekend together, and parted ways as long-distance lovers," I answer without missing a beat.

"Don't say *lovers*. That's weird."

"What am I supposed to call it? We fell in love, didn't we? You want me to say we were pen pals? Sexting buddies?"

He holds up his hand. "Just stop. We were in a long-distance relationship. There's no reason to elaborate on what that looked like."

"I think the people want to know how we went from a weekend together to engaged, Leo. If there wasn't any phone sex, then—"

"Please don't talk about phone sex. It's not the crowd. This is my family and all our closest friends who might as well be family." He rubs his temples.

I shrug. "Fine, but if they ask, then I can't make any promises. You want this to be believable, then we definitely had phone sex."

"Trust me, they won't ask. Now, let's just get this over with." He opens the door, revealing a scene straight out of a Vegas nightclub—the ones I've seen on TV anyway.

We walk through the foyer, passing a burlesque dancer holding a tray of shrimp cocktail, and I swipe one off the tray as I follow Leo into the living room. My eyes go wide as I take in all the characters. There are so many people here, and some of these costumes look like the real thing.

There's an oversized cage big enough for a tiger in the middle of the space, and I spot an orange cat curled up on the small platform, fast asleep. It's hilarious how he seems so unbothered, the large metal bars are easily spaced wide enough for him to walk through if he wanted to get away, but he looks too comfortable sitting atop his plush throne.

"Leo!" Mary calls out as she rushes to us with a martini in hand.

Leo's mom's wearing a crown-shaped birthday hat and a sequins sheath dress that falls to her knees. She looks classy and timeless and is even more beautiful than last time I saw her.

"Oh, honey, I'm so glad you came." She waves someone over, and a few moments later, Frank appears, wearing a white Elvis jumpsuit, complete with a wig and platform boots to match.

"Ivy, you remember my parents," Leo starts, but they're already hugging me.

"We're so happy you could make it! I can't think of a more perfect event for you to meet everyone. Leo, make sure you make the rounds. Everyone has been dying to meet your future bride," Mary says as she hugs Leo.

"Mrs. Kingsley, this is incredible."

"Please call me Mary. I think it came together rather nicely. We had a few hiccups with the entertainment, but I think it all worked out in the end. We love any excuse to bring people together, don't we, Frank?"

His slow nod says everything he doesn't. The man is so smitten with his wife that he'd do anything to make her smile. Even throw a cat's twenty-first birthday party.

"Which reminds me, we really need to start talking about your wedding shower ... and then there's the bachelor and bachelorette parties ..."

She looks to Leo, bubbling with excitement, and to my absolute shock, the ice man cracks a smile but quickly course corrects.

"Let's not get ahead of ourselves. Ivy and I are taking our engagement slow."

"You know it wouldn't kill you to show a little enthusiasm every now and then. I'd hate to think you were actually happy," Frank teases, and the remnants of Leo's smile fade into a hard line.

"Oh, trust me, he was *bursting with excitement* just before we came." I squeeze Leo's bicep and wink.

Leo stiffens. "She doesn't mean it like that—" he starts to argue, but Frank just laughs and shakes his head.

"I knew I liked you. It takes a strong, confident woman to be with a Kingsley man. We're a stubborn breed—that's for sure."

He plants a kiss on Mary's cheek, and her whole face lights up. It's the cutest fucking thing, watching them so clearly in love. If I ever settle down and it's not like that, then I don't want it.

It might not be my twenty-first birthday and technically not Vegas, but the party checks all the boxes in my book. Besides, I think Fern would make an exception if she were here to see this.

The music grows louder as a Britney Spears drag queen impersonator steps up to perform on the small platform in the center of the room, and we all spin to watch her. It's like nothing I've ever seen. Between the bass of the music vibrating in my chest and the flashing lights, I feel like I'm really in Vegas watching a show. I don't even want to know how much work went into this party tonight, much less the cost of turning their living room into a Vegas nightclub.

Ever since I crossed the county line into Ashford Falls, it's like Fern's list has come alive and is creating every opportunity written on it. At this pace, I'll be finished with the entire thing by the time the festival rolls around and I leave for Transylvania.

The thought of completing it and moving on to whatever's next sends a wave of panic straight to my chest, and I instinctively rub my palm over my aching heart.

It's rare that I don't have the list with me, but I didn't exactly have a place to put it in this tiny dress. I couldn't even wear a bra because the cutout in the back, and my nipples are rubbing themselves raw with every brush against the sequins.

"What's wrong? Is it too much? Do you need some air?" Leo's deep voice whispers in my ear, sending chills up my neck.

This man doesn't miss anything, does he? How is he

already so perceptive to my changes in mood when we only just met?

I shake my head and brush the ache away. Thankful for his well-timed distraction, I wrap my hands around his neck and pull him closer. He stares at me with a concerned look, like he's trying to solve a puzzle, like he's not buying my act for one second.

That's ridiculous, Ivy. He doesn't even know you. It's just the way his face looks. Stop making this bigger than it is.

I sway my hips to the music, ignoring his questioning stare as I look up at his massive frame that's encompassing me like a protective barrier, shielding me from the mass of dancing bodies. It's so dark and loud now with only a spotlight shining on the stage; we might as well be the only ones in the room.

He doesn't tear his gaze away as he studies me like he's just waiting for me to crack again. But I'm nothing if not a professional. Even the observant Leo Kingsley is no match for my ability to avoid the pain of my grief.

I spin around him as I dance to the music while he stands stiff as a statue, but his gaze doesn't waver as he watches me.

"Come on, Leo. Dance with me," I yell over the music.

He shakes his head. "I don't dance."

"Shocker." I roll my eyes, then spin around so my ass is pressed against him and begin to grind in a slow rhythm to the beat of the music.

"What are you ... doing?"

His hands move to my hips, and he squeezes, like he doesn't know whether to push me away or press me into him. I make the decision for him when I press my ass against him harder and fold at the waist as I begin to twerk.

"Jesus Christ, Ivy." He clenches my waist, then pushes me away ... but not before I feel the hard length of his cock through the thin layer of fabric of my dress.

We're both breathless now as I give him a playful grin. "Relax. I'm just having a little fun. It's what people in love do, remember?" I walk my fingers up the panel of his tux and run my hands over his freshly shaven jaw. "You're too uptight. They're never going to believe you're getting laid if you keep scowling like that. You need to loosen up. Have a little fun."

"Who says I'm not having fun? You don't even know me." His nostrils flare, and he holds perfectly still as I run my fingers through his dark, wavy hair.

I shake my head and laugh. "If this is you being fun, then I'd hate to see you angry."

The music blends into an Elton John song, and I pull his hands. "Come on. You can at least handle a slow song."

To my absolute shock, he follows me to the middle of the floor and pulls me into him as he begins leading me in a slow dance. I narrow my eyes, and he just shrugs.

"What? I didn't say I couldn't dance, just that I didn't."

I follow his lead as he spins me around and circles his arms around me like a goddamn professional.

"Someone has a hidden talent, doesn't he?" I tease.

"Mom made all of us take ballroom dancing classes every summer. Said it was important for men to know how to be gentle and graceful." He leans in and whispers, "But I always thought she enjoyed torturing us after having to watch all of our sports."

His thumb moves in soft circles over my hip, and now, my heart is catapulting in my chest.

"I'm with Mary on this one. I think a man who can dance is sexy. She did you a favor, my guy." I wink, and he shakes his head, letting out a small sigh before sending me twirling me in a circle.

When I snap back to his chest, I suck in a breath of surprise, which seems to please him because I catch the slightest twitch of a smirk pull at the corner of his lips. Maybe there's hope for him yet.

"You're good at this, you know." His voice comes out slow and deep.

I swallow the lump in my throat. "Good at what?"

"Pretending. They really like you."

He dips me, then traces fingers up my leg, but is careful to stop just above my knee. My pussy clenches in excitement, and it's all I can do to keep dancing. What the hell is happening to me?

Leo guides us through another slow dance effortlessly, and I only trip a few times, but thanks to his strong arms holding me upright, you can't even tell. And when the song comes to an end, the lights slowly turn on, and I realize everyone's staring at us.

"Good idea," he whispers in my ear, his warm breath tickling the skin on my neck.

"I told you those dancing lessons were a good idea," Mary says from behind me, then grabs my hand and tugs me away. "Come with me, Ivy. I want you to meet everyone."

Once I get a few feet away from Leo, I'm able to shake the fog from my brain and finally think a little more clearly.

What's in that cologne he's wearing? Some kind of pheromone voodoo? Or is it this place that has me all turned around and inside out?

I follow her on shaky legs through the living room and into the kitchen, where a group of people are laughing around the massive kitchen island. It's brighter in here, and I immediately recognize Dr. Stone and one of Leo's brothers from the hospital.

"You remember Dr. Stone. This is his wife, Evelyn, our lovely mayor and my best friend since childhood."

I shake each of their hands.

"And that's Roman, our middle son. Who's gone above and beyond helping me with this party."

Roman waves, then pops the top of his beer. "It's no big deal. You know I'm always happy to help," he says with a grin.

I can't help but notice how similar he looks to Leo, but in reverse. He's all smiles while Leo's signature facial expression is a judgmental scowl.

It almost reminds me of the way Fern and I were so opposite, but Ferny wasn't grumpy like Leo, just intense and mysterious. Maybe that's the happy medium.

"This is Silas, Dr. and Mrs. Stone's oldest—a pseudo cousin, if you will," Roman says as he points out the others.

There are so many names; I doubt I'll remember everyone, but I do my best to make small talk.

"Mary, you've outdone yourself with this party! A true experience, as always," a voluptuous, older redheaded woman says as she kisses her on each cheek.

Mary looks around and shrugs. "Thank you, Miss Scarlett. I'm just happy to be surrounded by all these friendly faces. This town really is special, isn't it?"

"That it is," she agrees before turning to Roman. "Now, a little birdie told me you're still looking for someone to volunteer to plan this year's Phantom Festival. Is that true? Please tell me you haven't waited to start planning. It's the hundredth anniversary and the biggest charity event of the year. We can't disappoint all the organizations who depend on us for funding."

Roman's eyes widen as he looks at Leo in a silent plea for help.

"Not at all, Miss Scarlett. I don't know where you're getting your information from these days, but I assure you the Phantom Festival will be better than ever this year. We've got a committee of volunteers working on it, and there's no need to worry."

Miss Scarlett lets out a heavy sigh and nods her head in relief. "Good. I'm so happy to hear that. I have to tell you, when Shir—ahem, the birdie told me, I started to panic. It'd have been a disaster if that were true. No one could plan something that big in less than four weeks." She taps Leo on the arm and laughs. "It's the hundredth anniversary. I'd hate for the town to drop the ball on such an important date. Not to mention, we wouldn't want to anger the Phantom, now would we?"

I catch the slight twitch in Leo's jaw before he plasters on a fake smile.

"Let's not ruin my mother's beautiful party with silly ghost stories. I assure you, the festival will be a hit, just as it is every year." His words come out firm and final, cutting the conversation off right there.

"Well then, I'm happy to hear. I'll have to tell Shir—the birdie to stop with the fear-mongering rumors. Lord knows this town doesn't need any help in that department," she says with a laugh, and everyone joins in, though I'm not sure why it's funny.

Consider my interest piqued.

"And don't you look beautiful tonight?" Miss Scarlett nods in my direction, taking the conversation in a complete one-eighty. "I don't think I've seen Leo take his eyes off you all evening." She winks.

"At one point, I thought we were going to have to pull Leo off of her and spray him with a water hose to cool him down," Frank adds teasingly.

"Well, with moves like that, how's a girl supposed to resist? I had no idea he could dance that well," I say with a laugh.

"Didn't you two meet at a gala?" Roman snaps his fingers as he thinks. "The fundraiser for the children's hospital—?"

"We didn't really have time for dancing. We got lost in conversation about climate change," Leo quickly adds, covering my mistake.

His eyes shoot daggers at me, and just like that, he's back to his rigid, grumpy self.

"Oh? Isn't that romantic?" Roman laughs and claps Leo on the shoulder. "Leave it to my brother to go up to someone and woo them through intellectual conversation."

"Oh, trust me, we did *more* than talking. We spent the entire weekend together. I could barely keep him off me, if you know what I mean. Seems Leo here got a taste of something he liked." I nudge him in the ribs, and he grabs my arm and tucks it down by my side, holding it there when I try to squirm free.

"It wasn't exactly the lust-filled haze Ivy's making it out to be. We built a deep connection of respect and trust. Took things slow and long-distance for a while." He nods his head as he looks at me, as if making sure I'm following him. "Eventually, deeper feelings grew, and Ivy decided to move here to be with me."

I don't miss the way Frank and Roman exchange a skeptical glance. He's making it sound so robotic and boring, like the least romantic connection ever. It's not believable, and even if it were, it's not doing what he thinks it is, convincing his dad he's not all work and no play.

I've got to spice things up if I want them to believe this.

"We had lots of phone sex," I blurt out. Leo tightens his grip on my elbow, but I keep going. "Trust me when I say, this man right here knows how to dirty talk."

"No, that's hardly—"

"He can bring me to orgasm without even touching my body. I'm talking the whole shebang, full-body tingles and—"

His hand covers my mouth before I can finish, and then he's pulling me away. "Excuse me. I just need a moment alone with my fiancée."

He pulls me into a small bathroom down the hall and closes the door behind us. He spins me around to face him. "What the hell are you doing? I said to stick to the script!" he hisses.

"What does it look like I'm doing? I'm helping you, giving them something believable!" I shove him in his hard chest, but he doesn't even flinch. "You're making it seem too rigid and ... contractual or something. They're not buying it, Leo. And even if they did, that's not the type of love your dad wants for you."

"You don't know anything about what my dad wants or

me for that matter. I asked you to stick to the script. Why is that so hard?"

"Because I can read people, and I'm telling you, they aren't buying it. How many years have you spent doing things your way? And how's that working out for you?"

His jaw tics, but he doesn't say anything.

I take a step back and cross my arms over my chest. "Let me help you. Let me make you seem fun. What's the worst that can happen? Your dad won't name you as his replacement?"

His nostrils flare, and he scans up my body slowly. There's that look from before, only this time, he doesn't hide it; instead, he stares into me so intently that I don't know whether to move closer to him or run.

"Fine, but keep it PG. I don't need my family knowing intimate details of my bedroom skills, whether they're made up or not."

A victorious smile spreads over my face, and I leap to hug him, wrapping my arms around his massive center. He stiffens for a moment, and then to my surprise, he pats me a couple of times, and it's probably the closest thing to a hug I'll get, but I take it as a good sign nonetheless.

"I'm going to make you look so good, just wait and see."

"Somehow, I feel like I'm going to regret this."

* * *

It isn't hard to see that Leo's uptight and takes everything too seriously, but after watching him interact with his family, I realize it's worse than I expected. It's like he keeps these walls up around him and doesn't let anyone really see him.

Now, I just need to figure out why.

We've moved back into the living room, and someone makes an announcement over the speaker. I recognize Roman's voice immediately.

"Ladies and gentlemen, thank you all for being here to celebrate the one and only Bartholomew Elvis Butterfinger Kingsley's twenty-first birthday."

We all clap and cheer as the lights blink several times, and a roar plays over the speaker.

"It is my great honor to introduce our main event of the evening ... a magic act like no other. May I present ... Siegfried and Roy!"

The lights go out, and a spotlight shines on the large cage in the middle of the room, revealing Bartholomew standing on the platform as a feather dangles from a string in front of him. Then, Leo's two youngest brothers pop out, wearing poofy-sleeved white shirts that are unbuttoned midway down their chests.

Everyone bursts into applause and laughter when one pulls a hula hoop out from behind the cage. A light flicks on that projects a holographic flame, and we're instructed to remain silent. The air is tense with focus and anticipation as Guy sprays a gust of catnip in Bartholomew's face, and he swats at the spray bottle, then wiggles his butt before pouncing to attack the feather. We all try to hold back our laughter, watching them attempt to lure the old, grumpy cat through the hula hoop. He takes a swing at one of them every chance he gets until he finally gets fed up and jumps through the hoop.

The crowd erupts in applause as Mary scoops him up and cuddles him to her chest. His little face wears a scowl that matches Leo's, but it's easy to see how happy he really is when he gently blinks up at her.

"Mom's the only person he likes; it's the only reason he tolerates all this shit," Leo whispers in my ear, sending a prickle of goose bumps over my skin.

He hasn't left my side the entire night. I'm not sure if it's because he's afraid of what I might say if he's not there to intervene or if it's because he knows I don't know anyone. His manners are nearly impeccable, so it's probably a little of both.

I could get used to the feeling of him standing over me like this, like my own personal guard dog on constant alert. Even though we're just at his family's house, he makes me feel safe.

The lights slowly get brighter, indicating the end of the show, and Roman calls Leo over to help him untangle one of his brothers from the string lights.

"I'll be right back," Leo says, and I wave him off.

"Go. I'm fine. Best behavior, remember?" I make my way back to the kitchen to see if I can help clean up when I bump into Frank.

"Well, what did you think of the Siegfried and Roy performance?"

"I thought it was hysterical. The perfect main act for a cat's twenty-first birthday. All of this is incredible."

"Mary does love her themed parties," he says with a laugh. "Listen, I've been meaning to talk to you about something." He looks around to make sure we're alone.

"Yeah, what's up?"

His smile falls, and there's a sad look in his eyes. "I'm just worried about Leo." He looks down and shakes his head like he's trying to keep his emotions at bay. "He's always taken the burden of what we do so seriously, and I ... I hate that I've put that on him. I've known he was stressed out for a long time, and I didn't say anything." He looks up to meet my eyes. "Would you please take care of him, make sure he isn't pushing himself too much?"

"Oh, of course I will," I assure him.

"It's just ... I've never seen him look so happy. When he looks at you, I can see this relief on his face. I don't want that to go away. It killed me to not give him that promotion, but I couldn't give my oldest son a death sentence. Can you please talk some sense into him? Make him take a day off every now and then? I'm afraid of what could happen if he doesn't figure out how to stop pushing himself so hard."

"Don't you worry, Frank. You have my word."

"Thank you, Ivy. I knew I could count on you."

CHAPTER SEVEN

Leo

Last night was torture in more ways than one. Everyone was so excited for me. Several people I'd barely spoken to even pulled me aside to congratulate me for finally putting myself out there. They told me they'd been worried about me and my one-track mind toward my career ever since Heidi—the only girlfriend I'd ever had—and I'd split over ten years ago. They'd wondered if I'd ever get over her enough to move on.

Jesus. I hadn't realized anyone still remembered that—much less ten years later—but I shouldn't have been surprised. Everyone in this town remembers everything.

The last thing I want is for people to feel sorry for me. Of course I've moved on. And as much as I wish I could erase it from everyone's memory as well as my own, that experience is what made me into the high-performer man that I am today.

Sure, it felt like a nightmare at the time, but I was barely twenty-five—my frontal lobe wasn't even completely developed. I was operating under the delusion that someone like me could have it all. No one gets to have it all, especially not a man with my tastes. It's not fair to anyone. That's why I can't go there again—there's too much at stake.

Everything changed that day she ended it ... and the timing couldn't have been worse. Her parting words still haunt me.

"*Of course I cheated, Leo. I had to get attention from somewhere, and you were certainly never around. Did you really expect me to sit around all day and wait on you? You're such a perv. I never wanted to play into your disgusting fantasies. It made me sick every time I had to call you Daddy ...*"

The memory slaps me across the face, and I scrub my hand over my jaw as if I can wipe the sting away. She didn't even wait for me to fully put my coat down before she unleashed those words, piling shame on top of the hate I'd already felt for myself.

It was the worst day of my life. I was so broken. I didn't feel the impact of those words at first, but years later, anytime I started to feel lonely or wonder if there was a way I could have both, they'd come flying back to snap me back into reality.

Honestly, I should thank her. If she hadn't destroyed me that day, then it would've been me ending things and pushing her away, blaming her for distracting me. At least I don't have to carry the guilt of that on top of everything else. It's a small consolation, but a man can only hold space for so much regret without it tearing him up inside.

I was able to channel all my pain and regret into a bigger purpose—committing myself to not only striving for excellence and growth for my family's company, but also to keeping people safe. It's all I have now, and I'm thankful for the reminders, no matter how painful they might be.

Which is why this thing between Ivy and me can't go any further. I've seen what happens on the other side of this, and it ends with *everyone* getting hurt.

It's already enough that my family's already so attached to her. My too-young-for-me fiancée, who is quite possibly the biggest handful I've ever met and on paper is the last person I'd choose to ask for help. And yet she was incredible last night—despite going overboard with some of the details of our relationship and how we'd met. She was charming and fun—all the things I am not—and I could see they all believed it.

I don't even want to think about how much this is going to break my mother's heart after it's all said and done. That's another layer of guilt to add to the weight I already carry on my back and a problem for another day.

Right now, I need to make it through this one.

Honestly, I should be thanking her for her convincing performance, but doing that would only encourage her, and that's not something anyone is ready for, especially not me.

She's got this innate ability to push me right to the edge of frustration. For fuck's sake, I've never met someone who could both identify and push my buttons within seconds of meeting me. It's intriguing *and* terrifying, the way she's already seemed to burrow herself into my mind, as if she's carving out her own little nook to settle into just to torment me anytime she likes.

Images of Ivy dancing, those pretty, pouty lips doing unspeakable things ... the way her shapely thighs are little bit fuller at the top and kiss each other, practically begging to be touched ... it's not a detail I should be privy to, and yet thanks to that fucking microscopic excuse for a dress, I am unable to forget. I splash cold water over my face as I stare at my exhausted-looking reflection, urging the images out of my mind.

I feel like such a perverted bastard, but my cock seems to have a mind of its own.

It's bad enough I have to live with her—*way to jump the gun with that idea, Leo*—but it seems she's infiltrated my dreams as well.

I had to jerk off before I went to sleep and again this morning just to get this raging hard-on under control. I don't think I was prepared for how devastatingly gorgeous this woman was. Thankfully, her loud, energetic personality is there to offset it; otherwise, I'd be so screwed right now.

I'm making my way into the kitchen for my first cup of coffee when I find her bent over, digging in the fridge, and of course, she's wearing only an oversize T-shirt. I stop dead in my tracks before tearing my gaze away and making a beeline straight to the coffee maker.

But it's too late. The damage is done.

As if I needed any more fuel for my too-old-for-her, perverted guilty conscience, now, I'll have the image of her perfect, round ass burned into my memory for years to come.

Fucking fantastic.

"Oh, hey, you're up early," she says as she closes the refrigerator with her hip, arms full of ingredients.

"I could say the same thing about you. Do you have something against pants?" I wait for the espresso machine to stop sputtering for what feels like hours.

She looks down at her shapely legs. "I don't like to be restricted when I sleep. I find that wearing pants limits my range of motion. Besides, these are boy shorts; they're practically shorts themselves." She moves to the stove as she starts stirring ingredients in a large bowl. "I'm making pancakes. Do you want any?"

Looks like she's made herself at home.

I sip my espresso, savoring the strong, bitter flavor. I'm not much of a morning person despite my rigorous work schedule, and even I can admit that I'm grumpy before I've had my coffee. "No thank you. I'm not big on breakfast. Clean up your mess when you're finished, please."

"Didn't Dr. Stone tell you not to have coffee on an empty stomach?"

She holds up the wooden spoon, and a dollop of pancake batter drips off onto the floor. My gaze locks on the mess, and my eye begins to twitch.

"I have very few vices in life, and my morning espresso is one of them. Why don't you just worry about yourself, and I'll worry about me? My health really isn't your concern."

I turn to leave, but she grabs my arm to stop me.

"You asked *me* to help *you*, remember?" She swipes the coffee cup from my hand and replaces it with something else.

"Hey, what are you—" I sniff the hot liquid and glare daggers at her. "Is this hot lemon water?"

"Drink the lemon water, take your medicine, eat something, and *then* you can have your coffee. That's the way things are going to go until your ulcer heals."

She spins around and grabs a long blue rectangle off the counter beside my medicine and shoves it at me.

"I separated your meds for you for the entire week,

Grandpa. Now, take your pills and shut up, or tomorrow, you'll find me in here, topless. Understand?"

I grit my teeth and take the pill container from her, feeling much like the grandpa she loves to compare me to— but at least she didn't call me daddy again. I hate to admit she's right; Dr. Stone did say drinking coffee on an empty stomach was among one of the worst things I could do to heal. I swallow down my pills, but I don't argue as she shoves a plate of pancakes toward me. She used bananas and blueberries to make a frowny face.

She slides onto the barstool next to me with her own plate, and I notice her pancake is happy.

"Hey, why'd you give me the sad one? And why does yours have chocolate chips?"

"Because I don't walk around scowling at everyone I come in contact with and you only had enough chocolate chips for one."

She shrugs and shoves a bite in her mouth. It's too big, and syrup drips down her chin. My dick twitches, and I have the strangest urge to lick the syrup away. I turn to my own plate and begin cutting my pancakes.

"You should cut your food in smaller pieces so you don't make a mess."

"I cut them fine."

Out of the corner of my eye, I see her tear a piece with her fingers and pop it in her mouth.

"Now, your fingers are sticky. Use your utensils like a civilized human."

To that, she picks up the largest pancake with two fingers and dangles it over her face, taking a bite from the very bottom.

"Now, you're just being a brat—"

I watch her nibble the pancake in horrified annoyance as syrup drips on the counter and down her cheek until it tears apart, landing straight in her lap.

"Dammit, Ivy. You've got syrup all over yourself!" I jump up to grab a wet towel and find her wearing a conniving grin.

"Oops. I'm all sticky." She licks syrup from her thumb without breaking eye contact, and my brain short-circuits.

"I hope you know you're cleaning this up." It's the only thing I can think to say as I hand her the wet towel.

"Yes, Daddy."

I don't like the way my pulse ticks up or the way my face gets hot, and I certainly don't like how hard my cock gets when she calls me that. I know she's just trying to get a rise out of me. If only I could've done a better job of concealing my emotions last night.

I blame that fucking dress. No man in his right mind would be able to think clearly around that.

Not that the thin white T-shirt she's wearing right now is any better. I should win a gold medal for the restraint I've shown by not looking at her nipples or the wedgie she's had all morning, revealing half of her round, plump ass cheeks.

This little act of defiance has gone too far, and if she's not careful, she's going to bring out a side of me that I haven't seen in a very long time. A side of me that I put away a long time ago because I don't think it's possible to satisfy both versions of myself.

I move toward her, bracketing her between my hands until her back is flush with the cold quartz countertop.

She smells like syrup, and my mouth waters for a taste.

"Listen, you little brat. I told you to stop calling me that. I don't like it," I growl in a low whisper.

She sucks in a small breath, and I can see her hard nipples poking through her shirt, like they're begging for attention. Everything about this woman commands attention; I don't know why her tits would be any different.

"Are you sure you don't like it? Because it kind of seems like you do ..." She moves her eyes down toward my raging hard-on that's straining through my gray sweatpants.

"I see what you're doing, and I don't know what kind of game you're getting at, but just because my dick's hard doesn't mean anything. So, you can stop with the teasing and walking around half naked. You're not going to win here. I've gone a long time without giving in to my urges, and I'll be damned if I break now—"

"A long time, huh?" She bites her lip and grins, making her nose scrunch up like she just learned some big secret. "I had a feeling that was the problem."

I shake my head, but I don't back away as I glare down at her cute fucking freckled nose. "You're way off there, so stop pushing me or else ..."

She trails her hands up my jaw, then rubs her thumb over my lips, and I have to fight the urge to keep my eyes from rolling back in my head from the intimate contact. Talk about touch-starved. How sad is it that she's got my dick ready to explode from a mere brush from her fingers? I am utterly pathetic and starting to realize how much trouble I've caused for myself. I don't think there's anything I can do to put Ivy back in Pandora's box now ...

"Or else ... what?"

I suck in a slow breath. "Trust me, you wouldn't be able to handle it."

I bite her finger, and she yelps. Then, I gently suck the syrup from it, never taking my eyes off her.

Her eyes widen, and I don't have to read her mind to know that I've just created the most exciting game of cat and mouse ... only I don't know which one I am in this scenario.

"I think you'd be surprised about how much of you I can handle." She flashes me a mischievous grin as she looks down at my aching cock, then shoves my chest away. "Remember, no coffee until after you've eaten your breakfast." She stands from the stool and heads toward the hallway, never bothering to fix that goddamn wedgie. "Excuse me while I clean myself up. I'm all sticky now."

I should be ashamed of myself, watching her cute little ass sway until she disappears down the hall, but I can't look away. I guess I really am a glutton for punishment.

By the time I've cleaned her breakfast mess and wiped all the syrup from the countertops and floor, my coffee's ice cold. I could make myself a fresh cup but decide better of it. Maybe I'll give my stomach a break ... just for today.

My phone buzzes several times on the counter, and I don't even have to look to know what it's about.

MOM

> Good morning, everyone! I'm hosting Sunday dinner tonight to celebrate Leo and Ivy's engagement! I hope you can all make it. Six sharp!

LEO

Wait a minute. Shouldn't you ask the person of honor if they're available BEFORE you invite the whole family to celebrate? I can't make it tonight. I've got too much work to catch up on before tomorrow.

ROMAN

Sounds good. See you then.

Dude, I think we all know you can carve two hours out of your busy schedule to celebrate.

DAD

There's nothing more important than family time. Your mother's excited, son.

LUKA

Will this require my participation? Because I'm struggling to get all the eyeliner off from last night.

GUY

Try baby oil. Trust me, bro, it works like a charm.

LUKA

How'd you figure that out?

GUY

Do you really want me to answer that on our family group chat???

DAD

That's enough, Guy. We're eating over here.

GUY

Don't say I didn't warn you.

MOM

Is Jett in the group? Jett, are you here?

ROMAN

Yeah, I added him back after he left last time.

JETT

Yes. I'm here... against my will... but here.

MOM

Oh, stop being dramatic. I expect you to be at dinner tonight. We're celebrating, and you're a part of this family whether you want to be or not.

JETT

I have work. Sorry.

MOM

Figure it out.

JETT

Mom, you won't even notice I'm not there. Leo doesn't even care.

LEO

I'd really like your support, Jett.

MOM

Aw! I love to see my boys getting along.

JETT

Bastard. I'll see what I can do, but I'm not making any promises.

ROMAN

It's Sunday. You normally close an hour early anyway because you're so slow.

JETT

Thank you, Rome. That's quite helpful.

MOM

I can't wait to have all my boys together! We'll take the group photo tonight since Jett will be there, so dress nice!

JETT

Fantastic. I can't wait.

LEO

That makes two of us then.

LUKA

I'm going back to sleep now.

I pocket my phone as I head upstairs to my office. Maybe I can squeeze in a couple of hours of work now that I know my evening is being hijacked by my family. When I turn the corner, I crash into Ivy. The smell of her shampoo disorients me—that and the fact that she's covered by nothing but a small towel clasped around her breasts.

"Sorry." I steady her, placing my hands on her still-damp arms and then quickly pull them away.

She gives me a sly smile. "Where are you off to in such a hurry?"

"I've got some work to catch up on." I nod in the direction of my office. "Listen, my mom's planning a dinner for us tonight. To celebrate our engagement. It's just family, I think. Do you think you can be ready to leave by five thirty?"

She pulls the towel off her head, letting her long, wet hair fall down her back, and begins dabbing the ends. "If that's what you need me to do, then I'll be ready."

My mouth goes dry as I watch a small drop of water slide down her collarbone over her sun-kissed skin. I have to fight the urge to trace its path. What the fuck is wrong with me? She's got my body responding like I've never been with a woman, and it's fucking with me in more ways than one.

Get your shit together, man. She's nearly the same age as your family cat, for fuck's sake.

"That'd be great. It's pretty casual, but she'll probably want to take pictures, so maybe wear something nice. Do you have nice clothes or just overalls and cutoff jean shorts?" It's a serious question, but it comes out a little sharper than I intended. Rather than get into a verbal battle, I just pull out my credit card and hand it to her. "Here, just get yourself some nice dresses and outfits to wear. There's a boutique downtown that should have everything you need."

"Well, since you're so eager to take care of me, I could always use some new clothes ..."

I pull the card back just before she grabs it. "Please don't do anything to embarrass me. It's a small town, and you're bound to have eyes on you now that word about us is out."

She pops a hip and narrows her eyes. "And how do you think I'd do that?"

"Oh, I don't know ... but I don't think it's bold to assume you can figure it out."

Biting her lip to hold back a cheeky grin, she stands on her tiptoes and swipes the card from me. "Yes, Daddy."

Fucking hell. I guess I walked right into that one, didn't I?

Without another word, I head to my office and slam the door behind me, putting as much distance as possible between us. I'm not saying I can't be trusted, but when she's walking around, freshly showered and smelling like a fallen angel, in nothing more than a hand towel ... a man can only expect so much self-control.

Ten minutes later, I check the security monitors and see her leaving, her little beat-up car driving down the driveway, and it's only when I know I'm alone that I let out a deep exhale. I pull my aching cock from my sweatpants and begin stroking myself right there at my desk, thinking about all the things I wish I could do to my bratty fake fiancée.

CHAPTER EIGHT

Ivy

I toss my shopping bags in the booth seat across from me and check the time on my phone. It's only just after lunch, and I feel like I've already walked ten miles.

The choice was simple since the only restaurant on the small downtown square was oddly named Restaurant. I still chuckle every time I see these hilariously precise business names. Nineties grunge music plays over the speakers of the edgy bar and grill as people file in and out. It's by no means packed, but considering the size of the town, I'm surprised to see it's this busy.

Like most of the architecture here, Restaurant is a sort of gothic-esque Victorian-style building with black beams that span across the massive ceiling. It feels old and elaborate and cozy, all at the same time.

Ashford Falls certainly has its charm. From the quaint little shops to the eccentric people who are in everyone's business, to the pristine landscaping, to the Victorian architecture. Everything here is beautiful and has an edge of something I can't quite put my finger on. Almost like they preserved the darkness as a memory of what once was, and I like that. I can't help but think how beautiful it would be in the fall.

Of course, I'll be long gone before then, on to check off the next item on Fern's list. I might live by the seat of my pants in all other areas of my life, but settling down at the ripe age of twenty-two is definitely not an option—that's for damn sure.

I pull the worn paper from my pocket and read it once again—not that these words aren't branded into my memory by now. It's good to have the reminder of what I'm really doing here, especially considering my current situation and all the distractions that come with him.

Seriously, how is anyone that rich *and* hot? Like, he's playing on a whole other level. He sent me, a practical stranger, on a shopping spree with his credit card. Who does that? And not only is he gorgeous, but I fear I'm going to develop carpal tunnel in my wrist from having to distract myself from tiptoeing into his room, pretending I'm lost.

Then, there's the whole alpha, grumpy thing he's got going on. I don't know what's happening to me. I've always hated being told what to do, hated any form of authority really. Hence the reason I'm sitting in this cute, spooky town in the mountains instead of finishing my college coursework. I've never responded well to criticism; in fact, I think I'm more sensitive to it than most. So, why do my panties get wet when he goes all Daddy on me, bossing me around?

There's something about his laser-sharp tone, all masculine and domineering, and his unyielding determination to keep his walls up that excites me. It's like I've gone my whole life searching for a worthy opponent, and I just met my match. All I can think about is shaking up his tidy, planned-out life until he finally breaks open and releases his armor of control.

Nothing like being told I can't have something only to make me want it more. I swear I'm the poster child for dysfunction.

I shake my head and laugh.

It's a dumb game I'm playing—I know that—but at the same time, I love the rush I get, seeing his nostrils flare and his jaw clench when I tease him. The man is one stressful event away from exploding, and that's coming from his doctor's mouth, not just mine.

Leo Kingsley needs to relax and stop taking life so seriously, and lucky for him, he's fake engaged to the queen of avoiding problems.

If I've learned anything in my short twenty-two years, it's that as much as we think we are in control of our lives, we're not. There's no planning, mental preparation, or secret stash of money that will save you if it's your time to go and sometimes, you just get dealt a crappy hand. So, why waste the precious moments we have, thinking we're the ones in control? I've felt pain and loss deeper than I could've ever imagined, so things like work, money, and the other minor details of life don't stress me out anymore, and I'll be damned if something as insignificant as a job makes me feel miserable. Maybe that's why Fern placed this uptight, grumpy man in my path. Because I'm growing more and more convinced by the day that she somehow orchestrated this whole thing.

Change someone's life for the better.

If only I could get through to Leo to show him another way of living, how he doesn't have to be so miserable all the time ... how life's pleasures are meant to be enjoyed ...

And then, just like I knew I would, I get an idea. I know it's a good one because I get the familiar buzz of belly flutters and tingles.

I can hear my sister warning me in her favorite parental tone, *"Ivy, are you sure about this?"*

Stirring my straw in my bubbly soda, I formulate the first step to my diabolical master plan.

Maybe I can't get him to listen to me because I've been trying to get through to the wrong head.

Looks like I've got one more stop to make this afternoon.

* * *

"Jesus, woman! Did you leave anything in the shops?" Leo grumbles as I pile shopping bags in his outstretched arms.

"I was merely following your orders, and since I know how picky you are, I wanted to make sure I had all my bases covered."

I slap another small bag to the top of the pile, and he has to adjust it so he can see.

"I'm not picky," he grunts.

"Okay, controlling. Is that a better word?"

He grumbles something inaudible under his breath as I run ahead to open the doors for him. When he gets to my room, he drops the pile on the bed with the rest of the bags he already carried inside.

I see the moment his eyes land on the bag from Adult

Store, and his face burns red. "What's that? I thought I told you not to go there again."

He takes a step toward the bag, but I move in front of him, placing my palm on his rock-hard chest.

"Excuse me, that is private—"

He pushes my hand away and lets out a frustrated sigh. "Seriously, Ivy, would it kill you to just listen? Or are you actually incapable of following rules?"

Rules.

My stomach does a backflip as soon as he says it, and I fear I might be in over my head this time.

But now, I'm committed. He's already mad, so I might as well see how it pans out.

"Relax. It's not what you think. Just a personal item. Nothing to do with *you*." I grab his elbow to usher him to the door, but he doesn't budge.

He crosses his arms over his broad chest, making himself impossibly bigger as he stares down at me and nods to the bag. "Show me."

"Show you? I'm not going to show you, you perv—"

This time, I try to push him through the door, and it's almost comical how weak I am in comparison, but the big guy still doesn't move.

"*I* bought it. So, show me what you needed so badly after I deliberately told you not to go in there again." His command comes out in a low growl that makes my toes curl and sends a wave of chill bumps down my arms.

I shake my head. "Fine. But don't say I didn't warn you." I stomp over to the bed and grab the bag, pausing to give him one last chance to change his mind.

He rolls his eyes and gestures for me to get on with it, and I have to bite my cheek to keep from smiling.

"You're about to feel really dumb, so get ready ..." My voice trails off as I pull out the hot-pink vibrator, complete with a flower petal clit stimulator. I present it to him like I'm at a dog show, making sure to highlight every bump and ridge before turning it on for the full effect.

Leo's face heats bright red as he glares at me, staring daggers in silence, so I take it as encouragement to keep going.

I hit another button, and the base pulses thicker while the thin silicone petals vibrate and the center of the flower makes a sucking noise.

"You bought a vibrator," he says in almost a whisper.

"More than a vibrator. It's more like a robotic dick," I answer, then hit another button that makes the shaft spin in circles.

He clenches his jaw and begins massaging his chest. And it looks like my little plan to get under his skin is working.

I chew on my lip to hold off my grin as I stare up at him in challenge. I don't know what I want him to do, but considering the tingles I'm getting at the thought of both positive and negative reactions, I think I'm in big trouble, no matter what.

"And exactly *how* much did I pay for that?" He takes a step closer, closing the space between us, and I have to force my legs not to buckle under his towering glare.

I will not let him get to me. I can't show any signs of weakness, or it'll all be for nothing. This is the only way to get through to him. I just have to make him more uncomfortable and stick to my guns.

I hold my hand over the clit stimulator and smile as it flicks and tickles my palm. "It's the latest model. There's even an app so I don't have to use my hands if I don't want to—"

"How much, Ivy?" He takes another step closer, so close that I can feel the heat of his skin, and my palms itch to reach out and touch him. He's angry—there's no question about that.

I swallow a gulp and keep going. "It's also waterproof. It has a suction cup at the bottom for hands-free shower play—"

"Ivy," he hisses before snatching it away.

"Hey, give me that—"

"I can't believe I actually thought you were capable of behaving without supervision."

I roll my eyes and jump to grab it, but he holds it over his head, out of my reach.

"I got a good deal on it. Miss Scarlett gave me a family and friends discount, so it was only four hundred ... plus tax."

"That's just great—"

"I thought so. Especially with all the updated features—"

I jump again, but he dodges me, pushing my head down and covering my eyes with his gigantic palm. I try to pry his fingers off one at a time, but he's too strong. I think the man's bones are made of lead.

"So, not only does the biggest gossip in town know that my fiancée needs a robot dick to get her off, but the top-of-the-line model at that. I'm never going to hear the end of this." He shakes his head.

"Will you stop freaking out? It's not that big of a deal. Miss Scarlett is nothing if not a professional."

I jump again when he's not paying attention and almost grab it, but he moves it out of reach.

"Can you please give it back? I was really looking forward to using this before we left tonight. I need to take the edge off."

At that, his body goes rigid, but then his shoulders relax, and the corner of his lips twitch like he's holding back his own grin.

My stomach flutters again as I stare up at him, unsure if I should be happy or terrified by his sudden change in demeanor.

"You're really nervous?"

I nod.

"Getting yourself off would probably help take the edge off," he says more like he's talking to himself than to me, but I nod anyway.

The thrill I get from not knowing what he'll decide, from having zero control as I watch him contemplate his decision, is something I should definitely see a therapist about.

"But what would that teach you?" His lips twist into a wicked grin as he slides a gentle palm behind my neck, his thumb caressing my jaw with a heated touch.

He takes another step, closing the space between us. Instinctively, I try to move back, but my knees bump against the wooden bed frame, pinning me in place against him.

"I see what you're doing here, and I should warn you that you will not win this fight. So, stop while you're ahead, yeah? You have no idea what you're going up against with me."

He slowly traces his thumb across my bottom lip, and I suck in a breath.

"Besides, why should I make things easier for you when you've done nothing but try to get under my skin every chance you got?" He shakes his head and tsks. "No, I think

I'll hold on to your robot cock for a while, make sure you're behaving like a good girl before I think of giving it back."

"Just because you—" I start to argue, but he shakes his head, his thumb brushing back over my lips to silence me.

He leans down and whispers, "Careful, or I'll forbid you from pleasuring yourself altogether. And then you'll really be in a bind, won't you?"

It's a rare thing for me to be stunned speechless, but when I open my mouth to argue or press him on how he'd prevent me from touching myself, I'm quickly distracted by the rush of arousal pulsing between my legs.

I look up, seeing a pained expression behind his dark eyes, like he's torn between leaning into this side of himself and bolting to get as far away from me as he can.

Before I can think twice, I act on impulse and bite his thumb. Hard.

"Ow. Fuck."

He yanks his hand away in surprise as I flash him my teeth, giving him a challenging grin.

"You're a fucking brat, you know that?" He doesn't wait for me to answer. "Get dressed. We're leaving in five."

He grabs a yellow sundress that's strewn across my bed and tears the tag off before tossing it at me. "And don't even think about acting out tonight, or I swear on everything I will make you regret it." His voice is all gravelly and laced with warning and does nothing to stifle my curiosity that's growing bigger by the second.

I don't *want* to know what he means ... I *need* to know.

Looks like my little plan of temptation backfired, and I'll be the one with blue balls tonight.

But this is far from over. Leo Kingsley doesn't know who he's dealing with.

CHAPTER NINE

Ivy

I gnaw on my bottom lip and stare out the window, replaying our argument over and over in my head, trying to make sense of what happened back there.

My plan was to antagonize him, get under his skin by giving him a little something to fantasize about. I knew he'd be annoyed—it's not exactly a difficult feat to annoy him—but I didn't expect him to take it from me, to threaten me.

And more than that, I didn't expect to like it.

I can't explain it, but there's something so exhilarating about pushing his buttons, like I've finally found the rush I've been chasing all these months. Being around him makes me feel alive, like I'm breathing pure oxygen after surviving my whole life off polluted air.

The rush of not knowing how he'll react feels like a drug that I'm quickly becoming addicted to. It's like I'm catching glimpses of the real Leo through the cracks in his armor every time I push back.

I sit back with a huff and prop my feet on the dash. It seems that I underestimated him before. Looks like I'm going to have to try a new angle next time.

"What did I tell you about putting your feet on the dash?" Leo scolds, breaking through the silence.

I jerk my gaze from the window and narrow my eyes. "You're literally pulling into the driveway. I think I'll take my chances."

"It's not about that. It's a bad habit, a dangerous habit, that you need to break. I'm not always going to be around to remind you," he says as he taps my leg with the back of his hand, his touch sending a jolt of electricity in its wake.

"Yes, Daddy," I tease, rolling my eyes as I pull my legs down.

He doesn't say anything, but I can see the slight twitch of the muscle in his jaw and the way his grip tightens on the steering wheel. The man's clearly on edge, and I wonder if he's thinking about what happened back there, just like me.

But before I can ask him, he puts the car in park and spins to face me. "I'll do most of the talking. I just need you to smile and look pretty. I think you've already taken enough creative liberties for the day with your little stunt this afternoon." His jaw muscle spasms, and his eyes darken as he stares at me like he's waiting for his words to sink in. His voice drops lower. "Do you think you can manage that, Ivy?"

Oh, hell no. Who does this guy think he is right now?

I force a fake sweet smile. "What's wrong, Leo? Are you scared that I'll act like a brat and embarrass you because you took my new toy?"

I lean toward him and run my fingers through his styled

waves, not missing the way his eyes drift shut for only a moment before he catches himself.

He grabs my hand and places it in my lap a little more forcefully than I'd expect. "Just save it for when we're alone, will you? We can fight until we're both blue in the face behind closed doors, but I've got a reputation to uphold. There's a lot at stake here for me. Remember that I'm helping you here just as much as you're helping me." He lifts his brow in challenge.

"Of course." I bat my eyes and flash him another fake smile.

He sighs. "Come on. Let's just get it over with."

He's out of the car and already opening my door before I can do it myself, and I take his offered arm, looping mine through his as he leads me inside. Wow, he's really putting on a show if he thinks they're spying on us in the driveway.

Mary and Frank meet us in the foyer, both pulling us into tight hugs, and I'm shocked at how quickly they managed to transform the space from all the Vegas decorations.

Leo loops a single finger in my palm, offering me the tiniest bit of comfort as I follow behind in awe, taking in all the personal touches I missed last time. A gallery wall filled with baby pictures, old family photos on the wall behind the staircase, a mixture of old and new furnishings.

This isn't just a big, fancy house; it's a home, and I can practically feel the years of memories that made it that way. And for the life of me, I cannot begin to understand how someone so serious and grumpy as Leo could've grown up in a loving home like this.

I drag my fingers across the ornate molding, my eye catching on the peeling wallpaper in the corner of the hall, and I don't know why, but I find it all that much more endearing. This big, rambunctious family has more money than I can even fathom, and yet they still have peeling wallpaper and scuffs on the baseboards. It's refreshing, so different from the everything's-for-show life I grew up with.

The sound of arguing grows louder as we approach a fancy sitting room, and Leo's four brothers come into view.

I recognize Roman and his younger brothers, Guy and Luka, so that must mean the raven-haired man sulking at the table is Jett.

Fern's gray eyes flash through my mind, her coloring strikingly similar, and I already know I'll have a soft spot for the black sheep of the family. Leo hasn't told me much, but I'm perceptive enough to notice when something's off with people, and there's definitely something beneath the surface with this guy.

"Finally decided to join us, did you? I've been sitting here for thirty minutes, practically starving because Mom wouldn't serve the appetizers without the *guests of honor.*" Guy rolls his eyes as he moves to the bar cart to pour himself a whiskey.

"You literally just ate, like, four dinner rolls. I'm afraid you don't understand the meaning of that word, little brother," Luka says, swiping the whiskey from Guy before he can pour his drink.

Guy shoves him away and snatches the bottle back. "Why do you have to be such a dick?"

Luka just laughs and shrugs as he moves to the table to take a seat.

"Boys, now, that's enough. If you're going to act like wild

animals, then you can go eat outside with Marty," Mary scolds, and they both apologize under their breath.

I look at Leo, confused that I missed someone. "Who's Marty, and why does he have to eat outside?"

He huffs a laugh, accepting the drink Frank passes him, but it's Frank who answers. "Marty would be the pig Mary adopted at the county fair three years ago." His words sound irritated, but his smile tells me otherwise.

"Do you know what they were going to do to him, Frank? They were auctioning him off to be turned into bacon," she whispers behind her hand, as if Marty can hear us talking about him.

"I'm well aware. You made your case, and thanks to you, Marty is now living the life of his dreams, feasting off the finest scraps a pig could want." Frank winks and kisses Mary on top of the head, and they both look to Leo and me like they couldn't be any happier.

"Well, sounds like I need to meet this special pig."

Leo wraps a heavy arm around my shoulders, tucking me into his warm, protective embrace, and I have to fight the urge to pull back and look at him like he's crazy. "I'll take you out to the barn to meet him after dinner."

"You two are just the cutest. I don't think I'll ever get tired of seeing my oldest boy so happy and in love. Come on. Let's sit down and catch up." Mary claps her hands together and leads us to the massive oak dining table, set like a fancy restaurant with origami napkins and more forks than feel necessary.

Leo pulls out a seat for me on the end, across from Jett, who only acknowledges us with a nod. "This is Jett. He owns

Restaurant downtown. Don't worry; he's like that around everyone. It seems like all he enjoys in life is work—"

Roman's laughter cuts Leo off. "And you're one to talk. I swear, I thought you'd taken some kind of vow of celibacy like a monk, committed your life to your work, until this one showed up." He shakes his head and laughs, and I can feel the heat of Leo's irritation boiling under his skin.

"He's not wrong," Frank adds as servers fill the room, placing small appetizer plates in front of everyone. "I can't tell you how shocked your mother and I were to run into Miss Ivy in the hospital of all places." Frank takes a swig of his cocktail and eyes us over the glass. "That just goes to show that people can always surprise you."

My eyes ping between the men, and I can sense there's more to the story. Why else would Leo feel so desperate for my help?

"Well, let's not talk about work. It's a rare moment where everyone I love most is here, together, under the same roof. Tonight, we're celebrating Leo and Ivy and their surprising engagement," Mary squeals, holding up her glass in a toast.

Jett's eyebrows furrow, and he whips his head to Leo in confusion. "Wait a second. Did she say *engagement*?"

Leo clears his throat and smiles, then places an arm around me, as if to prove it, but Jett just shakes his head, staring between us.

"You're telling me you're engaged? To be married? And this is the first time I'm hearing about it?" Jett narrows his eyes at Leo like he sees right through him.

"Don't be ridiculous. I know we told you in the group text." Mary pulls out her phone and begins searching for proof, but now, we've got Frank's attention too.

I can feel Leo stiffen. His leg begins to bounce under the table, and I slide my palm over it to still him.

"We, uh ... wanted to keep a low profile until we knew things were serious." I flash a smile to Leo, who looks half relieved and half terrified. "You know, because of the age difference ..."

The room falls silent, and if looks could kill, I'd be a dead woman from the glare Leo sends me. I can practically see the steam spewing from his ears, but he's already angry, so I might as well keep going.

"Thirteen years, to be exact." I nudge him in the ribs with my elbow and flash him a wink before I turn back to Jett. "Daddy didn't want the unnecessary judgment with your family's high-profile status and all—" My words are cut off when Leo's large hand clamps tightly around my upper thigh, sending a sting of pain and rush of tingles straight to my core.

Jett's eyes widen in shock, and then all at once, everyone bursts into laughter, doubling over, wheezing, and slapping the table.

Guy laughs so hard that he falls back in his chair, which only makes Luka laugh harder.

I have to say, I've always been quick-witted, but even I surprised myself, pulling out that masterpiece of revenge.

Leo clears his throat again, trying to brush it all off. "She's just joking." His hand moves a little higher on my thigh, his fingertips sliding just beneath the hem of my little yellow sundress, and I suck in a breath. "Ivy loves to joke around and get a rile out of me. Don't you, sweetheart?"

I swallow a gulp when his hand slides up further, fingers tracing dangerously close to the apex of my thighs. All eyes are on me, and I try to play it cool. I don't know what kind of game he's playing, but I will not be threatened twice in one day.

"I'm sorry. I forgot you only like me to call you that in the bedroom. Oops." I shrug as I begin picking at my salad.

"Well, one thing is clear: this family certainly isn't boring," Mary chimes in, and soon, everyone falls into conversation.

His thumb breaks underneath the elastic of my panties, and I jerk my head to look at him.

What are you doing? I mouth, but he just takes a long pull of his whiskey, his eyes staring at me as he moves his thumb closer in slow circles until he finally brushes over my now-throbbing clit.

I swallow a gulp, ready to argue, to slap his hand away, to do something ... but rather than any of that, I find myself parting my legs to give him better access. My traitorous vagina hasn't seen any action in months. Who am I to turn down a spontaneous fondling when the man is so clearly skilled with his trade? I don't know what kind of game this man thinks he's playing, but he needs to know that it'll take more than a public finger-fucking to teach me a lesson. Hell, if this is how he reacts to being called Daddy in public, maybe I'll start calling him that exclusively.

Another flick over my clit, followed by a gentle caress, and my eyes are threatening to roll to the back of my head as a wave of full-body shivers coat my skin. Pure, unfiltered pleasure shoots up my core at the faintest brush of his finger, and my needy vagina clenches in response, starving for more.

I suck in a hiss, and my fork drops to my plate with a sharp clatter. Once again, the chatter dies down as everyone looks toward the direction of the commotion.

I scramble to grab my fork just as Leo makes another delicious sweep over my clit, this time pausing for just a moment as he masterfully plays with my pussy.

"This Caesar salad is amazing! Maybe the best I've ever had," I manage to say, which seems to appease them as they go back into their conversations.

I nearly fall out of my chair when he adds his other fingers to his perusal, deepening his touch. He dips his middle finger deeper, teasing along my entrance as he methodically massages my clit with his thumb.

"Are you struggling to keep a straight face right now? God, you're such a whore, aren't you? You're so wet, parting your legs for me, begging me to touch your pussy right here at my family dinner," he whispers in my ear, making me choke on my own saliva.

"You two are being awfully quiet down there," Mary says, bringing the attention back to us.

Leo pulls his hand away for only a moment, and I take a deep breath of relief, but just as I open my mouth to speak, he slides a thick finger inside me, and I strain to keep a straight face.

"I think Ivy's a little tired from her shopping excursion today. Aren't you, sweetheart?"

"Uh-huh, yes, I did go shopping ..." My words come out blubbery, like I've had too much to drink, and then he's curling his finger, and my vision goes blurry.

It takes every ounce of focus I have to keep my body up straight, and I can't even think about the wet spot I'm leaving on the chair.

"Scarlett mentioned you came by her store when she called earlier to ask me about the festival sponsors—"

"Did she now?" Leo says between clenched teeth, and then he adds a second finger.

My fingers grip on to the seat of my chair as I try to maintain my balance, try to look unbothered, but I've never felt pleasure like this. It's like I'm aware of every nerve in my body, and they're all turned up and tuned in to Leo's impeccably skilled fingers as he plays me like an instrument.

I don't know if it's the fact that he caught me off guard, or that he's touching me underneath the dinner table and nobody even notices, or that the man has brought me closer to orgasm with only a few brushes of his fingers than I can get myself with my vibrator ... but my body's never experienced pleasure so intense.

A drop of drool falls from the corner of my mouth and lands on my hand, and I'm quick to wipe it away. Luckily, Jett seems to be preoccupied with his phone, saving me the trouble of having to look him in the eye while his brother finger-fucks me into oblivion. Because *that* would be uncomfortable ...

I'm so close, right fucking there, as stars start to cloud my vision. I suck in a hiss through clenched teeth, trying to hold back my moans as the warm fluttering builds low in my belly. Holy shit. My toes curl, and every muscle in my body braces for the most powerful orgasm I've ever had. My walls begin to clench around Leo's fingers, and I squeeze my eyes shut, ready to ride the waves and succumb to my much-anticipated release when, all at once, he slides his fingers out of me.

Cold air rushes in place of his warm skin, and my eyes fly open.

I croak out, reaching for his hand as confusion floods my mind, "Wait ... why'd you ... I was just about to ..."

He gives my leg a friendly pat, like he's telling me it's okay, as that cocky, smug smile spreads over his lips. And then he leans in and whispers, "Now, you didn't really think I was going to let you finish after that behavior, did you, baby girl?" He carefully spreads his napkin over his lap like he didn't just finger-fuck me to the edge of madness. "Maybe you'll think twice before you start something you can't finish."

My mouth falls open, and his eyes flash to my untouched plate. "Don't be rude, Ivy. You've barely even touched your plate. I know how hungry you were ..."

A piece of cherry pie sits in front of me—not sure when we moved on from dinner to dessert—and Leo dips his finger into the whipped cream. I watch as he licks it off, closing his eyes like he's savoring the flavor.

"Damn, that's sweet. Almost feels sinful for something to taste so good."

"Can someone pass me a piece of pie?" Guy's voice breaks through the sexually charged moment, snapping me back to reality.

I narrow my eyes and grab my fork, stabbing my own piece of pie with unnecessary force, but my threat goes unnoticed when Frank's voice steals everyone's attention.

"Speaking of the festival, Roman, how's the planning coming? We're only a few short weeks away."

"Actually, Dad, I've been meaning to talk to you about that." He looks around and shrugs. "I didn't want to impose on Leo and Ivy's celebration dinner, but I do have some good news myself."

"It's no imposition to us, is it, Ivy?" Leo looks to me, feigning innocence.

I force a smile. "Not at all."

Roman's smile grows wider, and his shoulders sag in relief. "Good. Well, I'm happy to announce that thanks to Leo securing our partnership with the Thompson Brothers deal, Kingsley Industries will be creating a new sister brand of eco-friendly cleaning products next fall."

Mary claps her hands excitedly.

"That's incredible, son. This is wonderful news," Frank adds.

"So, naturally, I'm going to be pretty busy as we create the new branding. We're starting from scratch and pulling a whole new team together to work on it. I'll be flying all over for the next six months at least, and that means ..."

"You're not going to be able to head up the festival," Mary finishes for him.

Roman offers her an apologetic smile and then looks at Frank. "So, looks like we're going to need to find a new lead and fast. I'll admit, I've been behind schedule, and I haven't done much to get started, so whoever you pick's going to have their work cut out for them."

I see my opportunity for revenge, and I jump. I was only halfway listening, but I heard all I needed to hear.

Festival planning. Work cut out for them.

Check and check.

"Leo would love to do it," I blurt, and everyone goes completely quiet.

I look at Leo, who's back to fuming, and return his pat of encouragement. "Leo was just telling me on the drive over how he's looking for more ways to get involved and give back to the community. He's been dying to get his hands dirty, and I'm sure he's more than capable of getting the job done."

"Leo, that would be ... wow, son ... that would be perfect." Frank's smile grows impossibly bigger as he looks between his boys, his eyes gleaming with pride.

"Look at that. I told you, don't count him out of the fight just yet," Mary says to Frank, but everyone's gone so quiet that we all hear.

We all look around in awkward silence, and then Frank claps his hands. "Well then, that settles it. I'm going to need you working on the festival full-time, starting tomorrow. I think this will be good, give you a little break."

Leo grips my shoulder like he's pinning me in my seat. "Oh, I don't know, Ivy. I'd hate to busy myself with more work after you just uprooted your life and moved here to be with me. I'm not sure that it'd be fair to you—"

I pat him on the chest. "I don't mind one bit. I think it's important to follow your heart. You know I'll be here to support you, holding down the fort while you go to the office every day."

Frank cuts in, offering another solution, "Why don't you let Ivy help you? Bring her into the office, and you two can plan the festival together? That way, you'll still be together, and you won't feel guilty for leaving her alone all day."

I clap my hands together. "Now, *that* is a good idea. I can't wait to see your office and what you do all day. Now, we'll never have to be apart!"

Leo's lips tighten, and I can see he's trying to bite back an objection ... because what can he really say? His dad's solution is sort of perfect.

"Problem solved," he says through clenched teeth as he flashes me a look that says, *Just wait until we get home.*

"Now, when we're at work, would you prefer I call you Boss Daddy, or should I just stick to Daddy?"

CHAPTER TEN

Leo

"Put me down!" Ivy screams as she beats her fists on my back.

The drive home was torturous, and it took every ounce of strength I had to keep my attention on the road. To not pull over and play out any of the punishments that readily came to mind.

Jesus Christ, I've never been so equally aroused and irritated. Never thirsted so badly for someone I couldn't have.

I've suppressed that side of myself with surprising ease for the last decade, and all it takes is for this bratty bombshell to waltz in and start tearing down walls and fucking everything up. It's like she holds my weakness in the palm of her hand, and I've never been more terrified in my life. Because as much as I fight it, I'm not sure who's in control right now—me or her.

"Someone needs to teach you a lesson on how to behave." I slap her on the ass, and she lets out a little yelp. Her tiny yellow sundress is so thin that I can feel the heat of her skin, and it pisses me off that much more.

I hate that I'm so attracted to her, hate that she has this much control over me, hate how badly I want to play with her ...

I don't know who I'm more pissed off at—Ivy for deliberately trying to embarrass me in front of my family or myself for losing control.

I grit my teeth as I climb the steps to the front porch and swing open the heavy front door with a loud thud. It's been a long time since I've let this side of myself see the light of day, but when I look at Ivy with her wild, long hair and that playful fucking smirk on her face, it's like the other piece of my soul's been woken up. And I don't know what to do about it.

My hands itch to spank her, to do unspeakable things to her, things I have no business even entertaining ... and yet I can't stop them from filling my mind. It's like a faucet's been turned on, and it feels so good that I don't know if I'm strong enough to turn it back off. Or if I even want to for that matter.

I can still taste her, still see the way her cheeks flushed and the way her pretty amber eyes hooded, the way her pouty lips parted as she gasped as I brought her right to the edge of release. Fuck, her pussy was so wet for me, so eager, the way she spread her thighs and welcomed me in. I nearly blew a load in my pants right there, just from feeling the way her body responded to my touch. Oh, the fun I could have with her ...

A sharp punch to my kidney snaps me out of my daydream, and I charge through the living room, down the hall, until I reach her bedroom, where I drop her on the mess of tangled sheets and pillows.

"Let's get one thing straight; all these little games you're playing end right now."

She lands on the bed and bounces with a squeak, and the little brat has the audacity to grin at me. She fucking grins like she's proud of herself, and I realize that I am once again giving her the exact reaction she's been begging for.

She bats her eyelashes innocently. "I don't know what you're talking about. I was trying to help you. Your brother saw right through you, and you froze."

She sits up on her knees, and I take a step closer, meeting her challenge.

"Is that so? Tell me how calling me Daddy in front of my entire family *helps* me?"

She crosses her arms over her chest and rolls her eyes. "I was giving them a *believable* reason that you'd keep your relationship a secret. And you know what? They bought it without asking another question. So, tell me, what does that say about *you*, Leo Kingsley?"

I clench my teeth so hard that my jaw twitches as I stare down at this feisty, infuriating woman. As much as it pains me, I know she's right. The moment the words left her mouth, I saw understanding spread across Jett's face. It does make sense, but that doesn't mean I have to like it. Maybe she did do me a favor, made our lie a little more believable, but she didn't have to go as far as calling me Daddy. She didn't have to be *that* honest.

Fuck, I guess that's what I get for reacting so strongly. I've given her all the fuel she needs to drive me insane, and judging by the proud smirk she's wearing, I know I've got my work cut out for me if I want any semblance of control back.

I take a step toward her, closing the space between us. "So, this is what you want, is it?" I wipe my finger along her full lips as I stare down into those warm sunshine eyes. "To drive me crazy, push all my buttons until I'm so pissed that I lose control? You want me to punish you, don't you, baby girl?"

She sucks in the faintest little gasp, but her eyes light up with excitement.

I move closer, tilting her jaw up so that her eyes meet mine. Towering over her like this—that yellow sundress riding up over her ass, her bare tan legs tucked beneath her, her wild, wavy hair falling over her sun-kissed shoulders, and those fucking eyes staring up at me like she's daring me to pounce, it's all too much to take. Fuck, I've got to get ahold of myself.

"I should punish you. I should bend you over my knee and spank your pretty little ass for that stunt you pulled tonight ..."

Her eyes sparkle, her teeth sinking into her plump bottom lip.

"But that'd be too easy. That'd be giving you exactly what you want, wouldn't it?" I trace my finger along her jaw and ever slowly down the side of her neck. Her pulse pounds with excitement. "I bet if I slid my hand between your thighs, I'd find your panties drenched right now, wouldn't I? All pent-up from having your pussy played with ..."

"Why don't you stop talking about it and see for yourself? Judging by the erection you're sporting, I'd say that you seem just as excited ... maybe even more." Her eyes flash to my cock, and she wets her lips.

I trail my fingers down her shoulder and then to the back of her neck, where I grab a fistful of her long hair and wrap it around my wrist. I hold her gaze, and she lets out the sexiest whimper, but she doesn't break eye contact. My little brat likes being dominated, and fuck if it doesn't make my cock that much harder. She gets off on pushing me, but what she doesn't know is, that's one of my biggest kinks as well.

"That might very well be true, but unlike you and your impulsive behavior, I'm more calculated with my decisions. Which is why I'm telling you good night."

Her eyebrows furrow, and she opens her mouth to protest, but I hold up my hand.

"We've got a big day ahead of us tomorrow, so get some rest. And don't you fucking dare even *think* about touching your pussy after I leave this room."

"What are you going to do about it if I do?" she bites back.

I tighten my grip on her hair as I stare down at her eager lips. "You don't want to know, trust me."

I take a step backward, feeling stronger as I put more space between us until I finally reach the doorway.

"I promise you next time won't be nearly as fun. I went easy on you tonight, and you'd be wise to not disobey me again."

I don't wait for her response before closing the door. There's no point in pretending that there isn't something here between us, that this isn't something we both want. But that still doesn't make it right. I've already crossed the line, and I can't let myself go there again.

Our bodies might want one thing, but if there's any part of me that's actually a good person, then I won't let this go any further than it already has. She's young. Too young. And she has her whole life ahead of her, and all I'd be doing is setting her up for another disappointment.

It might be the death of me, but I've got to at least try to resist her, if only for her own sake.

I make a beeline to my bathroom, stepping into the shower with my fist around my cock before the water even has time to warm.

I brace my hand on the cold tiles as images of Ivy flood my mind. What would it feel like to bury my cock so deep in her tight little cunt? To have her tan legs wrapped around my waist as I drove into her, her perky tits bouncing beneath us as I fucked the sass right out of her? Now that I know how tight her pussy is, how wet she was for me within seconds of touching her ... fuck, I can't stop thinking of what it'd be like to be inside her, to claim her as my own. She'd never be the same after I got finished with her, and that thought alone is more tempting than I care to admit. The things I could teach her ... because I know the men her age haven't fucked her like I would, that they didn't appreciate her the way I would. I'd fuck her so hard, edge her again and again until she was a blubbering mess, begging me to finally let her come.

And only then would I give her what she wanted so badly. I'd reward her begging and pleading, swallowing her moans as she fell apart on my cock again and again.

I pump my fist, picturing her naked body writhing and begging beneath me as heat soars up my spine, my orgasm just beneath the surface.

I imagine pulling out of her, the little gasp of surprise

she'd make from the sudden loss of my cock, as I shoot my hot liquid release, painting her sassy mouth and lips with my cum.

I can practically see her surprised smile, already know the little brat would love it. And fuck if I don't feel a little spark of something I haven't felt in a very long time.

Bracing myself to keep my balance, I pump my cock with one final stroke as I come so hard from the fantasy that I nearly black out, pleasure ripping through me. I let the vision consume me, let myself have this moment of pure selfishness.

And when I finally come back to earth and open my eyes, I already know I'm a fucking goner.

CHAPTER ELEVEN

Ivy

"I'm so excited! I've never had an office job before. Do you think everyone's going to like me? Will there be snacks? What if I get hungry before lunch?" I fire off a list of questions as Leo ignores me, like he's staring down at me from his high horse.

We're waiting for the elevator to bring us to the top floor of Kingsley Tower, and my grumpy fiancée turned boss has barely spoken two words to me. He's cold and detached and acting like last night he didn't finger-fuck me at family dinner ... and then threaten to punish me further if I touched myself.

Holy fuck, I'm getting turned on again, just thinking about it.

Where on earth did that come from, and how do I trigger it again? I'm not exactly sure what we're doing here. All I know is that no one has ever made me feel anything remotely close to what I felt from this man's *fingers*. If he's that skilled with his hands, I can't imagine what he can do with his cock.

I fan myself as a rush of heat burns my cheeks, feeling more and more frustrated that he doesn't appear the least bit affected. If anything, he's more closed off and rigid than usual.

After Leo left my bedroom last night, I was in such a flustered tizzy. I couldn't get the memory of his hands out of my mind, and I lay there, fighting the urge to bring myself the relief I was so desperately craving.

I didn't want to listen to his stupid commands, trust me. But every time I tried to find my own relief, I kept getting distracted by how much better it'd felt when Leo touched me. After several failed attempts and a charley horse in my hand, I finally gave it up and succumbed to my fate.

Who knew all it took to get me to listen was some pent-up sexual frustration and a firm tone from an older man? If I could harness this kind of willpower, there's no telling what I'd be capable of achieving. It's a dangerous power in the wrong hands, which makes sense that the responsible, controlled Leo Kingsley would be the only man known to wield it.

He can never know; his ego's much too big already.

That was the hottest thing anyone had ever said to me, so it was torture, not being able to give myself a release, but in the back of my mind, I just kept thinking that if I listened to him, then maybe he'd burst through my door and put me out of my misery.

So, despite my efforts to disobey him again ... I begrudgingly followed his orders, and I think that is deserving of some kind of acknowledgment, a special treat, something.

I just need to find the right opportunity to bring it up.

The elevator chimes, and we step inside. I turn to watch the gorgeous views as the elevator lifts us all the way to the top floor. Ashford Falls is breathtakingly beautiful, and Kingsley Tower has a prime location overlooking the waterfalls on one side and the old railroad station on the other. I'm sure this location was intentional.

"How many waterfalls are in this town?" I ask, trying to make small talk.

"Seven, but that's the largest one, and if you look to the east, you can see another one from this vantage point."

The elevator doors open, and I follow close at his heel.

"Oh, so you *can* speak. I was beginning to wonder if you'd lost your voice when you were moaning my name in the shower last night—"

He stops abruptly, and I run smack into his back. "Have you not learned your lesson about trying to embarrass me?"

I give him a shrug. "I don't remember it being so bad, having you finger-fu—"

He slaps a palm over my mouth and pins me with a glare. "Listen very closely. I might have lost control last night, but I promise you I have no intentions of doing so again, and you'll be wise to not push me."

I stare up at him in forced silence for only a moment before he pulls his hand away, probably realizing he's making a scene.

He straightens his tie and lowers his voice to a hushed whisper. "We're at work now, and I expect you to at least pretend to be a professional while we're inside these walls."

I shove my hands in my pockets and rock back on my heels. "So, you don't deny it?"

"What?"

"Does that mean you *were* moaning my name? Because I was just fucking with you but—"

He pinches the bridge of his nose. "Why the fuck did I agree to bring you here?"

"Your dad didn't exactly give you a choice if I remember correctly, but I was still glitching from having my orgasm withheld from me, so I might not have the best memory."

His jaw clenches, and he looks at me like I've exhausted him. "Please just try to keep quiet and don't make a scene. People are working, and I don't need you causing a distraction."

"Sure thing, boss."

"Don't call me that."

"Why not? We're at work. You're paying me to be fake engaged to you. It's either boss or Daddy, and you told me to stop calling you Daddy so—"

"For Christ's sake, do you ever shut up?"

"Only when my mouth's full," I say with a shrug.

"You're making me question how much I really want this promotion with every minute that passes," he mumbles under his breath as we step into the open office space, where a handful of staff members are already setting up for the day.

"Good morning, Leo."

"Good morning." He waves, then places his hand on the small of my back, as if he's afraid I'll run away and embarrass him if he doesn't have a hand on me.

It's not completely untrue ...

"We heard about your hospital scare over the weekend. I can't believe you came in today—wait, is this *her*?" the woman sitting at the desk in the center says, causing everyone to turn around and stare.

I smile wide and give them a little wave, but before I can introduce myself, Leo speaks for me. "This is Ivy, my fiancée. You'll see her around here, as she's helping me plan the festival this year. Please try to keep things professional. I know this seems unexpected and exciting, but we are all here to work—"

"I can't wait to get to know all of you!" I interrupt. "We're going to have so much fun together—"

He tightens his grip on my arm. "She means at the festival, of course. Well, I'll be in my office, showing Ivy the ropes. If you need anything, just shoot me an email ..." He opens his office door, practically shoving me inside, and hits a button, making the office-facing windows go black for privacy.

"Whoa. Now, isn't this fancy?"

I look around the moody office, painted in a dark green or blue—I can't really tell because it's so dim. There's a large mahogany bookshelf built into the wall across from his desk, and a huge floor-to-ceiling window overlooking the falls. With the privacy shades, the window gives just enough light to have a cozy, calming feeling.

I plop down in his leather desk chair and spin around several times, lifting my feet when I build up enough speed to propel the chair on its own.

He grips the chair, causing it to stop abruptly, and the sudden force makes me fly into the armrest.

"Ouch. Hey, why'd you do that?"

"Get out of my chair."

I cross my arms over my chest and sink down further. "Make me."

He moves closer and props his hip against his desk as he

glares at me. He smells amazing, like aftershave and a touch of something woodsy, and I do my best to keep from shoving my nose into his chest. That would be weird, and by the looks of it, he isn't in the mood to be sniffed. Maybe I can get a good sniff in when he isn't looking ...

"You're insufferable—do you know that?"

"So I've been told."

Just when I expect him to yank me up out of his seat, he walks to the corner of the room and lifts an armchair like it weighs nothing and sets it beside me.

"What are you doing?"

"I'm improvising."

He slides his keyboard and mouse in the space in front of him and scoots the monitor over so he can see. He begins going through his emails. Like I'm not even sitting here.

Fine, I'll just figure out a way to entertain myself.

I take the opportunity to walk around and survey his bookshelves.

There's not much personality in this office, mostly just your standard classics—probably all first editions, if I had to guess. I drum my finger along the old spines until I come across a title that surprises me. I pull it from the shelf, and just as I suspected, it's a signed first edition copy of *The Hobbit* in pristine condition.

He clears his throat, and I spin around, still holding the book.

"I wouldn't have guessed you were a Tolkien fan. And a collector at that."

I wave the book, and he grabs it out of my hand, smoothing the cover before placing it back on the shelf.

"You're so uptight—you know that, don't you? I wasn't going to break it, you know—"

"Maybe not intentionally, but considering you still have a little bit of jelly on your lip from your doughnut this morning, I'd rather not tempt fate."

I suck in a breath when he swipes his thumb across my bottom lip and down my chin. But to my disappointment, he pulls a napkin from his pocket and wipes his thumb clean rather than sucking it off.

Shame.

"Okay, well, if I'm not allowed to touch your stuff, can you at least give me something to work on for the festival? I'm so bored. There must be something productive I can do ..."

Leo moves back to his seat, and I follow him.

"I don't have time right now. Maybe after my next meeting, I can find a list of vendors—"

"Your dad said the festival should be your top priority. And I'm here to make sure you stay on the right task and to keep you from stressing yourself out with all this work—"

"The only thing stressing me out is your mouth. Now, can you please figure out a way to entertain yourself—quietly and without destroying priceless antiques—for ten minutes? I promise we'll talk about the festival soon enough."

"Can I leave this office?"

"No."

"But it's so dark and cozy in here, and the shades are pulled down, and it's making me really horny ..."

"That's enough, Ivy," he growls in warning, making the hairs on the back of my neck stand on edge.

I love the way my name sounds, rolling off his tongue.

Really, this man should narrate audiobooks with that deep, panty-melting growl.

I fan myself as I watch him work. He might look like Superman, but this office is definitely giving Batman vibes.

"What superhero do you think you're more like—Superman or Batman?"

He glances up, with a look of confusion. "Seriously?"

"My guess is, you like Superman more because he's more wholesome and polished ..."

He lets out a long sigh, but doesn't say anything.

"Oh, come on. You're just going to sit there and ignore me like I'm not even here?"

"I don't think I could pretend you weren't here if I tried. Between your fidgeting legs shaking the desk and your interruptions every thirty seconds, even a goldfish wouldn't be able to forget your presence."

"You say that like it's a bad thing."

"Can you please stop talking? I'm concentrating."

I rock back in the fancy leather desk chair and fold my legs under me.

"You can sit there and look pretty while I catch up on these emails," he answers without looking my way.

"So, you *do* think I'm pretty? You know I can't really tell with this whole Jekyll and Hyde thing you've got going on. One minute, you're completely ignoring me, and the next, you're confiscating my vibrator and threatening to punish me if I touch myself. Make up your mind, Boss Daddy. What's it going to be?"

He hits Send on his email and turns to face me, wearing a look of exhaustion.

"I don't have time for this. As I'm sure you've gathered,

I'm a busy man, and now, thanks to your little suggestion last night, you've just tripled my workload. So, even if I wanted to be your *Boss Daddy*, I wouldn't have anywhere near the time or energy it would require of me to take on that role."

My mouth falls open, and for once, I'm literally too stunned to speak.

"Now, please, do me a favor and be quiet for five minutes so I can think about how I'm going to bend space and time to get everything done." He rubs his temples and sighs before going back to his computer screen.

Several moments pass as I try to hold in my question, but eventually, my curiosity wins out, and I break the silence. "Now, when you say you don't have the time and energy to take on that role, does that mean that you've done this before?"

"It means, drop it. This is not the time or the place to have this conversation."

I start to argue, but the phone rings, slicing through the tension-filled air like a knife. And just like that, Leo switches back to his business professional persona as he discusses eco-friendly packaging substrates and pricing.

But that one little comment is all the encouragement I need.

"I can't imagine Leo saying that, much less right before bungee jumping with you," Janice, one of the ladies on Leo's floor, says.

"I thought he was scared of heights. Wasn't that one of

his fun facts during last year's holiday party?" Ricky, the only other man on the twentieth floor, asks.

"No, it wasn't heights. I'm pretty sure he said claustrophobic," Janice adds.

"Really, Janice? Now, you're the expert, are you?" Ricky snaps back, crossing his arms over his chest in annoyance.

Clearly, there's some unresolved tension between these two, as they haven't stopped arguing since we sat down for lunch. We're in the cafeteria, and I've drawn quite the crowd around me, as everyone wants to get to know Leo Kingsley's mystery lover.

I'm a good time. What can I say?

"Oh, well, he put on a brave face before we jumped, but one of the workers ended up having to push us over the edge because he tried to back out. He clung to me and screamed like a little girl the whole way down," I say with a laugh, trying to lighten the mood.

In the twenty minutes since Leo left me unattended for lunch—he's taking a working lunch that's too important for my *distractions*—I've managed to meet all the staff members working on his floor and some of the people in HR. I've told them how we met. I even stuck to Leo's boring script, but I took some creative liberty with some of the other stories, like the first time he'd told me he loved me—while we made love in his car on the way back from the airport. It was so romantic; he couldn't wait to get me to the hotel, just swooped into a Walmart parking lot, and I rode him to high heaven.

Sometimes, my imagination terrifies me with how quickly I come up with these things.

"He's got quite the wild side to him when he lets himself detach from work," I say with a shrug.

"Wow, I wish we could see fun Leo every now and then. Maybe then he'd actually be able to keep an assistant," Fran, from HR, says.

"What do you mean? His assistants quit a lot?"

Fran continues, "Oh, yeah. He's got about a three-month limit before he either overworks them, or pisses them off bad enough for them to either transfer to another department or outright quit."

My eyebrows knit together in confusion. It's not that I can't see Leo being hard to work for; his expectations must be through the roof, as he demands perfection from everyone around him, especially himself. But I'm surprised because this place seems so good to its employees. I see the way Frank's personality and gigantic heart for this company and the community shine through everything. How is Leo still missing the mark? I know he cares; it's why he pushes himself so hard ... but isn't he smart enough to see he's making his staff miserable, that they have to walk on eggshells around their boss?

No wonder his dad decided he wasn't ready to be promoted.

"Hey, you know what? We should do something after work on Friday! Like a team-bonding activity. What do you think?" I blurt out the idea as soon as it pops in my head.

Everyone's so tense around here; maybe if we shake things up with some after-work drinks and games, they'll be able to see Leo's not so bad.

"We stopped having happy hours after work when Leo moved over to our floor two years ago. He said he didn't want to be liable for someone getting hurt or something like that," another woman says.

"That's ridiculous. It's after work, and everyone is responsible, right? Leo might have decided that two years ago, but I'm here now, and the man doesn't tell me no about anything. What do you think we should do? Does anyone have any ideas?"

"Ooh!" Janice raises her hand excitedly, so I nod for her to share. "We could play trivia at Restaurant. Leo's brother Jett owns it, you know. I bet he'd make sure we had a table and enough space for everyone to join!"

"Yeah?" I look around as everyone nods in agreement, chattering among themselves, and dare I say, for the first time since I stepped in this building, there's a buzz of excitement in the air. "Let's do it then. I'll call later today and ask Jett to reserve a space."

"Reserve the space for what?" Leo's husky voice asks from behind me, and suddenly, everyone falls quiet.

The room feels ten degrees colder as he stands over me with one eyebrow cocked up. It's like he's a real-life fun sucker, a Dementor for joy.

I flash him a big smile as I try to boost the energy back to its previous level. "There you are. We were just planning a trivia night after work on Friday. Doesn't that sound like fun?"

I bat my eyes and nudge my head toward his staff, but his scowl only deepens.

"Absolutely not." He shakes his head, shoving his hands in his pockets.

"But I haven't even told you the theme—"

"It's a liability, and my decision is fin—"

I don't wait for him to finish before jumping up and wrapping my arms around him. I grip his tie and pull his head down so I can whisper in his ear as his heart beats violently in his chest. "You want to prove to your dad that you're ready, then just go with it. Or I can entertain them with more scandalous stories about us ... let them know your favorite pet name ..."

"I swear to God, if you even mutter a single syllable about that ..." His voice trails off in a growl underneath his breath.

"See, you keep saying that, but here's the thing ..." I trace my fingers over his rough stubble before grabbing the knot of his tie in my fist. "I don't think it's having the desired effect you think it is." I quirk a brow, tightening my grip on his tie.

He coughs, then shakes his head, looking irritated. "Fine, but keep it work-appropriate. And everyone will need to sign a waiver before drinking any alcohol."

I loosen my grip and tap him on the cheek, his afternoon scruff scratching against my palm. "Good boy," I say with a wink.

Everyone breaks out in cheers, and it's only then that I remember we're not alone. His hard chest moves under my palm as he breathes small, quick breaths, and judging by the way he's looking at me, I'm not sure if he wants to spank me or kiss me ...

Lucky for me, I'd be happy with either.

CHAPTER TWELVE

Leo

Fucking hell, I'm in over my head.

I need to get my shit together, rein in the stupid fucking urges that haunt me nonstop, and get over this *crush* so I can focus on what's really important.

But calling what I feel for Ivy Lane a crush seems like the understatement of the century. No, I'd say my thoughts of her are borderline obsessive at this point, and the only thing I can do is try to avoid her by smothering myself in my work.

I even went as far as moving her into her very own office, normally reserved for my executive assistant that I still haven't gotten around to replacing. She might have a shared door to my office, but at least I can somewhat keep her from causing too much trouble with the staff.

Every morning, we get ready and eat breakfast in silence, where she makes sure I have a full glass of water and breakfast in my stomach before she lets me have any coffee. Then, we drive to the office as I force myself to go along with her small talk, answering questions and pretending I'm not thinking about how wet her pussy got for me or the pretty pink flush of her cheeks as she held back her moans.

Fuck, I'm hard all over again, just thinking about it. I think I've had a permanent boner since the moment she stepped through my doorway and agreed to this stupid charade. I'm afraid my cock's going to get stuck like that because heaven knows jerking off to her every night isn't doing a goddamn thing to help.

I don't trust myself to be alone with her and have found an excuse every night this week to leave just so I don't have to be.

But not tonight.

Thanks to my temporary moment of weakness, agreeing to this trivia night, I've got to force a smile and play nice, no matter how badly it pains me.

I look around as people start to file in, all wearing smiles on their faces. Sure, Kingsley Industries is a good place to work overall, but these folks are from my department, and I've never seen them so happy. Hell, Ricky threw his back out, demonstrating how to do the worm at lunch earlier this week, and is walking on a cane. But judging by the grin on his face, you'd never know it.

"Leo, could you grab a couple of pitchers of water to put on the tables? I'm going to do one more mic check," Ivy says.

She's wearing denim cutoff shorts and a cropped white tank top that reveals her belly button when she lifts her arms or moves just right.

She's sexy as fuck. All smiles and sunshine.

"Sure. Yeah. I'll go grab some." I shake my head, trying to

get my mind back out of the gutter, but she's not making things easy for me.

I help myself behind the bar and into the kitchen, where I know Jett keeps the extra serving supplies, and grab four water pitchers from the shelf.

"What the fuck are you doing back here? You're not wearing slip-resistant shoes or a hairnet," Jett's voice calls from behind me, and I spin around to face him.

"Relax. I was just grabbing some extra pitchers. Didn't want to inconvenience you. It's really picking up out there, and as far as I can see, you've only got one server working tonight ..."

He crosses his arms over his chest. "Yeah, well, I had two servers call in sick, so we're making do." He tilts his head to the door. "If you hadn't invited your entire company, it wouldn't be a problem. I couldn't find anyone to fill in so last minute."

I scratch my chin, feeling like a dick. He's right; I told Ivy I'd make the reservation, but it totally slipped my mind, as I was too distracted by the actual work that needed my attention.

"You got an extra pair of shoes around here?"

Jett narrows his eyes. "Leo, I don't need any favors. I've got it under control—"

"We need all hands on deck back here. I've got thirteen tickets waiting, and we're approaching a forty-five-minute ticket time!" one of the guys on the line yells, and Jett just shakes his head.

"Let me bring these waters out, and I'll be right back. I'm going to need those shoes and a hairnet." I move past him, and I fill the pitchers with water and ice and head to the table.

"Leo, this is all amazing. I can't believe you approved it," Fran from accounting says as I place the waters on the table.

A smart-ass comment is on the tip of my tongue when Ivy gives me a wide-eyed look of encouragement, as if she's mentally telling me to accept the compliment.

I swallow a gulp. "Thanks, Fran. I hope everyone has a good time. You all deserve it. It's the least I can do."

This earns me a proud smile from Ivy, and fuck if it doesn't feel good to be on the receiving end of that smile. I'm so used to pissing her off that I don't think she's ever looked at me like she's proud of me. She seems to be the one to see through my bullshit, even when I'm trying to do the right thing.

Ivy leans a hip on the table and faces me. "Now, was that so hard? Look at them. I didn't know Ricky knew so much about superheroes, but he hasn't shut up since he got here, and we haven't even started with the trivia questions."

"It was fucking painful actually. I think I just got a lie bump on my tongue," I say as I start filling the empty glasses with ice water. "Listen, I know this is all supposed to help me look like a cool boss and everything, but Jett's drowning back there in the kitchen. I'm going to go back there and help him get out of the weeds. Can you handle running everything on your own for a bit?"

"In the weeds? Who are you, and what have you done with my billionaire boss daddy?"

I send her a warning glare, and she just smiles.

"I'm not all white collar. I worked in a restaurant all through college—Jett and I both did. It's where he fell in love with the idea of starting his own, and I realized I wanted nothing more to do with it." I place the last cup of water down as the lights start to dim, and the rock music in the background gets a little louder.

"Don't worry; it's just a little mood lighting. Go help your brother. I've got this under control."

She winks, and I grab her wrist before she walks away.

"Thank you for taking the initiative and pushing this. I think this is exactly what our team needed, and I never would've known that without your annoying nagging."

She places a hand over her heart. "Oh, Leo, your words are so touching. You should write greeting cards."

I press my lips together to keep from smiling. "Shut up and get up there before Ricky takes over and starts singing the Spider-Man theme song."

"That's an oddly specific example ..."

"Trust me, you'll have that song stuck in your head for weeks. I'm just warning you." I loosen my grip on her wrist and rub a thumb over her soft skin. "Remember to keep things professional, okay? I'll be back as soon as I can. I want everyone to have fun, but this is still a work event—"

She rolls her eyes. "Relax. I'm on your side, remember?"

At that, I drop her hand and head to the kitchen. I don't have time for her antics right now, and Lord knows, if I give her a reaction, it'll only prompt her to keep going.

I burst through the doors, and Jett shoves an armful of gear in my chest.

"You fucking took long enough. Get dressed and meet me on the line. We've got tickets piled high, and I just turned off the phone because we've got just as many to-go orders."

I strip off my work shirt, throw the apron over my white

undershirt, and replace my leather loafers with rubber -soled, slip-resistant shoes.

A flash of steam scalds my face as I add the chilled cream to the pan.

"You've got to lower the heat, bro. You're going to scald the sauce," Jett calls from beside me as we fall into a flow state, tackling tickets and moving in rhythm.

It's satisfying, working with my hands, seeing tangible results for my actions right before my eyes, especially after the frustrating week I've had. I let my body do the work and my mind take a back seat as the familiar skills brim to the surface. It feels oddly relaxing and comforting, working alongside my brother.

I feel closer to him back here, like how things were before, when life was easy and we were best friends.

I'm almost able to forget my spitfire, loose cannon of a fiancée ... almost.

I just hope she's not doing anything crazy while I'm preoccupied back here, but it's just trivia night. How much trouble could she really cause?

CHAPTER THIRTEEN

Ivy

"Who is James Howlett?" Ricky yells as he hits the bell on the table just as Janice slaps her bell and screams, "Logan!"

I lift the answer cards to cover my smile as the two teams begin arguing among themselves.

"You're wrong, Janice! You've only seen the movies; you didn't even bother to read the comics!" Ricky hollers behind his hand and rolls his eyes.

Who knew superhero trivia could get so heated?

I clear my throat, and they all look at me with bated breath.

"The tie-breaking point goes to ... Ricky and the Wolf Pack. Wolverine's real name is in fact James Howlett. Logan was his alias, as well as Weapon X."

Ricky jumps out of his seat and crosses his hands in an X across his crotch, then howls in victory. "Suck it, Janice! You're such a know-it-all in the office. Well, how does it feel to lose?"

"Why don't you shut up, Ricky? Before I come over there and make you—"

I hold my hands out. "Whoa, whoa, guys. It's just a game. Let's all take a deep breath and remember that this is for fun. It's just a bonding activity, not anything that matters."

Ricky does a victory lap around our tables, hands in the air like he's waving to all his fans, while the Wolf Pack cheers and Janice and the Smarty Pints scowl at him.

Shit, Leo was right. These people really do take their trivia seriously. I don't think I've seen a more competitive group ... ever.

I thought Fern and I were bad. We used to fight like mortal enemies over every board game we ever played until we learned we were stronger as a team. Our twin bond gave us an edge that didn't even feel fair at times, like we could read each other's mind. Once we figured that out, we were pretty much unstoppable in any game where we had to communicate and work together.

Janice jumps out of her seat, trying to steal Ricky's invisible trophy, and I panic.

"Hang on. Hang on. Let's not get physical—"

"I'm going to kick your ass, Ricky. Then, I'm going to CC you on every minor expense report correspondence that comes across my inbox. Now until the end of time!" Janice hisses.

Ricky audibly gasps. "You wouldn't!"

She pulls out her phone and types something, then looks back up, wearing a devious smile.

He grabs his phone from his pocket, swiping it open, and lets out a bloodcurdling scream of horror. "Three hundred unread emails! You bitch!"

"Those are just from after five. Just wait until you open your inbox on Monday morning." She throws her head back and cackles like an evil witch.

I have to admit, that was pretty harsh. Everyone knows Ricky can't leave work until he's read every email in his inbox.

I scratch my head, trying to think of something, anything to distract them because, right now, the Wolf Pack and the Smarty Pints are staring at each other like two gangs ready to brawl.

A server walks by with a tray of shots, presumably for the group of young people sitting in the corner, and I blurt the first thing that comes to mind. "Who wants shots?"

Ricky and Janice both pause and look at me like I've grown two heads, but I don't really have time to think of a better game plan, so I grab the tray from the server with a pleading expression. "I'm so sorry. I really need to borrow these unless you want this place to turn into a WWE wrestling ring in the next five seconds."

To my surprise, she obliges with no argument ... which makes me wonder if this is a normal occurrence around Ashford Falls.

"Could you send those guys another round on Leo's tab as an apology?"

"You got it." She winks. "Watch out with Ricky there. Too much tequila, and he'll be singing karaoke and trying to give everyone in here a lap dance."

I quirk a brow. "Is that right? So, he's a happy drunk?"

She laughs. "Oh, yeah. Total blast. I'd even be willing to bet that he wore his leopard-print thong just in case ..."

I nod my head. Now, that could be a fun time.

"Keep the tequila shots coming, would you?"

She just grins. "I knew I liked you. Looks like it's going to be one of those nights. Can't wait."

I grab three shots and head to Janice and Ricky, shoving one in each of their hands. "What do you say we make things a little more exciting tonight? No more competition, just bonding and having a good time."

I watch as Ricky and Janice stare at each other. Then, Ricky throws his shot back with a hiss. It's the closest thing to a truce Janice is going to get, and I think she knows it, so she follows suit, wiping her mouth with the back of her hand.

I down mine and wince, then grab the mic. "Who's up for a little karaoke?"

* * *

Ricky's in the middle of a particularly sensual rendition of "I Want to Sex You Up," and I look around the room, feeling a warm flutter of accomplishment. Everyone's gathered around the small stage, and they've pushed all the tables against the walls, creating a dance floor in the middle of the restaurant.

Smiling faces fill the space as far as the eye can see, and the Wolf Pack and Smarty Pints are blended evenly now; you wouldn't even know there was almost a brawl over X-Men trivia just an hour ago.

This is exactly how things should be. Leo would be pleasantly surprised if he saw everyone getting along so well, and I'm just glad a little quick thinking on my part and a few rounds of tequila shots were all it took to get everyone to bond and get along.

The spotlight shines on Ricky as he moves from the stage

and makes a beeline straight to Janice. To my surprise, she doesn't slap him or even flinch when he begins grinding himself on her. If anything, she looks ... flushed?

That can't be right. Janice hates Ricky ...

She fans her face as she sways to the music, encouraging him to grind on her more.

I nearly fall over from shock when he grabs the back of her hair and pushes her to sit in a chair, but she looks like she likes it.

The crowd goes wild as he unbuttons the top half of his oxford shirt and loosens his belt, rolling his hips and gyrating to the music. The song "Bump n' Grind" begins to play, and everyone claps their encouragement. I guess I'll get to see Ricky's leopard-print thong tonight after all.

I cup my hands over my mouth and let out a hoot when Janice grabs his tie and pulls him down, changing places with him.

Oh shit. I didn't see that coming.

Janice spins away from him and lifts her dress to her knees, putting her ass right in his face, then folds forward and begins to twerk.

My jaw unhinges as everyone loses it, whooping and hollering and chanting her name, which only encourages her. She finishes her twerking, then spins around, kicks a leg in the air, and lands in the splits, and I nearly fall over from shock.

Ricky jumps up, offering her a hand, and to my utter shock, she accepts, letting him pull her back to her feet like it was all a part of the show.

The energy in this place is so high; it almost feels like

we're in a nightclub as I look around, seeing everyone dancing and vibing together.

Fern would have fucking loved this place. This town. These people. She'd have been joining in dancing and making memories with everyone, making the most out of every moment. I can't help but see her here everywhere I look. I'm more and more convinced that she had a hand in bringing me here a month earlier than I planned. Of all places to crash my car, it just so happened to be here, where a billionaire CEO would need me to pretend to be his fiancée. It's too ironic to be a coincidence.

When the last chorus of the song plays, Janice grabs a pitcher of water from a server walking by and dumps it down the front of her dress. Her nipples harden beneath the material, and the fabric clings to her, leaving nothing left to the imagination.

The room falls quiet, and then someone yells, "Wet T-shirt contest!"

Suddenly, the crowd joins in, and they all chant together. I don't think I've ever seen such an unlikely group of people share such passion and unity.

A few guys run to the drink stations, filling up pitchers of water and lining them along the bar as everyone forms a circle around the dance floor.

Someone shoves me to the center, and I look around, confused and excited all the same. That's when I realize I'm standing in the circle of women—who are all easily thirty years my senior—as they shed their bras, slingshotting them overhead in every direction.

I think about Fern's list and once again how these

ridiculous scenarios keep falling in my lap. There's no way the stars aligned this perfectly to set me up for this.

No, this is one hundred percent my sister's doing.

I don't know how or why it's happening, but it's like I can feel her near me, like she's standing right here, cheering me on, wearing that knowing smirk of hers. Like she's daring me to do it, to live in the moment while I still can.

Maybe it's the warm buzz of alcohol flowing through my veins or the energy in the room of everyone being so in sync with each other, or maybe it's a bit of both. Either way, there's no denying there's something magical about this town and the people in it. I've never felt more right about where I'm supposed to be in life. Like this moment in time was carved out just for me.

So, when I'm handed my own pitcher of water, I reach behind my back and flick off my own bra, sending it flying across the room, slapping Leo Kingsley right in his grumpy, scowling face.

"Wet T-shirts on three!" Janice screams.

Oh shit. He looks really mad.

"One."

I should stop this before it gets any worse.

"Two."

Why is he just staring at me like that instead of stopping this?

"Three!"

Oh well, here goes nothing. This is for you, Ferny.

His stare bores into me, sucking me in like we're the only two people in the room. I keep my eyes trained on him as I dump the freezing pitcher of ice water over my chest, feeling my nipples harden beneath my thin white tank top.

I'm yanked out of the moment when the ice-cold water splashes down my body, soaking my legs and feet, and I suck in a shocked breath.

See-through wet T-shirts fill the room as titties of all shapes and sizes are on full display. Long ones, big ones, small ones ...

Who knew Janice was hiding such a great rack under those cardigans?

A laugh bubbles out of me at the ridiculous situation, and I don't think I'll ever forget this moment for as long as I live.

"This is the best day of my life!" an old man I don't recognize shouts, lifting his arms over his head in celebration.

Ricky moves to a now-soaking-wet Janice and pushes her up against a wall. They share a moment of intense eye contact before his mouth crashes to hers, and she hikes up her leg, wrapping it around his back to pull him closer.

Well, damn. Maybe all that competitiveness brewing between them was something else after all.

I feel Leo before I hear him, his anger vibrating in the air between us.

"What the fuck is wrong with you, Ivy?" he growls behind me and spins me to face him, holding up my hands.

"Leo, listen. It's not what it looks like. We're just having a little fun, and things got out of hand."

His eyes trail down my body ever so slowly, his gaze lingering on the see-through fabric of my white T-shirt and my whole body lights on fire. And it's as if his switch has flipped, revealing the real Leo once again, his eyes growing darker as he drinks me in.

When he finally tears his gaze back up to meet my eyes,

his nostrils are flared, and there's a pained expression on his face.

He moves closer, and I find myself walking backward until my ass bumps against a table as his massive body towers over me, shaking with rage.

"Do I need to remind you that you are my fiancée? You're supposed to be making me look good."

"I ... I ... am," I stammer out as I brace my hands on the table to keep myself up right.

He grits his teeth. "How the fuck is pouring water over yourself, exposing your tits to the whole town ... and encouraging my entire department to do it with you ... making me look good, Ivy?"

He lifts my chin with his hand, craning my neck to meet his eyes.

Fuck, it's so hot when he's mad. I know there's got to be something wrong with me if this type of attention is what gets me going, but I have to clench my thighs to keep my throbbing pussy from distracting me.

I press my chest out, feeling his eyes burning across my damp flesh, and my nipples harden even more from his hot, intense gaze.

I open my mouth to speak, but before I can defend myself, he swipes an arm around my back and pulls me flush against his chest.

"You're such a fucking brat. I left you alone for two hours, and you turned the whole place into a goddamn sex club." He reaches behind his back and pulls off his shirt, then pulls it over my head. The shirt easily hangs to my knees and engulfs me in the scent of his cologne. "Cover yourself up and go to the car while I deal with this."

I shake my head. "No, you don't have to do that. Let me help you shut it down. I don't want you to have to be the bad guy."

He quirks a brow. "Really? Since when are you concerned with my image? Go to the car, Ivy. You've done enough *helping* for one night. Don't you think?" His words are laced with anger and something that sounds like disappointment, and for the very first time, I actually feel guilty for being so impulsive.

I guess I'm not used to my actions affecting anyone else.

"Okay, people, enough with the water!" Jett says into the microphone rather calmly, considering the circumstances.

Again, I'm starting to wonder what really goes on here in Ashford Falls.

"Ricky and Janice, you guys can dry-hump all you want *after* you help clean up this mess you made. Come on, people. The party's over. Grab a squeegee, and let's get these tables back to where they belong. You want to have a rave, that's fine, but I'm too understaffed to clean this up by myself, and I happen to know where you all work."

Everyone grumbles as the lights flick on, and they all start cleaning up the mess ... like it's just another regular Friday night.

"I should help clean ..." I start to move, but Leo grabs my wrist and slowly shakes his head.

"I told you to wait in the car. You've done enough for one evening. Can you please just listen for once?"

"But ... I—"

"I said, go wait in the fucking car, Ivy," he barks. Then, in a calmer voice, he adds, "I'll be right there after I settle up the check with Jett."

I cower a little under his glare. I don't think I've seen Leo this mad ... ever ... and since I make it my daily challenge to annoy him, I find that truly terrifying. "Okay ... yeah. I'll, uh ... I'll just go wait in the car."

He doesn't say anything, but I feel his eyes on me as I hang my head in defeat and head to the car.

I know I'm in trouble ... I just don't know what that means.

CHAPTER FOURTEEN

Leo

I didn't speak a word to her the whole drive home. My hands hurt from gripping the steering wheel as I seethed with anger and annoyance.

I'd left her alone for less than two hours. I had known she was going to be a handful the moment I asked for her help, but I don't think anything could have prepared me for this. She's insufferable. It's like she's trying to get a rise out of me with everything she does and everything she says. Like she was created by God himself to be the fucking kryptonite that would bring me to my knees.

How could she do this to me? And what the fuck am I supposed to do about it when every fiber in my being is screaming at me to lean in and let myself out of this cage?

I don't think she could've picked a more inconvenient time if she tried.

Getting out of the car, I slam the door behind me. I stomp up the steps two at a time, trying like hell to get my temper under control. I hear Ivy's heavy breathing behind me as she runs to keep up, my steps taking at least two of hers as she jogs up the stairs. I'm not even winded.

"Leo, wait. I'm sorry, okay? Aren't you going to at least hear me out?" She bends over, propping her hands on her knees as she tries to catch her breath.

"What's to tell, Ivy?" I pinch the bridge of my nose. "You were bored, so you decided to make things more fun, right?"

I take a step toward her, but she doesn't move.

"You did what you always do, and now, I'm the one who's going to have to explain to my dad why we have to pay for Jett's restaurant to be professionally cleaned and why half the town had their tits out at a company event. Do you have any idea how big of a mess you created? Do you even care?"

She coughs out a bark in between her pants for air and begins to pace, her arms held over her head.

"You're so goddamn selfish. You never stop to consider how your actions affect anyone but yourself. Do you even feel remorseful, or is this some kind of game for you?"

She shakes her head, tears welling in her eyes, but she doesn't speak as she stumbles and leans against the front porch railing.

Something's not right. Are her lips turning blue?

I move toward her, my heart kicking up a notch as worry rises in my chest. "Ivy, what's wrong? Can you not breathe?"

I tilt my head and move in front of her as she claws at her throat, a panicked expression forming behind her eyes.

"Asthma attack," she says between coughs, then wheezes some more.

I look around, holding her steady. "Fuck. Okay, do you

have an inhaler somewhere? Do you keep one on you? In your purse or something?"

She shakes her head and closes her eyes as she tries to take another strained breath. "It's in my ... in my dresser," she croaks out.

I barely wait for her to finish before tearing off in a sprint through the house. I pull out her dresser drawer and dump the contents on the floor, then move to the next one, dumping everything out in a panic until I find what I'm looking for.

Who keeps their life-saving medication tucked away in the bottom drawer of their dresser, next to their workout clothes, and not with them in a purse or something?

I sprint back through the house and find her doubled over again, wheezing and coughing.

"Here. Here. Breathe this in." I shake it up and hold it out for her, encouraging her to take deep breaths.

She takes a few puffs of the inhaler before her wheezing quiets and she's able to take deeper breaths. She relaxes a little as I hold her to me, tucking her under my arm as my own breathing starts to calm.

"There you go. I've got you." I smooth her hair down and kiss the top of her head as I try to blink back the fear that flashed before my eyes, watching her struggle like that. Feeling like the biggest asshole for screaming at her while she was having an asthma attack.

Fuck. I didn't even know she had asthma.

"I'm sorry," she says with a cough.

I move to sit in a rocking chair, pulling her into my lap. My trembling hand rubs circles along her back to soothe her, but truthfully, it's more for me.

I take my own deep breaths, urging myself to calm down

now that I know she's safe. "Shh. Let's not talk about that right now. I just need you to focus on breathing and calming down, okay?"

She nods her head, and I feel a hot, wet tear land on my arm, and it almost kills me, knowing that I had anything to do with that tear. Despite my anger, I should've noticed she was struggling, and instead, I made her chase me up the steps and tore into her, unloading all my pent-up frustration.

Eventually, her wheezing turns to whimpers, and I realize she's crying, so I spin her to face me. We're both soaked now, my oxford shirt hanging off one of her shoulders. She straddles a leg on either side of me, and I cradle her to my chest, breathing in her sweet scent.

My heart aches with each and every sob she lets out, which just makes me hold her tighter as my protective urges settle back down in the place I've kept them trapped for far too long. Fuck, it feels good to hold her like this, to be the one who comforts her while she cries ... even if I'm the reason for her tears. I forget how much I've missed having someone to care for, how much I crave being needed. And more than ever, I am keenly aware of just how much I've been missing, of what I truly want.

I bring my hands to her waist, running my thumbs along the exposed flesh of her hips, hating how even the faintest of touches of her skin has my body responding. This is the last thing I need right now, but somehow, I can't seem to shake the desire from my mind.

What if it could be different this time? What if she was into it too?

I shake the thought from my head. This isn't the time for

that. The poor thing just had a fucking asthma attack, and I'm wondering if she'd fit into my lifestyle.

What the fuck is wrong with me? Get your head out of your ass, Leo.

She's shaking like a leaf, all pitiful and teary-eyed, and I think I'd do anything to put a smile on her face right now. The world is off-balance when Ivy cries, like a unicorn without its wings or a black-and-gray rainbow, and it knocks the breath from my lungs, making my heart hurt.

I lift her chin and wipe the tears from her cheeks. "Baby girl, I hate seeing you like this. Tell me what I can do to make it better. Do you need medicine? Water?"

She shakes her head and purses her lips as I brush her wild, wavy hair from her face, cradling her against me as she sobs.

"Are you hurting then? What's wrong? What can I do for you to make you feel better?" I ask, feeling helpless.

She sucks in a shaky breath and sits up. "It's not that." Cough. "I just don't want you to be disappointed in me." Cough. "I didn't do it on purpose, and I feel so bad about everything that happened." Cough. "It all just happened so fast, and I didn't think—"

"Shh." I press my finger to her lips. "You're getting yourself worked up again, and you're going to make your asthma flare back up. You need to take a deep breath."

She sucks in a couple of deep breaths through her nose, and when she's breathing easier, I pull her back to lie on my chest.

"Tell me about the asthma. Is it something you struggle with often? Because I really think you should carry your emergency inhaler on you from now on."

"No. It's usually only activity-induced, but I'm pretty good at catching it before it turns into an attack. I haven't had a flare-up in years. I used to get them when I was little though, when I'd get upset."

I rub my hand down her back in a soothing motion, trying to keep her calm as best I can. "And I upset you tonight. When I yelled at you." It's not a question. I know I caused this, and I don't need her to take it easy on me. I need her to tell me I did this; I need her to be angry with me.

She sucks in a breath, and her voice shakes. "I just felt so guilty because you were right. I messed up tonight, and I feel so bad about it, and I just want you to know that I didn't do it on purpose. Not exactly anyway ..." Her voice trails off, and my hand stills.

"What do you mean by that?"

"It's just ..." She sighs, and the tears start back up. "My twin sister and I had this list ..."

I tilt her chin up, silently encouraging her to keep going as my hands trace her small frame like they've got a mind all their own.

"Like a checklist?" I ask, she nods and scoffs a laugh.

"Something like that. Fern called it her Fuck It List. It was all the things we were going to do together after we graduated ..." Her voice trails off, and she wipes her eyes with the back of her hand.

"Okay, so you and your sister had a checklist ... of things to do together. I still don't understand what that has to do with starting a wet T-shirt contest during a work event."

She looks down, pulling the sleeves of my shirt over her hands. "My sister died when she was seventeen. From lung cancer."

"Ivy, I'm so sorry—"

"She told me she'd help me complete the list from wherever people go after they die ..." She bites her lip to keep from crying as her eyes well with tears. "It all just happened so fast ... I guess I just felt like she was making it happen. She had *enter a wet T-shirt contest* on the list." She looks to me and shrugs. "I know that sounds crazy, but it's like ever since I got here, I can feel her. Not like when she was alive, but like the veil separating us is thinner ..."

"Ivy, that's ..."

"Insane. I know." She shakes her head and wipes her nose on my sleeve, and that little gesture almost makes me laugh. Only Ivy would use a five-hundred-dollar shirt as a hankie.

"That's not what I was going to say at all." I slide my hands up her toned thighs, feeling a rush of bravery come over me. It's almost like since I'm consoling her, these touches don't count, so I want to get in as many as I can before I come back to my senses. "What else is on the list?"

She fidgets in my lap, then crosses her feet, tucking them behind my back, and suddenly, I am keenly aware of our wet bodies and how thin the fabric separating us actually is.

Her soft body feels so good, pressed up against mine, and I urge my cock to calm the fuck down because this is neither the time nor place, but images of Ivy's perfect nipples flash through my mind anyway. The way her shirt clung to her tits, carving out the shape of her curves and confirming she was even more perfect than I'd already imagined.

I bite my cheek, urging the thoughts from my mind, focusing on how angry she made me instead. But somehow, that just excites me more, and my cock strains beneath her, growing harder and harder by the second.

"And camping," she says, and I realize I just zoned out when I see Ivy biting her lip, eyes curious and twinkling with mischief. Just how I like them.

For a moment, I forgot what we were talking about, but I quickly put it together as I dig my fingers into her hips that are beginning to roll across my lap. Fucking hell, she saw right through me just now, didn't she?

I clear my throat. "Camping, huh? Seems pretty mild compared to a wet T-shirt contest. Sounds like your sister had quite some range."

"She specifically wanted to go camping in the Appalachian Mountains. I was thinking I'd go tomorrow evening if we don't have any couple plans or events to be at? I know I probably caused enough trouble tonight—"

"Absolutely not." I shake my head and tighten my grip on her waist to stop the rocking.

And just like that, the bubble clouding my vision pops.

"What do you mean, *absolutely not*? I wasn't asking for your permission. If we don't have an event or anything, then I'm going camping—"

"Do you really think I'd let you go camping—which involves hiking sometimes up very steep cliffs—alone after you just had an asthma attack from running up the stairs?" My voice comes out a little harsher than I intended, but for fuck's sake, I'm still coming down from my own freak-out, watching her struggle like that. There's no way I'm letting her out of my sight to spend a night in the mountains alone. No way in hell.

She crosses her arms over her chest. "You don't get to tell me what I can do. You're not my boss ... well, not for real."

"Do you even know how to camp? To set up a tent? Any basic survival skills whatsoever?"

She just blinks.

"In the Appalachian Mountains?" I shake my head. "That's good, Ivy. Do you not remember what those mountains were like the night we first met? You practically threw yourself down a cliff because you thought something was chasing you. Hell, you were lucky it was only me. It could've been anything out there."

She rolls her eyes. "You're so dramatic. Of course I was scared. I wasn't prepared, and you were making scary sounds, stalking me like a creep."

I tuck a strand of hair behind her ear. "Let me set you up a little tent in the backyard. You can spend the night out there under surveillance, and I'll feel better knowing you're safe."

She pulls her legs from around my back and climbs off my lap, sending a cool gush of air in her absence. "No. That's not how the list works, Leo. It has to be in the mountains. You might control everything else around here, but not me."

She opens the front door to go inside and tries to slam it in my face, but I catch it just in time. I keep in step behind her as she stomps through the house, down the hallway, only stopping when she makes it to her bedroom door.

"Don't you walk away from me when we're in the middle of a conversation!" I grab her arm and spin her to face me.

"Stop telling me what to do. I'll do what I please, when I please."

Grabbing the top of the doorframe, I brace myself and lean in closer. "Listen to me, you little brat."

She lets out the faintest of gasps, and I know I have her

right where I want her. The push and pull of power hangs heavy as the space between us grows hot and charged. We're like two magnets fighting to keep from colliding, and I have to physically brace myself against the doorframe to hold myself back.

Everything about Ivy Lane is maddening—from the way she fights with me about anything and everything just for the fun of it to the way her pulse kicks up when I push back. The way she looks at me with those warm honey eyes that are full of sunshine and curiosity, like I'm some kind of puzzle she wants to piece back together or a toy she can't have.

As much as I'd love to give her what she wants, I can't afford the distraction.

I know a handful when I see one, and I simply do not have the capacity to go there ... no matter how much fun it would be.

I shake my head. I can't let myself think like that right now.

"You're not going camping in the fucking mountains. It's too dangerous. That's final."

Her eyes scan me up and down, and my breathing is now ragged as something like white-hot rage seethes through me, fueled by a fear so intense that my stomach is tied up in knots.

"You know, for someone who hates being called Daddy, you sure do love acting like one ..."

My body goes completely still, and the silence around us is deafening. "Let's not do this tonight, Ivy. Please, I'm begging you not to start your shit ..." I stare at her, my eyes pleading as a small ember of something that feels a lot like hope sparks in my chest.

She pops a hip, looking like she isn't the least bit affected by my warning. "You could just go with me." Her eyes trail down to my tented erection, and she gives me a coy smile. "You're getting awfully worked up over ... camping." She presses a finger to my chest. "Or is it the power struggle that you enjoy so much?"

"You think I enjoy this? Constantly fighting with you? I'm exhausted in every sense of the word while it seems like it's your life's mission to annoy me. Is this all a fucking game to you?" I ask through gritted teeth.

She cocks her head to the side and shrugs. "I think you enjoy my *games* more than you care to admit. The sooner we stop lying to ourselves, the sooner we can work some of this frustration out of our systems ... and start having a little fun."

Her words are like a wet blanket, pulling me back into the present moment and sobering me. I take a step back, putting some much-needed space between us.

She's right; I can't really tell her what she can't do, but I do have the choice whether I join her. All this back-and-forth, mixed with the way she was just grinding on my lap, has my body all mixed up. Hot and cold. Aggravated and protective ... and so fucking horny that I can hardly see straight.

It's Ivy's signature move, and fuck if I don't love to hate it. Maybe I am a masochist after all.

"I hope I bought you some hiking boots on your shopping haul because you're going to need them."

"Really?" Her eyes light up, and a smile breaks across her face. "You're seriously going to take me?"

I roll my eyes as I tuck a loose strand of hair behind her ear. "Apparently, I have a hard time saying *no* to you. Trust me, I'm just as surprised as you are. I'll take you camping, but you have to promise to listen to me. I don't want you to get hurt, and the woods are dangerous ... especially at night." A cold chill works its way up my spine, and I shiver at the thought of it.

I can't believe I'm doing this ... but if anyone could get me to go camping in those woods, it's this beautiful, spirited woman standing in front of me.

"Thank you, Leo," she squeals, wrapping her arms around my midsection in a surprisingly tight grip. "This is going to be so much fun!"

I don't know if Ivy and I have the same definition of the word *fun*, but I'd be lying to myself if I didn't admit that making her happy feels better than just about anything I've experienced in all my thirty-five years.

And that thought alone scares the shit out of me.

CHAPTER FIFTEEN

Ivy

"You took long enough," Leo mutters as I slide into the car.

"I'm sorry. I didn't realize we were in a hurry, Boss Daddy. Are we going to miss our appointment with nature?"

I slam the door a little harder than necessary, and he flinches with annoyance. I know it's on the tip of his tongue to tell me to be more careful, but to my surprise, he just clenches his jaw shut.

"Here, I got you this. Be careful with the straw. I don't want whipped cream to get everywhere." He passes me an iced coffee, and I hesitantly take it.

"What's this?"

"What does it look like? It's one of those froufrou coffee drinks all you girls love."

"You got me a coffee?"

"It's not a big deal. I was already in the drive-through and figured you'd like something too." He makes a gesture, waving me off.

My eyes go wide as I take a sip, the rich, sweet flavors exploding on my tongue. "How did you know I loved pumpkin spice?"

"It was a lucky guess."

"You know, if I didn't know any better, I'd think you might actually be getting a soft spot for me," I tease.

He shakes his head and smiles. "Don't count on it. I was just being nice. I am, in fact, capable of being kind every now and then."

Silence fills the space between us as I fold my legs in my lap and savor my first PSL of the season. It's the perfect preview of fall and a far cry from the Phoenix summer heat I'm used to. There's a nip to the air as trees blow in the breeze, and if I close my eyes, it almost smells like fall.

Fall was always Fern's favorite season while I was more of a springtime lover. We used to fight about it constantly, whose seasonal preference was superior, but every year, on the first day of PSL season, we made it our little tradition to take a long car ride while we indulged ourselves.

Fern was always the driver while I was the passenger princess with the perfect playlist for every occasion. We'd drive and sing our sappy breakup songs until our tank of gas ran empty. When I look back on it now, it was such a small thing. I never dreamed it'd be one of my last core memories of my sister living pain-free. I wish I could go back and make myself enjoy it just a little bit more, play all Fern's favorite songs without complaining they were too sad. I wish I could go back and have just a few more minutes with her, hear her laugh or ask her for advice on what I should do with my life.

A painful knot forms in my throat, and I take a swig of my coffee to force it down. The flashbacks come so vividly; even the good memories feel like my heart is tearing open. I can't afford to let myself go there, not right now.

That's not what today's going to be about. I'm checking this box on her list, and I don't want to feel sad about it.

I swipe away the threat of tears with the back of my hand. I need something to distract me.

I glance over at Leo, who looks hot as sin in his sunglasses, hair wavy and messy, and his day-old stubble. He's drumming his fingers to the beat of the music, and if I didn't know any better, I might even say he looks a little relaxed.

When I kick my feet up on the dash, Leo swipes them down, giving me a warning glare, but it fades quickly and is replaced with the slightest twitch of a smile at the corner of his mouth.

I narrow my eyes. "What's got into you today?"

"What do you mean?"

"You're driving seven miles over the speed limit; you surprised me with an iced coffee ..."

He holds up his hand. "In my defense, I was already getting myself one and figured you'd whine if I didn't get you something too."

I fold my arms over my chest and look out my window. "That sounds nothing like me."

He laughs and takes a sip of his own coffee.

"So, where are you taking me? We've been driving for a while. I figured we'd just go somewhere close since you're so terrified to be out there alone."

"About that ..."

I spin to face him. "Yes?"

"We won't exactly be alone ... I sort of invited my

family to tag along." He tilts his head side to side. "Well, they invited themselves when I showed up, looking for camping gear at my parents' house." He shrugs. "Either way, there was no stopping them. My parents love camping. They used to make us go all the time when we were growing up. Said it was forced family bonding because we couldn't escape each other out here." He nods as he pulls off the road onto a hidden path. "We've got a spot that overlooks the waterfall. It's a Kingsley family secret, so don't tell anyone, or my parents will disown both of us."

I gesture like I'm locking my mouth shut. "Don't worry about me; my lips are sealed."

We go a little farther underneath the trees until Leo's satisfied that his car is completely concealed, and then he walks around the car to open my door for me.

"Come on. We've got to hike the rest of the way. It's just about a mile or so."

He hoists a backpack on his back, and I can't help but laugh at how adorable he looks in all his hiking gear. It's the first time I'm seeing him, and the man's decked out to the nines in hiking boots, vest, and cargo pants.

I scan my eyes over him. "Wow ... you really look the part. Did you buy the entire Patagonia catalog just for this occasion?"

"Make fun all you want, but don't come crying to me when you've got a blister from wearing the wrong shoes or you find a tick on you." He shrugs his shoulders as he starts walking. "Besides, you're one to talk ..." He shoots me a glare over his shoulder.

"What? What's wrong with what I'm wearing?"

He gestures to all of me. "You're dressed like a professional wrestler."

"What are you talking about? This bodysuit is both functional and adorable."

"You look like André the Giant."

"Who's André the Giant?"

His feet abruptly come to a stop, and I nearly run into the back of his giant backpack.

"Seriously? The Eighth Wonder of the World? Seven foot four, five hundred pounds?"

I shake my head.

"He's only one of the greatest wrestlers of all time. Had a huge career in the '80s. He wore this black spandex unitard that only had one strap."

He pops the single strap of my bodysuit playfully, and I swat him away.

"God, sometimes, I forget how much younger you are than me. Wrestling was all the rage when I was growing up …" His voice trails off.

I prop my hands on my hips. "So, I remind you of a giant. That's just great. You certainly know how to boost a girl's ego, Leo Kingsley. That dry spell's starting to make a little more sense now," I tease, and just as I take another step, he hooks a finger under the strap of my bodysuit and tugs me back toward him.

"Trust me, it's taking all the restraint in my body to tear my gaze from that perky little ass of yours. I've nearly tripped over my goddamn feet ten times since we started this hike."

His finger caresses the skin beneath my strap stopping just as he reaches the swell of my breasts. Heat builds in my core and my nipples harden.

"But you already know that, don't you? That's why of all the outfits you could've chosen, you picked this thin piece of spandex that clings to your every curve because you knew it'd torture me and I wouldn't be able to resist staring."

"Maybe you should stop fighting it so much and just let yourself have what you want." I tilt my chin up in defiance as my eyes search his.

He looks like he's in pain, like he's struggling to keep the darkness inside of him, the darkness that so badly wants to come out and play.

"Because"—he blows out a sigh—"that's not the type of arrangement we have, now is it?" His hand moves down my back, sending waves of goose bumps and electric jolts in every direction before his palm cups my ass.

"And what exactly *is* the arrangement we have?" I say, keeping my eyes trained on his, daring him to keep going.

He pulls his hand away. "One where I'd be smart to remember that no matter how badly I want to do horrible, dirty things to you, this can never happen." He turns and begins walking, leaving me with my mouth hanging open.

"What the fuck? You can't just tell me you want to do *horrible, dirty things to me* and then take off like nothing happened," I pant as I jog to catch up with him.

"Look, Ivy, I see the games we're playing, and all of this has to stop. We can't do this. It's not right ... no matter how tempting you are to me." He gives me a glare over his shoulder. "I'm too old for you."

I run to catch up to him. "Age is just a number—"

"I'm not having this conversation with you. I acknowledged your plea for attention. Now, drop it."

I move in front of him so that I'm walking backward and

he has no choice but to look at me. "What if I don't? Then, what will you do? Are you going to spank me?"

His jaw clenches, and his nostrils flare as he tightens his grip on the straps of his backpack, like it's the only thing keeping his hands under control. "Maybe," he confesses through clenched teeth.

I don't know if the threat is supposed to scare me because it seems to do the opposite as a flare of excitement ignites in my core.

"What if I want you to?"

"Ivy," he hisses, his pleading stare boring into me. "You're playing with fire, and sooner or later, you're going to get burned."

I narrow my eyes in challenge. "Maybe that's the only way I'll learn."

"Then, I suggest you find yourself someone with a little more patience because I don't have time for your games."

"I think you're full of shit. You're making excuses because you're afraid of what will happen if you let yourself have what you want. It's like you don't think you deserve to be happy, like you're addicted to tormenting yourself and depriving yourself of anything that would bring you pleasure," I challenge back.

"Or ... I have more important things that require my *full* attention." He brushes me to the side as he moves to pass me.

"I'm so sorry, Boss Daddy. Please forgive me for distracting you with my tight clothes and great ass. Besides, you're the one who insisted on tagging along on my camping trip," I retort.

"Forgive me for worrying that you'd get yourself killed

out here alone. I guess I'm just the bad guy for actually giving a shit about your well-being."

"Don't get all defensive. I'm just saying it's only one night. I would've been fine. I'm smart. I can figure things out."

He rolls his eyes. "Which is exactly why I insisted on coming with you. This isn't one of those times where winging it is a good idea. Anything can happen out here, and you need to be prepared."

I nudge him with my shoulder. "Or ... you can go with the flow and see that things have a way of working out. It's called an adventure."

He scoffs a laugh and tugs on my long, braided pigtail. "If you call getting ticks and blisters an adventure, then you can keep your adventures to yourself. Besides, someone had to plan ahead so you can roast s'mores over the campfire tonight."

That makes me perk up, and I spin to face him. "You packed stuff for s'mores too?"

"Yeah, but I'm not sure I'm in the mood to share anymore."

I bump into him a little harder, but he doesn't move, just looks down at me with a teasing smile. We walk like that in silence for a while, and it almost feels like this could be real, like this could be my life. But it's all a show, and we both know it.

When we get to the top of the hill, I lean against a tree as I try to catch my breath.

"You should've told me to slow down if you were struggling." He pulls my inhaler out of his bag and hands it to me.

I take a couple of puffs, immediately breathing easier.

That's two thoughtful gestures today. Where am I, and where has my grumpy fake fiancée gone?

He points to a waterfall up ahead. "The campsite's on the other side of the waterfall. Can you make it the rest of the way, or do you need me to give you a piggyback?"

I narrow my eyes and grin. "You know, my legs are pretty tired from that hike ..."

He rolls his eyes. "Seriously?"

I shrug. "Hey, you offered. I just want to conserve my energy."

He moves his backpack to his chest and squats down for me to climb on without complaint. I could get used to this princess treatment even if it comes laced with sarcasm and snide remarks.

Without missing a beat, I climb on his back, wrapping my legs tightly around his waist and pressing my body flush against him. I don't miss the way his thumb traces soothing circles over my thigh as he holds me without any complaint, and I can't help but think he enjoys this as much as I do even though he'd never admit it.

Yeah, a girl could definitely get used to this.

"There they are, the two lovebirds," Mary calls out as Leo places me down to sit beside her. "Ivy, dear, tell me you didn't hurt yourself on the hike up."

"She's fine, just got a little winded on that last hill," Leo answers for me.

"Well, I'm glad you were able to put those muscles to use." Mary gives us each a hug. "I hope you don't mind, but we had to give you the little tent. Guy and Luka insisted they each needed to be able to spread out, and your father's air mattress takes up so much room, so we needed the big one."

She points to the line of tents set up in a row and a small one set off to the side. It looks like it's barely big enough for one person, much less Leo's six-four frame.

I rub my palms together. "That's fine. We do love to snuggle, don't we, babe?"

Leo forces a grin. "Yeah ... snuggling. That's something we do."

"Good. I knew you'd understand. I'm going to go find your father. I think he's down at the creek, fishing." She blows us a kiss, then gets up to leave.

"Don't worry; I'll get one of them to trade tents," Leo says as soon as she's out of earshot.

"Really? How are you going to do that?"

He shakes his head like it's obvious. "I'm the oldest brother. I have an arsenal of methods up my sleeve."

I sit back, propping my arms behind me. "Whatever you think is best. I thought you had the whole self-control thing locked down, but I guess not. If I didn't know better, I'd think you were afraid to spend the night with me."

He snaps a twig, grumbling something under his breath that I can't quite hear, then abruptly stands, in search of one of his brothers.

I look around the picturesque campsite, shaded by dense trees, and I can see why they hike all the way out here. It's so peaceful, like a scene right out of a painting.

If I close my eyes, I can almost feel Fern beside me, whispering spooky stories in my ear or giving me a history lesson about how old these mountains are. God, I miss her.

How am I supposed to know what to do next without her planning for our perfect futures?

Tears sting behind my eyes, but I don't let them fall, urging the sadness back down, where I keep it locked up tight. The pain's getting stronger; it's harder to push it away with each and every check I make to the list, and I'm starting to worry I'll be worse off by the time this is all over.

I'm supposed to be moving on with my life ... so why do I find myself clinging to the past, terrified to let go? I hate feeling like this.

I think it's about time for another distraction.

CHAPTER SIXTEEN

Leo

"Please, you have to do this for me. I'll owe you one ... whatever you want. I'll offer Scout a job, make her an offer she can't refuse so she'll have no choice but to move back." I snap my fingers as another idea hits me. "Oh, I know. I'll hire you in the same department and make you partners so she can't escape you."

Luka narrows his eyes at me before swinging his axe down, splitting a piece of firewood in half. "I don't get it, dude. Why are you over here, trying to bribe me into swapping tents? You're the only one out here getting laid ..."

"And offering a helping hand so you can do the same," I say, still hoping to convince him.

He shakes his head. "I appreciate the offer, but last I heard, she's happy—engaged, I think—so I'm afraid my chances with her are long gone by now." He places his hands on his hips and shrugs. "You can always try to bribe Guy; I'm sure there's a favor he'd like to cash in. Not sure how desperate you are to avoid sleeping next to your fiancée ..."

"It's not like that. I told you, I sleep hot. I don't want to sweat her out in that tiny child-size tent—why was that the one you grabbed? I know we have more to choose from in storage."

He swings his axe again with a thud and stops to wipe the sweat from his brow. "It was on top. You didn't exactly give us much notice to pack—"

"Because you weren't invited! I showed up to get tents, and everyone just decided to tag along and invade our private camping trip like some kind of fucking *Christmas Vacation* bullshit," I snap.

"Now, Leo, we both know you wanted us to come along, so cut the shit. You always loved family camping trips growing up. I think the only time I've ever seen you genuinely happy was when you were out here, and it's certainly the only time I've ever seen you come even remotely close to being relaxed. Forgive us for wanting to spend time together without you and Dad hijacking the entire conversation and making it about work."

I bend to start stacking the wood into a pile, not wanting to look him in the eye. "I don't hog the conversation. I just don't always have Dad's attention at work, so when I get the opportunity to discuss things and he's listening, I guess I just take it."

He places a hand on my shoulder tenderly. "I appreciate your honesty, bro ... but you're not getting my tent. If you're so worried about getting too hot, maybe you should sleep nude. That's what I'm planning on doing. Makes me feel dangerous and uninhibited." He winks, and I brush his hand off.

"Fuck you, man. Don't ask me for any favors because I'm going to remember this." I point at him as I walk away.

"Hey, aren't you going to help me carry all this firewood?" he calls, but I just give him the middle finger and stomp off.

"Real mature, Leo. If I didn't know better, I'd think you're afraid of being alone with your fiancée. Tell her my tent's always open if she needs someone with a little more stamina and youth on his side."

Fucking idiots. They all are.

I kick at a rotting tree log, sending slivers of wood flying as I stomp through the thick, wooded forest, trying to blow off some steam.

Of course, Guy and Roman both had similar reasons to say no. Luka was my last hope, and as the most reasonable of all my brothers, I was really counting on him to throw me a fucking bone, but alas, I came off too desperate.

This is bullshit. I'm just going to have to pull it together and power through the night with my tempting-as-fuck fiancée.

* * *

A thin sheen of sweat beads at my brow as I weave through the dense, rows of trees. I should get back to camp, make sure Ivy isn't getting into trouble, but I need to clear my head, and the best place I know to do that is the falls.

When I was younger, I was obsessed with all things

outdoors. It's not surprising. Anyone growing up in Ashford Falls shares the same sentiment. It feels like holy land out here, both frightening and reverent at the same time. We have a healthy respect for these woods, and the falls are no different.

I can hear the pure power of the water flowing as I approach, and my nervous system immediately begins to calm. As far as danger goes, this one lies somewhere in the middle. It's nothing as powerful as the biggest waterfall, the one our town is known for, but depending on the water levels, it's dangerous all the same.

For decades, this has been the place for teenagers to gather. We'd come here for everything from graduation parties to first dates, everyone sharing in the thrill of jumping to the ice-cold water below.

The memory feels like a warm blanket, bringing me back to a time before I felt the weight of the world on my shoulders, before I knew the pain of mistakes and the heavy price of penance that comes along with it.

What I would give for another taste of that freedom, to be young and carefree with no ties, no responsibilities weighing me down, driven only by my desires and interests. A strangled laugh bubbles out of me, and I shake my head. Basically, I dream of being like Ivy.

Maybe that's why I'm so protective of her freedom—because I see that one wrong decision can take it all away in the blink of an eye. I'll do everything in my power to preserve that because, fuck, if I can't have it, then I'm so happy she can. I'm happy to survive off the warmth radiating from her even if it's only temporary.

I wind behind the small cliff, following the beaten path until I'm at the very top of the waterfall. Cupping my hand over my eyes, I scan the clear blue pool of water beneath me, framed with dense green hemlock trees that are just beginning to fade to orange.

"How'd you find me? Do you have some kind of tracker on me I don't know about?" Ivy holds out her arms and does a little spin as she looks down.

My eyes land on the small wooden box she's holding. It looks vaguely familiar. I think she was carrying it the first night we met.

I start to ask her what's in the box, but when she kicks off her shoes and unties the flannel from around her waist, I freeze.

"I was just about to go for a swim. Care to join me?"

She places the box on a rock and quickly covers it with her flannel. Then, to my shock, she pulls the strap of her adult onesie off her shoulder. The tight fabric clings to her like a wetsuit as she rolls the material down, revealing a thin, strapless bra.

My brain short-circuits at the sight of her exposed tan shoulders, my eyes catching on the curve of her collarbone and the shallow divot between her perky breasts. Fuck, I've never wanted to touch someone so badly, to run my palm over her supple skin, to explore every curve and freckle.

I tear my eyes away, blinking several times, and hold my hand out in a pathetic attempt to block her from my view. "What ... what are you doing? Stop taking off your clothes. We're in public. Anyone could see you."

She makes a show of looking around. "Yeah? Maybe I want them to watch?" She pulls the bodysuit down around her ass, then carefully steps out of it.

I swallow thickly.

"Relax. I just don't want to get my clothes wet. Your chastity is safe with me. No need to freak out."

When she turns to add her clothes to the pile, I catch a glimpse of that sweet, round ass, covered in a small triangle of fabric that gets bunched between her cheeks. My dick grows hard at the sight of it, and my palms itch to touch her.

She reaches behind her head and begins to braid her long hair, all while keeping her eyes trained on me, like she knows I'm teetering on the edge of my last ounce of self-control.

"Can I ask you a question?"

I watch her through my lust-filled haze, unable to tear my eyes from her breathtaking body. It's what dreams are made of, truly. The perfect balance of soft flesh and sculpted muscle. She's so petite compared to me, and I have the sudden urge to wrap my hands around her hips to show her all the things I fantasize about doing to her.

"Sure," is all I can manage.

"Why won't you let yourself have me? It's like you're punishing yourself or something." She pulls the hair tie from her wrist and secures it on the end of her braid, then moves toward me. "I see the way you look at me. That fire burning behind your eyes. The glances you sneak when you think no one is looking."

She places a hand on my chest, over my rapidly beating heart, and I grit my teeth.

"You want me, Leo. And I want you too. So, why are we pretending like we don't? Why do you feel like you always need to be in control when all I want is for you to let loose and show me the real you?"

She trails her hand down my abs until she reaches the hem of my T-shirt.

"Ivy," I warn, but she doesn't relent as she moves her hand over my rib cage and back down, like she's trying to memorize my form with her hands.

"I know you think I'm too young, but I'm a big girl. I know what I'm getting myself into, and I'm not afraid of you."

She traces her thumb lightly over my nipple, and I grip her wrist to stop her.

"You have no idea what you're asking. I'm ... I'm all wrong for you, and the sooner you realize it, the better."

A mischievous smile stretches across her face. "I think you'll find that I can be pretty stubborn when it comes to getting what I want. I don't like to be told no."

This makes me laugh because it's not exactly a secret. Ivy wears it proudly all over her face, the way she moves through the world with her golden eyes and confidence, so charismatic and playful. I feel like *no* isn't a word she hears very often. It would take someone made of steel to tell this woman no.

"I ... I can't ..." I force the words out of my mouth, and they feel unnatural, like lies that have my insides twisted into knots. I take a step back, putting some much-needed space between us.

Ivy just pouts and shrugs. "Well, it was worth a shot." She spins around, giving me a wink over her shoulder. "It's your loss, Leo." Then, she takes off into a run, cannonballing off the side of the waterfall, squealing the whole way down.

My heart races in my chest as I rush to look over the edge just as her head pops above the water.

"Come on. Take the leap and join me. Unless you're too chicken," she calls from the clear blue pool of water.

Call it a momentary lapse of judgment or self-sabotage to

the millionth degree, but for one split second, I want to feel that rush again. I want to shed this heavy armor and free fall, trusting that everything will be okay when I land in the deep, cool water beneath.

I shake my head as a million thoughts bombard me, but before I realize what I'm doing, I'm stripping off my clothes.

Here goes nothing.

I jump from the cliff and plummet toward the bottom, my body twisted and thrown from the force. I land with a cold splash, and it's as if I were being recalibrated, baptized in the freedom of the moment. When I push to the surface, I find Ivy staring at me in misbelief, her blonde hair slicked back from her face, wearing a smile that could bring anyone to their knees.

Fuck, she's pretty, and the sight of her nearly knocks the air from my lungs.

But my attraction to her is so much more than surface level; it's her essence that draws me to her like a moth to a flame. She's magnetic in every sense of the word and embodies all the qualities that I don't.

She's warm, excited about the future, optimistic, and she lives every day in the moment. She's not afraid to be herself even if it means she'll be judged for it. She's pure sunshine in human form, warming everyone lucky enough to cross her path. And I'm the rainstorm that ruins the last day of your beach vacation.

I've come to accept my role; we can't all be the life of the party. Some of us have to create safety nets and boundaries. Some of us are here to provide the structure so others can enjoy their sunny days to the fullest. But I'd be lying if I said I didn't wish I could be both, have both. I know it's selfish, but right now, I don't care. Right now, I want to pretend that I could actually be worthy of this incredible woman.

Ivy doggy-paddles toward me and splashes me in the face. "What the hell was that?"

I wipe the water from my eyes and brush my thick strands back, feeling a smile cover my own face. "What was what?" I ask, splashing her back.

"You just jumped ... like you've done it a thousand times."

She moves toward me, and I grab her waist, unable to keep myself from touching her, as if it doesn't count if we're underwater.

"Maybe I have. You don't know everything about me." I run my fingers along her hips, the rush of adrenaline fogging my brain.

She bites her lip. "I knew you had a fun side deep down in there. I just needed to keep poking you until it came out."

She wraps her legs around my waist, cinching herself flush with my core, and my hands trail lower, cupping her ass as I kick my legs, keeping us both afloat.

It feels so natural, holding her like this, and every cell in my body feels alive, charged with false hope and delusion. Our mouths are dangerously close, and I flick my eyes down as she wets her lips. There's a heat growing between us, an electric current that sizzles when two unlikely souls meet their match. I'm a clown fish, and Ivy is my anemone—or maybe it's the other way around. It shouldn't work, but somehow, I can't imagine anything fitting together more perfectly. All I know is that when I look into her eyes, it terrifies me.

"We could do anything out here, and no one would

know," she whispers as my hands caress her soft hips, savoring each stolen moment.

I would know, and that's all that matters.

"Can I ask you a question?" I ask, mimicking her from earlier.

"Ask away. I'm an open book."

She opens her arms wide and leans back, trusting that I'll keep her head above water. I love that about her—that she trusts me so completely. And yet I don't think either of us realizes the lengths I'd go to prove it.

"What's in the box?"

Her smile falls as her brows pinch together. "Oh, that ..." Her voice comes out almost weak, like I just struck a nerve, which only piques my curiosity. "That's my sister's ashes." Her eyes drop as she seems to disappear for a moment, as if she's lost in a memory. "I know it sounds weird and morbid or whatever, carrying it around with me ... but ... I don't know ... Fern asked me to spread her ashes somewhere beautiful. She said I'd know the spot when I found it, and I've been looking for the perfect place since I got here. I haven't found it yet though."

I cup my hand over her jaw, rubbing the pad of my thumb over her cheek. "Is that why you're really here? Is that the reason you decided to stay?"

She looks up at me with those big, vibrant eyes, and there's a darkness to them now that I haven't seen before, a darkness I'm all too familiar with. She's hurting.

The thought of Ivy suffering silently, wearing that contagious smile that lights up every room as her own armor, feels like a dagger in my heart.

"Yes, and no," she admits. "She was so obsessed with

ghost stories and cryptids, growing up. She used to tell me all these terrifying stories about the creatures that lived in these mountains before bed. I had nightmares for years because of those stupid stories, but I never told her because she loved them so damn much.

"I was just supposed to be passing through, biding my time and checking off as many things from her list as I could before I left. I planned to visit the Phantom apparition site, but I didn't expect to be spending the rest of the summer fake-engaged to a billionaire in the cozy small town of Ashford Falls." She pinches my side playfully, but her smile doesn't quite meet her eyes.

"Then, I saw the sign for the waterfall, and I thought it could be a perfect place for her ... but I couldn't bring myself to do it. I'm not ready to say goodbye. Not just yet."

A tear falls from the corner of her eye, and I wish I could soak up every ounce of pain she feels and take it on myself because the look of her face nearly kills me.

"Hey, it's okay. There's no rush for these things. You'll do it when you feel ready. I can be there to help you if you want?"

"I just don't know if I'll ever feel ready. I'm scared to let her go ... but I know it's what she wanted." Her voice cracks, and I pull her to my chest.

"You're so much stronger than you give yourself credit for. You're a fighter, Ivy. Anyone can see it. You don't have to do this alone, okay? I'm here for you."

She wipes the tears from her eyes and pinches her nose before dunking her head under the water, and when she comes up, it's like she's flipped a switch, turning off her sadness.

"Okay, enough being sad. What do you say we start a little wager?"

Her sudden mood change doesn't fool me for one second. There's no way someone can simultaneously hold that much unprocessed grief and still be the ray of fucking sunshine she pretends to be.

I'm starting to see a pattern that Ivy doesn't like to dwell in her sadness for longer than a couple of minutes, always flipping the script to look on the bright side. She reminds me of my dad in that way, always focused on the positives and finding the silver lining to everything. In a lot of ways, it's a good quality; it's why my dad is the incredible leader he is, but there's something to be said for digging into your pain and sitting in it too. Maybe I'm guilty of staying there too long, but I'm worried that if she keeps running from it, it's going to catch up to her in a big way. I'm not exactly sure how to get her to realize that though.

Bringing my attention back to the present, I quirk a brow. "What did you have in mind?"

I might be the only one in the world who sees through this act, but maybe that's the point of our paths crossing. Maybe she needs a cynic like me to call her out so she can process her grief and eventually move on from it.

She's clearly not ready to take that step, so right now, I'll have to give her the next best thing—a distraction.

"I was thinking we could race all the way to the falls. Winner gets to tell the loser what to do. No questions asked." She tilts up her chin like she's waiting.

No questions asked ...

Immediately, my mind is flooded with a plethora of *ideas*, most of which I should feel downright ashamed of, but if it's a distraction she seeks ... *that* might be something I can give her.

I narrow my eyes. "You should know I'm a very fast swimmer. It wouldn't be a fair competition."

"I know what I bring to the table, *Boss Daddy*," she tosses right back.

"Fine then." I rub the scruff on my jaw. "I can't wait to rub my victory in your pretty face."

"Bring it on, old man." She splashes a wave of water in my face and then plugs her nose before dipping under the water.

I swim after her all the way to the edge of the rocky cliff, feeling lighter than I have in years. I finally feel like there's a purpose for my schoolboy crush, which more accurately borders on the line of obsession.

I brace myself on the rocky cliff as I listen to her directions.

"The rules are simple. Whoever reaches the other side of the falls first wins."

"Seems easy enough. Are you sure about this? I don't intend on going easy on you after I win. I don't want to see you pouting about it either. It's not too late to back out."

"Cocky much? Why don't you focus on racing and save your victory speech for *if* you actually win?" She props herself on the rocks. "Are you ready?"

I nod.

"We go in three, two, one!"

I push my feet off the cliff as hard as I can, and I pump my arms through the water, propelling myself forward in a practiced movement. The cool water glides across my burning muscles as I move closer and closer to the falls with every stroke.

What I didn't tell her was that I swam competitively for most of my life and into college. Swimming is my favorite form of exercise, and I try to do it at least three times a week. It's how I keep all my demons at bay. Admittedly, my workouts have been on the back burner since this deviant woman walked into my life, and it feels so good to exert myself.

I can't wait to see the look on her face when I beat her. A flood of ideas crash through my mind, of the things I could make her do, and it only fuels me further. In one final stroke, I dive below the surface, feeling the heavy pounding of water crash against me, and I swim until I'm on the other side in the hollow space between the cliff and the falls.

I push my hair back from my face as I come to the surface, where I find Ivy sitting cross-legged on the rock's ledge, grinning like she just stole something.

"How ... how did you ..." I look around the hollow space for some type of explanation.

"I never said we had to *swim*."

CHAPTER SEVENTEEN

Ivy

"Cheater!"

He climbs out of the water, winded from the exertion, and I take the moment to admire the ridges of corded muscle he keeps hidden underneath those dress shirts.

Leo Kingsley has the most incredible body I've ever laid my eyes on. His abs flex with definition and his bulging biceps practically beg to be touched. He's all muscle and testosterone, and when he glares at me like that, with that fire burning behind his eyes, I want to melt in a puddle at his feet. I like to give him a hard time about being older than me, but truth be told, that's part of his appeal. He's a nurturer through and through ... even when he's looking at me like he wants to bend me over his knee ... maybe *especially* then.

I hold up my hands. "It's not cheating if it wasn't stated in the rules."

"It might not've been stated, but it was certainly implied,

and you know it," he growls out, and I pop my arms behind me, stretching myself as if his protesting doesn't bother me in the least bit.

Of course, my apathy only annoys him more ... which is exactly what I was going for.

His dark eyes scan my body, his gaze lingering on the thin, wet fabric of my bra. It's hot and heavy and almost uncomfortable, but I don't flinch despite the kaleidoscope of butterflies swarming to life in my belly. My nipples are hard and puckered beneath the wet fabric, begging for him to touch me, begging for him to give me even an ounce of relief.

"How did you beat me here anyway?" He looks around again, and I laugh, pointing to a small opening behind him.

"There's a tunnel behind the rock where we started that leads straight to the waterfall. I found it when I was exploring before you showed up. I'm surprised you didn't know about it, considering you used to come here all the time."

"Oh, *I* knew about it. I just didn't realize *you* did." He huffs under his breath and rubs a hand behind his tense neck. "You played me ..."

"Like a fiddle," I say with a smile.

"Well, I only make honest deals, so the bet's off. You can forget it. Whatever you're thinking, I'm not doing it."

I look him up and down, my eyes lingering on the massive bulge of his erection. "I guess we'll have to see about that, now won't we?"

He glances at his watch. "Come on. It's getting late. We should head back to camp. I don't want everyone to find us out here ... like this."

"You mean, soaked from swimming in nothing but our skivvies? The horror." I feign shock.

He shakes his head as he helps me up. "Why don't you lead the way since, apparently, you know all the shortcuts around here?"

I shrug. "Are you sure it isn't so you can stare at my ass?"

"Fine. You've got me there. I'm going to stare at that perky little ass the whole hike back, all while picturing all the things I'd love to do to you. Happy?"

His admission makes my jaw fall open, but before I can press him on it, his massive palm envelops my neck in a firm hold, and I go completely still.

His voice is a low growl in my ear. "I said, lead the way, baby girl. Don't look back at me. Let me enjoy this rare moment of peace before I go back to hating myself and you go back to pressing all my buttons. Can you do that for me? Can you do that for Daddy?"

I swallow a gulp, "Yes, sir."

"Thank fuck for that," he groans.

By the time we make it back to the camp, the sky's painted in streaks of pink and bright orange as the sun sets behind the horizon, and the butterflies fluttering in my belly have mostly calmed down. It was an awkwardly quiet walk, but the tension between us said more than any words could. Leo goes back to pretending he's unaffected by me, almost as if the moment we shared back at the waterfall never happened.

But when our eyes meet, there's no denying the hurricane of attraction brewing between us, growing heavier and stronger with every passing minute. It's only a matter of time before it's too powerful to contain.

I untie my flannel from around my waist and shrug it over my shoulders.

There's a chill to the air now that the sun's gone down, another preview of what's to come with the changing seasons.

"There you are. We were beginning to worry you got lost. I was about to send out a search crew to find you," Frank says as he drops a few pieces of wood on the fire.

"Oh, honey, they're engaged and in love. Probably sowing their oats all over these woods, if I had to guess."

"Mom—" Leo and his brothers all say at the same time.

"What? You were all thinking it too. I don't think there's anything wrong with a little exploration every now and again. Right, Franky?" She gives Frank a wink, and even in the dimly lit sky, I can see him blush.

"All right. That's enough of that." Leo claps his hands together. "What can I do to help with dinner?"

"Nothing at all. We've got it all sorted out. Ivy, I hope you like hot dogs? It's a Kingsley tradition. We've got all the fixings to go with it," Mary says as she gestures to a folding table with an assortment of sauces, peppers, and cheeses.

My stomach growls at the mention of it all. I must've worked up an appetite with all that excitement back there. "Hot dogs sound amazing."

"You heard the woman. Leo, grab your lady a wiener, would you?" Frank calls.

I start to argue, but Leo shakes his head, pointing at the empty seat in front of the fire.

I do as I was told, taking a seat while he takes my order and serves me the perfect hot dog. It's funny now that I notice it, but Leo loves to take care of me. As much as I'd like him to know that I don't need him to, I don't want to rob him of the joy he gets from doing it.

Roman, Guy, and Luka all sit in a line next to me, already eating their hot dogs, and we fall into a comfortable conversation as the sun slowly disappears beneath the horizon. I tell them about the little trick I pulled on Leo at the waterfalls, leaving out the part about the wager we made, and he teases me about looking like a professional wrestler and how he's afraid of me. Everything about it feels right, this place, these people. I have to pinch myself to remember it isn't a dream.

Even before my family was broken apart, before my sister got sick and my dad ran off to start a new family with his mistress, it was never like this. It didn't feel this easy and comfortable. My parents didn't look at each other with hearts in their eyes, but rather resentment.

My parents didn't create intentional moments for us to bond or grow closer. They were both miserable and doing their best to survive. Mom was depressed, and Dad was always traveling for *work*. If we wanted happy family memories, we had to create them for ourselves.

Then, when Fern got sick, I had to step in to play peacemaker to keep everything from imploding on itself. The last thing my sister needed to see in her final days was our family crumbling apart, knowing she'd be gone and she couldn't do a thing to stop it.

So, I stepped up, took the weight of Fern's treatment decisions off my mom's shoulders, and took on a role I was never meant to hold. I kept her from falling apart, and I made excuses for my father's absence so my dying sister wouldn't have to know he'd already moved on with his life as soon as she was declared terminal.

And now that she's gone and I don't have to worry about taking care of my mom anymore, it feels like I'm finally close to finding my own peace. The thought of that terrifies me because the familiar always feels safer even if the familiar means clinging to the past. I thought I could run from it forever, but the more time I'm spending with Leo, in this town, the more I'm realizing I'm just delaying the inevitable.

One of these days, I'll have to face my grief head-on … but luckily, today is not that day.

By the time we're finished with the s'mores—and I've got sticky marshmallow covering every finger—I nuzzle my head into Leo's neck, feeling so grateful for all of this. He wraps an arm around me, pulling me into him as he gently traces his fingers along my arm in a soothing, nurturing way. It feels so natural, and I don't even think he realizes he's doing it.

Everything about this feels natural, and for a second, I find myself wishing this were real.

But I'm quickly pulled out of that daydream as the ping of grief stabs at me, reminding me all too well what the pain from losing someone feels like. I don't think I could survive that kind of heartbreak a second time.

The thought has my walls pulled back up as I remind myself that this is just for fun. I can't let myself get attached or get caught up in the fantasy that this could ever be my life.

"Tell me, how's the festival planning coming along? Your dad said you two have been quite busy at the office," Mary asks, pulling me from my spiraling thoughts.

"Oh, it's coming along great." I clear my throat. "We've added all kinds of activities, something for everyone. I think it's going to be perfect. Don't you, Leo?" I bump Leo with my shoulder. "We've had so much fun, coming up with ideas. Leo can hardly shut up about it." If I'm here to help him prove that he's a changed man, I might as well lay it on thick.

Frank wipes his mouth. "Is that so?"

"Oh, yeah. It's all he talks about these days. Sometimes, I have to flash him to get him to stop yapping about it." I lean into Leo and squeeze his biceps.

"That'll do it every time." Frank laughs. "It's good to see you enjoying yourself, son. I worry about you working yourself so hard."

"Yeah, I've been guilty of that ..." His voice trails off. "But this one keeps me pretty distracted."

I shiver as a gust of wind blows toward us, and Leo wraps his arm around my shoulder, pulling me back into his warmth. He smells like aftershave and cedar and something else that's unique to him. I wish I could bottle it up or make a candle out of it so I could take it with me everywhere I go and never forget it. I let myself relax, snuggling into his warmth.

I know it's just for show and that we're pretending, but I could get used to being held like this. I trace my fingers along his corded forearms and up his biceps, loving the way his body feels wrapped around mine. I feel safe and protected, like when I'm with him, even the pain of my grief can't hurt me.

"You two look so happy. You have no idea how relieved I am to see my oldest son finally living his life," Mary says, and guilt pinches in my chest. I hate that we're lying to her like this, and I hate I'll be the reason her heart breaks when it's over.

I'm relieved when Guy changes the subject. "Ivy, have

you ever heard the story about the infamous Ashford Falls Phantom?"

Leo's muscles stiffen, but he doesn't take his arm off me. "Guy, don't start with the ghost stories; Ivy doesn't like being scared."

"Oh, come on, big brother. It's all a part of the camping experience," Luka adds.

I brush a hand over his jaw, sensing his protectiveness over me, or maybe it's his own fear rushing up to the surface. "It's fine, Leo. I can handle it. Besides, it's just a story, right?"

"We'll take this as our cue to leave," Mary says, and Frank stands to join her. "Please don't scare my future daughter-in-law off. I'd like her to at least give Ashford Falls a shot before you send her running to the hills." Mary gives them a warning glare, and I don't miss the sharp tone in her voice. Whatever the story's about, it's obvious she believes it.

We say good night as they make their way to their tent. Leo stands to add more wood to the fire, and I take the opportunity to move closer, warming my body from the chilled air.

"I think I'm going to need a drink for this. Who wants to join me?" Luka asks as he pours whiskey in his compostable plastic cup. He doesn't wait for an answer before he's passing us each one of our own, and when he gets to Leo, he gives him a knowing wink.

It's a small gesture, microscopic even, but something tells me there's more to it than meets the eye.

"Here, sit in my lap if you're that cold." Leo pulls me into him, and I gladly take the warm seat and snuggle into him, sipping my own whiskey.

"You might've heard of the Phantom, but has Leo told

you how he's connected to our family?" Guy asks, bringing my attention back to him.

I shake my head, thinking back to the spooky stories Fern loved to scare me with.

"Stop with the theatrics and get on with it," Leo says as he takes a long pull of his drink.

Guy holds up his hands. "I'm merely setting the tone, big brother. No reason to get your panties all twisted."

He stands from his seat, moving closer to the fire, stoking it with a long stick. As if part of the performance, the fire roars to life, flames lapping higher and brighter.

"Now, where was I? Oh, right. As the story goes, the very first encounter with the Phantom happened almost exactly one hundred years ago in a cavern inside what we know now as Phantom's Reach.

"A poor woman, whose husband had fallen ill due to the toxic fumes emitted from the mines, was down to her last crumb of bread. Her husband's health was rapidly declining with the sickness, and she had no way to feed her four children. So, in a desperate attempt to put some food on the table, she disguised herself and set out to work the mines while her husband recovered. However, her plan didn't work out the way she'd intended.

"When she arrived at the mines, her own chest began to hurt, and she quickly found that the men were acting odd, many of them confused and bickering among themselves. She tried to push through the fog in her brain, but quickly found herself just as disoriented and confused.

"She tried to find a way out of the cavern, but only seemed to be walking in circles as people began collapsing all around her. Hours passed, which soon turned to days, as she searched for a way out, pacing back and forth until her feet were blistered and bloody.

"She began hallucinating with visions of rescue, only to come to and realize she was still trapped in that cave. On the third day of her entrapment, something happened that would change the course of our history ...

"A sickly, rancid odor filled the cavern, and suddenly, the air grew cold. She opened her eyes to find a monster towering over her. He had massive wings that spanned across his back; his skin was black and smooth, like leather; and on his head sat a crown of antlers, as if he were a king or royalty of some kind. He stared down his nose, his fluorescent-green eyes illuminating the space around him in a soft glow, as the woman crumbled helplessly beneath him."

Leo's hand tightens its grip on my thigh, and I cover it with my own. I take another sip of my whiskey, feeling my muscles loosen as I listen to the eerie story.

"She scrambled to her knees and began pleading for her life, begging him not to kill her. And when he finally spoke, he didn't open his mouth, rather she heard his voice in her mind. It was gravelly and deep with a strange accent she didn't recognize. The words she heard were, 'I've come to warn you about the sickness in this land, sickness brought on by you and your people. I come to you as a harbinger that if you should continue your destructive ways, there will be deadly consequences to pay.'

"The woman told him that her husband had fallen ill, promised him that if he spared her life, she would do everything in her power to stop the mining. The Phantom saw the truth in her eyes and took pity on her. He took her word, agreeing to give her six months before he returned. But just as he was about to leave, she felt a searing, stabbing pain on her thigh as a reminder of his threat burned into her flesh.

"As the story goes, he marked her with the tip of his wing on the inside of her thigh. He carved out a gash, shaped like a crescent moon, which was rumored to have never quite healed completely and would start to throb the closer she was to him.

"Then, he was gone. The cavern air cleared of the rotting stench, and the other miners began to stir awake. The woman found her head had cleared of the fog and was able to find her way out of the cavern with ease.

"That night, she found her husband sitting up in bed, awake. It was as if he'd been magically healed. Although she was terrified, she knew she'd been blessed by the Phantom and soon began telling the story of her encounter to anyone who'd listen.

"They called her a fool.

"She became the laughingstock of the town, but she never stopped telling her story, never stopped pushing for change.

"As the weeks passed, she began to dream of the Phantom, as if he were reminding her of the ticking clock before his return. She was haunted by nightmares of explosions, seeing the people she knew and loved blasted into oblivion every single night and knowing there was nothing she could do.

"Despite her warnings, there was no change with the mining; in fact, they increased their production, adding more crews than ever. People were growing sicker by the day, and the land was barren of nutrients, making them solely dependent on the processed food they could buy from the few grocers that were left.

"Before she knew it, her time was up, and she was terrified to see his threat come to life. She intended on pleading with the Phantom to change his mind; it was her only hope. So, on the six-month anniversary of her sighting, she snuck away in the night, not even telling her husband where she was going, for fear that he'd stop her—or worse, follow her and get himself killed.

"When she arrived at the cavern, she called for him to show himself. And just like the time before, the air turned cold, and the sickly smell that she'd committed to memory returned. The Phantom appeared before her, even larger than she remembered, and when he spoke, he wasn't pleased.

"He cast a curse on her and all her descendants for the next one hundred years, holding them responsible for the damage being done to the land. As the story goes, the curse would bring bad luck to those who poisoned the sacred ground where they stood.

"But should they choose to turn from their ways and heal the land, great luck and fortune would rain upon them with blessings and abundance.

"He warned her that because of the continuous harm they caused to the land, destruction would follow when they least expected it and made her mute for the next year as a punishment for failing.

"The woman ran home, horrified by her inability to tell anyone what had happened, and waited as the dreams and visions visited her night after night.

"And then, one beautiful summer day, not much different from this, they filed into the mines, where a massive explosion took the lives of sixty-three men and injured hundreds of others.

"Her voice returned the very same day... though, by then, it was too late.

"That woman was our great-great-grandmother and the founding member of Ashford Falls."

"Wow, that's sort of a buzzkill. So, why exactly is there a festival to celebrate this Phantom?" I ask, breaking through the tension in the air.

The brothers all share a look before Leo finally speaks. "We, uh ... it's more of an appreciation for what he represents rather than celebrating him. The part my brother failed to mention was that in the years that followed, most of the original town members died from illnesses caused by the mines. It wasn't until our grandparents closed the mines completely that things started to improve."

"And our luck," Luka adds.

"Uh-huh. So, is that why your family started an eco-friendly company? You wanted to break the curse?"

Leo scratches the stubble on his chin and considers me for a moment. "Curses aren't real, Ivy, but it was still the right thing to do."

"And look at us now. We're wealthy, healthy, and so is everyone else who lives here. I don't need any other proof than that," Guy chimes in.

"Well, cheers to creepy monsters and breaking curses, I guess!" I hold up my cup in a toast, and we clank our biodegradable cups together.

Suddenly, this man in front of me is starting to make a hell of a lot more sense.

"Now that I'm officially spooked ... who's up for a little fun?"

"Hell yeah, that's what I'm talking about. What do you have in mind?" Guy says as he high-fives Luka and Roman.

Leo tightens his grip around my thigh. "Ivy, what are you doing?"

But I ignore him. "I thought we could play a little drinking game ..."

CHAPTER EIGHTEEN

Ivy

"Okay, gentlemen, the rules are simple. It's your standard game of Truth or Dare, but with a few more choices. You can pick from the following: truth, dare, double dare, kiss, command, and promise." I move from Leo's lap to the chair beside him as I explain the rules.

Guy gets up to refill everyone's drinks. "Hell yes, this is going to be so much fun."

"What happens if you refuse?" Leo asks, looking a little worried and uncomfortable.

Roman rolls his eyes. "Oh, come on, Leo. We haven't even started playing, and you're already looking for a way to get out of it."

I've noticed in the short time I've been around these guys, there's some unusual tension between Leo and his middle brother, Roman. He's quieter and nicer, so it feels slightly out of character that he'd give his brother a hard time. Maybe it's a work thing?

"Or ..." Leo drags out. "I know who I'm playing with ..."

"Now, boys, let's not fight. We're here to have fun. To answer your question, Leo, the penalty for not completing your question is an automatic command that will last for twenty-four hours and will be voted on by the group. However, if you choose to not fulfill a double dare ... then your punishment lasts forty-eight hours. Oh, and you can't pick truth twice in a row. I think that just about sums it up. Everyone understand?"

I flash my fiancée a devilish smile, and he nods. I swear I've never seen the man look more terrified.

Interesting. I wonder what skeletons he's got in his closet. I guess there's only one way to find out.

"Great. I'll go first." I turn to Guy, who's sitting on the other side of me. "Truth, dare, double dare, kiss, command, promise?"

He waggles his brows and winks. "Let's start off with a bang. Double dare."

I tap my finger to my lip. "All right, I double dare you to ... read the last text you sent out loud to us, no exceptions."

Guy's face falls a little, as if he's trying to remember his last message, and then Luka's grabbing for his phone.

"You heard the woman. Let's hear it. Don't worry; I'll watch over his shoulder and make sure he doesn't lie."

Guy takes the phone, and swipes open his texts, pausing until he has our full attention. "It's supposed to be enjoyed along with the accompanying photo ..."

"Spare us the jump scare and get on with it," Leo bites out before Guy reveals whatever photographic evidence hides behind his screen.

"Fine, but it's probably not going to make sense without

context." He clears his throat and reads, *"Come on, Mama. I'll two-step my wild stallion across those titties as many times as you like, if it means you'll sit on my lap and call me Cowboy."*

Leo's lip curls in disgust. "Oh God, it's worse than I thought."

"I would ask, but I've got a feeling I don't need to know," Roman says, as we all try to hide our snickers.

"Again, it'd make more sense if you saw the photo—"

"No thank you. No need for show-and-tell. You've already given us more than enough," Roman cuts in before he goes any further.

"Your loss, dude." Guy shrugs, pocketing his phone. "Cool. So, it's my turn then." He points to Leo with his cup. "What's your poison, big brother?"

Leo grunts, shifting in his chair. "Truth, I guess ..."

"Shocker," Guy says under his breath. He rubs his hands together maniacally as he considers his question. "I need to make this good. Leo Kingsley, tell us, are you still afraid of the dark, or is that something you've outgrown?"

Everyone goes quiet, and I don't miss the way Roman cuts his eyes at Guy.

Leo takes a long pull of his whiskey, as if he needs the liquid encouragement to get through this game, and then his gravelly voice cuts through the silence. "It was never the dark I was afraid of, but you knew that." He doesn't elaborate or explain any further before he turns to Roman. "Truth or dare or whatever ..."

Roman smiles. "Truth."

"Did you purposely schedule your travel so you could pawn off the festival planning on someone else?"

Roman's lips quiver before pulling into a smile. "You caught me. But, hey, can you blame me? I've been stuck on the planning committee for the last five years. I needed a break."

"I fucking knew it!" Leo throws his empty cup at Roman's head, and the brothers all burst out laughing.

"Stop your bitching. It was time you did something to give back for a change. Besides, you of all people should know why the festival is so important."

"Who's next?" Leo says, changing the subject.

All eyes land on Luka. "Command," he says without missing a beat.

Roman leans back in his seat, propping his feet on a piece of firewood. "Let's see ... I command you to ... read us the last five things in your search history."

Luka pulls out his phone, and Guy looks over his shoulder, no doubt watching to make sure he's honest. "*Robot for fucking. Is robot pussy wet? Most common robot sex injuries. Sex robot for sale. Sex robot for sale near me.*"

"And you guys thought I was the perv in the family. Looks like Luka just pulled ahead for the lead," Guy says.

The game continues for several rounds, and we all start to loosen up as the alcohol flows freely. If there's anything this game has taught me, it's that the Kingsley brothers are ruthless when it comes to airing out each other's dirty laundry.

In the last hour, I've learned that Roman frequents the local hardware store for special rope to practice his knot tying; Luka's had a threesome with a married couple who wanted an extra for their tenth wedding anniversary—he was explicit that there were no swords crossed; Guy admitted to making a masked-face porno under a fake name when he was nineteen; and apparently, Leo told everyone his name was Danielsan for two years after watching *The Karate Kid* when he was eight. He was so persistent that his teachers all called him Daniel, and all his papers were sent home under that name.

My side hurts from laughing so hard at Leo's confession, and I don't think I've ever heard so many scandalous stories in one evening. And I thought I was a handful; these guys could write a manifesto on leading secretly kinky lives.

Leo's finally loosened up. His eyes are slightly hooded, and I haven't seen the frown lines between his eyebrows all night. I know it's the alcohol, but more than that, I think he feels comfortable out here. It's like getting away and not having his normal surroundings as a reminder helped him get out of his head. I love this playful version of him. I only wish he'd let him out more.

"Okay, Danielsan, what'll it be?" I ask as the laughter dies down.

Leo pauses, his eyes meeting mine, and I catch a flicker of something that looks like challenge. "Well, since I can't pick truth again, I guess I'll go with kiss."

His eyes flick to my mouth, and I wet my lips as a rush of nerves envelops me.

I shouldn't be surprised. I knew our whole arrangement came with some physical stuff, and it's not as if the man hasn't had his fingers inside me, but a kiss feels so much more ... I don't know ... intimate?

Guy lets out a frustrated sigh. "Nice job reminding us that you're getting laid tonight and we're not."

"By the sound of that text you read us, I'd say you're not

too bad off yourself," Luka says to Guy, and they break off into an argument about whether robot sex goes toward your body count.

But their voices all fade away when Leo wets his lips and pats his thigh for me to come sit on his lap. It's a slight gesture, like I'm a pet he's calling toward him, like this is something we do all the time and not a monumental moment.

Maybe it's all for show, maybe he wants to make sure his brothers don't have any questions about if this is real or not, or maybe he's finally taking what he wants.

I don't have time to consider his motives. All I know is, my body is already moving toward him, obeying his command like a damn puppet, and my heart's beating so hard that I'm afraid everyone can hear it.

I perch myself on his knee and wrap my hands around the back of his neck, and when I'm close enough for only Leo to hear me, I whisper, "You don't have to really kiss me if you don't want. I'll be convincing ..."

The words are barely out of my lips before Leo's hand grips the back of my neck, pulling me into him with a possessive grip.

"The fuck you will."

And then his mouth is on mine, his hand tightening around my hair in a fist as he kisses me with pure abandon. It's slow at first, sweet even as we move together as if our lips were made for exactly this reason. Then, Leo's tongue slides in my mouth, caressing and teasing, and never in my life have I felt so connected to another person.

He sucks my bottom lip into his mouth, giving me a little nip, and he tugs my hair, tilting my head up as he moves to my neck, kissing and sucking my sensitive skin for just a moment before his lips return to mine. He's a man starved, and I'm happy to be the object of his desire because kissing Leo Kingsley feels like exactly that—desire.

If there was ever a question in my mind about whether this was real or for show, Leo's racing heart and hitched breathing tell me everything I need to know. He wants me ... and I can't think of a single reason to deprive him of even his darkest desires ...

I wiggle in his lap, throwing a leg on either side of him to bring our bodies closer as his mouth devours me like his life depends on it, like I'm the air in his lungs and the blood running through his veins.

Our kiss is needy and possessive and so fucking raw, and I'm about five seconds away from throwing caution to the wind and dry-humping myself to completion on his thigh when Guy's voice catches my attention.

"Jeez, save it for the tent, will you? I'm getting a boner, watching you two make out, and I'm feeling conflicted about whether that's fucked up or not ..."

Leo's fist tightens in my hair before he bites my lip one more time and pulls my head away, breaking our kiss with a sly grin. "Sorry, guess I just got carried away. Where were we again?" He's talking to his brothers, but he doesn't take his eyes off me, and holy shit, this guy never ceases to surprise me.

I touch my fingers to my now-swollen lips, feeling like I just had some kind of out-of-body experience, and all he did was kiss me. If his kissing is this good, I can't even imagine how amazing he fucks.

"It's Ivy's turn, I think," Roman adds, bringing us back to the game.

"Double dare," I say, looking to Leo, but before he can give me a dare, Luka jumps in.

"What do you say we take this game to the next level?"

I quirk a brow. "How so, robot boy?"

Everyone bursts out laughing at my dig, and Luka just beams, like he isn't the least bit embarrassed. They're starting to feel more like family by the minute, and it catches me off guard to realize I could ever feel this comfortable joking ... like siblings ... with anyone besides my sister.

Luka gives Guy a knowing look before his face breaks into a sly grin. "How about a game of Sardines? For old times' sake ..."

Leo shakes his head and checks his watch. "It's getting late. I don't want Ivy wandering the woods alone at night—"

"You're on," I blurt out before he can finish. Call me crazy, but I'm actually having a good time, seeing glimpses of Leo with his guard down, and I'm not ready for this night to end just yet.

Guy and Luka both laugh, shaking their heads.

Luka says, "Looks like you're outnumbered, big brother, but if you're too old to hang, we'd be happy to entertain Ivy for you."

Leo's jaw clenches, and so does his grip on my leg, reminding me that I'm still straddling him like we're going to start fucking at any second. "Fine, but only one round. It's pitch-black out here, and I don't need Ivy getting herself hurt tonight. She doesn't know these woods like the rest of us."

I wiggle back and forth, grinding myself on his rock-hard cock for just a moment, and then swing my legs around to a more appropriate position.

"Aw, look, the curmudgeon does have a soft spot for me," I tease, running my palm over Leo's scruffy jaw.

His hand comes down on my leg, securing me in place when I attempt to get up and move to my own seat.

Roman laughs and jerks his head to look at us. "I certainly hope so ... I mean, you guys are engaged, aren't you?"

Leo grips my hand, his eyes flashing me a reminder to watch my mouth. "Of course I do. Ivy sometimes forgets *how much* I care about her. She forgets that I'm protective of her *because* I care so much," he says in warning.

I swallow a gulp. "I just like to give you a hard time. You know I love your bossy, overprotective side ... especially in the bedroom."

Roman slaps his hands over his ears. "And I could've gone my whole life without knowing that."

"Right on. You know what? That makes sense. I can see the appeal—" Guy nods.

"Let's all get back on track, shall we?" Luka says, commanding everyone's attention. "It's your basic game of hide-and-seek, only in reverse. One person hides, and we'll set a timer for two minutes. Then, we'll all join. If you find the person hiding, you'll hide with them. Everyone can use the flashlight on their phone. Stay on this side of the creek. Trees are fair game. Ivy, since it's your turn, you can hide first."

Leo's hand shoots out to grab my arm. "Why don't you pick someone else? I don't like the idea of her being alone out there—"

I shrug him off, moving my hand to his chest, and feel his

heart pounding beneath my palm. "Then, I guess you'd better be the first one to find me."

CHAPTER NINETEEN

Leo

"This is so stupid. I can't believe I let you talk me into this. What if she trips over a tree root and knocks herself out or, God forbid, she runs into a pack of wolves or a bear?" I wipe a sweaty palm over the rough fabric of my pants as I pace back and forth by the campfire.

"She'll be fine, Leo. It's cute that you're so worried about her though," Luka says.

Roman stands from his seat by the fire and claps me on the shoulder. "It's refreshing, seeing you like this. Sometimes, I almost forget you have a heart underneath that cold exterior."

I swat his hand away with a grunt and check the timer on my phone.

Luka and Guy sit idly, chatting about something, like they don't have a fucking care in the world as I watch the seconds tick by, impossibly slower than normal.

When the timer finally beeps, I let out a sigh. "Are we

setting a time limit for the game? How do we know when it's over?"

"You're a big boy, Leo, and you have your phone. Stop trying to make unnecessary rules. It takes away from the fun," Guy says, propping a hand on my shoulder for balance as he stretches his quads.

Clearly, we're not playing the same game of Sardines because I have no intention of running or exerting myself. Hell, I'm happy to lose just so we can be done with all this juvenile bullshit.

"Everyone ready?" Luka asks as we approach the forest opening.

Guy bounces in place. "Let's fucking go!"

"Ready as I'll ever be," I mumble under my breath.

"Three. Two. One. Go!" Luka yells.

He and Guy take off in opposite directions. Roman and I take a slower approach, nodding before we go our separate ways.

The eerie quiet of the night is interrupted only by the crunch of the forest floor under my boots. Nights like this remind me of why these woods are revered as Guy's story plays in the back of my mind.

My heart picks up speed as I weave through the trees, shining my light in search of Ivy's blonde hair. Panic knots in my throat as more time passes, and I have to talk myself down, remembering the breathing techniques my therapist taught me when I was a kid.

"Ivy!" I hiss in a whisper. "Ivy, where are you?"

I don't know why I even bother. If I know anything about this woman, it's that she's as stubborn as they come. Hell, I wouldn't put it past her to spend the night out here alone just to prove that she won the game.

The thought has my blood boiling. I'm a tight ball of nerves and only growing more irritated with every passing minute.

I make it all the way to the creek before doubling back to check the opposite end. I'm careful, stepping over decaying logs and maneuvering around thick ferns as I shine my light all around me.

"Ivy! Where the fuck are you?" I hiss again as my foot crunches through a rotting tree log. I shake my leg free as my frustration rises.

I'm thankful to be wearing pants and boots. Which reminds me that Ivy's out here in a fucking spandex unitard and sneakers, probably covered in scratches and bug bites by now.

I clench my jaw. I fucking told her to dress appropriately, but of course she didn't listen. Hell, she's probably wrapped up in poison ivy, thinking she's got the best hiding spot in the world—or worse, hiding near a den of some kind ...

I can't let myself go there. I'm being ridiculous, my imagination taking too many creative liberties. If I'm going to find her, I need to calm down and think. Where would she hide?

I hear my brothers in the distance, ruffling around and laughing, which can only mean they haven't found her either.

Fuck, I don't know if that makes me feel better or worse.

"Goddamn it, Ivy!" I hiss again as my eye catches on a dense bush ... too dense to be natural.

I shine my light and study it, and that's when I see the

broken branches jutting out at the top. Someone added some extra leaves to this bush.

I shield my light as I inch forward and pull the top branch out, revealing Ivy crouched next to a massive, hollowed-out sycamore tree.

"Caught you!"

"Shh!" She gestures for me to be quiet before grabbing the collar of my shirt and pulling me closer. "Get in before they see you!"

Relief floods me, and I push through the limbs, carefully placing the branch back where she had it before crouching down beside her.

Damn, this is a good hiding spot. If I didn't know this forest so well, I don't think I'd have ever found her, and I don't know if that makes me more proud or pissed. I'm starting to realize the two usually go hand in hand when it comes to Ivy.

The moon shines bright, illuminating the sky through the pocket of trees surrounding us. Now that my eyes have adjusted, I barely need a flashlight at all.

She's practically sitting in my lap, as we sit squeezed in the tight space inside the hollowed out opening of a sycamore tree, the citrus and vanilla scent of her shampoo doing more to calm my nerves than I care to admit. This fucking woman is so radiant and warm that she even smells like sunshine, and I've been living in the darkness for far too long.

She slides a hand over my thigh, massaging me in soothing strokes, and, fuck, it feels too good to stop her. It's like she knows I need her touch, if only to calm my worried thoughts. She's here, and most importantly, she's safe.

I close my eyes, letting it sink in, and relief floods my chest in warm currents.

"I can't believe you found me," she says, breaking the silence.

"Yeah, well, it was only because I'd spent so much time out here when I was young. I knew there weren't bushes this large in the middle of the forest, but I can't say that the three stooges out there will be able to tell."

Her hand moves up my thigh, fingers brushing just beneath my balls as she gives me her signature mischievous smirk. "Then, we need to be quiet, so we don't give our awesome hiding spot away."

Goose bumps erupt all over my skin, and my heart rate skyrockets as her wandering touch moves from the top of my thigh to my knee. "Ivy, what are you—" I stand, attempting to put some distance between us. I need to get my head on straight. I need to think clearly before I do something we'll both regret.

But she's not making this easy on me, and she stands, too, which only makes things worse. My cock grows harder at the feeling of her soft breasts nuzzled against my core as our bodies press together in the narrow space. My palms itch to pull her into me while my brain fires off warning sirens. I know I should stop this, but, goddamn it, I don't think I can. I don't know how much more torment my touch-starved body can take.

I hiss a breath through gritted teeth as her hand moves back to my thigh. This time, she grazes my balls, and I nearly see stars.

"What are you trying to—" I grab her hands, pressing them against the tree, desperate to catch my breath.

But there's not enough space, and when she wiggles, she still somehow manages to rub my cock with her thigh.

Fuck me. My cock twitches as her soft body moves against mine, creating the faintest bit of friction.

"Ivy, this is not the time to play games—"

Her hand breaks free of my distracted hold, tugging my shirt to pull me closer as she hooks a knee behind my back. She stands on her tiptoes while she grinds against me, as if that could make up for our eleven-inch height difference. Fuck, she feels incredible, and I can't fight it any longer. I need this. I need this so badly that I think I might die if I don't get relief soon.

Without thinking, I cup her ass as she rolls her body over mine, and, fuck, it feels amazing. She feels amazing. It's all too much.

I squeeze my palm over her ass as she rubs her needy pussy over my painfully hard cock. I could come from just feeling her like this, our bodies rubbing together, breathless and starving for touch.

She loops an arm over my shoulder before wrapping her other leg around my waist, and then we're kissing.

I should stop this. There isn't anyone around to perform for. We shouldn't be doing this ... but I can't help myself. I'm a starving man who's gone so long without romantic touch that I've almost forgotten what it feels like, and Ivy's the walking wet dream of a woman, sent to remind me of everything I've been missing.

I suck on her bottom lip before nipping at it with my teeth as I lose myself in her kiss. Our bodies move as one, and I pin her, using the tree as leverage. Jolts of pleasure shoot straight to my cock as the threat of my release intensifies.

It's almost painful how incredible she feels. I swallow all her whimpers and moans as my hands roam over her petite frame, desperate to trace every inch of her skin. I shouldn't be doing this, but I don't think I could conjure the willpower to stop if I tried. I'll have the rest of my life to thoroughly punish myself, but right now, I'm going to enjoy this rare moment where all my dreams come true.

She grips my shirt before sliding a hand beneath, trailing her palm over my abs like she's trying to memorize my form with her touch. The darkness heightens my senses, intensifying every brush of skin as she dips her hand beneath my waistband, gripping my eager cock in her palm.

I nearly blow a load right there.

"Holy shit, Leo. You're massive." She slides her hand up and down my length, alternating her pace and pressure, and I breathe in a hiss.

It's like she knows exactly what I need and how I need it. My balls clench, and my vision blurs as she works me so good that I can barely remember why we're out here to begin with.

After a few more strokes, I feel myself getting painfully close, and I grab her hand so I can catch my breath.

"Whoa now, baby girl. Keep that up, and I'm going to come. And I'm not ready to come yet."

I pin her again as my lips crash against hers, but she doesn't stop her wiggling; if anything, she grinds her pussy harder over my cock, moving faster until I'm so distracted that she breaks a hand loose.

Heat pools at the base of my spine as our tongues twist and tangle, our lips moving in frantic need as we all but fuck each other through our clothes. Real sex has never come close to feeling this amazing, and that says a lot, considering the bottom of my shaft's currently pressed against the metal zipper of my pants. But I don't care. Somehow, the pain and *almost* of it all make it that much hotter, and I'll take whatever scraps I can get right now.

Her hand slides up my shaft again, and I bite the inside of my cheek to calm myself down, trying to think of anything to bring me back from the edge. But it feels too good, and when I close my eyes, all I can see are those mischievous amber eyes staring back at me, and I know I'm a fucking goner.

"Hold on, baby, just give me a second to—" I move my hand to stop her, but my arms feel like limp noodles, like I'm moving in slow motion.

"How close are you?" she teases as she moves her hand over me, somehow managing to stroke every sensitive spot on my cock like she's using fucking magic against me.

My hand moves over hers in a pathetic attempt to stop her. "Ivy, stop. I'm going to—" But as soon as the words leave my mouth, I feel my balls clench, and then I explode. "Fuck." Liquid heat shoots through me in waves of pleasure, and I come right there in my pants like a goddamn teenager.

I take a few moments to catch my breath as my racing heart returns to a normal rhythm, and then the post-nut clarity hits me like a freight train.

I don't know if I'm more embarrassed that I just came in my pants from a few minutes of heavy petting or annoyed that I told her to stop and she didn't.

This fucking brat.

Ivy's grin is almost too much to take as I stare back at her, looking so smug.

I've long forgotten about the game, that we're supposed to

be quiet and hiding. I don't care about whether or not I should be doing what I'm doing with a woman thirteen years my junior. None of that matters anymore because all I see when I look at her is *my* fucking brat that needs to be punished.

And I've been dreaming of the day when I get to be the one to do it.

I adjust myself, feeling the warm jizz drip down my cock as I glare at her. "You're feeling pretty proud of yourself right now, aren't you?"

She nods, her lips twitching at the corner as she tries to contain her smile, but her eyes tell me everything I need to know. She fucking loves this, loves seeing me fall apart, loves knowing that she has so much power over me that she could make me come in my pants, even against my fucking will.

I reach for my belt and begin unbuckling it, the high-pitched sound of the metal clinking filling the silence, and her eyes widen ever so slightly, but she doesn't move.

This is the moment she's been waiting for, isn't it? This is what she's been pushing me to do, so who am I to deny her what she wants? It's time for me to teach my little brat a lesson ...

"Get on your knees." I don't wait for her to catch on before I'm pushing her head down, and she reluctantly follows.

I see the confusion pulling between her brows, and fuck if it's not exactly what I needed, the cherry on top of this whole scenario.

"You act like a fucking brat because you want me to punish you, isn't that right, baby girl?"

I run my thumb along her jaw before tracing her full bottom lip. The sight of her on her knees, those big eyes staring up at me with anticipation, almost sends me over the edge. Hell, I can already feel myself getting hard again.

"Answer me," I bark, tightening a fist in her hair.

She nods several times before whispering, "Yes."

"Fuck, you look so hot like this. God, I want to fuck that smart mouth until your eyes water and you're gagging on my cock." I lean down and whisper, "And trust me, I intend to ... but first, you're going to clean up this mess you made ... every fucking drop."

I grip her hair, bringing her face closer as I shove my pants down with my free hand, and when she looks up at me ... she has the fucking nerve to smile.

Jesus Christ, this woman is going to destroy me, but I can't make myself care about that right now, not when she's playing her part so well. I never thought I'd consider doing this again with someone, but here I am, throwing caution to the wind because the thought of missing out on this once-in-a-lifetime woman terrifies me more than my fear of rejection.

She wraps her hands around the back of my thighs as her bright eyes flick up to meet mine, and she licks her lips. "Yes, Daddy. I'll clean up the mess."

My head falls back against the hollow tree with a heavy thud as Ivy sticks out her warm pink tongue, and she does just that.

Fuck me, I'm in over my head. I've always had a sweet spot for brats, but I don't think I've ever met one this headstrong, this fucking good at it, and as she licks every drop of cum clean from my body, I realize I've met my match.

I swipe the excess saliva from her lips with my thumb as I

stare down at her in appreciation. "Such a good little slut. You love having my cum on your tongue, don't you, baby girl?"

She reaches to stroke my once-again-hard shaft, but I swat her away. As much as it pains me, this is still a punishment even if she did enjoy it more than I'd anticipated.

"Ah-ah, let's not get ahead of ourselves. You might have cleaned up your mess, but I'm not finished with your punishment ..."

Her eyes fall, and I swear I see a flash of disappointment on her face.

Fucking hell, I don't know what I'm going to do with this woman.

"Did you see that? I think they're back here?" I hear Roman's voice just before his flashlight shocks us both back to the present moment and we remember what we're supposed to be doing.

I pull Ivy to her feet and barely manage to buckle my belt before all three of my brothers burst through the tree branch barricade, flashlights and booze in hand.

"We found you! I knew we'd find you if we worked together!" Guy yells, throwing an arm around Roman's shoulders in triumph.

"You two are really good hiders." Luka points with the mostly empty bottle of whiskey and stumbles before catching his balance on a tree.

I yank the bottle from his hand, then help myself to the little bit that's left. "I see you three have been busy."

"We had to entertain ourselves somehow. Do you know how boring it is, searching for over an hour?" Luka says, now propping himself on Roman for balance.

"We almost gave up. Thought you two might be out here, bumping uglies or something. Figured maybe you didn't want to be found." Guy hiccups and jumps like he's just startled himself, which makes Roman and Luka both double over in laughter.

Nothing like my three drunk younger brothers to sober me back to the present.

"Well, you certainly did ... find us, I mean." I grab Luka's arm and throw it over my shoulders as Ivy moves to help Guy, and we make our way back to the campsite.

My neck is still hot, and my mind's racing a mile a minute, thinking of all the things I wanted to do to her had we not been interrupted.

"What's all over your pants, Leo? Did you fall in a puddle or something back there? Why is it only wet around your dick?" Luka asks, which prompts Guy and Roman to offer their own explanations of what they think happened.

"Do you think he peed his pants?" Guy asks.

"No, it's not spread out like a pee stream—trust me, I know what that looks like," Luka offers, and I truly don't want to know how he knows that.

"It's weird though, isn't it? There's a distinct area of wetness—"

"All right, that's enough," I snap, cutting them off before anyone has any better guesses.

We deliver them to their tents, and I make sure to supply them each with a bottle of water, a puke bucket, and a couple of painkillers.

Talk about things taking a left turn. It's annoying as fuck to have to babysit my brothers, but I can't say that I'm mad about their interruption. It's giving me time to finally think with a clear head and figure out my next move.

I start toward my own tent, and it's only then that I remember how inconvenient our sleeping arrangement is going to be.

Fuck me, this is going to be a long night.

CHAPTER TWENTY

Ivy

"Coffee."

I blink open my heavy eyes to find Leo crouching down in front of me, his face masked from all emotion. He passes me a cup of the steaming hot liquid as the scent of freshly brewed coffee fills the tent.

I sit up, accepting the offering as all the images of last night come rushing back to me. I rub my scratchy eyes, feeling the tiniest twinge of a headache growing at my temples, and as if Leo can read my mind, he passes me a couple of painkillers.

"You'll feel better once you take this."

"Thanks." I toss back the pills as an awkward silence fills the air, both of us staring like we're waiting for the other to speak first.

Last night, things got pretty heated, and to say Leo surprised me is the understatement of the century. I was so worked up, so turned on, that I couldn't wait to pounce on him as soon as we were alone, couldn't wait to finish what we'd started back in the woods.

But Leo being Leo wouldn't hear of it. So, after he made sure his brothers were all set with what they needed and tucked into their own tents, he helped me into my sleeping bag and promptly turned out the lights without another word. He even went as far as sleeping on top of the sleeping bag with his head in the opposite direction.

I was tired and delightfully sated after the activities of the evening, and I figured he needed a little time to think. So, rather than pushing it, forcing him to talk to me—or God forbid pick up where we'd left off—I turned over and snuggled his muscular calf and slept better than I had in years.

I'm not so sure he can say the same, judging by the dark circles under his eyes and the look of remorse on his face.

"Listen, Ivy, about last night—"

I hold up my hand to stop him before taking a cautious sip of my hot coffee. "Let's not do the whole *I shouldn't have let myself get carried away* bit. It's too early for me to deal with your self-deprecation, and I'd like to keep my memory of last night untampered with."

His lip twitches, and he brushes my wild mane out of my eyes. "I wasn't going to apologize."

I snap my eyes up, and this time, when he looks at me, I don't see regret. Actually, he looks more at peace than I think I've ever seen him.

"If anything, I went easy on you last night."

I take a gulp of my coffee, not caring as it burns all the way down my throat. Is he being serious right now? Is this real life?

I go in for another gulp, but Leo's hand moves over the top of my cup.

"Slow down. I don't need you burning that pretty mouth before I have time to enjoy it."

And I think my panties might have just incinerated.

Leo smiles, wiping a drip of coffee from my chin with his thumb. "You're so fucking adorable when you wake up. You have no idea how hard it is to not crawl into that sleeping bag with you and forget about my entire family right now."

My mouth falls open as I stare at him.

Who is this, and what have they done with my self-righteous curmudgeon? Did I finally manage to break the emotionless robot? I can't help but feel the tiniest bit of pride at the thought. I knew I could break him ... eventually.

So, I guess the real question is, what the hell happens now?

Before I have time to spiral over that thought, he pushes my open jaw shut and laughs. "Why don't you get dressed? My dad's making breakfast, and I've got to help rouse my hungover brothers. I've got a surprise planned for us after breakfast."

He tugs the end of my hair, and then he's gone, leaving me equally surprised and confused in the best way possible.

Holy shit. I think I'm going to need more coffee.

* * *

"There she is," Frank calls at the same time Mary asks, "How did you sleep?"

I take a seat on the log bench beside Leo, and he wraps an arm around me, sliding me closer to him.

Leo is looking wholly unbothered and, dare I say, comfortable. "Like a baby. I could get used to being out here."

"Well, I'm happy to hear it. By the sound of it, you all had quite the eventful evening. I hope the boys aren't hurting too badly this morning after finishing off that entire bottle of whiskey." Frank laughs as he pulls the skillet from the hot rocks in the fire, and Leo jumps up to clear a space for him.

As if on cue, Roman and Luka climb out of their tents with a groan, wiping their sleepy eyes with their fists.

"Good morning, family," Roman says as he pours himself a cup of coffee and takes a seat by the fire.

"Why does bacon have to smell so bacony?" Luka grumbles, pulling the hood of his sweatshirt over his head.

"Ah, there they are, the party animals who kept us up well into the night. How're you feeling, Luka? Regret any of your choices last night?" Mary gives them each a pat on the head before passing Luka a bottle of water.

"I feel perfectly fine. Slept like a baby on a tiny boat in the ocean," Roman says. He nudges Luka with his elbow. "Some of us know how to hold our liquor while others are still learning."

Luka grunts, pressing his fingers to his temples. "Stop yelling, would you? My head is pounding, and your voice is making me nauseous."

"Here, eat this and stop whining." Leo tosses Luka half a sleeve of graham crackers, to which Luka doesn't even try to catch. Instead, the crackers smack him in the head and land at his feet.

"Thanks." He reluctantly takes a bite, looking absolutely miserable.

"I guess you and your brothers will think twice before getting piss drunk again."

"Oh, come on now, Frank. Let them enjoy their youth while they can. I'm glad everyone seemed to have had a good time. I just wish Jett had wanted to join us. I miss having all my people together like this. Now that we have more reasons to celebrate, maybe we can do things like this more often." Mary's smile beams as she looks around the campsite like she wouldn't rather be anywhere else.

My stomach twists at the thought of disappointing her, but the guilt is soon forgotten when Leo places a plate in my lap.

"And for my beautiful bride-to-be, eggs and bacon, cooked just how you like them."

I look down and smile when I see he used the yellow scrambled eggs to form a circle in the middle of the plate and added two blueberries and a piece of bacon to form a smiley face.

"Hey, why didn't you make mine cute? You know I love that shit," Roman says as he takes his plate and plops down on the log beside us. "Just because you got laid in the tent last night doesn't mean you shouldn't share the wealth."

Luka, who seems to be feeling a little better, perks up. "I'm pretty sure that's exactly what that means."

"Can we not talk about my sex life over breakfast, please?" Leo comes to sit beside me with his plate and wraps an arm around my waist to move me closer.

"Yeah, well, maybe we're just jealous," Roman says between a mouthful of eggs.

There's an awkward silence in the air as I think back to the moment Leo and I shared last night, the way he spoke to me and took control. I don't think I've ever been so turned on, and I don't know what any of it means or what happens next. All I know is, I liked it. And I can't stop wondering about what would've happened if we weren't interrupted.

As if he senses my racing thoughts, Leo places a warm hand on my knee, tracing comforting circles of distraction.

"I think I'm going to take Ivy down to the lake after breakfast to do a little fishing. Is the boat still in the same spot?"

"Should be. Pretty sure you were the last one to use it," Frank says as he begins packing up the breakfast supplies.

"I hope you don't mind us cutting the camping trip short, but Evelyn's hosting book club tonight at her place, and I already RSVP'd to bring dessert." Mary holds out her hand. She glances at her watch. "We'll need to hurry though, so I'm not rushed ..."

"Okay, well, I guess that's my cue to leave too," Luka says before heading back to his tent.

"Can you wake up your brother so I can start loading the truck?" Frank calls, and Luka gives him a silent thumbs-up.

"I guess I'll leave you two lovebirds to it," Roman says before swiping a cup and scooping it full with ice.

I watch as he creeps toward Guy's tent, where Luka waits, holding a finger over his lips. They slowly unzip the tent and disappear inside.

I turn to Leo, who's looking at me with a curious gaze. "Did you say you're taking me fishing? In a boat? On the lake?"

He inches his hand higher, tucking it securely between my thighs. "I did. Is that okay with you?"

I narrow my eyes. "Why are you being so touchy all of a sudden?"

"I think you and I have a lot to talk about. We're leaving in ten." He kisses me on top of my head before heading to pack up the tent.

"Yowwww! Fuck, that's cold! Not cool, man!" Guy screams from the tent behind us just as Luka and Roman come flying out, bending over as they laugh their assess off.

"It's never a dull moment around this family, is it?"

Leo smiles, shaking his head. "Never."

* * *

"How is it that you've never been fishing? Not even off a dock or in a pond?" Leo holds out a hand to help me step into the wobbly canoe.

We're on the pier right next to the bank, and the lake stretches as far as the eye can see in the distance. It feels strangely quiet out here, like we're the only ones here—and I'm starting to wonder if maybe we are. What's stopping the Kingsleys from buying a lake? They already own the whole town.

Everything about the Kingsley family is larger than life. Sometimes, I feel like it's all too much, and I wonder if I'm going to wake up and realize it was all a dream. Especially since we still haven't talked about what happened last night.

The boat sways as Leo steps in after me, using his momentum to push us out.

"My parents weren't really outdoorsy people, and they definitely weren't into the whole family bonding—hell, I don't think I can remember the last time both of my parents were in the same room ..." My voice trails off as I think back on it, making my stomach twist in knots.

I notice the slightest twitch in Leo's hand, as if what I said angered him, and then he moves it to my thigh in a gentle caress.

I don't know why, but that small, protective gesture gives me more comfort than either of my parents ever did, and soon, the knot is replaced with butterfly flutters.

I never share these personal stories with anyone, but for some reason, I find myself *wanting* to open up. I clear my throat and continue, "And then when my sister got sick, it took everything we had just to survive the day-to-day. I think I've spent more time in and out of hospitals than anything else." I shrug. "I guess that's why she added it to her list. Fern was always trying to create the fullest life possible; she wanted to try everything at least once." I laugh to myself, thinking about all the horrible food she'd insist we'd love, only for us to throw it away and order a pizza.

"I'm so sorry you had to go through that. You deserved to be a kid too. You shouldn't have had to worry about all of that at such a young age, and it wasn't fair for them to expect you to. I can't imagine the pain you must feel, living through something like that. If it makes any difference, I think you're incredibly brave, and I'm in awe of your resilience."

He can't imagine the pain I must *feel*.

I don't miss his use of present tense when referring to my grief, and I think Leo's the only person who's ever spoken of it as if it's an ongoing thing rather than something I should've moved on from by now.

Feeling a little too vulnerable for my liking, I shrug. "Yeah, it sucks, but Fern wouldn't have wanted me to dwell in sadness. She'd have wanted me to enjoy my life. It's why she made the list."

His mouth turns down for a moment, but his eyes don't leave mine. "Ivy, you don't have to do that, you know?"

"I don't have to do what?"

"Pretend to be strong. Pretend that you're not sad or that your sister's death wasn't painful or that it still doesn't hurt."

He places a hand on my shoulder, and I feel that familiar knot start to form in my throat.

I force myself to cough, pushing it back down to the empty hole in my heart, where it belongs. "I'm not pretending anything. Now, are we going to fish, or did you bring me all the way out here to give me a therapy session?"

Leo's lips press into a flat line, like he's holding back his words, but then he reaches down and pulls out a shiny pink fishing pole that he no doubt bought just for me. I don't bother to ask him when he had time to get it because if there's one thing about Leo Kingsley, it's that he can be incredibly thoughtful when he wants to be.

He's only known about Fern's list for a few days, and he seems to have committed it to memory. I hardly expected him to join me jumping off the waterfalls yesterday, and I guess this is no different.

At this rate, I'll have checked off the entire list by the time the Phantom Festival rolls around, and then I'll be off to Romania for the final hurrah. That thought used to excite me, but lately, I've been feeling more anxiety than anything. Probably because it'll be over, and then what am I supposed to do with myself?

I shake the thought away, bringing my attention back to the moment, back to the sexy man sitting in front of me, teaching me about different baits and where to cast, depending on what kind of fish I'm trying to catch.

I stare at his hands as he ties a bobber to the line, remembering how they felt when his fingers were inside me and how desperately I wanted them to touch me last night.

I can feel the blush creep up my neck, and when his eyes meet mine, I swear I see a flare of desire igniting behind them. Maybe I'll get to pick up where we left off last night after all? A girl can only hope.

"I prefer to use live bait, but since I didn't have much time to prepare, rubber worms it is."

Images of last night keep rushing back into my mind, and we're really sitting here, talking about bait?

He passes me the rod. "Here, use both hands and hold the bottom like this ..."

He moves behind me so my back's nestled against his chest, his muscular thighs caging me in as he teaches me how to cast in slow motion. I can feel his heart beating in his chest, and mine picks up speed to match. I feel safe and protected; it's a feeling I've come to associate with Leo, like I don't have to think quite so hard when I'm with him, like my survival instinct can finally relax and I can let down my guard.

"Then, you release, just like that," Leo says as the line soars ahead, landing in the water with a faint plop.

He holds the fishing pole lightly as I stay seated between his legs, neither one of us moving even though the lesson's finished.

I brush fingers along his jaw, which is scruffier than I've ever seen it, noticing the patches of silver and white hair that sparkle in the sun. He's got a faint crinkling around his eyes, a testament that he does indeed smile enough to form a wrinkle or two. Or maybe those are old ... from an earlier time when smiling was more common than furrowing his brow or scowling.

"What are you doing?" he asks as I trace my fingertip over the fine lines around his eyes.

"Just admiring your gray hair and wrinkles. I forget how much older you are than me sometimes."

"Thanks for the ego boost." He grabs my hand and places it back on the fishing pole, covering it with his own. As if to remind my wandering mind that we're supposed to be fishing.

"I didn't mean it as an insult. I like your wrinkles and your gray beard hairs. It makes you look distinguished and gives you character." I try to spin around to face him, but he tightens his hold around me to keep me in place.

"You have an interesting way of complimenting someone."

I glare at him from the corner of my eye. "Are we really just going to sit here and pretend that either of us cares about fishing right now?"

Leo doesn't even flinch, just keeps his eyes on the water as he casts his own fishing rod. "You know what makes a great fisherman?" he asks rather than answering me.

I roll my eyes and stifle a frustrated laugh. "Do tell, Boss Daddy. What makes a great fisherman?"

I catch the slightest twitch of his lip out of the corner of my eye. This man is so frustrating, always dodging my questions and deflecting.

"Patience." He slaps a palm over the exposed skin of my thigh, and it makes a loud thwack, stinging for just a moment before he rubs the pain away in soothing circles.

Great. And now, I can't stop thinking about how badly I want him to do it again.

What the hell is this man doing to me? And how does he know what turns me on better than even I do?

"I think you could stand to learn a thing or two about patience, don't you?"

He slides his hand a little higher on my thigh, and I have to clench my thighs together, feeling that all-too-familiar ache, the ache that is a persistent reminder that my body still very much needs a release.

My head falls back against his shoulder as I melt, opening my thighs in a silent invitation. I'm practically panting, and I don't care where he touches me. I just need him to put me out of my misery.

But as soon as I start to drop my fishing pole, he pulls his hand away, taking the promising electric tingles with him.

"I don't remember telling you to drop this." He places the fishing pole back between my hands, waiting for me to tighten my grip before he continues his exploration.

Fuck me, this man knows exactly how to torture me. He can't ever let it be easy, and I think that's one of the things I love the most about us. Leo understands me in ways that I don't even fully understand myself. It's like I'm learning new things I like every time he touches me.

"Very good. I'm pleased to see you're eager to learn this morning. I thought you might need a little more convincing, but it seems like you got a taste of something you liked last night," he hums in my ear, and I tighten my shaking hands around my fishing pole, gripping it like it's the only thing tethering me in place.

He slides a hand underneath the hem of my cropped T-shirt and bites back a growl. "You and these fucking crop tops are going to kill me—you know that, baby girl? Now, hold your pole steady—unless you want me to stop. We're not leaving this boat until you catch a fish, so however long this takes is up to you."

I swallow a gulp as I cling to my fishing pole, saying a silent prayer to the orgasm gods that something happens soon. I don't know if I can survive much more of this. I'm so desperate that I think he could tell me to jump in the lake and catch a fish with my bare hands and I'd give it my best try.

"You have no idea what you do to me, the way you drive me crazy with need, the restraint I've shown from the moment I met you and you opened this pretty mouth." He slides a thumb across my bottom lip, and I melt against him, boneless and floaty.

"Then, why don't you stop talking about it and show me?" I say in challenge.

"Trust me, I'm planning on it, but first, I need you to know something about me, and I want you to listen carefully because I'm only going to say this once ..."

A shiver runs down my spine as my heart races in anticipation, and I don't dare move.

His hand moves to my neck, grazing over my skin in a soft tickle before blanketing his palm over my throat. He doesn't squeeze; he just holds me like he's commanding all my attention. It's so possessive, like he's claiming me, and I've never been more eager to be claimed by someone.

"I can't give you anything more than this. I can't give you normal. I'm sure you've noticed by now that I have very specific tastes... are you okay with that?"

I blink innocently, though I'm sure my racing pulse gives me away. "Am I okay with what? Sorry, I need to know what you're insinuating before agreeing. I need to hear you say it ..."

He exhales heavily then says, "I require a certain amount of control, and not only in the bedroom. I think we both know by now that I have a certain weakness..."

"You like to be called Daddy," I supply for him, and I swear I feel his dick grow harder.

"Yes. I do. Is that something you're comfortable with? Are you creeped out that I want to hear you call me Daddy while I play with your pretty pussy, while I slide my tongue over every inch of your perfect, golden skin and show you what it's like to be worshipped by a real man?" He drags a finger slowly down my body, igniting a rush of heat inside me, and I let out an involuntarily whimper.

"Answer me, Ivy. *I need to hear you say it*," he demands, mocking me with my words from just a moment ago.

"No, I ... uh ... I actually think it's hot," I finally say and I feel him relax at my admission.

"Good." He lets out a sigh. "So we're clear what this is. I can't afford you getting attached. I decided a long time ago that my work is too important to have distractions, and you, baby girl, are a hell of a distraction."

His erection grows harder, pressing against my ass, and I take the opportunity to rub myself against him.

"It doesn't seem like your dick shares the same sentiment."

He tightens his grip on my neck. "You're right about that, which is why I'm offering to bend my rules for you, only until the festival. We'll have a little fun, fuck each other out of our systems, and then you'll leave. You'll move on to your next adventure while I stay here and dedicate the rest of my life to my work." He drags his hand from my neck, grazing his fingers over the side of my breast before settling at the apex of my thighs.

I wiggle a little more, my soaked panties an ever-present reminder of just how much my body craves him. At first, I feel a tiny twinge of disappointment at his offer, but who am I kidding? This is exactly what I've wanted since I met the guy, and he's being up front and honest about his boundaries. What else do I really expect?

"Can you handle that?" he presses, and I realize he's waiting for me to respond.

"Sounds perfect. When do we start?"

"If we do this, then I'm not going to hold back from taking you exactly how I want. Does that scare you?"

"No," I answer immediately because the only thing that could scare me about Leo is missing the chance to be with him, of living my whole life with the regret of not listening to my entire body, which is screaming and begging me to say *yes*.

"I won't coddle you, and I won't give in to your bratty demands for attention—"

"I don't want you to."

He shakes his head, like he's frustrated that I'm being so agreeable, like he wants me to say no and make the decision easy for him. "I will punish you when you act out, but I'll only push you as far as I know you can handle ..."

"I know that. I trust you." My words come out in a whisper as a rush of adrenaline soars through me, lighting me up with excitement.

"Fuck. Why do you have to be so goddamn perfect?" he grunts, blowing a heavy breath through his nose. I feel it on my neck, and I shiver at the rush of warmth.

My legs fall open, begging him to touch me. I hear him stifle a groan just as a hard yank pulls the fishing rod, jolting me forward with it and startling us both.

"Holy shit ... I think ..."

I tighten my grip to keep it from flying away, but suddenly, the tension is too strong.

Leo quickly jumps in, shaking the cobwebs of lust from his brain and grabbing the pole to hold it steady. "Looks like you got a bite."

CHAPTER TWENTY-ONE

Ivy

"You look ridiculous." I laugh as I attempt to wipe the mud from his face, but only manage to smear it in his eye.

Leo winces and tries to wipe it with the back of his arm, but it's no use; he's got mud on top of mud caked all over him.

"Well, if you had listened and watched where you were stepping, maybe I wouldn't have needed to break your fall."

"You should've seen the look on your face. I think you slipped in slow motion. I think it took you an entire minute to finally hit the ground." I hold my side as I double over laughing. "You looked like a cartoon character running in place."

"I'm glad that my self-sacrifice amuses you. Next time, I'll let you eat the mud and spare myself. Hell, maybe I'll even take a video so I can enjoy it again and again." Leo wraps an arm around me, pulling me into his cold, muddy torso, and I squeal, pretending to get away from him.

"No, you won't." I poke him in the ribs, and he jumps. He's much more ticklish than I anticipated. "You don't have a mean bone in your body, especially when it comes to seeing me hurt."

He presses a kiss to my soaking wet hair, his lips lingering a little longer than usual, as if he's savoring the feeling of finally being able to touch me. "You're right about that. I'll throw myself over every mud puddle I come across if it means you don't get a speck on your shoe. Now, help me get this door open, will you? Before I make an even bigger mess."

After I reeled in my fish, the rain started pouring so hard that we could barely see. Of course, Leo wouldn't let me help him paddle, saying that I'd only slow him down. He insisted on rowing us to safety, instantly going from dangerous and flirty back to his rigid protector self, which seem to be Leo Kingsley's only two speeds.

I help him shuck off his mud-soaked boots and place them in a neat pile by the door. If I've learned anything from staying here, it's that this man is a neat freak, and he'd never be able to relax, knowing there's a mess strewn about.

A pile of soggy clothes lands beside me with a loud thwack. When I glance up and see Leo stepping out of his soaking wet pants, I nearly combust right there.

Nothing could've prepared me for the image of this sexy-as-sin man, shirtless, nearly pants-less, with that dusting of hair across his broad chest, which is built to perfection. He's exactly how I envision a man to look. My cheeks heat as I remember all the things he said to me before the clouds opened up and decided to quite literally rain on my parade.

He pushes his pants down to his feet and steps out of

them, his erection tenting beneath the black boxer briefs, and my mouth actually waters from the sight. This man is built like a fucking Greek god, and I don't know how he's managed to stay single for so long. What is wrong with the women around here? One look at that sculpted chest, and I am absolutely feral.

My eyes catch on the crescent-shaped scar on his thigh, and I reach a hand down to trace it. "I haven't seen this scar before. What happened?"

He catches my hand, bringing it up to his lips. "I broke my leg when I was a kid. Compound fracture. It hurt like hell." He plants a gentle kiss on my hand as his eyes darken with need. "Is that really what you want to talk about right now? Because I sure as fuck don't," he growls as his eyes drop to his massive erection, a bead of pre-cum already leaking from the tip that's sticking out above his waistband.

I lick my lips, remembering the way he tasted last night as my pussy starts to throb with desire. Holy shit, this man is going to absolutely destroy me, and I can hardly wait. My lack of response and deer-in-headlight stare at his dick is the only answer he needs.

"Shower. Now," he grunts, pulling me up to him before his lips find mine. His soft lips cover mine in needy kisses as he fists a hand in my messy, wet hair, pressing us closer.

I begin stripping off my own wet clothes, our lips only breaking apart long enough to pull my shirt over my head. He pushes my shorts down to my feet, and I toss my shirt behind me, leaving a trail of soaked clothes in our path as we kiss our way through the hallway. So much for my attempt at a neat pile.

"Fuck, I've been dreaming of this moment for so long. I can't believe this is finally happening."

I give my nonverbal agreement by tightening my legs around his waist as he carries me through his bedroom and straight to the shower.

He sets me down gently before turning on the shower. Steam floats in the air around us, and I catch sight of myself in the mirror—mud smeared across my forehead, hair a tangled mess with random leaves sticking out. I can't help but wonder what Leo sees when he looks at me. I'm a mess in every sense of the word, but somehow, I don't feel like it when I'm with him. When I'm with Leo, I feel like I'm smart enough to do anything I want, free to try things out, and patient to see things through.

For the first time in my life, I feel like the parts of me that I have always considered my weaknesses could actually be my strengths. Like no matter what, he'll catch me if I fall.

I feel so beautiful and desired when he looks at me, especially the way he's looking at me now.

Leo takes a step toward me, pulling me closer, and traces over the muddy, wet fabric of my bra. "You're quite a mess, aren't you, baby girl?" His eyes catch mine in the reflection of the mirror, as if he knows what I was just thinking, and his lips pull into a smirk. "But you're my mess, and there isn't a thing about you that I'd change." He picks a leaf from my hair and tosses it into the trash can. "Well, maybe just the parts that aren't attached."

I slap his chest playfully, pushing him away, but he catches my hand and tugs me closer, so close that I feel the heat radiating off his skin. My eyes drift to his erection, and I swallow a gulp.

"We don't have to ..." He closes his eyes, taking a long inhale when my hand grazes over his hard length. "Fuck, just when I start to feel like I'm being too much, you're always one step ahead of me."

He doesn't wait for me to respond before flicking the hook of my bra and shoving my panties down to my feet. And then he's pulling me under the steamy shower stream, and our naked bodies slip and slide against each other, our bodies saying all the things our words can't.

He lathers shampoo in his palms and gestures for me to spin around. I can't help but laugh because of course this man would insist on washing me too. Hell, I think it's just as much for him as it is for me. He works his fingers through my thick strands, massaging my head with the utmost care as he washes my scalp with careful precision.

All while completely ignoring the rest of me as my pussy clenches in eager anticipation, waiting not so patiently for her turn for attention.

"I can wash my own hair, Leo. I don't need you to do it for me."

"And then you'd be depriving me of doing something I wanted. Let me take care of you. We're in no rush."

He presses a light kiss on my neck before guiding my head back underneath the warm shower stream. It feels heavenly. All my senses are on edge as the warm water and fragrant soap create an extra layer of arousal. My clit throbs, and my nipples stand painfully erect as Leo massages the sudsy soap over my shoulders and arms, touching me everywhere, except where I crave it most.

It's torturous and euphoric at the same time, and I don't

know how much more I can take. And now, I'm thinking two can play this game.

I squirt a handful of soap in my palm and begin massaging my hands down his broad shoulders, over his pecs, stopping when I get to his lower abdomen. Holy hell, this man is built. I don't think I took the time to appreciate how immaculate his body is before, but now that I'm seeing him—feeling him rather—with the lights on, I feel infinitely inferior, standing next to him.

I reach for his cock, but Leo moves out of the way, blocking me.

"Not so fast. Let me at least finish cleaning you before you attempt to get yourself dirty again."

"Now, you're just being mean." I cross my arms over my chest and turn my back to him when I feel a sharp slap on my ass cheek, stinging pain radiating for only a moment before the soft brush of his palm returns, rubbing the pain away.

I glance over my shoulder, finding him wearing an amused smirk.

"Oh, come on, baby girl. Don't pout. I promise I'll make the wait more than worth it."

He tugs my elbow, spinning me back to face him, and his hands continue their perusal, tracing across my belly.

"Fuck, your body is perfect. I knew it would be, but somehow seeing it in person is so much better than any of my fantasies."

"So, you did fantasize about me?"

He tightens his grip on my hip as he trails the other along my collarbone, his eyes devouring me as he drinks me in with his dark gaze. "You have no fucking idea how many times I fantasized about you, baby girl, how many times I stroked myself, thinking of these perfect tits bouncing above me as you rode my cock ..." He closes his eyes for only a moment, as if remembering, and then his touch deepens as he slides his hand from my hip down to my ass, where he grips me in an almost-painful squeeze.

"I've dreamed of this moment, where I can touch you, possess you, mark you as my own, and now that I have you, I intend to savor every fucking minute of it. So, don't you dare rush me while I appreciate the most beautiful woman I've ever seen. I promise to make it worth your while, but you're going to have to trust me. Do you trust me, Ivy?"

I wet my lips and nod my head ever so slightly as Leo brushes a knuckle over my sensitive clit, making me buckle forward at his faint touch. Holy fuck, talk about pent-up energy. The man's barely touched me, and I'm already on the verge of completely falling apart.

"This pussy is so goddamn tempting. Fuck, you're so beautiful and ..."

I suck in a breath, and Leo's eyes grow darker as he lathers more soap on his hands, taking a moment to stroke himself with one hand while he massages my ass with the other.

Steam billows in the air around us, and the warm heat has my body feeling so relaxed and boneless. I press my thighs together, feeling the slickness of my arousal between my legs as my clit pulses with need.

"Fuck, you've got the prettiest tits I've ever seen, and this ass is just begging to be spanked."

He tightens his grip on my ass as he draws a line between my breasts with his thumb sending a jolt of pleasure straight to my aching clit. His massive cock slides against my belly, grazing the bottom swell of my breasts. His pre-cum is slick on my skin, and my mouth waters at the memory of his taste. I'd only have to hinge at my waist, and I could have his cock in my mouth ...

He must sense my idea because before I can act on my impulse, he moves his hand from my ass to grip the back of my neck. "Don't get any ideas. I know your pussy is so needy right now, and I'd hate for you to miss out on yet another orgasm. I can do this all day, so you can either play nice or I can draw this out as long as it takes." He lifts my chin, guiding my gaze to meet his, and his eyes stare into mine, searing this moment into my memory forever.

He traces a thumb over my hardened nipple, and my head falls back as I let out a faint whimper of relief.

I can feel a slight tremor in his hands as he grips me tighter, like he's holding on to the last bit of restraint he has. "Fucking hell, baby girl, how am I supposed to keep it together when you make noises like that?" he growls, and then he's palming my breast as his fist tightens in my hair, and his mouth is on my neck, kissing and sucking.

I dig my nails into his thick hair, arching my back as he devours me, no doubt leaving a trail of evidence everywhere he kisses.

"I've never needed to have my cock inside anyone like I do right now."

"So, do it. Fuck me already. What are you waiting for?"

He pauses, looking up at me, a wolfish smile stretching across his face. "There's that smart mouth that I love. I was wondering how long it would take before you broke your silence."

His fingers lace together with mine as he pins my arms

above my head, pressing me against the cold tiles. He peppers my skin with painful pinches of teeth and soft, soothing licks as he feasts on every inch of my skin like he's worshipping my body with his tongue.

Our bodies move against each other, slick with arousal as the steamy water falls around us, rinsing all the suds away. It's an intoxicating mix of pain and pleasure, and it lights up every one of my senses, bringing me to a new level of heightened awareness. I've never been kissed like this, and I know that he's ruining me for every kiss that will follow. And still, I don't care. I'm a glutton in his arms, greedy to soak up every touch, every kiss, every moan until he has nothing left to give me.

I grind my clit against his leg, needing any friction I can get to ease the pressure growing between my legs as he trails hungry kisses along my collarbone. Between the possessive sucking and biting, there's no doubt I'll wear his marks as souvenirs, and that thought only makes me wetter.

I want him to mark me, so when this is all over, I can look in the mirror and know that it was real, that it wasn't a dream, that passion can feel this explosive and euphoric.

He cups my breast, and then he slides his hand down lower, his thumb circling my belly button as he continues to tease me with every brush of his skin. "I have no business touching you this way. I shouldn't be doing this with you. I shouldn't even be allowing myself to think of all the things I want to do with you ..." His voice comes out in a croak, and I don't know why, but the thought of him struggling so much, fighting with his own internal set of rules, makes this feel that much hotter.

I bite my lip, my gaze meeting his as I part my legs a little more.

Leo's eyes grow darker, taking in my naked curves like he's trying to memorize every inch of my skin and burn it into his memory forever. "I don't know how I got so lucky ... but holy fuck ..."

He grazes a thumb ever so gently over my throbbing clit in a quick little flick, but that's all it takes to make my back arch as pleasure rips through me.

"I should build an altar to worship this pussy; it's so pretty."

He falls to his knees as the mist of the shower stream falls all around us. He hooks my knee behind his head, bringing my pussy right to his face, and blows a cool breath over my throbbing clit before going in for his first taste.

"Jesus Christ, baby girl, your pussy is so fucking sweet," he moans as he licks me and sucks me in delicate strokes, teasing and giving me what I want, all at the same time.

Pleasure racks through my body as he flicks his tongue over my sensitive clit, and I'm thankful he's supporting me, so I don't lose my balance. I dig my fingernails into the soft skin on Leo's back as waves of pleasure shoot through me.

"Whoa now. For someone who talks a big game, I'd expect you to last longer than two seconds. I'm just getting warmed up."

The vibration of from laugh has me seeing stars as every nerve in my body stands on end.

I tighten my grip around his neck as he dips back down to taste me. He teases me, circling his tongue around my aching clit, every touch adding a layer of arousal that builds low in my belly. It's torturous and satisfying, and it's almost too much to take ... but I still can't get enough.

He's pushing me to my limit and showing me just how much pleasure is possible. He's opening my eyes to a whole new world of satisfaction. I feel like I've transcended into another dimension, hovering over my body because there's no way sex has ever felt anything like this. I think he's creating new nerve endings down there as he devours me, rewarding my mewls of pleasure with the deep strokes of pressure to my clit, bringing me to that euphoric place on the edge of combustion.

"See what you can have when you behave? If you listen to Daddy, I'll kiss your pretty little pussy like this every day." He slides a finger inside me, then adds a second, and my back arches even more, so desperate for relief.

"That's it, baby girl. Your pussy is so wet and tight around my fingers." He dives back down this time, licking me exactly where I want him to, as he curls his fingers inside me, sending jolts of pleasure ricocheting down my legs.

"Oh God. Yes!" My moan comes out like a plea, echoing off the tiles, and hearing myself get so loud has me turned on even more.

I'm right there, so close to falling apart. My nipples ache to be touched, and as if reading my mind, he slides his free hand up my body, giving each of my nipples a hard pinch. The sensation of pain, mixed with the pleasure growing between my legs, has my eyes rolling back in my head. My legs start to quiver and buckle in anticipation, and I don't know how I'll be able to keep from collapsing, but I trust Leo. I know he won't let me fall.

"Is my little brat ready to come now?" he growls out, pinching my nipple again.

"Yes." My voice is a whisper; it's all I can manage.

"Come on then. Beg me." He pauses for only a moment, commanding my full attention. "Be a good girl and beg me to let you come."

He licks me again this time, sucking my clit into his mouth and giving it the tiniest nibble.

Oh my God. Wherever this man learned to fuck, it should be required education for all men. He's doing God-level moves that I didn't even know existed before now.

"Fuck. Ah. Please!" I cry out.

"Please what?" He pauses again, and I'm so close that I can hardly form words; all this teasing has my mind in a jumbled mess.

"Please. Please. Please, Daddy. Please let me come," I cry out in a breathy whimper, and that must be the right answer.

Curling his fingers with impossible precision, he sucks my clit as an orgasm rips through me, so intense that I swear it has to come from the depths of my soul.

I let out a moan, riding my orgasm out as my legs shake and my toes curl, but Leo doesn't stop. I've somehow managed to wrap my other leg around his neck, too, so the only thing keeping me upright is the force of him holding me against the wall. And, fuck, he doesn't even seem to be struggling to do it, reminding me once again just how powerful he is.

"Come on, baby. You can give me one more. Be a good girl and come on my face one more time."

He licks me in slow, steady strokes with his flat tongue as he holds me up with one arm and curls his fingers inside me with the other. It's a skill set I never knew possible and yet another thing that Leo Kingsley has mastered.

I grip my fingers in his thick hair as pleasure tears through me in every direction, and in the next breath, I'm coming again and then again until my screams turn into strained wheezes.

Holy shit.

I am a boneless pile of flesh, satisfied, sated, and fucked within an inch of my life. And I know without a shadow of a doubt that nothing will ever be the same.

CHAPTER TWENTY-TWO

Leo

"Are you sure you're okay?" I ask, taking the inhaler from Ivy and placing it on the bathroom counter.

"I'm fine. Really. Just got a little too excited. I promise I'm fine. I didn't even need the inhaler that time." Ivy stares up at me with her big amber eyes, and I finally let myself relax.

Thank God I stocked up on rescue inhalers after I found out about her asthma. I placed them all over the house, just in case she ever had another episode. Luckily, I even put one in my bathroom, though I could never have expected to need it ... especially like this.

Ivy's wrapped up in a fluffy white robe, and her cheeks are pink from the shower steam. She looks so fucking cute that I can hardly contain myself. I've never lost control like that, but having her wet and naked, pressed up against me, was all it took to short-circuit my brain. It's been a long time coming, and now that I know how incredible her pussy tastes and all the noises she makes when she comes ... fuck if I'm ever going to be able to resist her again.

I might as well hang it up because this woman's got me wrapped around her little finger so tightly that I think I'd do anything to make her smile. The realization is surprisingly freeing, but I don't have time to dig into that right now because I'm too busy feeling guilty for being so negligent with her.

What would've happened if I'd slipped? Or if I'd dropped her? Not that I was anywhere close to doing so—hell, I could've held her like that all day, no problem—but what if she had flipped over my head or something? She could've been seriously injured, and it would've been all my fault.

"Fuck, Ivy. I'm so sorry. I got carried away. I didn't mean to hurt you." I kiss the top of her head, smoothing her wet hair from her face.

"You didn't hurt me." She laughs, running a hand over my jaw. "You were perfect. I just need to build up a little more stamina before you deliver the holy-shit package again."

"I could've hurt you ..." My voice trails off as I bend down to face her.

She rolls her eyes. "But you didn't. Why can't you let yourself enjoy this? Just be happy for once without punishing yourself or feeling guilty about it."

She slides a hand over my chest like she's testing to see if I'll bite, but I'm going to need a little time to come down after going from on top of the world to sheer panic in less than five seconds.

I grab her hand from my chest and kiss it, letting her

touch soothe me as all my endorphins start to come down and level out.

Dom drop isn't an entirely new experience for me, but I've never felt it this deeply before right now. I suppose it's only natural to feel the effects of a sudden change in emotions, especially after I've spent so much time building it up beforehand.

"Hey, are *you* okay?" she finally asks, breaking the silence between us. She tilts her head, assessing me, her eyebrows knitted together in confusion.

I blow out a breath, and I'm just about to lie, to tell her I'm fine and it's no big deal, but there's something about her that makes me feel safe to let her in, and fuck if that isn't refreshing. It's exactly what I've been missing ... *she's* exactly what I've been missing. I haven't felt this comfortable in my own skin since ... Heidi, the only other woman I've shown this side of myself to, ended things all those years ago, her hurtful words leaving scars of shame so deep that it altered my very being.

"I ... I just need a minute to calm down after that. I'm kind of having a war in my brain right now, and I think I panicked when you started wheezing. Sometimes, when people are in heightened states of emotion, like the extremes I tend to prefer during sexual acts ... the comedown can feel like a lot. It's, uh ... it's called a drop."

I clear my throat, feeling so vulnerable and mildly embarrassed, but to Ivy's credit, she doesn't even break eye contact. She stands and leads me to the bed, and then she climbs on my lap, wrapping herself around me.

"What are you doing—" I start to ask, but she cuts me off.

"I'm cuddling you. What does it look like I'm doing?"

"Why?" I ask, as she straddles a leg on either side of me and nuzzles into my chest.

"Because you look like you could use a hug and also because I want to."

I wrap an arm around her, squeezing her small body against me, and all my worries slowly melt away. I've never in my life felt so understood or seen, and who would've known that this little ball of sunshine and sarcasm would be the one to bring me to my knees?

Actually, I did.

The moment she kicked her sneakers on my dash and opened her smart mouth to argue, I knew I'd be a goner. But fuck if it isn't so much worse than I imagined.

"Why are you so goddamn perfect?" I ask, kissing her on top of her head. I don't even bother correcting myself or trying to backtrack because, honestly, that's how I feel.

She pulls away, breaking her death grip of a hug, wearing a satisfied smirk. "I just got a great idea ..."

"Oh, yeah? What's that?" I tuck a loose strand of hair behind her ear as I drink in her bare face, free of any makeup, not that she wears much anyway, but I love how clearly I can see her freckles right now.

"Can we have a movie night?" She claps her hands together at her chest as her eyes sparkle with excitement at the idea.

I don't know how anyone could tell her no. Not when something as menial as watching a movie has her this excited.

"Why don't I order us some dinner while you pick the movie?"

Her smile grows wider, and I can practically see the wheels spinning as she tries to pick the perfect movie for the occasion. "Can we have popcorn? And those chocolate-covered frozen raspberries you brought home last week?"

I nod, trying to hold back my grin. "If that's what you want, I'll place a grocery order right now."

She beams a smile and hugs me. "This is going to be so much fun."

I slap her ass, though the towel muffles the blow, so it isn't nearly as satisfying as I'd like. "Why don't you get dressed before I change my mind and tear that robe off of you?"

She hops off the bed, and tugs at the tie of her robe, making it fall open, revealing the shallow curve of her cleavage. "Is that supposed to be a threat? Because I can think of worse things ..." She kicks out her leg, parting the robe open further, and that pretty pussy of hers comes back into view.

I rake a hand over my face and stifle a growl. "Ivy ..."

"What?" She lets the robe fall down one of her shoulders, blinking up at me with big doe eyes. "Oops." The other side falls off her other shoulder, so her bare breasts are right in front of my face, and then she drops it to the floor completely.

I tighten my fists in the sheets as I drink in her perfect body—the subtle curve of her hips, those incredible tits that fit so perfectly in the palms of my hands, and the prettiest pussy in the whole goddamn world that's practically begging to be played with.

Just when I think I've pushed her too far, the little minx has to push back even harder. I shouldn't be surprised. It's one of the things I love the most about her. Ivy isn't afraid to be herself, and she damn sure isn't afraid to take what she wants.

"Get over here. On your knees," I command, dropping my towel from around my waist.

I'm already hard—or still hard, however you want to look at it. I feel like we've been in a perpetual state of edging from the moment we met, and it's going to take more than a few happy endings to get each other out of our system. Hell, at this rate, I'll be licking my wounds for the rest of my pathetic life.

She's worth it though ... a million times over.

With an almost-feverish excitement, she drops to her knees before me, and the sight nearly has my heart beating out of my chest.

"Is my needy little slut horny again already? You just can't get enough, can you, baby girl?" I ask, testing the waters to see how she'll react.

She swallows a gulp as her eyes widen, looking so fucking eager as she hangs on to my every word. And just like that, I know exactly what she needs from me—a little degradation, sandwiched between plenty of praise. And judging from the way she's looking at me right now, my guess is that she's only just realized it herself.

I grip my cock and line my head up with her mouth as I stand over her. The sight of her naked and on her knees, so eager for my cock, is enough to send me over the edge, but this time, there won't be any interruptions.

I fist my hand through her hair. "You drive me so fucking crazy with that smart little mouth. You're desperate for more already, aren't you? Open up and show me then. Show me how bad you want my cock, baby girl."

She parts her lips, and I slide my cock over her hot, wet tongue. When I hit the back of her throat, I see her lips twitch in a smile. She braces herself with one hand behind my thigh and uses the other to grip the base of my shaft as she flattens her tongue and sucks me down her throat.

"Fuck, baby, just like that."

I hold the back of her head as I fuck her mouth, loving how enthusiastic she is. She keeps her eyes trained on me, watching my every reaction. She's so eager to please me, and it feels so fucking good to finally let my walls down, to be seen for who I really am. For better or for worse, she welcomes both sides of me, and she doesn't make me feel guilty for my kinks ... hell, I think she might even enjoy them too.

She's so greedy to take all of me, despite gagging as my cock fills up her sassy mouth. I wrap her hair around my arm, loving the visual, the teary-eyed look of pleasure she wears as she looks up at me from her knees. I don't hold back as I drive deeper down her throat. Her tits bounce with every thrust I make, and my fingers itch to touch her again.

I let my hand drift from the back of her head and cup her breast in my palm, and she lets out a moan of pleasure before swirling her tongue around the head of my cock.

I nearly black out.

Fuck. I need more. I need to feel her. I need to taste her.

Before I realize what I'm doing, I'm lifting her off the floor like she weighs nothing and carrying her to the bed. The momentary loss of her warm, wet mouth gives my cock a much-needed moment to recover as I flip her around, and then her mouth's back, sucking my cock again, but now I've got my face buried in her pussy, and I'm ready to impart my own form of torture.

She moans when I flick her sensitive clit with the tip of

my tongue, and I don't hold back. She's already warmed up, and judging by the way she's grinding herself on my face, I'd say she's pretty close.

That makes two of us.

I flick my tongue side to side, keeping a steady rhythm as she grinds her needy pussy over my face, coating me in her intoxicating arousal.

Her body is so soft and malleable as I toss her around and maneuver her however I like, palming her tits and squeezing her ass every chance I get. I've got my face buried beneath her pussy, and thanks to a lifetime of swimming, I don't even feel the urge to come up for air. Hell, I might risk never breathing again if it means I don't have to stop tasting her. Who needs oxygen when you can drown yourself in pussy?

I slap her ass, she lets out a little yelp of surprise, and I immediately feel her get wetter. It's a satisfaction I've never known and all the encouragement I need to not hold back on any of my desires. My girl loves this shit just as much as I do.

"Fuck, baby, your pussy is so wet for me. You're making a mess all over my face. Do you like having your face fucked while Daddy licks your pussy? Fuck, you're such a dirty little slut, aren't you, baby girl?"

She nods her head, and with a renewed determination, she cups my balls in her free hand as she swirls her tongue over the head of my cock. The combination has my release rushing to the surface.

"Fuck." I let out my own moan, biting my cheek to hold myself back a little longer.

I'm so close, but I'm not quite ready for this to end yet.

I grip her hips, lifting her just enough to change the

pressure of my tongue, and lower her back down as I lick her in deep, steady strokes.

"Oh my God," she croaks.

Fuck, I wish I could see the look on her face as I repeat the movement, creating a new rhythm that already has her toes curling as her orgasm builds.

She likes when I toss her around like a little rag doll. Good to know.

I repeat the movement again and again, as if she weighs nothing, increasing the pressure of my tongue on her clit little by little, until she's writhing and trembling over me. I smile a satisfied smirk, feeling like the luckiest man in the goddamn world as I give her clit one final flick of my tongue, and then she's falling apart, moaning around my cock. She swallows her moan, and that little spasm of her throat is all it takes to send me over the edge.

I come undone.

"Fuck, baby, I'm coming," I croak out as I grip her ass, holding her steady against me as I completely fall apart.

She deepens her strokes of my cock, sucking me further down her throat as I shoot the liquid heat of my release right down her throat. And just like last time, she takes every single drop.

We both sag in relief, and I reach down and pull her up so that she's lying upright on my chest. Our skin is damp with sweat, and I brush her loose waves from her face, planting a gentle kiss on her forehead.

"You're so fucking incredible. Holy shit, I don't know how I got so lucky."

A lazy smile pulls at her lips, and she leans up, tracing the ridge of my jaw with her finger. "You're not so bad yourself, Boss Daddy."

I shake my head and laugh. "What am I going to do with you?"

She leans in, brushing the tip of her nose against mine, and laughs. "What do you mean? You promised me a movie night. No takebacks and don't even think about falling asleep because I've already decided on what we're watching." She jumps up and grabs her robe off the floor, giggling as she dodges my pathetic attempt to catch her before she takes off down the hall to no doubt set up the perfect movie night.

I grab my phone off my side table, and I swipe open the grocery delivery app. I add Ivy's chocolate raspberries to my cart and fall back on the bed, wondering how the fuck I've already fallen so hard, this fast.

Holy shit, I'm in trouble ...

CHAPTER TWENTY-THREE

Ivy

"Good morning, Jeff. Hey, is that a new tie?" Leo waves to the smiling stranger in the lobby as we wait for the elevator.

"Good morning, Francis. Your hair looks nice today. Hey, thanks for getting me that report last week on such short notice. Your hard work doesn't go unnoticed."

I look up at him in confused bewilderment and almost don't recognize him. Rather than the uptight boss, dressed to the nines in a suit, Leo stands beside me in a casual navy polo shirt and dark gray khaki chino pants that hug his ass in all the right places. Not to mention his signature early morning scowl's been replaced with a smile.

A smile.

I've seen him flash those pearly whites at least three times, making it an all-time record high. And he's chatty. I think he's managed to greet everyone he's seen within a ten-foot radius with some kind of personal message. It's like he's done a complete one-eighty, although I don't even think he's aware of it.

I think he's just in a good mood.

I guess finally having your dick sucked after a long hiatus will do that to a man.

Don't get me wrong; I had my theory that all he needed was to get laid, but I had no idea it'd have this much of a change on him. Come to think of it, I don't think I've seen him take a single antacid since last week.

I knew I was a miracle worker. I happen to believe that a good orgasm will solve most of the world's problems, but nobody listens when I tell them that.

The elevator dings its arrival, and we step inside. Like every morning, I turn to face the window as we climb up the building, giving me the best view of the falls below.

"I never get tired of that view," Leo sighs. "It's certainly not a bad way to start your morning."

He sips his coffee from his favorite mug he brought from home, making a sound of satisfaction. I could be mistaken, but I could've sworn I saw him add a spoonful of sugar to his cup as he made mine.

So, orgasms and a touch of sugar are all it takes to keep the curmudgeon at bay. I'll have to make a note of it, should anyone need it after I'm gone.

My stomach drops at the thought of leaving, making the pancakes I had for breakfast churn in my belly—another surprise from Leo. I swear he told me he wasn't a morning person, but I guess only under the right circumstances ...

"You coming, baby?" he says it like he's repeating himself, holding out his hand for me.

I take his hand and let him lead me through the office.

Baby. Baby girl. Brat. I've never had a pet name before. I could get used to being treated so ... how is it that he treats me? He's bossy and domineering one minute, scolding me and completely annoyed, and the next, he's taking off my shoes, making me breakfast, and surprising me with coffee.

I can never keep up, but I love it all the same, the way I feel like I'm the center of his universe, like he's thinking of me at all times, even when he's supposed to be working. I see it in the way he looks at me, like I'm the only one in the room, like he'd move mountains just to give me a better view of the moon.

No one has ever given me so much attention. Not my parents ... and certainly not anyone I've ever dated.

Maybe it's because I was born a twin, but even as a small child, I felt like my parents' love was divided between us rather than multiplied.

But not Leo. Leo treats me like I'm the only woman to have ever existed, giving me his full attention. Whether he's annoyed with me or comforting me, everything he does is with intention. And when he looks at me, it's like he actually sees me for who I am. The only other person in the world who's ever understood me was my sister, and it's not exactly like she had a choice; we shared the same womb after all.

It's like the universe decided to play some kind of cruel joke, giving me everything I never knew I wanted at the worst time imaginable, making me choose between honoring my sister's memory and whatever *this* is.

As if there's even a choice. A fresh pang of grief smacks me square in the chest as I realize how badly this could end. Because the only thing worse than walking away from someone you care about is having them ripped away against your will.

I don't think I'd survive losing anyone else, and I can already see the writing on the wall of where this is headed, but for the life of me, I can't make myself stop. Not before I have to.

Maybe I'm a sadist, or I just have an affinity for the drama of it all, but either way, there's only one way off this train, and I'm not ready to take that leap just yet. So, instead, I'll enjoy my distractions while I still can because if losing my twin sister taught me anything, it's that life will knock me down soon enough.

"Hey, Ricky. How was your weekend? Did you get any projects done?" Leo asks as we pass Ricky's desk.

He glances up, looking confused, and I give him a slight wave. "I, uh ... yeah. I finished changing the entire fleet's costumes from orange to blue. And I spent a little time in my garden."

"That's great. I'm glad you were able to make time for doing what you love. It bleeds over into your work—that's what my dad always says anyway." Leo rubs a thumb along the inside of my wrist, like he can't help but touch me.

"Everything okay with you, boss? You're not firing me, are you? Because I'm really sorry about the whole ... well, everything that happened the other night. I got carried away, but I promise it'll never happen again—"

Leo holds up his hand. "Forget about it, Ricky. I know I have. Besides, maybe it just means we need more social events. Let's not wait so long before we do something again, okay?"

"Who are you, and what have you done with our boss?" a woman asks from behind a pile of file folders on her desk.

Leo lets out a laugh. "I'm the new and improved Leo Kingsley, at your service. Get used to it. Things are going to get a lot more fun around here."

"Well, damn, who knew all this time, all he needed was steady sex?" someone whispers.

"Right?" another whispering voice agrees.

"I heard that," Leo says loud enough for everyone to hear, and the chatter goes silent as he leads me into his office, where he doesn't immediately pull the shades.

Like everyone else, I stare at him with my mouth agape, wearing a look of utter confusion.

He pulls up the big chair beside his desk chair and takes a seat. "Are you going to stand there with your mouth hanging open, or are we going to finish planning this festival?"

Don't get me wrong; I like the grumpy curmudgeon Leo, but this guy right here is taking my attraction to an entirely different level.

Seeing the way he handles his work with such attention to detail and professionalism, how competent and smart he is, always asking the right questions ... and his charisma ... it's no wonder the man's has a shot at becoming the next CEO. People practically throw themselves into action as soon as he asks them to do something; everyone's always so eager to please him.

And it isn't hard to see why.

As much as I love to get under his skin, it's the way he

looks at me after I do what he asked—like remembering to pack my inhaler when I leave the house or keeping my shoes stored in the designated shoe basket he bought just for me— that makes me feel so appreciated. I feel so supported and seen, and I know I could try anything, and he'd still be standing on the sidelines, cheering me on.

I could get used to having someone look at me like that, like he's proud of me. It makes me want to do more positive things, like plan for my future.

For the first time in my life, I've found myself actually considering what I want to be when I grow up, as if I'm not the twenty-two-year-old adult who's been living on her own for the last four years, all while working odd jobs to pay for college classes and picking up the tab for my mother's medical bills.

I know I signed a contract to work whatever hospitality job they need me to do when I get to Romania, but maybe I can pick an area to specialize in and see where it takes me.

I've never been picky before, always taking whatever job paid the best while giving me the most freedom, but now, I'm starting to wonder if that was just me wanting to avoid the commitment of having to stick to only one thing.

I don't like being tied down to any job, anyplace, and certainly not to anyone ... do I?

Maybe I don't know anymore. It's not like I have to decide either way. The decision's already been made for me in the form of a list, scribbled in pink marker by a teenage girl. That list is calling the shots, and I carry it in my overall pocket, right next to my heart, as a constant reminder.

"It looks like you two have been busy," Frank says as the board meeting comes to an end.

I look down at my page of notes—or the page of *doodles* in the place of the notes I was supposed to be taking. I guess I was daydreaming just now.

It was just a financial something anyhow, not anything to do with me ... unless they discussed the budget for the festival, which is directly related to me. Oh well, I'm sure Leo took his own notes.

"We've nailed down all the food vendors and invited all the top-rated food trucks in a hundred-mile radius, and I've ordered enough apple butter for everyone who buys a ticket to have as a free gift." He wraps his arm around me. "Actually, that was Ivy's idea."

Frank just smiles as he looks at Leo with a newfound appreciation, or maybe he's also thinking the same thing everyone else is. Either way, it's like the worry he's been carrying around for his son melts away, making the lines on his face disappear.

"I'm so proud of you, son. Proud of you both actually. Keep up the good work. I can't wait to hear what else you've got planned for this year's Phantom Fest." And then he turns to leave.

I spin to face Leo, who looks so relieved, so happy that he's almost unrecognizable, and it's crazy to think that I somehow had any part of making that happen. For the first time in my whole damn life, I finally recognize this invisible feeling I've been chasing.

It's purpose.

CHAPTER TWENTY-FOUR

Leo

"You're really good at this." I look up from the planning spreadsheet Ivy created, mapping out every detail, down to the allocated bathroom breaks for the festival performers and three alternate plans of action if a show goes on for longer than expected.

To say this will be the biggest Phantom Festival we've ever had is an understatement. I had no idea what I was doing by giving Ivy free rein of the planning, but seeing the details from her imagination laid out into tactful plans feels like pure alchemy, like she's brought our little festival to life with the twitch of her nose.

"Don't act so surprised. I might not look like I have my shit together, but I can be responsible when I need to be, especially when it's something that's important to me."

She rolls her eyes and tosses a throw pillow in my direction. I duck just in time, and it knocks down an unlit candle and several framed photos.

I shoot her a warning glare, and her shoulders creep up her neck.

"Oops." She bites her bottom lip, looking so fucking cute and not at all apologetic—which I can tell by that crooked grin she's hiding and the way her eyes sparkle with mischief, like she's begging me to do something, to react and give her what she wants. What we both so desperately want.

It's been almost a week since she had my cock in her mouth right here on this couch, and I'll admit, it's been the highlight reel playing in the back of my mind ever since. As much as I'd love to cancel all our plans, lock the doors, close all the windows, and do nothing but fuck her until I get this feral urge out of my system, I've actually had to work.

This festival is important to my family and to this town, and for the first time in my life, I want to be a part of creating an experience that serves no other purpose other than to be fun. It's a novel idea to me, but being around Ivy Lane is like sitting in the sun and expecting not to feel warm. She has this effect on me, like she's thawing out my frozen heart, making me all warm and tingly and filled with ... hope? All I know is, I've found myself examining my motives for everything I do, asking myself the hard questions about why I want the things I want, and challenging my beliefs about everything.

I can't say that it's been comfortable, though I suppose going from one extreme to another so quickly wouldn't be ... but there's a pleasure in the pain that's almost as addictive as Ivy herself.

A shard of glass hits the floor with a tink, and I lift an eyebrow as I send her a warning look, loving the way her eyes light up as she holds my gaze. The little brat is practically begging for a punishment.

"Do you really think that breaking my belongings is the right way to ask for attention?"

She shrugs like she can't be bothered to answer, knowing that her lack of response irritates me.

"Get up." My voice comes out clipped. "Come over here." I toss a throw pillow at my feet. "Get on your knees."

It takes a moment for my demand to register, but then her eyes widen, and she hops off her chair, moving to kneel on the pillow in front of me, her chest heaving just a little. I bet if I felt her pulse right now, I'd find it racing from excitement, and the thought of how eager my girl is to please me has my cock twitching behind my jeans.

We haven't gone past oral, not because I haven't wanted to, but because I've been holding out for the right moment. I want Ivy to feel sure about this because, truth be told, I'm happy with any scrap of her body she'll give me.

I slide my hand around the base of her neck, pulling her hair just hard enough to make her smile as I force her head up to look at me. Fuck, she's so pretty, sitting on her knees for me, looking like she'd love for me to shove my cock down her throat, make her drink my cum.

"Look at you, so desperate for my cock." I swipe my thumb over her full bottom lip, and her tongue traces behind my finger, wetting her lip in anticipation.

I unbuckle my belt with my free hand, then slide down my zipper, freeing my painful erection. Fuck, it feels so good to be longed for. No one's ever looked at me the way Ivy looks at me. It's like she can't get enough, and nothing I do is too much for her, rather it's the perfect amount.

I work my cock with my free hand, pulsing and pumping myself as I hold her chin steady in the other. I watch those shapely, pouty lips, so jealous of my hand, and her hands move to my thighs, ready to help me.

"What makes you think I should let you suck me off after you've been so disrespectful?"

She opens her mouth to argue, but I shake my head.

"You think I haven't noticed those little outfits you've been wearing to work all week."

I trail my hand down her neck, where I trace her delicate collarbone. I fucking love her neck, how fragile it is and the way her whole body responds when I touch it.

"You think I like the idea of everyone in the office looking at my girl?" I slide my hand further down her chest. "You think I want anyone knowing how fucking perfect these tits are?"

I flick my thumb over her hardened nipple, and her head falls back as she lets out a whimper. Then I pinch it, making her whole body jump.

"If you wanted my attention, you should have asked me nicely. There's no reason to throw pillows at my head." I tug her chin, directing her gaze to the shards of broken glass on the floor. "Just look at the mess you made. Are you even sorry?"

Her smirk, which she quickly tries to hide, is all the answer I need.

This fucking brat.

I am going to have so much fun with her punishment.

"Here's what I'm going to do." My fingers graze to her other breast and then back up to her neck. "I'm going to set a timer and let you suck my cock for five minutes, but after that, I get to play with you however I like. Is that a deal?"

She tilts her head to the side, as if she's considering.

"What if I don't want to stop after five minutes? What if I want to finish you off and make you come down my throat?"

A slow smile spreads over my face. "You will stop after five minutes. You remember what happened last time, don't you? Orgasms are only for good girls, and I can tell by the way you're squeezing your thighs together that your pussy is already wet and throbbing for me. So, if you want to come tonight, then you need to follow the rules. Understand?"

"Yes, Daddy." She wets her lips as she wraps one hand around my shaft while cupping my balls with the other.

I grab my phone and set a five-minute alarm just as her warm tongue licks up the base of my cock, swirling around the head before sucking me into her pretty little mouth.

"Fuuuck," I sigh as my head falls back against my chair, loving the feel of her mouth on me, loving how eagerly she takes me, like she can't get enough.

I don't know where this girl learned how to suck dick, but she should patent her technique and teach classes on it. She has no idea how much power she has over me in this moment. I think I'd give her anything she asked, and that thought is terrifying and exciting all the same. The rush I get from this exchange of power makes me feel so alive. One minute, I hold all the control, and the very next, she's flipped it as she brings me to the intersection of my deepest fantasies and the most euphoric pleasure I've ever felt.

My palms start to tingle as I fight to keep my composure, not wanting this to end. A fantasy of something I've always wanted to do flashes through my mind, pushing me closer and closer to the edge of my orgasm.

I grip her hair and tug to get her attention. "Slow down,

baby. I don't want this to end. Trust me, I've got big plans for you tonight," I say in a breathy pant.

Her round siren eyes meet mine, holding my gaze, and she starts to hum on my cock, alternating between sucking me down her throat and licking my head.

I try to slow my breathing, taking long, deep breaths through my nose as I clench my fists in a white-knuckled grip.

Glancing over at the timer, I notice there's one minute left.

I can do anything for one minute. *Come on, Leo. You can hold out.*

As much as I want to enjoy this fucking incredible view in front of me, I will my brain to think about work, spreadsheets ... Ricky fumbling through this morning's meeting ...

Pleasure builds at the base of my spine, and my mind flashes through a tornado of images. Some erotic memories of Ivy's body, naked and dripping wet as I devoured her pussy in the shower; or the way her perky little tits fit perfectly in the palms of my hands; the sated, glazed-over look in her eye after I made her come; mixed with images of spreadsheets and quarterly reports, flashes of rebranding our cleaning products line and packaging substrates ...

The swirl of chaos slows down my release, if only by a few seconds, as I dig my fingers into the arm of the chair, leaving a permanent indentation.

Just as my release threatens to explode, her mouth disappears, and I suck in a much-needed breath to steady me.

She works my length with her hands, and then her hot mouth is back. Only this time, I feel a strange texture coating her tongue. Little beads of something scrape along my shaft, and I'm about to ask her what it is when I feel a tiny pinch.

Suddenly, all the tiny beads pop and pinch in a rotating succession, creating a stinging vibration.

"What the fuck did you—" I startle in my seat, eyes flying open in surprise, only to find Ivy wearing a wicked grin.

I try to pull her off, but she just grips my shaft tighter, tugging my balls in an almost-painful grip as tiny explosions erupt all over my cock. There's no getting out of this. She has me right where she wants me, and all I can do is ride it out.

I'm racking my brain, trying to figure out what the fuck's in her mouth—all while holding in my orgasm that's only moments away—just as the five-minute timer rings.

She releases my cock with a gentle pop, wearing a smug grin, and pulls a little black package from her back pocket.

"How long have you been carrying Pop Rocks in your pocket, waiting to pull that stunt?" I swipe the package from her and shake it. "You think it's funny to prank me?"

"I just wanted a little treat." She makes a show of licking her lips before wiping her mouth with the back of her hand.

"Such a fucking brat. You're going to pay for that stunt tonight." I stand, pulling my pants up, but not buckling them, and then I lift her from the floor and toss her over my shoulder.

She lets out a little squeal and kicks her feet as I move down the hall, passing my bedroom until I'm in the library.

"Leo, wait. What are you doing? Why are we in the library?"

I pull the spine of the third book from the right corner, and a door pops open, revealing a dark staircase.

"What the hell? You have a secret staircase hidden

behind your library?" She kicks her legs, trying to break free. "Wait! Where are you taking me?"

I slap her ass, the sound echoing off the bare concrete walls as I walk us down the staircase, careful to follow every single step.

The room is nearly pitch-black, save for the dimly lit flame-free candles filling the corners, and it takes my eyes a few moments to adjust.

It's been far too long since I've had a reason to come down here, and, holy shit, if I'm not itching to finally let myself out of this cage and have some fun.

I set Ivy down carefully, placing my hands on her shoulders as I spin her to face the room. "This is where I come to play. I feel like it's time I finally showed it to you."

She sucks in a sharp breath, and, fuck, I wish I could be inside her head to know what she's thinking. Is it too much? Is she afraid? Does she want to leave?

Her eyes move to the Saint Andrew's Cross on the far wall and then to the rack of bondage equipment in all shapes and sizes.

"You really use all this stuff? I thought you were out of the game ... for, like ... a long time."

I shove my hands in my pockets, feeling more vulnerable than I ever have, hoping I haven't scared her off. "I was. This is from my previous life, when I had time to indulge in my fantasies."

She moves to the king-size bed in the middle of the room, tracing her fingers along the pillows. "Do all the homes in Ashford Falls come standard with a sex room, or did you have to pay extra for it?"

I laugh, relieved that she isn't too spooked, remembering

how Heidi seemed to enjoy it at first too ... until she didn't. But Ivy hasn't given me any reason to believe she doesn't like the way we play. The two women couldn't be any more different.

"I can't speak for everyone in town, but ... what people do in their own time is none of my business." I shrug and move to the bar cart to pour myself a whiskey. "It cost me a pretty penny to have everything custom-built ... but it was a worthy investment. You wouldn't believe the resale value you get, having a sex room in your basement."

Her eyebrows knit together like she's trying to figure out if I'm kidding, and it's so fucking cute that it takes all my strength not to kiss her right now.

"So, you brought me down here to *play*?"

I nod, giving her time and space to process everything, to consent whether she's interested in playing with me.

She picks up a rocks glass and dangles it in her fingers, her way of asking for a drink. "So ... how does this work?"

I take the glass from her and fill it with ice. I pour her a shot of gin, topping it with a mixture of lime juice and simple syrup and garnishing the glass with a lime wheel and a cherry.

"You tell me. We can go slow if you'd like, work you up to everything ... or we could just keep using our mouths on each other. I'm happy to have you in any way you'll give me. You're the one in control here, Ivy. You say the word, and I'll follow."

Her eyes twinkle as I pass her the drink. "I'm going to need to know all the choices before I agree."

"That can be arranged."

She sips her drink, eyeing me over the rim. "What if I want *you* to decide?"

A warm smile pulls at the corner of my lips. I take a sip of my whiskey, then loop a finger through her belt loop and tug her toward me. "I was hoping that's what you'd say. So, is that a yes?"

The air between us sizzles with anticipation and energy and promises of things we don't know about yet and everything in between. I drain my glass as I wait for her response, my skin buzzing with hope and excitement.

She flashes me a grin, her eyes flicking from my cock back to meet my gaze as she crosses her arms over her chest. "It's about time you finally caved. If only I had known you had all this hidden away, I wouldn't have been so impatient." She drains her glass and walks over to the bed, pulling herself up to sit on the edge. "All right, Boss Daddy, where do you want me?"

CHAPTER TWENTY-FIVE

Ivy

The words have barely left my lips before Leo's got me pinned underneath him.

I can feel his hard length pressing into me, and I can't imagine how needy he must be after my little performance upstairs. His body vibrates with desire as he cradles my neck in one hand and cups my cheek with the other.

His kiss tastes like relief, like a glass of cold water after walking through the desert on a hot day, relief with a hint of the whiskey he just had. He sucks my bottom lip into his mouth and bites down in a hard pinch, the metallic taste of blood adding another layer of desire between us.

"Fuck, I want you, Ivy. I want you so bad. It's all I think about; it's all I dream about," he whispers between frantic kisses, hands palming my ass and thighs as he pulls me closer.

I wrap my legs around his waist, craving friction and pressure from whatever piece of him I can get.

He slides his palm over the inside of my thigh, and I'm

already so close. I can still taste him on my tongue, and my pussy clenches with need.

"Are you on birth control?" he asks in a low growl as he teases my body, never touching me where I want him to.

"I ... I ... have an IUD," I pant as he kisses and sucks along my neck.

I love the way he kisses my body, branding me with hickeys and teeth marks, like he's claiming me. I want him to claim me. I want everyone to know I belong to him. I want to be a walking billboard with flashing neon lights, letting everyone I come across know that my body belongs to Leo Kingsley ... and maybe a little bit of my soul too.

"I've never been with anyone without wearing a condom ... and even then, it's been *a while*. I'm clean." He brushes a thumb across my cheek as he meets my eyes.

"I trust you."

We stare at each other like we're trying to communicate telepathically, and then he says, "You'll tell me if it's too much?"

I nod.

"All you have to do is say the word, and I'll stop. You understand?" He sits up and pulls off his shirt, revealing his chiseled abs, covered in a dusting of hair.

I run my hands over his hard muscle, like I can't physically keep myself from touching him. He's so masculine. Everything about him oozes testosterone. He's powerful, demanding, domineering, and at the same time, he's nurturing and protective of me. I might not fully understand the extent of his feelings, but I can see glimpses in the way he's always aware of wherever I am in a room, the way he never takes his eyes off me, and I catch him smiling more and more as time goes on. I don't think I'm ready to admit how much I'll miss this ... because then maybe it won't hurt so bad.

"What word? *Banana? Pineapple? Shazam?*"

He yanks my cropped T-shirt up at the hem and pulls it over my head in a smooth motion, leaving me breathless in my tiny shorts and thin cami bra.

"How about *stop?*" He buries his face in my neck, nipping at my shoulder with his teeth. "It doesn't have to be that complicated."

"All right. I think I can remember that ... though it usually isn't part of my vocabulary when I'm having sex."

"Then, it doesn't seem like we'll have any issues ... though I don't know if I'd be so sure, baby girl. I have no intention of taking it easy on you after that prank you pulled upstairs." He drags my bra strap down my shoulder, covering me in kisses, and repeats the motion on the other side before stripping my bra off completely and tossing it over his shoulder.

A thrill of excitement shoots through me at his not-so-threatening threat. Being with Leo makes me feel more alive than I ever knew possible. Hell, I might have to take up skydiving just to replace the rush of dopamine after this is all over because I am quickly becoming addicted to everything about this man and his lifestyle.

"Jesus, baby, you are so beautiful. I want to embed myself in every inch of your skin."

He kisses the space between my breasts, the spot that every other guy seems to ignore. I feel like a goddess being worshipped with the way he touches me, like he's savoring every kiss and brush of my skin. I am the center of his attention, and somehow, that sends a thrill straight to my core.

Sure, I've had my fair share of good sex. I needed to distract myself from my pain somehow, and sex always got me out of my head—for a little while anyway. But no one's ever touched me like this. No one's ever been able to evoke this longing so deep inside me, this burning desire that feels like I'm discovering a whole new sensation of pleasure every time he touches me.

"Lift your hips," he tells me as he hooks his fingers around my G-string and slides my panties and shorts off at the same time, leaving me completely bare.

It's hardly fair that he gets to keep his pants on while I'm helpless and naked beneath him, and I don't know why but the thought only turns me on more.

"As much as I'd love to take you right here, I'm afraid we still have your punishment to deal with."

"Or ... just hear me out ... you could just let me finish the good work I was doing upstairs, and we can call a truce?" I offer, suddenly feeling nervous.

Leo's lips pull into a smirk. "And what kind of daddy would I be if I didn't teach my brat the consequences of being naughty?" He doesn't wait for me to protest, not that I have anything to counter his argument. He lifts me from the bed and carries me across the room to a large X-shaped contraption attached to the wall. "Give me your hands."

The leather feels a little cold at first as he fastens the cuffs around my wrists and ankles, but I'm quickly warmed by the heat of his gaze. He stands before me, shirtsleeves rolled up to his forearms and his belt still undone, looking like the fucking god of sex—is that a thing? If not, I propose a movement to name him as such.

His eyes roam over me, drinking me in as I stand bare before him, my body yielding to his mercy.

My pussy pulses in anticipation of what he'll do next, and I wet my lips as if in challenge. "All right, *Daddy*, now that you have me tied down and helpless, what do you plan on doing with me?"

"Fucking hell."

He shakes his head as he drinks me in, the head of his cock sticking out above his waistline. I can't wait to feel him inside of me, stretching me beyond any toy or anyone I've ever had.

"I'm going to play with you now, try out a few things to see what you like best. I want you to tell me if it gets to be too much, and I'll stop. You're the one in control here, but I think we both know you deserve to be punished for your behavior …" His voice trails off as he plucks a skinny stick with a flat leather tip from the wall.

I suck in a breath as he runs it over my skin, needy desire burning like a fire in my belly.

"This is called a crop or a riding crop." He pops it against my leg, leaving the slightest sting behind, goose bumps erupting all over my skin.

"You like that, don't you?" He pops me again, this time a little higher on my thigh, and I let out a little whimper. "I fucking knew you'd like to be spanked. You're such a naughty girl, always playing tricks, begging for attention. You wanted me to spank you, didn't you, baby girl?"

Another slap, slightly harder, and I buck, straining against the cuffs.

"How does it feel to be tied up, knowing I can do anything I want to you right now?" He moves to the ground, kneeling in front of me as he slides a hand over my mound and in between my legs. "So wet already."

He licks my arousal from his finger, and as if he can't help himself, he slides his tongue over my clit for a breath of a moment before pulling away.

"Now, that was for me." He looks up at me from his knees, eyes dark with desire and lust as he traces the tip of the crop over my clit. Then, a sharp slap leaves a burning sting in its wake. My head falls forward as the rush of pain and pleasure floods my system, and it's almost too much to take—*almost*—but it's somehow perfect at the same time.

He leans in and kisses my clit, sliding his soft tongue over me in a gentle caress, and I nearly buck off the wall from the contrast in sensation.

"Look at you, such a needy brat. You like being my whore, don't you?"

"Yes." My response comes out in a breathless moan as I nod my head. No one's ever spoken to me that way, and, holy shit ... I really like it.

Leo's green eyes grow darker, the corners of his eyes squinting in an almost smile as he continues teasing me with the crop. "Your needy cunt is already getting wet for me, isn't it? I bet if I touched you right now, you'd make a mess all over my fingers, wouldn't you, baby girl?"

He pops the whip again, and when I buck my hips forward, his hot tongue licks the sting away, giving me a little more pressure than before.

My legs shake, and I ache to press myself into him, to give me the pressure and friction I so desperately crave, but I can't move. I can't lift my legs to wrap them around his head or use my hands to pull him in closer, and the longing builds to something that's almost painful.

Sensing my discomfort, he inserts two fingers inside me as he licks my pussy, bringing me back to that place on the edge of pleasure and release. Time seems to stand still and speed up, all at once, as he brings me into a sexual trance-like state, where nothing else matters and we are the only two people to exist.

"Fuck, you're practically dripping, and you taste so goddamn sweet. I'm going to fill this tight little cunt with my cock, but I want to make sure you're ready for me." He curls his fingers inside of me, and my legs grow so weak that the only thing keeping me upright are the cuffs around my wrists.

"I could keep you tied up like this all night, torturing you while you squirm, but I'm too fucking hard to wait." He removes his fingers, planting a gentle kiss on my clit, and then he's unbuckling the restraints.

There's a sweet relief that comes when I pull my arms back down and the blood rushes back to my limbs. I massage my wrists, feeling an odd sense of freedom, but like something is missing.

He scoops me up, carrying me over to the bed, and sets me down in front of it.

Just when I think the freaky torture is over, he fastens another cuff to each of my ankles, securing my feet open with a bar stretching in between.

"What's this for—"

No sooner does the question leave my lips than he has me bent over the bed, ass up and legs spread. "Bend over."

I feel the sharp, stinging slap of his palm against my ass cheek and then hear the clinking sound of his belt as he pulls down his pants. I brace myself for whatever he decides to do to me next.

"This cute, perky ass drives me so fucking crazy." He rubs a soft caress over my skin, soothing the remnants of the sting. "You see what being a good slut does to me?" He presses his hard cock against my ass, rubbing himself between my cheeks.

"I want to fuck your ass so badly, but we'll save that for another night. Tonight, I'm going to fuck this tight little cunt until you can't take it anymore and the only word left on your lips is my name."

He wraps a hand around me, rubbing my clit as he teases my entrance with his cock, and grips the back of my neck with his other hand as he pushes my face into the mattress.

Electricity shoots through every cell in my body, and I want him inside me more than I've ever wanted anything in my life. I need him to fill me, to end this agonizing torture of emptiness.

"Leo. Please. Please ..." I beg, feeling every sensation magnified.

The cool fabric of the sheets feels incredible against my heated skin as he presses me harder, his possessive grip holding my neck.

"What's wrong, baby girl? Is your needy cunt aching for Daddy to fill it?"

He pushes himself right at my entrance, and I buck my hips into him, catching him off guard.

He jerks back, but not before the head of his cock nudges inside me; it's thick and big enough to make my eyes water.

"Fuck, baby, not so fast. Let me ease you into it. I don't want to hurt you," he growls out, tightening his grip as he tries to regain his composure. There's a slight tremor in his hands, which tells me it's taking a massive amount of restraint to keep himself from taking me right here.

Leo Kingsley, always the picture of control, even when he's fucking—and I'd really like to change that.

He moves himself back to my entrance, this time holding me at my waist. I love the way his hands feel, so possessive as he holds me, like he can't decide which part of my body he wants to touch first, like he can't get enough of me.

He slaps my ass again, and I let out a yelp of surprise and flinch.

"Fuck, I've wanted to do this since the very first moment I laid eyes on you, with your cute-as-fuck overalls and that smart mouth of yours, always saying the first thing that came to your mind, no fucking filter whatsoever ..."

He runs a palm over my ass like he's trying to wipe the sting away, and then he pushes inside me ever so slightly, letting out a tortured sigh.

My body tenses as his cock stretches me past the point of comfort. Jesus, this man is huge. For once, I'm grateful for his incredible patience, making sure I'm ready.

"Shh, baby, just relax and breathe. You can take it. I know you can," he whispers encouragingly as he laces his fingers in mine, watching my face for any sign that I've changed my mind.

But I've never wanted anything more than this.

I relax a little more, feeling the worst of the pain subside as I grip the fluffy bedding and brace myself for the rest of him.

"Goddamn it, you're so fucking tight," he grunts as he slowly inches himself inside me, being extra cautious to not hurt me. "But you can take it, can't you, baby? You're such a good little slut for me, so hungry for Daddy's cock."

He pinches my nipple as he pushes himself in fully, and I suck in a sharp breath.

He wasn't lying when he warned me it would be a tight fit. I've never been stretched so full, but the pain quickly subsides as I relax my muscles around him. He fucks slowly at first, each stroke bringing a new sensation of pleasure as he moves harder and faster.

Another hard slap to my ass in between thrusts, and I can't do anything but hold on to the sheets as he drives his cock harder and deeper inside me, wringing out more and more pleasure by the second.

I don't know if it's his perfect cock, or the angle of my hips in this position bent over the bed, or that I'm pinned down and unable to move, but it's almost too much in the very best way. It's like Leo has a remote to the inner workings of my pleasure and has the dial turned all the way up to the top—another millimeter, and I'd spontaneously combust.

"Such a good girl, taking me so well," he hisses, and then he grabs the bar between my legs and flips me over onto my back, pushing my knees up to my head. He uses the bar to maneuver me exactly where he wants, pushing my legs open wider as he fucks me in deep, rhythmic strokes.

The position hits an entirely new angle, and it's like I'm experiencing sex for the very first time because there's no way this is the same as the sex I'm used to. No, Leo's tapped into some kind of secret power that only the professionals know about. He's got me feeling tingles in places I never knew existed before tonight, places I'll never be able to find again without his help ...

It's the kind of sex that makes you forget your name, who you are, and your reason for living. It redefines everything about you, rewiring your brain and baptizing you into a whole new state of being.

It's only when I'm panting for air and my legs start to shake that he changes his rhythm.

"What are you—no—just keep going ..." I shake my head, trying to urge him back.

He flashes me a wicked grin. "I can feel your pussy clenching, and I don't remember giving you permission to come."

CHAPTER TWENTY-SIX

Leo

I knew it would be mind-blowing, but this? This is something straight out of my darkest fantasies, played out in real life, and I don't even think this woman knows how much power she has over me.

Fuck, everything about her has me ready to throw it all away just to make her smile—hell, to hear her make that sound again. I love the noises she makes, like she's truly surprised or caught off guard by her pleasure. I want to record her moaning and listen to it before I need to do anything competitive or perform because she's got my ego sky high right now, and I feel like I could do anything with that power.

I grind myself inside her, rolling my hips and doing all that I can to keep myself under control. I'm not ready for this to end, and those whimpers she's making aren't doing anything to help my cause.

I fucking love having her pinned down like this, her legs

spread open, knees by her ears, as I drive into her impossibly deep, burying myself all the way to the hilt. But what I love even more is how much she loves it too—the hungry look in her eyes, the way her bee-stung pink lips part as she moans, and how she's so confident in her body, letting me maneuver her exactly how I want.

"You love being my fuck doll, don't you, baby girl?" I growl in her ear, knowing she's so close to the edge.

I told her to hold off mostly because I want her orgasm to be powerful, but also because I fucking love teasing her, especially after that stunt she pulled with the Pop Rocks. My little brat loves her punishments, and I love being the one to give it to her.

"Fuck, yes. Use me, Leo. Fucking use me however you want," she moans out, and I nearly blow right there on the spot.

I tuck a wedge pillow under her back as I push my hand on her belly to create more friction between her G-spot and my cock. And in a matter of seconds, she's screaming and fighting through her orgasm as it racks through her body in violent shudders.

It's like winning a Nobel Peace Prize, knowing I did that, that I'm the reason her pussy's clenching around my cock so hard that it nearly makes me pass out. I wish I could collect her orgasms like gold stars and wear them on a medal for everyone to see.

"Holy shit, that was incredible."

She closes her eyes and shakes her head, and I can't help but smile at how beautiful she looks when she's freshly fucked. Her wavy locks spread around her like a halo, all tangled and disheveled, and she's got mascara smeared down her cheeks. Her lips are swollen, cheeks tinted pink. She looks so fucking sexy and adorable, all at the same time. I could die right now and have zero regrets, just from the satisfaction of making her come.

I kiss her on the forehead as I unclamp her ankle straps. "I'm glad you enjoyed yourself, but we're far from done."

Gripping her waist, I flip us over so that she's straddling me, and I nearly lose my breath from the view. Perky tits, tanned skin, golden hair, and I have the very best angle to watch.

She runs her hands over my pecs as she works her hips over me, rolling and grinding until she's whimpering again, and I know she's so close.

"Come on, baby. Ride my cock. Let Daddy watch you make yourself come on my cock."

She pinches my chest in her grip as she rides out another orgasm, then collapses on my chest in a heap.

I don't wait for her to come down this time. I slap her ass. "Get up, doll. You can rest when we're done."

"Leo ... I don't think I can. It's too much," she protests, but I've waited too fucking long for this, and I'll be damned if I let her off so easily.

"You can, and you will," I growl, finding her swollen clit, rubbing circles around it. Her body melts at my touch, and I know I have her right where I want her.

I scoot myself up so I'm sitting against the headboard and flip her around, giving me a prime view of her ass.

"I want to watch you fuck me like this, and if you do a good job and make me come, then I'll let you rest." I move her hair over her shoulder and kiss the back of her neck, making goose bumps cover her skin.

Her hips begin to rock as I let my hands trace over every curve, loving the way our bodies fit together like they were made for each other. After this, I'm convinced that they were.

How cruel of a joke it is to find your other half, only to know she isn't meant to be yours, that you can't keep her. That just means I need to make every moment we have count because I'll be living off these memories for the rest of my life. Hell, I might as well become a monk after having her because there's no pussy, toy, or jerking myself off that could even come close to the pleasure I feel when I'm with her.

"You feel so good, baby. Use my cock to make yourself come. I want to feel your pussy spasm and watch you fall apart." I trail my finger along her cute little ass, teasing her entrance and palming her cheeks. I'm close. I just need to hold off a little longer, let her get one more before I take my own.

She shakes her head. "I don't think I can. It's too sensitive."

"Do you need help?"

"I don't know."

"Close your eyes." I reach a hand around her, finding her swollen clit. "You're doing such a good job, taking me so well," I whisper as I work her clit with one hand, guiding her hips with the other.

"Such a good girl," I hiss as my orgasm builds. I grit my teeth and slow my breathing as I try to hold on for her. "Your pussy is so tight and wet; you feel so good when you're stretched full of my cock. I want to fill you up with my cum while you scream my name. Do you think you can come one more time for me, baby?"

I pinch her nipple, and her head falls back as she lets out the sexiest moan of pleasure.

"Yes." Her voice is faint, but it's all the encouragement I need. She likes when I talk her through it.

I slap her ass, catching her off guard, then push myself in a little deeper until she lets out a surprised moan, and I know I've hit the spot I was looking for.

Her hips begin to rock in a frenzied rush as she chases her orgasm, and all I can do is hold on to her as she loses all control.

"Fuck, yes. Come for me. Be a good little slut and come all over Daddy's cock," I say as my own pleasure moves to the surface.

"Yes. Yes. Oh my God ... Leo!" She throws her head back as she rides out her orgasm.

My vision blurs, and all I can do is hold her as time seems to stand still. "Fuck, you're so goddamn perfect," I say as liquid heat shoots through my core, and I fill her up as she rides out the last of her pleasure.

She collapses against me, her back against my chest, and our hearts beat violently in a steady rhythm, blending with the sounds of our panting breaths. I wrap my arms around her, holding her against me as we both come back down to earth.

"That was ..."

"Fucking perfect," I answer for her, tucking her against me.

I smooth her hair from her damp face. She's so fucking beautiful; it nearly takes my breath away, and I know that I'll never feel like this with anyone else.

"Come on. Let's get you cleaned up." I lean up, but she doesn't move.

"I can't. My legs are Jell-O. Just leave me here to rest."

"Not happening." I go to the bathroom and start the shower before returning for her. "Come on. I'll carry you." I scoot her up in a cradle-carry before she can protest and carry her to the bathroom.

"You have a shower down here too?" She perks up, looking around the now-foggy space as the shower steam fills the air.

"Of course I do. It's a sex room. Things can get messy, and it's much easier for cleanup."

I wait for her to use the bathroom, and it's like we've been doing this for years, so comfortable around each other. It feels so natural.

Opening the glass shower door, I lead her inside, guiding her underneath the hot spray, and fuck if I'm not already starting to get hard again. You'd think I'd be satisfied after what we just did, but it's like my cock knows this is only temporary and wants to make every moment count. He's going to have to wait though. My girl's exhausted, and all I want to do is wrap her up in my arms and cuddle the shit out of her for the rest of the night.

I work the shampoo suds in her hair, massaging her scalp, and to my surprise, she doesn't protest. I'm learning the secret to managing Ivy's smart mouth is keeping her fed and fucked ... which also happens to be two of my favorite things. I love taking care of her, and for the first time in my life, I actually feel complete, like I'm finally satisfied and there's not something missing.

Maybe I need someone to take care of, to fill this void. I

used to think I couldn't be my whole self and do my job well, but since Ivy walked into my life, it's like she handed me a pair of glasses, and I'm seeing things clearly for the very first time. She's changed me. She challenges me to question why I want the things that I want. When I'm around her, it almost feels like I don't have to try so hard, like I don't need to be perfect, like I'm good enough just as I am and I'm not too much either.

Ivy gives me hope that, someday, I'll be able to trade the armor of guilt I wear as a shield for a clean slate, where I don't have to hate myself or atone for my past mistakes.

The scent of vanilla and citrus fills the air as I rinse out the conditioner and lather her in shower gel.

"Why do you always insist on bathing me?" she asks as I bend down to wash her.

I tap my knee, indicating she give me her foot, to which she obliges. "Maybe I just really love taking care of you ..." I realize the word choice as soon as I say it, but I don't backpedal.

I just look into her warm sunshine eyes as I wash her, daring her to prod further. Maybe I want to tell her; maybe I want her to hear me say it.

"I love it too," she answers, and fuck if that's not the best goddamn thing I've ever heard.

"Good." I trade for her other foot, and she giggles when I scrub the bottom.

"I hope you're ready to carry me up those stairs because I don't think my legs can manage. Maybe I'll just sleep down here in the sex dungeon tonight until I can muster the strength to walk."

"You'll do no such thing. I plan on cuddling you all night

long." I stand and begin washing myself. "I'll carry you up the stairs. I'll carry you anywhere you need me to for as long as it takes. You just tell me what you need, baby girl." I work the shampoo through my own hair and rinse my head underneath the shower stream. "Say the word, and it's yours."

She narrows her eyes mischievously, making her nose crinkle. "Anything?"

I scan her face, my eyes lingering on her lips. "Within reason ..."

She moves a little closer as she grips my cock in her palm, and I suck in a hiss. "Even my vibrator?"

My laugh comes out in a loud boom, surprising both of us, and I take her face between my hands and kiss her gently on the forehead.

"If you think you'll still want to use it after I'm done with you, then you have even more stamina than even *I* can manage. You thought tonight was exhausting? Just you wait. I was going easy on you. You think I have an entire room dedicated to sex and I only use a little bondage and a riding crop?"

Her smile falls, and she bites her lip, looking a little nervous.

I tilt her chin up. "I'm only just getting started. I did try to warn you." I glance down at where she's gripping my cock. "You might want to save a little energy for tomorrow, but that's up to you." I flash her a challenging grin, and she slowly pulls her hand away. "Smart girl."

We towel off, and just as I promised, I carry her upstairs and help her into one of my T-shirts before tucking her into bed beside me, right where she belongs.

"You know, I didn't take you for a cuddler," she says as I

pull her into my chest, wrapping an arm around her to keep her close.

We feel so natural like this.

"Why is that?"

"I don't know. I guess because you seem so rigid all the time. You keep this wall around you and everyone at arm's length. Why is that? What happened to make you so closed off?"

I let out a sigh, considering if I should tell her. She's been nothing but accepting of my lifestyle, so I don't see why I can't trust her.

"Around ten years ago ... I was in a pretty serious relationship. I'd had plenty of flings before then, slowly discovering my kinks along the way ... but this was the closest I'd gotten to settling down with someone."

Ivy runs a hand over my chest in soothing strokes, as if to tell me she's here and she's listening.

"I was still pretty young, and I had a big head, thought I knew everything. I'd recently gotten a promotion to be the VP of safety and sustainability for the entire North American region, and the added responsibility was more than I'd realized. The company was growing so fast, which meant I needed to hire more safety managers to supervise all the new factories we were building.

"I started working longer hours. The woman I was seeing —her name was Heidi—started expressing she was unhappy about never seeing me. She lived a few towns over, so we only saw each other a few nights a week as it was. Anyway, I did everything I could to make time for her, but she didn't exactly make things easy on me either. Nothing I did was ever enough, and I found myself cutting corners at work so I didn't have to stay so late.

"We were engaged in a Dom/sub dynamic, and after years of suppressing what I wanted, I finally started to open up and show her the real me. It was the first time I asked someone to call me Daddy. She was only a year younger than me, and she acted like she was into it—she never gave me a reason to believe she wasn't. I realize now that what we had was toxic because our words didn't mean anything. She'd promise me one thing and change her mind without telling me, but expect me to somehow know anyway.

"She was giving me heat about a work trip she didn't want me to go on—I was supposed to be meeting a new safety manager candidate for our biggest factory yet, but it meant that I'd be gone during the week of her birthday. She threw a fit and gave me an ultimatum—said if I went on the hiring trip that we were done."

I brush my hand over my face, feeling the painful memory stir back to the surface. "I made up some lie about having a mutual friend with one of the candidates, told my dad that he'd vouched for him, and promised him that the trip wasn't necessary because I was confident in my decision. It was the first time I'd ever lied to my father, so he had no reason not to believe me ...

"So, I didn't go. And to make things worse, I skipped over countless candidates with more work experience in favor of some guy around my age, fresh out of school with the highest level of education I could find. I didn't even call all his references; I just gave him the job."

I blow out a sigh and shake my head, and Ivy runs her fingers through my hair, encouraging me to keep going.

"About three months later, I walked in one morning and found my father sitting at my desk, waiting for me. His eyes were swollen and puffy, and he had tears running down his cheeks. When I asked him what was wrong, he didn't answer me; he just turned on the news. And that's when I saw the headline—*sixty-three workers killed in an explosion with over two hundred others critically injured.* I'd been warned not to cut corners, but I didn't listen. I knew what would happen eventually ... I just hadn't believed it until it actually came true."

That chilling number sticks in my mind, and I have to shake the other memories back down.

Ivy's face falls in horror, and then her brows cinch together like she's confused. "What do you mean, you'd been *warned?*"

Of course she picked up on that. I shake my head, not wanting to get into it right now. It's already so much to take in without explaining my childhood nightmares.

"Nothing. It's not important."

"So, what happened to cause the explosion?" Ivy asks.

"Turned out, the guy I'd hired to head up safety for the factory had a drug problem. If I'd done a thorough background check, I would've known that. He'd been fired from his previous job for showing up to work drunk and had a history of DUIs that he'd had someone remove from his record. He showed up to his graveyard shift strung out of his mind and missed a critical safety check. It was something so small that could've been easily fixed, but then a freak accident happened—a small fire ignited near the leak, and the factory exploded.

"That's when we moved to being one hundred percent

chemical-free in our manufacturing, so nothing like that could ever happen again."

"Leo, that's terrible, but it was a mistake. Please tell me you aren't still punishing yourself for that."

"It was a mistake I made from negligence, and it was unforgivable. I was on the phone all day, trying to clean up the mess, dealing with insurance companies, and writing settlements for all who were affected. I could hardly process the weight of it, but it hit me all at once in the car on my way home. I was so numb, hating myself for making such a horrible mistake, and when I walked through the door and I saw her sitting there, pouting and pissed off because I'd missed our dinner reservation without calling, I knew I couldn't do it anymore. I knew I couldn't have both.

"Lucky for me, she made it easy, so I didn't have to end it. She was screaming and crying, breaking shit as she packed her bags. I didn't even try to stop her; I wasn't upset when she told me she'd been seeing someone else because I didn't make enough time for her. It was the worst day of my life, and I hadn't thought anything could make it any worse. But right before she left, she told me I disgusted her … that she felt like I'd forced her to play into a role she didn't like.

"She said, 'You're such a perv, Leo. I never wanted to play into your disgusting fantasies. It made me sick every time I had to call you Daddy.' "

Ivy moves from my side, straddling her legs on either side of me as she covers me in a blanket of her body. She slides her hands from my chest and up to my jaw, where she holds each side of my face as she looks at me. Tears brim her eyes as she stares down at me like she can feel my pain as her own. "That was a horrible thing to say, but hear me right now, Leo

Kingsley. There is nothing wrong with you, and you are far from any of those horrible things she said to you. There is nothing about you that needs fixing. You are perfect just as you are, and you deserve to finally forgive yourself and let go of this guilt you insist on torturing yourself with.

"I see you, Leo, and I'm not leaving ..." My heart catches in my throat for only a moment before she adds, "Before I have to anyway."

I wrap my arms around her, savoring her comforting words as the clock in my mind counts down, reminding me of how little time we have left.

She yawns, and I kiss her head and click off the lamp.

"Good night, Daddy," she whispers, sending a gust of reassurance I didn't know I needed straight to my calloused, bruised heart.

I let out a heavy sigh of relief, feeling that spark of hope expand a little more. "Good night, baby girl."

CHAPTER TWENTY-SEVEN

Ivy

"That about does it on my end. We'll be all ready to set up next Friday. Can't wait to see what's in store this year. It sounds like you two have really gone all out."

I shake Richard's hand before marking the dunking booth off my massive checklist.

Leo comes from around the corner, towel-drying his damp hair, in a fresh set of dry clothes—someone had to be the test dummy to make sure the dunking booth worked smoothly, and honestly, how was I supposed to resist?

I flash him a smile and wave with my fingers.

"You know, I never thought I'd see the day the reclusive Leo Kingsley willingly sat inside a dunking booth to make sure it worked." Richard shakes his head and laughs as he claps Leo on the shoulder. "You, my friend, are what they call *whipped*." He winks and gestures toward me. "Not that I blame you in the slightest. If I had a pretty lady like Ivy on my arm, I reckon I'd do just about anything she asked me to as well."

"Thanks for taking the time to meet with us, Richard. I know we sprang this on you on short notice, but I think these dunking booths will be the perfect addition to the festival. And thanks for the clothes." He laughs, gesturing to his bright purple Fighting Phantoms T-shirt and matching sweatpants from the local high school.

This carefree—and dare I say—happy man is almost unrecognizable. Peace looks good on him.

Me, on the other hand? I'm a frazzled ball of nerves, waiting for the other shoe to drop.

I'm having the best sex of my life—life-altering sex that has me feeling like I've grown fairy wings, gliding weightlessly through the world around me. I see colors brighter, food tastes better than it ever has, I'm moved to tears anytime I listen to music. It's like I've transcended dimensions and I'm living in an enhanced version of reality.

And honestly ... it's pissing me off.

Don't get me wrong; I love to have fun. I love to enjoy myself. I live for experiencing joy and pleasure—hell, I center my whole life around finding it—but this ... this is suspiciously perfect. Leo is being suspiciously delightful—too perfect—and it's going to be that much harder when it's time for me to leave.

My stomach twists in knots when I think about it, which makes me feel guilty, like I'm somehow cheating on my sister's dying last wishes. I've never felt so mixed up and confused about what to do in all my life. Before a few weeks ago, I didn't even question that moving across the country to work in Dracula's Castle would be something I'd be struggling with ... which can only mean one thing. I've lost sight of reality, and I need to take back the reins before I let this delusion of happily ever after wash me away.

I've never let myself get this stressed, and it's really messing with my head.

So, I decided to take out some of my pent-up frustration on Leo. I came up with a whole list of obnoxious errands for us to do today, but so far, he's just happily obliged, never once complaining, no matter how ridiculous. I expected him to buck back, to fight me on it, to distract me with a little back-and-forth verbal sparring before he'd finally put me in my place and fuck my attitude away ... but that's not what's happening at all.

I thought asking him to take the day to run errands rather than go into the office would be enough to get a reaction, but no. In fact, he seemed excited to skip work today, even insisted on taking me to breakfast.

Then, when I told him I needed him to model the full-face paint for the Phantom design and make sure the paint didn't irritate his skin, he just agreed! He's been walking around with his face covered in black and purple face paint all morning.

He didn't complain when I told him I needed pictures in various spots around town because I wanted to see what it would feel like on the day of the festival to make sure the vibes were right.

We've been walking around all morning, testing photo ops, eating, picking out craft supplies for the children's craft area, where I pretended I couldn't decide between dark purple or medium purple thread for the friendship bracelets. I thought for sure he'd tell me it didn't matter, but, no, he pulled out his phone and made a list of pros and cons for each color in his Notes app until we ultimately decided to get both!

And I just knew the dunking booth would be the last straw, and he'd finally show signs of irritation ... but instead, he agreed—*because it would be quite the letdown if the booth was faulty.* He even bought Fighting Phantom merch to wear after since his clothes were wet.

"So, what's next on your checklist? Do we have time to grab some lunch?"

He wraps an arm around me as we saunter out of the store and onto the downtown cobblestone street. There's a cool nip in the air, and the sun shines bright in a nearly cloudless sky. It's the perfect day with the perfect weather and the perfect man ...

"I'm not really hungry," I say just as my stomach grumbles, contradicting me.

Leo quirks a brow. "You might not think you're hungry, but your grumpiness is telling me something else. Come on. Let's grab a bite to eat, and then we can get back to checking off your to-do list." He takes my hand and leads me across the street, careful to check both ways.

His mention of my to-do list has the warning bells blaring in my head ... and my heart—a visceral indication that I'm in way over my head here and I don't know how I'm going to dig myself out of this mess.

He opens the door to Restaurant and ushers me inside to a booth tucked in the back. My mouth waters as soon as the delicious aroma of food hits me, and suddenly, I'm grateful for his persistence. I didn't realize how hungry I was. I guess all that walking worked up an appetite.

For a moment, my nerves calm down, and when the server brings out our drinks and an appetizer of fried pickles —which I swore I didn't want, but Leo insisted we get because *he* wanted them—I feel much better.

"So, tell me, what's left on the list?" he says, popping a pickle slice into his mouth.

The man never used to eat fried food when I met him, and now, he's drinking a beer in the middle of the day, eating fried pickles, and even added bacon to his cheeseburger. And the crazy thing about it is, he seems so much healthier now, despite indulging in normal people food from time to time. He's got this healthy glow about him, and he hasn't needed his antacids in weeks. He doesn't fight me in the morning about drinking water and eating before he has his coffee ... and he's smiling at me.

If I didn't know any better, I'd think he was abducted when I wasn't looking and replaced with an alien look-alike, but seeing him in his sex room is all the proof that I need. He is, in fact, my same Leo ... only lighter.

He's so happy, and the thought of leaving him after all this is over, of him losing this side of himself and getting his family's hopes up ... that's the part that really kills me.

I thought I was helping him, but I'm afraid that when it's all said and done, he'll be worse than I found him, and I don't know how I'm supposed to live with that.

I shiver and fold my napkin in my lap to cover my bare thighs.

"Are you cold?" He doesn't wait for me to answer, just moves to my side of the booth and wraps an arm around me, tucking me into his warmth.

"Better?"

I nod. "Thanks. You didn't have to do that. I always get cold after I eat."

He slides a palm over my thigh and squeezes. "I'll take any excuse I can get to touch you."

I smile, but it falls flat.

"What's wrong? You've been acting off all morning. Are you worried about the festival? Because I think you've thought of everything. I was going to tell you this later, but I really think you should lean into this kind of stuff—planning parties, events, festivals. I think you've got a knack for creating a bigger vision than most people can see, and you're executing it incredibly. Seriously, I'm rarely surprised by people, but you've surprised the fuck out of me. In a good way."

"Thank you."

His compliment piles on an extra layer of guilt, and my lip begins to quiver as I try to hold it all in.

He tilts my chin up, examining my face. "I'm sorry, baby. I didn't mean to upset you. I know you've worked really hard on this. I was just trying to tell you how impressed I am. I guess *surprised* wasn't the best word choice. Of course, I knew you were capable of doing this—you're so smart and hardworking ..." I look away as his voice trails off.

"It's not that. I just ..." A traitorous tear falls from my eye, and I try to wipe it away before he sees.

"Hey, what's going on? What's got you so worried, baby girl?"

His words are like a punch to the gut, reminding me of how badly he's going to be hurting after I leave, how we both are.

I shake my head. "It's nothing. I'm just stressed, I guess."

"It's not nothing. You're upset. You're never upset. Tell me so I can make it better." He stares at me with those forest eyes that swallow me up, so open and vulnerable, so trusting ...

"I ... I just don't want you to hate me ... when this is all over." I wipe my eyes with the scratchy, unabsorbent napkin, probably making my face redder than it was before.

He cranes his neck, searching for my eyes. "Where is this coming from? I could never hate you. How could you even think that?"

"Not right now." I suck in a sob and wipe my eyes. "But you will—after this is over and I leave."

He grows quiet, and when I look back at him, he's wearing a pained expression, his eyebrows fallen and his mouth pressed into a tight line.

"Ivy, baby, look at me." His voice is commanding, and I look up at him automatically.

He traces a thumb over my lips and wipes a tear from my cheek. "I'm not going to pretend for one minute that it won't hurt to tell you goodbye. Jesus, I'm already prepared to have my heart knocked right out of my chest ... but, baby girl, you aren't responsible for anyone's happiness—not even mine—so please stop carrying that burden on your shoulders. I'm a grown man. I knew what I was getting myself into, and I made a choice.

"Just because it's going to hurt doesn't mean you need to feel guilty for putting your life first."

He tugs at the end of my braid, making me smile. "You are so young; you have your whole life ahead of you." He taps the pocket of my overalls, knowing exactly what's underneath. What I always keep tucked away right beside my heart. "You've got big plans to move to Romania, you've got your sister's list to guide you, and you have your whole life to figure out what you want to do next. If you think I could ever live with myself for preventing you from doing any of that, then that's where you're wrong."

I suck in another sob, my eyes blurry with tears, and now, I'm crying for a whole new reason. Why did I have to meet my perfect person at the worst possible time? It's a cruel joke, and it makes me wonder what I did so bad to deserve it. Losing my sister and the love of my life in the same lifetime feels brutally unfair, and I don't know how I'm supposed to get back in the ring after this.

"I might be a cruel bastard, but I'd go to the ends of the earth, crawl through hot coals and shards of glass, just to make you smile. You've lost so much in life already, baby girl. There's no fucking way I could live with myself if I took your future from you too."

He slides my soda toward me and holds out my straw for me to take a sip.

"Now, let's enjoy the rest of our lunch. We can worry about tomorrow when tomorrow comes, but right now, you're still mine, and I'd like to hold on to that feeling for as long as I can. Okay?"

"Okay." I nod, feeling slightly better.

I can't explain it, but I've never had anyone tell me that their feelings weren't my responsibility. I've always been the one to clean up everyone's emotional mess, to carry the burden of cheering them up when they were down, to keep the peace between my parents. Ever since I was a little girl, I felt this weight to make sure everyone was happy around me. I was the one responsible for cheering our mom up, so she could take care of us and go to work after our dad left. I carried the burden of giving Fern something to hope for, to keep her going during her chemo treatments.

I've been the emotional birthday clown to everyone my entire life, carrying the burdens of everyone's happiness on my shoulders, but I've never had anyone tell me they didn't need me to do it.

Not once has anyone given me permission to only worry about myself the way Leo just did, taking responsibility for his own emotional wellbeing. I feel like a weight's been lifted off my shoulders as I take in a deep, cleansing breath and wonder if this is how it's supposed to be.

What would my life look like right now if I hadn't tried to solve everyone's problems, throwing myself on the ground so they didn't have to walk through their own sadness? Would I still be in school? Would I be following my sister's checklist like a map, letting it guide my every move? Or would I have dreams of my own instead?

* * *

"Where are we?"

"Just hold on. Watch your step. We're almost there." Leo's hands cover my eyes as he leads me to my surprise.

We spent the rest of the day doing *real* errands—meeting with Miss Lucy to pick out cookie designs, paying the deposit for the carnival rides, and stopping by the rental place to order enough tables and chairs for the eating spaces and concert area.

Leo was a great sport about it, never complaining. I even saw him decline a last-minute meeting request. Of course, I didn't call attention to it, but it gave me a warm, fuzzy feeling in my chest. I can't believe how far he's come, but at the same time, I feel like I'm finally seeing the real Leo, the man he's been too afraid to show the world.

"Here we are," he says as he removes his hands.

We're standing in front of a massive chain-link fence somewhere in the middle of Phantom's Reach. Behind the fence, I can see what looks like an old mine with a dilapidated building beside it, and there's a small railroad-looking track that spans from inside the cave to the back of the building.

My eyes take in the No Trespassing sign that Leo's standing beside, and I narrow my eyes in confusion.

"Do we have an appointment to be murdered I don't know about?"

He laughs and rubs my tense shoulders, and I close my eyes, relaxing into his touch.

God, I didn't realize how tense I had been, trying to plan everything for this festival. I started out doing this for Fern, but after getting my hands dirty and seeing my vision come together, I want to do it for me too. All of a sudden, I find myself feeling motivated to finish something—to know that I'm capable of following through with a commitment even if it's just a festival. It's one small thing I can move to my own nonexistent list of accomplishments, one thing I can do for *me*.

"This is the largest mine in Ashford Falls. It's the place where the Phantom was first sighted. I thought you'd want to see it—you know, for your sister's list," he says with a shrug, then holds out his hand to me.

A knot forms in my throat, and I try to swallow it down,

but it's lodged in there, like I just took a pill without anything to drink.

I blink several times, glancing from the clear signage that states it's illegal to enter and back to Leo.

"Don't tell me you're afraid because I've been hyping myself up for this all day."

I shake my head. "Why? I don't get it. I thought you were afraid of the dark or something, and you were so freaked out when your brother was telling the Phantom story. Isn't that what your brothers were teasing you about?"

He shrugs, trying his best to look unbothered. "I'd say I'm more claustrophobic than afraid of the dark." He walks toward me and takes my hand. "Look, I know this was on your list, and I want to help you check off as much as you can before you leave …" He scratches the back of his neck, looking down. "And I can't imagine how hard this is for you or how much pressure you're probably feeling about finding the perfect spot for your sister's ashes … so I figured I'd try to help." He looks up to meet my eyes. "I put your sister's ashes in the car this morning, and I thought maybe this would be a good place—no pressure or anything. I just don't want you to feel rushed … since we only have a few days left."

I push my hand through my hair as I begin to pace back and forth. Overwhelmed by so many emotions all at once. "Leo, that's …" My voice trails off as I try to figure out what to say.

"Please don't feel like I'm pressuring you. I'm only trying to help, offering you whatever support I can. We don't have to go in. I just knew it was on the list and—"

My feet come to a stop, and I spin to face him. "Thank

you. You have no idea how much this means to me. Fern would love this so much ..."

He shoves his hands in the pockets of his purple sweatpants and nudges his head toward the car. "Good. I'll just go grab your sister then. Be right back."

When he jogs away, I can't help but crack a smile at the absurdity of it all. Never in a million years could I have expected to end up here, but I guess Ferny's been working her magic this whole time.

My amusement is quickly replaced with dread when he reappears in front of me with my sister's urn tucked beneath his arm.

"You ready?" he asks, passing me the urn as a wave of nausea rips through me.

I swallow a gulp, trying to ignore the ball of pain that twists in my stomach at the thought of saying goodbye, not only to my sister, but to Leo too.

"I think so ..."

CHAPTER TWENTY-EIGHT

Leo

I stare up at the dilapidated building and press my lips into a flat line. I never thought I'd be anywhere near this place again, much less willingly walking in at night, but this is so much bigger than my stupid fear. I need to be there for Ivy. I want to be there for Ivy, to help her through this.

I don't know when it happened exactly, when she managed to wiggle her way past the steel walls I'd put up, infiltrating my heart from the inside out. All I know now is, she's the sun I revolve around. She's sunny spring days and beams of sunshine that warm your skin after a bitter, cold winter that seemed to never end. She's the best thing that's ever happened to me. She's everything I never knew I needed.

"Watch your step." I take her hand and lead her through the old metal door dangling on broken hinges.

We duck inside, letting our eyes slowly adjust to the darkness—a darkness that seems almost unnatural, blacker than any night sky. I turn the flashlight from my phone on, illuminating the dark, dusty space as we work our way inside, the floorboards creaking underneath us with every step.

It's so eerily quiet, I can almost hear the dust stirring in the air from our footsteps.

We move farther inside, past piles of bricks and mangled steel, stepping over rubble and debris. You can't make out anything from the original setup, but it's not hard to imagine how it used to look.

Ivy spins around, taking it all in. "I can't believe this is where it all happened. How many people did you say died in the explosion?"

"Sixty-three," I answer automatically.

The number's been burned into my memory since I was a kid, the same number that's haunted me from my own past. The past I never talk about.

"Didn't you say that's how many people died in your factory explosion too?"

I grit my teeth. "Yeah. Sixty-three."

"That's so ironic," she says, squatting to pick up an old black-and-white photo.

In the picture, a young woman beams as a man stands behind her, his arms wrapped around her playfully as he kisses her cheek. They look so happy, so in love. It's probably an engagement photo, if I had to guess. Their smiling faces are like a punch straight to the gut.

"Do you think they knew? Before it happened?"

I turn to Ivy, confused by her question.

She pulls at her hair—her tell that she's nervous or uncomfortable. "I just mean, my sister used to say that people have a sixth sense about when death is near, like a way to help prepare them or whatever." She shrugs. "Fern knew. She told me two days before she died. She'd actually just gotten some really great news about her levels. The doctors thought she was going into remission, but she knew. She predicted it down to the hour." She bites her thumbnail nervously.

I kick the dirt at my feet, unable to look her in the eyes. "I don't know. Part of me hopes they didn't know ..."

"Yeah. Me too." Her voice is small and quiet, like we're both talking about something else entirely.

Not a day goes by that I don't think of the people who lost their lives because of my negligence. If I could go back in time, I'd do so many things differently. But that's the thing; I can't. I've done everything I can to try to atone for my mistakes. With my own personal funds, I paid their families a generous settlement, as well as a monthly stipend for the next fifty years, and I've tripled our company's safety requirements.

Torturing myself isn't going to bring anyone back to life, but maybe it's possible to remember them without the soul-crushing guilt I've been carrying.

For the first time in my life, it's like I can see a light at the end of the tunnel, but the light isn't some mystical thing; it's Ivy and her rays of sunshine slicing through the edges of my darkness. It hardly feels like a coincidence that I'd meet her while walking alone in the woods at night, and at this point, divine intervention seems like a better explanation than happenstance.

"What's that over there?" She points to a hatch door leading to the bunker below.

My chest pinches at the sight of it. Swallowing a gulp, I say, "It's a bunker; it was supposed to be a safe space to protect people in the event of an accident ..." I trail off, and the unsaid words hang in the air between us.

I open the door, revealing the top of the metal ladder, and shine my flashlight, illuminating the narrow space below. "It connects to the cave underground. They built a tunnel system so they'd have access to both sides. It's ... actually the exact spot where the Phantom allegedly appeared."

Her eyes widen. "Can we go down there?"

I knew this was coming, but that doesn't make it any easier, and there's no way I can deny her this, not after everything she's told me today. "Yeah, I'll take you down there, but you have to promise to stay close to me. It's pretty far down."

"Promise." She loops her little finger in mine before kissing her hand.

"Let me climb down first, and you can follow me. That way, I can catch you if you slip."

I take a deep breath as I squeeze through the narrow opening, slowly making my way down the ladder. I breathe through my nose, counting backward from one hundred. I try to imagine a spacious room, full of fresh air rather than the dank, cramped cave surrounding me.

When my foot touches the solid earth, I let out a sigh of relief as I reach to help Ivy down the rest of the way. At least this way, I know she won't hurt herself.

I lead her through a wide pathway, and it's so much tighter than I remember when I was twelve. I almost lose my battle to keep my panic at bay when I have to turn to the side just to squeeze through, but then the tight space opens up, and we're inside the bunker area. It's still pretty cramped but light-years better than what we just came through.

Rows of cots and metal bunk beds line the space, and a large metal shelf sits on the opposite end with century-old soup cans and supplies.

"Whoa, this is so cool." Ivy moves to explore the decade-old stash of supplies, covered in a thick layer of dust and soot. She holds up a pocket watch. "Look at this stuff. I can't believe all of this is still down here ..."

When I don't respond, she turns around to find me bent at the waist as I try to calm my breathing. I hold up a hand to wave her off. "Don't worry; I'm fine. I just need a minute."

She's by my side before I can even finish. "Are you okay? Here, why don't we sit down?" She leads me to sit on the cool stone ground beside her.

"It's fine. Really, I'm fine," I try to assure her, but the worry on her face says she's not buying it. "I'm just a little claustrophobic—that's all."

"It looks like it's more than a little. I can feel your heart racing, and you're white as a ghost. Why'd you bring me down here? You could've said no. I would've understood."

I wrap an arm around her, letting the scent of her shampoo ground me back from my panic. When my breathing finally returns to a semi-normal pace, I find Ivy staring at me like she's waiting for an explanation.

"Have you always been claustrophobic like this? Is that what your brothers were teasing you about that night when we were camping?"

I clench my teeth and brush my hand over my jaw. "Sort of. I, uh ... remember when you asked me about my scar?"

She nods, placing a hand on my thigh.

"I actually got it the first time I ever came down here—the *only* other time I've been down here. I was twelve, and everyone at school was obsessed with the Phantom. We'd all grown up hearing the stories, and we used to argue about whether or not he was real. I, of course, didn't believe in him while all the other kids in my class did. One day, I made a big deal about how I wasn't afraid of the Phantom. I was just trying to be cool, but they called me on it. They dared me to spend the night down here and provoke him, to prove that I wasn't scared. And if I survived, then they'd believe me too.

"It was so stupid, idiotic actually, but I did it even though I was scared shitless.

"Anyway, I waited for my parents to fall asleep, and as I was sneaking out of my window, Jett walked in and caught me. He's only eleven months younger than me, so he knew about everything from the kids at school. He tried to talk me out of it and finally threatened to wake up our parents if I didn't let him tag along.

"We were both scared; we'd never done anything like this, and the only knowledge we had of the Phantom had come from the scary stories we'd grown up hearing. But neither of us talked as we walked the two-mile hike, cutting through the forest, and made our way inside.

"We came down here to the bunker and laid out our sleeping bags on the cots, both of us pretending we weren't terrified. Somehow, we eventually fell asleep.

"At some point during the night, I woke up shivering and realized our lantern had gone out. There was a horrible stench in the air, and when I reached for my flashlight, it wasn't there.

"I was growing more terrified by the minute. I tried to call for Jett, but I couldn't see anything. It was pitch-black dark, and I started to feel like the walls were caving in on me. I had this bone-chilling fear wash over me. I know now that I was having a panic attack, but I felt like I was suffocating.

"I couldn't find my flashlight anywhere—I guess it'd rolled underneath my cot or something when I panicked. All I could do was scream for my brother. Jett woke up, not knowing what was going on, and I know I must've scared the shit out of him too. He couldn't find his flashlight either, but he was able to lead us back to where we had come in.

"He went ahead of me on the ladder so he could open the hatch door as I struggled through panicked tears right behind him. My arms and legs were shaking so violently that I had a hard time keeping my balance, and when I got to the top of the ladder, my foot slipped. My hands were so sweaty that I wasn't able to get a good enough grip to catch myself.

"I fell almost thirty feet, landed on my leg so hard that the bone snapped completely in two, breaking all the way through my skin. I'd never experienced so much pain in my life, and there wasn't anything Jett could do to help me.

"He ended up running the whole two miles home in the middle of the night to get my parents. They had to send a rescue crew to pull me out. I had to have two surgeries to repair my leg and spent the rest of the school year in a wheelchair."

"Oh my God, Leo, that's awful. You must've been so afraid, waiting down here all by yourself, not to mention hurting."

I nod, remembering that fear all too well. "I had nightmares for years after that. I'd dream the Phantom was there with me, watching me, taunting me for being reckless. At one point, I was convinced he'd been the cause of it, that he was the reason I slipped.

"Eventually, my parents had to put me in therapy because the dreams wouldn't go away. After a while, they stopped, but the weird thing was, as soon as I got promoted and put in charge of safety, they came back. Only this time, rather than being trapped and alone, I would see an explosion. Sometimes, I was working with the crew, and other times, I was spectating, but every single time ... I was the one responsible, and the number was always the same. Sixty-three."

I let out a sigh and shake my head, and Ivy runs a hand over my jaw.

"You think the Phantom was warning you because you were being reckless again?"

I shrug. "I don't know what to think, but when it actually came true, I vowed I'd never be that negligent ever again."

"And you never told anyone this? Not even your brother?"

I shake my head. "No, Jett and I have always had a rough relationship. We were hardly speaking at that time in our lives. Besides, he's got his own shit to deal with.

"So, that's all of it. Now, you know every dark secret about me ..."

She loops her hands behind my neck and pulls me into a hug. "Thank you for trusting me with that. I get why that would make you so uptight. I just wish you'd told someone about it before now. You might've been able to let go of some of your guilt."

"Yeah, I'm starting to see that you're right." I push myself up to stand and offer my hand to help her up. "Enough about all of that stuff." I gesture over my shoulder with my thumb. "This could be a pretty awesome place to sprinkle your sister's ashes if you want to check out the cave."

Her eyes fall, and she shoves her hands in the pockets of her overalls as she shuffles her feet. A few moments pass before she finally speaks, the usual brightness in her eyes replaced with something dull and heavy. "I don't know, Leo. You're right; this is exactly the type of place my sister would've loved ..."

She bites her quivering lip like she's trying to keep her emotions trapped inside. It kills me to see her in so much pain, but there's nothing I can do. As much as I wish it were possible, I can't take it away from her. All I can do is support her and hold her hand, show her I'm here for her.

I brush a stray hair from her face, my palm moving to cradle the back of her neck as I meet her gaze, our eyes saying everything our words can't. "You don't have to do this right now. If you're not ready, then we'll wait until you are. Okay? This place isn't going anywhere."

She looks around and huffs a laugh. "As if I'd ever ask you to come back here after everything you told me tonight. Trust me, Leo, I'm not that delusional to expect you to overcome your biggest fear a second time just to impress me."

She nudges me with her elbow, and I playfully rub my rib cage like she wounded me.

"You know, I think you'd be surprised ... I know I am ..." I say more to myself than to her.

"Now, for the love of God, can we please get out of here?"

She shivers, and I wrap an arm around her.

"I thought you'd never ask."

CHAPTER TWENTY-NINE

Ivy

We're silent as we make our way downstairs. We both need this distraction after all the painful memories we dug up tonight.

The heavy thud of the door closing behind us is like a starter pistol. Our lips crash together and we both begin shedding our clothes. Leo stifles a growl as he pushes me against a wall, his kisses devouring as he lifts me with one arm and removes his pants with the other.

I wrap my legs around his waist as I yank his sweatshirt over his head before attempting to remove my own.

"Fuck, baby, I need to be inside you so bad, but there's no need to rush," he says as he unclasps my overalls, sliding his large palm over my hip and moving it up my back, where he unhooks my bra with a flick of his fingers.

My bra falls down my arms, the cool air and the heat of his gaze making my nipples harden into tight peaks. I arch my back as he removes my shirt and bra in one smooth motion.

Immediately, his hungry mouth is on me, sucking and licking my exposed skin as his grip tightens on my ass like he's trying to hold himself back.

He adjusts his grip on my ass so he can pull my overalls off, and I take the opportunity to grind my clit against his erection. We're both in only our underwear now as I reach my hand down to stroke him, cupping his balls and teasing his massive length.

It's dark down here, the red accent lights giving the whole room an edgy, moody glow.

"Leo. I need you to fuck me," I say in a breathy moan as I edge myself closer just from rubbing my clit against him.

I'm so worked up, so desperate, that I don't need anything more. I just need him, bare, inside me. It's all I can think about.

"Fuck, baby, you're so goddamn perfect." He carries me over to the bed in the middle of the room, the cold sheets on my bare back catching me off guard.

I suck in a hiss as I look around in confusion.

Leo must sense my body tensing, as he breaks our kiss and pulls away. "What's wrong? Did I hurt you or—"

"Why are we in the bed?" The question falls out of my mouth before I can filter it.

Leo lifts a brow before following my gaze and looking over his shoulder at the various equipment.

"I thought you'd want to tie me up or do something ... kinky," I add, just in case he doesn't quite understand. Honestly, I thought we'd be on the same page about this after everything tonight.

A wolfish grin spreads over his lips as he stares down at me, raking his gaze ever so slowly over my exposed breasts as he holds himself up so he doesn't crush me. "Is that what you want, baby girl? You want me to edge you tonight? You want me to *punish* you? To *play* with you?"

I swallow a gulp, suddenly feeling nervous, thinking of all the choices, but rather than waiting for my response, he reaches over to the side table and clicks a remote. R&B music starts playing softly in the background, and then he lights several candles, dimming the red lights a little more.

He moves back over me, grabbing my wrists and lifting my arms above my head. "Do you trust me?"

He holds both wrists with one hand as he gently traces a thumb underneath the swell of my breast, and my back arches off the bed, desperate for more.

I part my thighs and wet my lips as I look into his dark eyes, hungry with lust and desire as he watches me like a predator stalking his prey.

"Yes, I trust you," I whisper.

His mouth twitches in amusement as he reaches over me to grab something behind the headboard. "Fuck, that's what I hoped you'd say. I've been dying to have you like this."

A moment later, both my wrists are tied with a small Velcro cuff. He hooks a finger in the hem of my panties and slowly drags them down my legs as he unwraps me like a goddamn present.

"Fuck, baby, you're already soaked for me, and I haven't even touched you. Just look at this pretty pussy."

He brushes his fingers over my sensitive skin with the slightest touch, and my legs spread open further on impulse.

Taking advantage of my new position, he moves down to secure my ankles. I'm spread out like a starfish, completely bare, helpless, and at his mercy ... and I wouldn't want it any other way.

I close my eyes, savoring this moment. The anticipation of what he'll do to me, knowing how amazing he'll make me feel, has my heart racing like a snare drum.

"You have the prettiest pussy I've ever seen—do you know that, baby girl?" He slides a hand up my leg, his fingers dipping into the apex of my thighs as he gently brushes a finger over my aching clit. I let out a mewl of protest when he removes his hand, bringing a finger to his mouth to taste my arousal. "And you taste so fucking sweet."

"Yeah?" I part my legs a little further, as much as I can with the restraints holding them down. "Then, why don't you show me? If you love it so much, why isn't your face between my thighs right now?"

I have no idea where that boldness came from, and judging by the look on Leo's face, I'd say he's just as shocked.

He clicks his tongue, and then he reaches over and grabs the lit candle from the side table and holds it over me as he straddles his legs over my waist, careful not to put his weight on me. "This is a massage candle. It burns at a lower temperature, making it safe to be used on the skin, but it can still be intense. I'm going to drip this wax on you, but if the pain gets to be too much, all you have to do is tell me to stop, and I will. Do you understand?"

"Mmhmm," I moan as I wiggle beneath him, my body buzzing with anticipation and need.

"Words, Ivy. I need your words right now," he growls, his deep voice commanding as he pinches my nipple.

"Yes, Daddy," I gasp, my hips bucking up from the jolt of pleasure, mixed with pain, that shoots to my pussy.

"That's my good little slut." He drips some wax on his wrist to test it before shifting to the side. "This one is a little cooler and melts to an oil. We'll see how well you tolerate it before we go for the real wax."

He pours a small drop over my thigh, watching my face for any sign of discomfort.

The wax is so warm, and my senses are immediately heightened as the smell of something citrusy and earthy fills the air. I squirm as my eyes close, and I brace myself for the next drip.

Leo's palm rubs the warm oil into my thigh, massaging me with a practiced touch, and I let out a whimper when I feel the warm oil drip over my other thigh. Holy shit, this man knows exactly how to touch me. I've never had a proper massage before, but I'm afraid my expectations are now through the roof. He's ruined me, and I can't make myself care, not when he's so fucking good at it.

"Do you want more? How's your pain level right now?" he asks as he brushes a caress over my aching pussy, his fingers applying the slightest pressure as he rolls his thumb over my clit.

"Yes. More. Please, Daddy. I need more," I plead, feeling like I'm going to combust if he doesn't touch me.

"Jesus, you're so needy, aren't you?" He dips two fingers inside me as another drip of wax coats my stomach. The warm oil slides down my belly for only a moment before his other hand is there, massaging it into my skin.

"Yes," I gasp as he curls his fingers inside of me, his thumb swirling delicious circles over my clit.

He massages the oil up my stomach, his touch melting away all the tension in my body. I'm so close, teetering on the edge as his fingers move inside me, filling me and bringing my pleasure to the surface. My legs begin to quiver, and I feel my orgasm building as I clench my jaw, and my thighs fall open even wider.

"You are so fucking beautiful. I can't get enough of you, your fucking whimpers, this bratty mouth. I want to keep you down here all to myself, teasing you while you beg me to let you come." He kisses me, biting my lip and tugging it with his teeth when he pulls away. "Is that what you want, baby girl? Do you want Daddy to make you come?"

"Yes, please. Please, Daddy, please make me come," I cry out, feeling no qualms about begging because it turns me on just as much as it does him.

"Fucking hell, I don't think I've ever heard anything more perfect."

The wax feels hotter now, coating my chest. I suck in a hiss and brace myself for what I know is about to come when I feel the hot sting drop on each of my nipples.

Euphoria shoots through me as the pain subsides, the hot sting quickly replaced with a warm touch of Leo's palm as he rubs the oil over my chest, pausing to hold my neck for only a moment before he takes my breast in his palm.

It's all so much, all at once, and if I didn't know better, I'd think he grew two more hands because I don't know how he's touching me everywhere, all at once, like this. My eyes roll to the back of my head, and my back arches off the bed as pleasure rips through me, making every muscle in my body tense. Leo keeps his pace, curling his fingers inside me as he alternates, caressing my nipples, giving them each a hard pinch just as my legs begin to shake. And then I'm screaming as I fall apart, limbs violently tugging against my restraint as I writhe beneath his torturous gaze.

When the pleasure finally subsides, my chest is heaving, and Leo places his large palm over my heart. "You okay?"

I nod enthusiastically as I finally catch my breath, and Leo unties the restraint from my wrists and then my feet. When he's finished, he helps me sit up, then slaps my ass before he lies down and positions me on top of him.

He must see the look of confusion on my face because his lips curl into a grin as he slides his underwear down his body and props his hands under his head. "Now, I want *you* to fuck *me*."

CHAPTER THIRTY

Leo

My erection springs to life, and I release a calming breath as she grips my length in her small hand, stroking me as she warms me up. As if I need to be warmed up ... I just spent the last thirty minutes rubbing hot oil over her naked body while she begged me to let her come. I can't think of anything sexier ...

My thought's interrupted when she shifts her weight, bringing the head of my cock to her tight entrance. Goddamn, it's a hell of a visual, and I selfishly hope she enjoys riding my cock because this view is what wet dreams are made of.

"That's it, baby girl. Take Daddy's cock inside your tight little cunt. I want to watch your perky tits bouncing in my face as you fuck me and make yourself come."

I reach out and pinch her nipple, loving the way her back arches as she sucks in a hiss of pleasure. Gripping her hips, I guide her down, slowly sliding inside her as her silky, wet heat clenches around me, and I have to force myself not to move. She's so fucking tight; even after I made her come with my fingers, she needs a minute to adjust to my size, so I don't hurt her.

Her skin is slick with oil as I run my palm over her breast, loving the slight weight in my hand as I squeeze. Once I'm completely inside her, she begins rocking her hips in circles, and it's fucking torture the way her pussy grips me so tightly.

She bites her lip as her hands move to my chest, her fingers sliding through my chest hair and tugging as she finds a rhythm that feels good.

It's almost too much to take, and I'd be lying if I said I didn't have to think about work a couple of times to keep myself from blowing too soon. I let myself go to the edge and then bring myself back, knowing I'll be fine now that I've got it under control.

"You look so hot, riding Daddy's cock, baby girl. Your little cunt takes me so fucking well."

I slap her ass a few times as her hips begin rolling faster, and I take a moment to appreciate my view. Her eyebrows pinch together, and she bites her lip as her pace grows more frantic. I grip her hip with one hand and tease her breast with the other, wishing I could touch her everywhere all at once.

She's so fucking close. Her hips buck harder, and I can feel her pussy clenching around my cock as she throws her head back, crying out moans of pleasure. Her fingernails dig into my chest so hard that I have no doubt she's drawing blood, but I don't mind the pain. Hell, it makes it that much hotter, knowing my cock is what's doing this to her right now, making her lose all control and fall apart.

"That's it, baby. Come for Daddy. Come all over my cock

like a good little slut," I say as I grip a fistful of her hair and pull.

That sends her right over the edge.

"Oh God, Leo!" she cries out as she rides me harder, her sexy ass clenching as she fucks me with all her strength.

It's the most beautiful sight I've ever seen, and I feast my eyes on her as I commit every fucking second to memory.

Her fragile limbs collapse on top of me in a heap as she buries her face in my neck. There's a thin sheen of sweat coating her skin, and I move her long hair over her shoulder as I pepper kisses over the side of her neck.

"Holy shit, Leo. That was ... that was incredible," she says through gasps of air as I caress her damp skin, giving her a second to catch her breath.

I grab a bottle of water from the side table and twist off the top before handing it to her. She rolls her eyes, then takes a big gulp before wiping her mouth with the back of her hand and passing it back.

I quirk a brow. "You good?"

She takes another deep breath and nods, and I don't know why, but seeing her so exhausted, the way her cheeks are flushed pink, knowing she looks like this from fucking me ... it's feeding my ego in a whole new way.

I grip her ass and flip her over so that I'm on top, but we're still propped up at an angle against the pillows and the headboard. At first, it takes her by surprise, but when I start driving my cock deep inside her, she quickly wraps her legs around my waist to take me deeper.

Fucking hell, this woman is so damn perfect. It's painful knowing I can't keep her. But I can't think about that right now. I need to savor every touch, every glance, every goddamn stroke while I can, which is exactly what I plan to do.

I reach for the other candle on the side table, pausing my movements for just a moment as I hold it between us. Her eyes widen with excitement, and she bites her lip.

"This one's a little more intense. You'll tell me if it's too much?"

She nods, and I pour the wax over my forearm to test the temperature. It's hot, but not unbearable and quickly dries. That's going to be fun to get out of my body hair later ... but at least Ivy doesn't have that problem.

I drip the wax over her shoulder, a little at first, but when her head falls back with a moan, I add a little more, letting it pool on her shoulder and drip down her chest.

"Oh fuck, Leo. It's so hot; it feels amazing on my skin," she moans, sticking her chest out as she rolls her hips over my cock.

Christ. I should've known it wouldn't be too much, that she'd get off on the pain, just like I do.

I tilt her chin. "Open your eyes, Ivy. I don't care how good it feels. You want me to make you come again, then you keep your eyes on me. Do you understand?"

I move my hand to the back of her head, cradling her fragile neck and gripping her hair to keep her from moving as I drip another bead of wax lower. This time, it lands on the top of her breast.

She sucks in a hiss, but she does as she's told, never letting her eyelids flutter closed.

"That's my good little slut. You like the pain, but I'm not

going to let you use it as an escape right now. I'm not going to let you deny this connection. You're going to look at me in the eyes while I make you come because what we're doing right now is so much more than fucking, and you know it as well as I do."

I pick up my pace, driving my cock inside her more forcefully now as I take her with long, deep strokes. Fuck, it feels too good to be true. Her tits bounce in my face with every thrust as she digs her nails into my shoulders, holding on as we both lose ourselves to each other.

It's like an out-of-body experience as we stare into each other's eyes; it's like there's a magnet between us pulling us together, like we never even stood a chance of being apart because the universe would always bring us back here, back to this perfect moment.

My balls clench as my release builds, and I know I'm dangerously close. I feel the walls of her pussy clenching around me, and I know that she's right there too. She lets out a whimper, her fingernails digging harder into my shoulders as her orgasm rushes to the surface.

I take the opportunity to pour more wax on her. This time, it lands on her breast just above her nipple, the thick, hot substance slowly sliding down.

"Oh God. Yes, Daddy. Daddy, I'm coming!" she cries out, and I feel her walls tighten all around me in an almost-painful grip.

She sucks in a breath and her eyelids flutter, but she doesn't allow them to fall closed.

It's a small victory, but it's all I need because that little act of submission tells me that she feels this too.

I let myself fall. A rush of pleasure ripping through me, so intense that I see stars as I pump my cock, riding out the warm currents of my release.

Holy fuck, I'm in trouble.

CHAPTER THIRTY-ONE

Leo

I lace my fingers with Ivy's underneath the table as Roman goes on and on about a new tenant in one of his rental properties.

It's the night before the festival, and we're at my parents' house for family dinner, celebrating all our—and when I say *our*, I mean *Ivy's*—hard work. She's done so much to plan this festival, and thanks to all her creative ideas, I know it's going to be the best one yet.

It's hard to believe it's already here. I can't believe I only have three more days with her. I've already upgraded her flight to first class—though I haven't told her about it yet—and upgraded her luggage to something bigger, something that can hold all her new clothes I bought her even though she still mostly wears the same three pairs of overalls all the time.

Fuck, I'm going to miss her.

I'm going to miss her so damn much. Falling in love with Ivy wasn't something I ever saw coming, and I can't say I didn't put up a fight, but really, how could I have expected it to be any other way? She's a ninja like that—gets under your skin and burrows herself inside you, and before you even realize it, she's got her name carved in your heart.

Though I'd love nothing more than to tell her how I feel, I can't bring myself to do it. The last thing I want is to confuse her any more than she already is. I don't want her worrying about me or feeling guilty for leaving, not when she's got her whole life ahead of her. She's moving across the world, and even though I'd love to be selfish and ask her to stay, I could never do that to her.

So, I'll keep my feelings to myself and love her through my actions. I'll savor every moment while it lasts, and I'll spend the rest of my life picking up the pieces of my broken heart and still consider myself the luckiest man in the whole goddamn world.

"I cannot believe the festival is already here. Can you, Frank?" my mom says as she nudges my dad.

Dad takes a swig of his drink. "You're right; it feels like just yesterday, we were all sitting right here when these two offered to help run it."

My dad's eyes move between us and narrow in on me like he's picking up on something that's not quite right. Since I was a little kid, he's always been able to see straight through me, always known when something was bothering me.

I purse my lips and smile. "It's been quite an undertaking, but if anyone could make it fun, it's Ivy."

I squeeze her hand under the table, and she flashes me a quick smile. I immediately recognize it as a forced smile—I know every expression this girl makes; I've been studying her from the moment we met.

Maybe she's thinking about the list?

Or she's nervous about the event?

I don't have time to overthink every possibility because my mom raises her glass for a toast.

"Here's to another successful Phantom Fest and the best one yet!"

We clink our glasses, and I hold Ivy's gaze and mouth, *What's wrong?*

She shakes her head quickly and brushes me off. "Nothing. I'm just tired." But then she releases my hand from under the table to grab a roll and never returns it.

It's not like her to dodge my physical affection; in fact, I halfway expected her to fuck with me, try to give me a hand job under the table as payback. But she's not acting like her playful, spunky self, and all I want to do is get her alone so I can fix whatever's going on in her head right now.

"So, I've been meaning to tell you something, Leo. I know I already announced Carl as my successor, but it was always meant to be you who took my place, son. You were born to run this company, and there isn't a soul I trust more to do it ..."

My eyes snap to my father, and everyone's side conversations go silent. Ivy's hand finds mine, and she gives me an encouraging squeeze.

"I ... I don't understand. Are you serious? What about Carl?"

My dad grins, his eyes finding my mother's. "Carl put on a good front; he was in on it the whole time, but he never really intended to take the job. I just needed a way to get your attention."

My mouth falls open as I try to understand what he's

saying, and then I notice my mother attempting to hide her own grin behind her napkin. "Wait a minute. Did you know about this too?"

She puts her napkin in her lap, her smile now fully on display. "Of course I did. Who do you think gave him the idea? Don't get me wrong; your father is a smart man, but I know my son, and I know how to get through to him."

"I can't believe this. So, all this time, you two were playing me ..."

Roman lifts a hand. "Uh, I was in on it too."

"We also knew about it." Luka gestures between himself and Guy.

I shake my head in disbelief, feeling a sense of overwhelming relief that my dad never really doubted my ability, that I hadn't lost his trust.

Suddenly, the realization that I've been lying to him this entire time about my relationship hits me, and I don't feel so relieved. Instead, there's a new layer of guilt that's beginning to creep in. I can't keep doing this. I can't keep lying to him, especially now that he's telling me how proud he is, how much he thinks I've grown.

I sneak a glance at Ivy, who's biting her lip uncomfortably. She's no doubt thinking the same thing I am. She gives me a little nod as she squeezes my hand. This is going to suck, but I know what I need to do.

"I've watched you grow so much over the last month, and I think you're finally ready for me to pass you the baton. You've proven that you're ready—"

"Wait." I hold up my hand to stop him. "I think you should know something before you say anything else ..." I pause, taking a deep inhale. "I've been lying to you this whole time. Ivy and I aren't really engaged. Hell, I'd only met her the night before you did, and that was just by chance—"

My mother's laughter is what interrupts me, and I clamp my mouth shut, feeling once again completely lost and confused as my entire family joins in with her. My eyes find Ivy, who thankfully seems to be just as confused as I am— thank God for that, I guess, as we watch everyone laugh at a joke we aren't in on.

"Do you think we didn't know that? Honestly, son, how blind do you think I am? I knew the moment I called her by name in the hospital. The poor girl didn't have the faintest idea who any of us were, and I saw the panic in your eyes when we all walked in with her."

She tilts her head side to side and gives me a little shrug. "I can't say I expected you to keep the lie going. I only meant to ruffle your feathers after all." She bursts into another fit of giggles, wiping a tear from her eye. "We even got Dr. Stone in on the joke. Everyone in town knew, and we were all having the best time, watching you pretend ... especially at first."

"You should've seen your face when you realized we'd packed you that child-sized tent," Luka cuts in, and he and Roman high-five.

"That was all my idea," Roman says, waggling his eyebrows.

I shake my head. "I can't believe this. I feel like such an idiot."

"Oh, honey, you're far from an idiot by a long shot. We were going to tell you we knew, but we did hope you'd come clean and tell us yourself. We are so proud of you, despite all the lies; you really seem to have found yourself in all of this."

My brothers join in, taking turns as they all share their

own stories of how they knew I was lying. The noisy chatter and laughter fill the space, and I can't help but notice Ivy isn't sparkling as much as usual. She's being awfully quiet and skipped out on several opportunities to share her own embarrassing stories about me, which isn't like her at all.

Are you okay? I mouth, trying not to draw attention to us.

"Yeah, I think I'm just tired," she responds in a whisper.

I know it's a lie. Even when she's exhausted, she's never this quiet.

I try not to worry about it, but I can't help myself. I don't think I'll ever be able to not worry when it comes to Ivy.

After we all finish eating and my brothers and I help clean up after dinner, I find my mother and Ivy in the sitting room. They're laughing and talking, looking so comfortable, like old friends, as my mother shows her my baby pictures from our family photo album.

"Leo, why don't you join me for a drink?" my dad's voice calls from over my shoulder.

I spin around to find him holding two glasses of whiskey. He nods his head toward his study.

Feeling a whole new rush of nerves, I slowly follow him, taking a seat in an armchair in front of his massive shelf of books.

"I'm sorry I didn't tell you about Carl sooner. I was just so worried about you, and I didn't know how to get you to listen. Then, your mom came up with the idea, and I figured I didn't have anything to lose."

"It's okay, Dad; you weren't wrong. It was the reality check I needed. So, I guess Mom's plan worked."

He lets out a chuckle. "It always does. Don't tell her I said that though."

I take a sip of whiskey and laugh as he tells me about his plans for transitioning, filling me in on upcoming expansion plans and Roman's rebrand that's starting to take off.

"I know you've always put pressure on yourself to be perfect ... especially after the explosion incident in Texas ... but I want you to know it wasn't entirely your fault, and you've never given me the chance to tell you—"

I shake my head. "Dad, you don't have to say that. I know what I did—"

"Let me finish. I need you to listen, and I need you to hear this. Yes, your guy was a poor hire, and he was a drug addict who came to work under the influence, but the problem started before all of that. There was an issue with the machine; it'd been assembled improperly when it was built. That explosion would've happened one way or another regardless because it was a flaw in the actual machine. It was a ticking time bomb, and it just so happened to blow up when your guy was in charge. It wasn't your fault, son, and nobody blames you. Even if it was your fault, you've done everything right to make up for it."

I let this new realization wash over me, feel the knot in my stomach finally loosen. Hearing my father tell me he doesn't blame me is everything I didn't realize I needed, and I let myself drop the last bit of guilt once and for all.

"You have no idea how long I've waited to hear that, but I don't think I was ready to listen until now," I finally say as my throat squeezes with emotion.

My dad claps me on the shoulder, looking so proud and relieved. "I'm glad you're finally able to hear it. You're going to need to be a little more flexible now that you're CEO ... which brings me to my next question ..."

I sit back in my chair, not knowing where this is going. "What's that?"

He nods to the other room, where my mother and Ivy are sitting. "When are you going to tell her?"

I furrow my brows, feeling confused. "Tell her what?"

His face breaks into a big grin. "When are you going to tell her you love her? Don't you dare try to lie and tell me you don't ..."

My face falls as I lean forward, propping my elbows on my knees. "I really wish I could, Dad, but I love her too much for that ..."

Then, I fill him in on everything because God knows I need any help I can get right now.

CHAPTER THIRTY-TWO

Ivy

I rub my sleepy eyes as Leo loads the last of the supplies in the car, and I try to wake myself up. It's the morning of the Phantom Festival, and we've got a big day ahead. Everything seems to be accounted for and going surprisingly smoothly, but I still can't seem to shake this feeling that something is missing.

Maybe it's just exhaustion. I hardly slept a wink last night as my brain spiraled, thinking of everything that had happened the night before. I still can't believe his family knew we were lying this whole time. I can't get over the relief I feel to finally be honest with them, but there's still this ping of sadness that the charade's up.

It's not like it really matters. My flight to Romania leaves in twelve hours anyway. Maybe it's better like this. We get a clean break, and I won't have to feel guilty for hurting anyone when I leave. Leo won't feel responsible for his family's disappointment, which will keep him from spiraling, and he'll be able to move forward.

I'm so proud of him for how far he's come. He's finally going to have the title he's spent his whole life preparing for. When I set out to help him, I had no idea the impact my silly antics would actually make, but in a lot of ways, I think we're both coming out stronger on the other side of this. It's a rare thing to have a front-seat view of watching someone catch the dream they've been chasing, and I think it's shaken something awake in me too.

For the first time in my life, I'm starting to think of what I'd do without Fern's list guiding my every step. I find myself considering the type of career I want, dreaming of the life I want to live, places I want to travel ... and maybe even starting a family someday or settling down somewhere that feels a lot like Ashford Falls.

I wouldn't be having any of these thoughts without the not-so-gentle shove from my dead sister and the silly list she'd created all those years ago. Maybe that was her plan all along. Maybe she really has been my guardian angel all this time.

Which reminds me, I have a few more things I need to check off.

"We're leaving in five minutes if you still want to stop for coffee on the way," Leo calls from the living room as he finishes loading the iPads I had charging overnight for everyone to have the live schedule I created.

"Be right there. I'm just double-checking I have everything," I call back.

I know five minutes really means ten, but Leo is nothing if not prepared for me to get sidetracked. The man always inflates every timeline he gives me, and it's one of the things I love the most about him—he helps corral my squirrelliness. I don't know how I'll survive a real job without him ... but I guess I'm going to have to learn.

I open the top drawer of my dresser to grab my inhaler and my sister's list, like I always do before I leave the house these days. Leo's all but drilled it into my mind by now, making it a habit more than anything else.

I slide open the drawer to find my inhaler, but my sister's list isn't there beside it, like it's supposed to be.

That's weird. I always put it here after I change. Maybe I forgot to remove it from the pocket of my overalls the last time I wore them.

I rush to my overly stuffed suitcase, dumping the contents out on the floor. I begin searching through the pockets of all my overalls, growing more and more panicked by the second.

It has to be in here. I always keep it with me. What am I missing? It couldn't have grown legs and walked off.

"Hey, baby, are you rea—whoa, what happened in here? Did your suitcase explode? I told you I thought overalls and sneakers were the best option. It's going to be a long day, and you're going to want to be comfortable—"

"Have you seen Fern's list?" I say, cutting him off. "It's not where I remember leaving it. I've searched everywhere I can think of, but it's not here." My voice comes out shaky and panicked, and I have to bite my bottom lip to keep it from quivering from the fear of losing the last piece I have left of my sister, her final wishes for me.

Leo rushes to my side, rubbing his hands down my arms in soothing strokes. "It's got to be around here somewhere." He falls to his knees, digging through the pile of laundry and checking every pocket just in case I overlooked it. "Try to think back, when was the last time you remember having it? Where were you? What were you doing?"

He lies down on the floor, using his phone's flashlight as he searches under the bed.

I close my eyes and will myself to think. My heart races, and I have to take a hit from my inhaler to relieve the tightness forming in my chest.

Think, Ivy. What were you doing the last time you remember having it?

A vision of myself standing in the middle of the factory in the old mine pops in my head. I pulled out the list to mark off *Visit the home of the Ashford Falls Phantom.*

"What's wrong? Do you remember where you had it?" Leo's voice breaks through as my heart drops to my stomach.

The alarm on Leo's phone goes off, the real one indicating we only have exactly enough time to make it. He doesn't know that I figured out his code, but the man's not nearly as sneaky as he thinks he is. He hits silence as he waits for me to respond.

I wipe the tears from my cheeks. "I remember having it when you brought me to the mines a few days ago. I guess I was so busy that I didn't realize it was missing before now ... but it could be anywhere. I mean, we had to climb the fence and hike to get back there. It could've fallen out of my pocket anywhere. It could be long gone by now ..."

"Don't worry, baby; we'll find it. As soon as we get the first chance, we'll go look for it—"

I shake my head. "We don't have time. We have to leave right now. We have everyone's schedules and the passes ... they can't open the gates until we get there ... and it'll be dark by the time it's over ... and my flight ... my flight leaves as soon as the festival is over. We don't have enough time or daylight, Leo."

The realization hits me all at once—how everything is happening so fast and there's nothing I can do to slow down time, no matter how desperately I want to. Of course I'd make it all this way, get to the final leg, and drop the ball at the end. God, this is exactly like me, always the fuckup who needs her sister—and now Leo—to clean up my mess.

It's a painful reminder not to get ahead of myself with all my high hopes and dreams for the future. There's a reason my sister created that list, a reason I always let her take the lead. When I'm in charge, I make everything a mess … just like the current state of my life.

"I promise you, I'll figure it out," Leo says, pulling me into a hug.

And the thing is, I know he will because he always does … I just wish he didn't always have to.

I shake my head, feeling defeated and oddly relieved that the pressure's finally off. Once the worst thing you can imagine comes true, what else is there to worry about? It was bound to get lost or destroyed eventually. I should be proud that I managed to keep up with it for five years. At least I've got the monkey off my back now …

"Let's just go. We're already going to be late because of me. I don't want the whole day to be ruined because I can't remember to keep up with precious, irreplaceable things."

"Baby girl, please don't beat yourself up about this. I promise you, if I have to spend the whole night searching, I'll find that list, and you'll have it in your hand the moment you walk into that castle tomorrow evening. You have my word."

Rather than argue, I just nod.

Maybe this is for the best. I still have her ashes to deal with. Maybe this is ripping off the Band-Aid so I won't feel so sad when it's complete. I've never been good at goodbyes anyway.

* * *

"You ready, Miss Ivy?" James, the security officer working the front entrance, asks, and I wipe my sweaty palms against my overalls.

There's a small crowd gathered at the front entrance, and people are slowly filing in behind them.

I check the time on my phone, seeing it's exactly eight a.m. Thanks to Leo's impressive driving—honestly, I hadn't known he was capable of driving that fast—we managed to swing by Bakery to grab doughnuts for the whole crew and get our coffees with only seconds to spare. But the important thing is, we weren't late.

Leo's stationed on the other side of the festival, helping coordinate the dunking booth and fair rides, while I'm set up at the entrance.

I could beat myself up over losing the list—hell, I'll have plenty of time for that on my fifteen-hour flight tonight—but right now, the most important thing is making this festival run as smoothly as possible.

Let's do this.

"James, open the gates." I give the all clear, and I sit back and wait for the chaos to finally begin as the chatter from the crowd of excited people fills the air.

Oh, the sweet sound of distraction. It's exactly what I need, giving me a break to allow the initial shock to wear off.

Nothing like delaying the pain I'll inevitably feel for a little while longer.

James clinks the metal hook from the railing, and a line of people file in, tickets in hand and smiles on their faces.

"Welcome to Phantom Fest. Here's a booklet with an itinerary of events, and there's a bingo card in the back. If you fill it out and turn it in, you'll be entered to win a vacation package to next year's event. There's a total of ten winners, so that's pretty good odds."

I add the booklets to the bags and stamp hands, then point them toward the first show of the morning, watching as they take in the expansive decorations and list of events.

"Wow, this is incredible. I've been coming to this festival for years, and it's never been this big. What sparked the change?" a woman says as I stamp her hand.

I shrug. "We felt inspired by someone who wasn't able to make it."

"Well, be sure to tell them thank you. I'm obsessed with the Phantom. Been listening to stories about him since I was this big." She playfully tousles her little girl's hair. She can't be older than four or five years old.

"I certainly will. Have a good time today and make sure to stop by the kiddie area. There's free face painting and a photo op to have the Phantom Photoshopped into your picture so it looks like he's attacking you." I waggle my brows at the little girl.

"Him's not mean," she says, shaking her head. "Him's a nice monster. Can I take a picture with him smiling?"

Her question catches me off guard, and I lean in. "Uh, yeah. I'll have to check ... but we should be able to do that."

She smiles brighter, looking excited, and tugs on her

mom's shirt. "Yay. Mommy, can we please go there first? Can I hang my picture over my bed so he can watch me sleep?"

I jot down a note to call the photographer. "You're a brave little girl, aren't you? I would've been terrified to see something like that on my wall at night when I was little."

Her mom gives me a knowing smile. "It's natural to be afraid of things you don't understand, but that doesn't mean those things are scary. Right, Violet?"

"Right," the little girl says, flashing me a grin.

"Well, maybe you're right. I guess I never thought about it like that. You know, you remind me of someone I cared about very much."

"You don't care about them anymore?" she asks.

"No, I do ... but she's gone now, so I only have my memories of her." I tap my finger on my temple, and the little girl's eyes widen in understanding.

"You can still talk to her though," she says like it's obvious. "That's just pretend stuff anyway. You just have to hold your breath like this ..." She sucks in a breath and crosses her fingers and then lets it out in a gasp. "And you think really hard in your head, and then if you are good and pray the right things, you can talk to her in your heart."

I laugh. "Oh, well then, if it's that easy, I'll have to try it."

Her mom ruffles her hair again. "Violet has quite the imagination ..." She looks at me for a little longer than comfortable and says, "But she's not entirely wrong."

She takes her daughter's hand, and then they're gone, disappearing into the crowd that's seemed to grow exponentially in the short time of our conversation.

I find myself playing back what she said, about talking to my sister in my heart. What an odd, extremely descriptive thing to say. Honestly, it sounds like some shit my sister would've said ... which is why I actually find myself wondering if that's what I've been doing all along.

"Hey, Ivy, we've got an issue over here at the petting zoo. Someone left the gate open, and there's a pony out on the loose somewhere," a male voice says over my walkie-talkie.

I pinch the bridge of my nose and sigh. "All right, I'll be right there. Call Andie over at the face-painting station and tell her to section off the area until we find the pony. Surely, it couldn't have gone too far."

"Roger that."

"James, can you send out a call, asking everyone to keep their eyes out for a runaway pony? Keep it discreet. I don't need the guests panicking. The gates have been open for less than an hour. You remember the codes we came up with?"

"Yes, ma'am. Can't say I ever thought we'd need 'em, but you really thought of everything, didn't ya, Miss Ivy."

I throw my backpack on and sigh. "We'll see about that. It's only eight thirty. We've still got all day ... anything could happen."

"Don't I know it?" James laughs.

* * *

Five hours later, I'm icing a goose egg on my forehead with a snow cone as sticky blue syrup drips down my arm.

After I left to find the missing pony, I got another SOS call about the jumpy house deflating. Apparently, the teenager running it didn't pay attention and forgot to make sure everyone took off their shoes before getting inside. One tiny cowboy later, and the whole thing was caving in. It took five of us to get all the kids out. Luckily, no one was hurt, but there went our security deposit.

We found the pony after following the screams of a disgruntled vendor, who discovered it eating apples out of the bobbing-for-apples trough. The woman's scream startled the poor pony, which took off into a run, barreling straight through a row of porta-potties. Needless to say, we had some very unhappy guests who fell victim.

Thank God it was still early enough that they were mostly empty ... not clean enough, however ...

And to make matters worse, there was a hiccup with the trailer for Frank's big surprise float during the parade. It's only the biggest event of the entire festival, where Frank Kingsley—dressed as the king of the Phantom Festival—will pass the throne to Leo, officially naming him CEO and the new head sponsor of the event. Leo was the closest one to the float, so he took the lead on finding a last-minute replacement part.

Which means I got to lure the terrified pony across the festival solo. Everything seemed to be going fine until a dog broke free of its leash and came charging toward us out of nowhere, barking. Naturally, the pony got startled when the dog nipped its ankle, resulting in me getting kicked at. I barely managed to escape, hitting my head in the process. Don't worry; the dog was perfectly fine—and the pony ran off. At least it ran in the right direction this time. They were able to get it back in the trailer to calm down.

"Hey, Ivy. Can you stop by the stage when you get a minute? The band's out here, saying something about needing a beer keg to perform," Luka says over the walkie-talkie.

"There was a keg delivered this morning. I signed for it myself," I answer.

"Yeah ... he's saying it's not cold enough or something. I offered him some ice, but he called me a lazy, good-for-nothin' pretty boy and said I was too young to know how beer's supposed to taste ..."

"Aren't you, like, twenty-five?"

"Twenty-six actually," he adds. "That's what I told him, but he said I was lying. I can't help it that I got good genetics and the skin of a young child."

I laugh for the first time all day at the absurdity of it all. "Tell him I'll be right there."

"Ten-four. Oh, and if you're close ... don't go out of your way or anything ... could you grab me and Guy a corn dog? Extra mustard and ketchup packets, please."

I look up at the lemonade stand in front of me. "Sure thing. How about a lemonade to go with it?"

"You're the best fake future sister-in-law a guy could ask for," Luka says in a teasing tone.

I should be relieved that they know it was all a ruse, but there's a part of me that finds myself wishing it were true— that somehow, I could be part of this family I've grown so attached to. But it's too late for that now. I've got a keg to track down and a festival to run.

I order the corn dogs and lemonade and make my way over to the stage to find Luka and Guy in a heated debate with all five members of the folk band ... who are supposed to be performing right now.

"Hey, guys, what seems to be the problem?"

The next ten minutes are spent listening, and making promises to fix the warm beer situation.

"If you could excuse me for just one second, I need to make a quick call." I pull out my phone and call the only person I know who'd have a backup keg in their possession.

Jett answers on the first ring, and I tell him everything and beg him to help, even promising to pay him double for his inconvenience if he can deliver it in the next half hour.

To my utter surprise, he agrees, and I have no doubt in my mind if Leo—or any of his brothers for that matter—would have asked him for the same thing, he would've insisted he didn't have enough. It makes me curious what skeletons he's got hiding in his closet. After hearing how Jett had to run home that night to get help for his injured brother, I can only imagine he's got his own set of issues ...

I hang up the call. "There. I promise we've got an ice-cold keg on the way. How about I grab you all some lemonades in the meantime?"

After a little grumbling, they finally agree, and I call for backup to make the delivery. My feet ache, my head is pounding, and the mental countdown in my mind is steadily growing louder ... and it's only midafternoon.

"Where'd my horrible liar of a brother run off to? I don't think I've seen him all day. You'd think he'd at least try to look like he cares about this festival since he's going to be the new head honcho around here," Luka says more to Guy than to me.

"Didn't he say he was going to track down the pony?" Guy says with a shrug.

This catches my attention because I specifically sent him to deal with the float while *I* went pony hunting. We had a whole conversation about it.

"Why do you say that, Guy? Leo's dealing with the float

trailer ... isn't he?" I swipe open the iPad, revealing the newest schedule, including everyone's assignments, broken down in thirty-minute increments.

Guy just shrugs before sucking down the rest of his lemonade. "That's what he told me when he asked me to wait with the float until Big Dan showed up with the replacement parts."

I press my fingers to my temple as the beginning of a headache starts to form. "Wait. Are you saying Leo called Dan to fix the float? Dan isn't even working the festival ... so where is Leo then?"

Luka tosses back a mouthful of ice and crunches it between his teeth. "How am I supposed to know? I thought you were the one with the master plan, fake sister."

I'm genuinely confused and worried about the scheduling. This event can only run smoothly if everyone's in the correct place, and we've got a lot riding on this with the surprise parade event for Frank's retirement.

Guy holds out his phone and dials Leo's number. It goes straight to voice mail, and then Luka tries calling him on his.

Finally, I try to call him on the walkie, not expecting a different result. He always has his phone on him, and I know he charged it last night before we went to sleep.

Seconds of silence pass before someone pipes up. "I thought he went to get you the coffee you'd asked for?"

"What are you talking about? I didn't ask him to get me a coffee."

Someone else speaks up. "He told me he needed to help with an emergency with the dunking booth."

"Uh ... I'm at the dunking booth now. Everything's running fine. I haven't seen Leo though," another voice says.

I drop the walkie-talkie and look at his brothers, and we all stare at each other in confusion.

Where would he have disappeared to? And why hasn't anyone seen him since ... I check the schedule, confirming his last known station.

"So, no one's seen Leo in four hours?"

I pull out my phone and dial Frank's number. He answers on the third ring. I can barely hear him over the noisy chatter around his sponsor booth.

"Frank—er, Mr. Kingsley," I correct myself, suddenly feeling weird about addressing him by his first name. "Yeah, uh ... I just wanted to check to see if you've heard from Leo recently. He isn't answering on the walkie or his phone."

"No ... I ... I haven't heard from him." He covers the phone with his hand as he asks Mary and whoever else is working the booth with them. "No one's seen him since the gates opened. Do you think something's wrong? Ivy? What's going on? Is everything okay? Do you need us to help you look for him?"

I shake my head, feeling worry set in. "I ... I'm not sure. But I'll let you know. I just need to think ..."

"Listen, I'm sure he'll turn up around here somewhere. You two have worked too hard to put this festival together. It's not like there's anywhere more important he'd need to be ..."

My eyes fly open as realization hits me square in the chest. I sink down to the folding chair beside me.

Guy crouches beside me. "What is it? What's wrong?"

"Do you know where he is?" Luka asks, pocketing his phone.

I let out a sigh, remembering the fear in his eyes he tried

so hard to keep me from seeing when he brought me there ... nobody's heard from him for hours and his phone's not working ... which means there's only one place he *could* be ...

"I think I know where he is."

"Where? I'll hop on my bike and go check," Luka says.

I swallow a gulp and look at Luka. "The old mine in Phantom's Reach."

"What? Why the fuck would he go there? He's terrified of that place—"

"I think he might've gone to the mine to look for something I lost ..."

I see the understanding wash over them as Luka and Guy share a knowing look.

"Oh shit," Luka says.

Oh shit is right ...

CHAPTER THIRTY-THREE

Leo

I jump down from the ten-foot barbed-wire fence, the earth crunching beneath the heel of my boot, and stare up at the old mine.

I had to tell a couple of white lies and make up an excuse that Ivy needed me to bring her coffee, but as soon as I told Big Dan why I needed to leave, he didn't hesitate before offering to help me. That's the thing about Ivy—she's had everyone in this town smitten with her from the moment she showed up. They'd probably stop the festival just to help me find this list if I asked them to—I'll have to reserve that as my backup plan.

I pause at the doorway, taking a deep breath to psych myself up before I go inside.

I just need to get in, find the list, and get out. If Ivy's memory is correct, this shouldn't take more than a few minutes, and I'll be back in position at the festival before she even realizes I'm missing.

I step inside, and the darkness envelops me even though it's daylight outside. Good thing my phone has a flashlight. I wasn't exactly prepared to come back here today; it was more of a last-minute decision than anything.

Then, when I saw an opening and knew I could count on Big Dan to hold down the fort, I jumped at the opportunity to help.

I promised her I'd find that list, and I have every intention of keeping that promise. She deserves to have that piece of her sister with her when she leaves, and what kind of man would I be if I let her leave here without it ... especially since coming here was *my idea* in the first place?

My light cuts through the darkness as I search the main floor for any glimpse of the list.

It's got to be around here somewhere.

I make another loop around, searching everywhere I remember Ivy standing. She was so busy checking everything out, opening drawers and digging through old treasures. I think she touched every surface of this place with her curious fingers. After several minutes of searching, I don't see any trace of it. I glance at the time on my phone, trying to remember what station I'm supposed to be at now.

I've already been gone longer than I planned, and the last thing I want to do is mess something up by not being where I need to be. Ivy's counting on me. This festival means a lot to her, and I don't think it's just because of her sister. She thrives with all this planning and coming up with new ideas. She's a genius with last-minute emergencies and moving schedules around. It's like her chaotic mind works as her superpower, and she doesn't even realize it.

The loose wooden boards beneath my feet creak in a

loud, high-pitched squeal as I catch sign of a footstep in the dust. I crouch down to a squat to get a better look.

I'd recognize that Converse print anywhere. The girl with wings on her shoes and stars in her eyes.

And it leads straight to a hatch door.

Of course it'd come to this. I don't know how I could've expected it to go any other way.

The last thing I want to do right now is crawl down this hole, where my nightmares were born—especially without Ivy here, giving me a reason to pretend like I'm not afraid—but it's the only place left to look. If she lost it somewhere in the woods, it's going to take a whole lot more manpower to find it—which is my backup plan—but I have a very strong feeling that it's down in that bunker.

I pry open the heavy hatch door, its rusty hinges squealing as I squeeze through the opening. The dank smell of the cave makes my stomach coil, and I do my best to push my fear away. I'm doing this for Ivy, and it's going to take more than a dark, cramped space to stop me.

Taking a deep breath, I use my phone's flashlight to illuminate the rusted metal ladder until it disappears into the darkness beneath—my own personal hell.

"Let's get this over with."

I lower myself inside, clinging to each rung of the ladder with a steel-like grip as I try to distract myself by counting backward.

The darkness swallows me whole, and the putrid smell grows stronger, triggering all the painful memories that fueled my nightmares as I go deeper inside. Bile rises in my stomach, and I spit, trying to rid myself of the scent. It feels like it's worse today than it was last time, but maybe that's because I don't have Ivy's comforting scent to distract me.

I cover my nose with the neck of my shirt as I descend the last few feet, breathing a sigh of relief the moment my shoes connect with the earth.

Now, for the fun part.

I suck in a breath to calm my nerves, but the smell's only growing worse, and the damp, stale air swallows me up, coating my skin like a film. My back brushes against the wall as I maneuver my broad frame through the tight space.

My blood goes cold, and my palms begin to sweat as a fresh wave of fear shoots up my spine.

I'm halfway through the narrow opening, pinned sideways between the tight cave walls, using every panic-attack coping strategy I can conjure from my memory when I hear the haunting squeal of metal hinges, immediately followed by a loud thwack. The noise is so loud that I can feel the vibration through the cavern walls surrounding me.

I don't have to go back to know that my worst nightmare just came true ... yet again.

I'm trapped, with no phone signal, locked in from the outside.

CHAPTER THIRTY-FOUR

Ivy

"I don't understand why he'd take you there. Leo's terrified of that place. He had to go to therapy for two years after his accident. I remember waking up from him screaming from his nightmares. Mom had to move his bedroom downstairs because he kept waking everyone up every night," Luka says.

I check the time on my phone again, trying to come up with all the logical reasons I haven't heard from him. Maybe he dropped his phone when he was crossing the creek, just like I did that night we met.

Who am I kidding? Of course, he's got a waterproof case on his phone, and he wouldn't be so careless to leave it lying around, not on a day as important as today. Besides, when we tried to track him with my phone, I got an error message, saying his location was unavailable.

I can't believe he'd do this. The man willingly drove straight toward his biggest fear, just for me. I'd almost think it was sweet if I wasn't so worried about him.

"Hey, guys. Do you think I could borrow one of your cars?" I say, interrupting their argument over who remembers Leo's hot therapist's name.

"It was definitely Gillian because I remember every time I saw a G name for a girl, I'd get a boner ... for, like, three years or something."

"That doesn't make any fucking sense, Guy. *Your* name starts with a G. Tell me you're full of yourself without telling me."

"Hey, I'll not have you, of all people, kink-shaming me," he says pointedly.

And after hearing Luka's search history, I don't know if I want to know what he's suggesting. If these two are anything like their brother, then there's not a doubt in my mind that they've got some hidden kinks buried under their conventionally handsome exteriors.

"I don't mean to interrupt this extremely important argument you two seem to be having, but I'm really worried about your brother."

They stand nose to nose, and neither one of them bothers to look at me before Luka finally answers, "We can take my bike. I'll get us there in half the time."

"God, you think you're so cool because you drive a motorcycle." Guy pushes Luka in the chest and rolls his eyes.

"I mean, yeah, that's kind of the whole point," Luka says like it's obvious and turns to face me.

I want to argue with him, but there's no time. Leo's been missing for over four hours, and I need to know that he's all right. Even if it means reassigning my responsibilities to the questionably reliable and *only* other person in front of me.

"Guy, do you think you can stay here and hold down the fort? Jett should be here any minute with the keg."

"I've got a delivery," Jett says from behind me, as if on cue.

I spin to face him, feeling a tiny bit of relief that Guy will at least have one adult to supervise him.

"Thank God. You can set it up over there on the side of the stage. There's a tent—make sure it's in the shade, please. I don't need these guys walking out before the parade." I cover my face with my hands. "Shit, that's in two hours ..." I look at Guy with a pleading expression. "Can you please help me out? I need someone to distract them in case we aren't back in time. We can't have your dad pass his *crown* to Leo without *Leo*."

Jett appears again after setting up the keg. He wipes his hands together, then crosses his arms over his chest. "What's going on? Why do you need this needle dick's help?"

I breathe out a sigh, but thankfully, Luka answers for me. "Leo's missing. Ivy and I are going to look for him, so she needs Guy to make sure shit doesn't go off the rails."

Jett narrows his eyes and takes a step closer, his broad shoulders looking impossibly larger. "What do you mean, he's missing?"

I blow a stray strand of hair from my face. "He went back to find a checklist I must've dropped while we were there a couple of days ago. It was the last thing I had left of my sister's ... and I lost it." I sigh, feeling so stupid for causing all of this. "Anyway, I think he went back to the old coal mines to find it ... but it's been over four hours since anyone's seen or heard from him ..."

"You're saying that *Leo* went to the mines ... alone ... of his own accord ... to find something you'd lost?"

I nod, trying to figure out where he's going.

Jett blows out a huff, looking shocked. "Jesus, the man's more whipped than I thought."

His words punch me in the chest, nearly knocking me off-balance as I look between his brothers in shock.

Jett shakes his head in disbelief. "Are you really going to tell us you didn't know? Your relationship might have started out as a lie, but there's no denying our brother is head over heels in love with you ... and judging by the look on your face right now, I'm guessing you just realized you feel the same way."

I open my mouth to speak, but I'm not sure what to say. Of course, I knew he cared for me, but if he really feels that strongly, if he is really in love with me, why hasn't he said something? Why hasn't he asked me to stay here with him instead of moving across the country?

He knew you'd feel guilty, for making you choose, I hear my sister's words in my head and immediately think back to the little girl this morning, knowing she was right. Which makes me wonder ... if I can still hear my sister now, why am I clinging to a list she created in the past?

"So, are we just going to leave Leo to fend for himself out there with all his worst nightmares, or are we going to find him?" Jett finally asks, breaking through the awkward silence.

"Luka and I are heading there now on his—"

"I'm coming with you," Jett says before I can even finish my sentence.

I nod in understanding, realizing how scared he must be and the traumatic memories he's likely remembering.

Guy pulls out his phone and begins typing notes for himself. "So, I just need to transition from the afternoon concert and buy you time until the ceremony? That all?"

I bite my cheek, hating that I have to ask him to do this. "Yeah, there's a list of step-by-step directions on this clipboard, and I have a detailed itinerary here on the iPad." I grab the iPad and swipe over to my Excel sheet. "It's color-coded, but if you swipe, you can see all the events happening, broken down by half-hour chunks. Click on the event, and there's a primary contact in charge with their contact information if you can't get them on the walkie-talkie." I grab the walkie-talkie and my backpack full of supplies—the one Leo packed ahead of time that's already saved my ass multiple times today.

"Wow, this is really thorough." Guy scrolls through the document and looks up at me, wearing a surprised look on his face. "You really thought of everything, didn't you?"

I shrug. "I didn't have your brother going missing anywhere on that list, so I guess not everything ..."

He places a hand on my arm. "Don't worry, Ivy; he'll be all right. You've given him something to fight for."

I force a smile. "Yeah ... I hope you're right."

"I'm going to get a head start; I'll meet you two there. And, Luka, drive safe. I know we're worried, but I don't need you crashing and giving us two reasons to panic."

Luka holds a hand over his heart. "Aw, Jett, you do love me. Don't worry; I'm not an amateur. It's like you have no faith in me."

"Or we've seen you wreck too many times to count," Guy says, but Jett's already walking away.

"Cars are different than bikes. And I barely nudged that guy. It's not my fault he parked in my blind spot."

I step in between them. "Enough, you two. Guy, please call me if you have any questions and ... improvise if you have to. Just don't let anyone see you panicking. No running. Keep things easy and light."

He makes an okay gesture with his fingers. "Easy and light. Got it."

"Oh, and please don't do anything that could get us sued. This is a family-friendly event after all. We don't need Leo's first task as CEO to be damage control," I say as I take off toward Luka, following him to the alley where he parked his bike.

He passes me a helmet, then puts on his own.

"Do you always keep a spare helmet?" I ask as I climb onto the small seat behind him.

He grabs my hands and tucks them around his waist. "You never know when you'll meet a pretty girl who wants to be your backpack ..."

He revs the bike up and takes off down the alleyway, swerving on side roads and in between rows of cars as I hold on for dear life.

This is amazing ... and so convenient. Maybe *I* should look into getting a motorcycle?

Leo would never go for it.

I find it interesting that my automatic thoughts involve Leo now, like he's more than just a speed bump of fun along the way.

"Hold on," Luka says as we pull onto the highway, and he swerves ahead of the line of cars.

So, I do. I hold on, hoping and praying Leo's okay ... because there's something I really need to tell him.

CHAPTER THIRTY-FIVE

Leo

No. No. No.

I force myself back up the tight space, climbing the metal rungs of the ladder two by two despite the growing tightness in my chest and the increasing struggle to breathe.

When I finally reach the top, I pound as hard as I can, fist crashing into the metal that sends a reverberating vibration in my bones.

Maybe it's just stuck?

I pound my fist against the heavy metal door again and again as I try to keep my balance on the flimsy ladder, but it's no use; the door is rusted shut. It'll take someone prying it from the outside to get this thing open.

My vision begins to blur as a fresh wave of panic sets in, and it takes all my concentration to climb back down the ladder. At least if I'm on the ground, I know I'll be safe.

The thought of how long I'll have to wait down here

before they figure out I'm gone, before Ivy realizes *where* I've gone, has my stomach in knots.

What if I ruined the festival for her?

What if they don't find me in time for me to tell her goodbye?

Would she still leave? Do I want her to? Of course, I don't want her to leave, but I also don't want to be the reason she doesn't fulfill her sister's list. It might seem silly, but she's come alive from following the things on that list, and who am I to tell her to stop now?

The thought of causing her any more stress than she's already dealing with is like a knife in a wound.

I shake the thought away. I can't let myself go there. I can't start spiraling because it will only make my anxiety worse, and I already have enough triggers to deal with right now. I take a slow inhale in my nose for seven seconds, hold it for seven more, breathe out for seven seconds, and repeat. I just focus on my breathing and nothing else, trying to ignore the rancid smell.

When I finally feel like I'm halfway calm, I pull out my phone one more time, desperately hoping that I'll have reception.

No service available.

Shit, what am I going to do? What *can* I do?

A flashback of me lying here with a bone sticking out of my thigh, screaming in agony and completely alone in the darkness, rips through me. I catch myself on the smooth, rock wall to keep from falling over as a sense of dizziness nearly knocks me over.

You're going to be fine, Leo. You just need to find

somewhere to sit down and wait this out. They will come for you.

I nod my head as if agreeing with someone other than myself. I begin to weave through the narrow pathway, trying not to panic when the space becomes so tight that I can hardly shuffle my feet. Jesus, were people that much smaller one hundred years ago?

After what feels like an eternity, I finally make it into the larger space of the bunker. I let out a heavy sigh and fall to my knees, savoring the small improvement. At least I don't have memories of lying in here with my bone sticking out of my leg.

There was that creepy draft and the smell though ...

The smell was the naturally occurring scent of sulfur, and the draft came from the wind somewhere inside the cave, I remind myself.

I was a scared kid back then, and the idea of something supernatural taunting me seemed just as likely as any other explanation. But over time, I was able to convince myself there was a reasonable explanation for everything I couldn't explain at the time.

I wipe the sweat from my brow with a trembling hand as I hang my head, feeling so many emotions all at once. I take in the small room, where cots and broken metal bunk beds sit in rows. It's like I'm seeing it again for the first time after all those years of nightmares.

There's the cot I was sleeping on that night, and Jett slept on the opposite end. We were both terrified but trying to pretend like we weren't, especially me. I always thought I needed to be the bravest because I was the oldest.

I acted like I was so annoyed that Jett had forced me to let him tag along, but really, I was relieved that I wouldn't have to be alone.

Who would've thought I'd end up trapped down here, back where all my worst nightmares were born? And willingly. Well, not the trapped part anyway—that was just my terrible luck.

I think of Ivy's smiling face, the golden freckles that stretch across her nose and the way her honey eyes sparkle with mischief. Fuck, she's so pretty, it hurts, and I don't think I've ever met someone with such a massive, welcoming presence. She sucks you in, like a tornado of giggles and deep conversation. She's so damn funny and quick-witted. She keeps me on my toes and pushes me in ways no one else ever has.

I feel the fear start to dissipate, so I let my mind drift further, remembering all the moments we shared, the way I felt when I first laid eyes on her, and how she propped those white Converse sneakers up on my dash like she'd been riding shotgun with me for years. I don't think a single day's gone by that I don't play that conversation back in my head.

God, she infuriated me that night ... and just about every day since.

But that's what I love about her. She knows how to get under my skin. She knows how to get through to me in a way no one else has. She's the first person who's ever looked at me and really seen the man I kept hidden beneath, the real me I was too scared to show the world.

Suddenly, I realize that this place isn't half as terrifying as the thought of losing her.

Maybe that makes me selfish, but how the fuck am I supposed to let her go? I don't know what the answer is, but

I'll be damned if I'm going to sit here, rotting in this hole, now that I know what I'm missing.

I swipe my phone open again, trying for the millionth time to see if I have service, but this time, the glow of my screen illuminates something small and white.

And there, tucked beneath one of the old, mangled cots, is the very thing I came down here to find. I pick it up, taking in the bubble letters of Ivy's name written on the side in glittery blue ink and hold the list to my heart.

I don't know how long it'll take before someone finds me, but at least I know one thing: my efforts were not in vain. I might have ruined everything she'd planned today and caused a whole lot of panic for my family, but at least I was able to keep my promise. At least I'll be able to return her most prized possession.

I carefully unfold the paper like it's a precious antique, ancient and fragile, and I take in the words that have guided Ivy's every decision for the last five years. I read the list as I remember everything I did to help her and some things I didn't realize were even on there.

My eyes catch on the words *Make something better than it was before*, where she checked the box with an arrow pointing to *The Phantom Festival.*

I smile when I think back to the wet T-shirt contest she accidentally started at a work trivia night and the way she checked off that she partied in Vegas for her twenty-first birthday, *Bart's Party* scribbled to the side. I had no idea some of these things were on here, and I laugh, thinking of how they came up with some of this stuff.

Learn to fish. Check.

Jump off a waterfall. Check.

Make out with someone rich and famous. Check.

That one really makes me laugh. Honestly, I don't think I could've written a more accurate list of things we did together. It almost feels like the list was created in reverse.

I scan my eyes down further, pausing when I see *Change someone's life .. for the better.* My name's there, too, circled and underlined three times with a giant check mark right beside it.

Holy shit, this girl is full of surprises, isn't she?

But when I see the last one, I find my eyes welling with tears, and all my worries fly right out the window.

Fall in love, the kind you read about in romance novels. Check.

And there's my name again, written in big, bold letters. She even drew a heart in place of the O in my name.

Now, I know that no matter the circumstances, she feels the same way... everything else is just semantics.

CHAPTER THIRTY-SIX

Ivy

"We have to climb that?" Luka says, looking up at the ten-foot-tall barbed-wire fence spanning the perimeter of the mine.

I wipe my hands on the front of my overalls. "Yes. Have you never been here before? I thought this was some kind of teenage initiation."

I begin climbing the fence with a practiced technique, and I hear Luka grunt as he jumps up to follow me.

"What part of this being illegal is so hard for you to understand? Some of us don't need to prove anything. Some of us are content with riding motorcycles and playing video games; we don't need to break the law and provoke monsters too."

I get to the top and pause. Last time, Leo brought a sweatshirt to cover the barbed wire, but naturally, I didn't think of that. I hike my leg over, carefully balancing my weight to keep from slicing my leg open.

"What are you doing? Are you fucking serious right now? You want me to climb over that—"

"At least you're wearing pants. Stop whining, and let's go."

I carefully pull my other leg over, but my bottom foot slips on the fence, and my top leg crashes down on the barbed wire, snagging my thigh. It's the only reason I didn't fall.

"Shit. Ow. Fuck." I wince, finding my footing and pushing myself up enough to pull the sharp wire from my thigh. A stream of blood drips down all at once, like turning on a water hose, covering my overalls and socks.

I hear Luka's audible gag behind me as he heaves several times.

"You okay?" I ask when he gets to the top, but he just gives me a silent thumbs-up, probably too afraid he'll puke if he opens his mouth.

I land on the ground with a thud and call up to him, "Just go slow over the top and watch your footing."

He carefully swings his long legs over, clearing it with ease. Must be nice to be tall. I guess Leo didn't even need the sweatshirt, which means he remembered to bring it because he was thinking of me.

The realization feels like salt in my wound. Leo's always thinking of me. Even when he seemed to hate me. It's in the little things he does, like bringing an extra sweatshirt because he knew my legs weren't long enough to clear the barbed wire, or checking to see if my coffee was the right color and temperature before bringing it to me, or packing my backpack before the festival with all the things he knew I'd need without me having to ask...

Meanwhile, all I've done is taunt him and try to get under

his skin. He shouldn't have come back here by himself. He shouldn't have to face his literal worst fears because of me ...

"I don't know if I would've offered so willingly if I had known I'd be climbing barbed-wire fences and—oh my God, that's disgusting." Luka climbs down and covers his mouth when he sees the stream of blood pouring down my leg.

I probably look like something straight out of a horror movie, but there's nothing I can do about it right now. "Come on. Let's find Leo."

"Listen, I don't know what kind of freaky shit you and my brother are into, but I'd appreciate you never bringing me in the middle of it ever again—"

I shove him forward as we move inside, stepping over piles of rubble, planks of wood, and ashes as far as the eye can see.

"Where do you think he went?" Luka asks, eyes growing wide as he scans the large front room.

"I'm not sure, just keep your eyes out for any signs of him ..." I duck under a fallen sheet of roofing, scanning the hallway. "Leo! Leo, are you here?" I call, my voice echoing off the empty walls so clearly that it sounds like someone else entirely.

"Leo!" Luka yells somewhere behind me.

"Leo! Leo, can you hear me? It's Ivy!" I call, the threat of tears beginning to burn behind my eyes as I really start to worry.

I really thought he'd be here. I don't know what I was expecting exactly. That I'd walk in, and he'd be sitting there, waiting for me, ready to hear my apology and welcome me back into his life with open arms?

"Leo! Dude, don't play with me right now," Luka says, and I can hear the fear in his voice too.

I look at him as a fresh wave of worry falls over me, and my heart races in my chest.

"What if he's not here? I really thought he'd be here." My overactive imagination offers me an assortment of other terrifying scenarios to consider.

"Is this everything? Have we searched all the rooms?" Luka asks, breaking me out of my anxiety spiral.

Bang. Bang. Bang.

I stop in my tracks and look at Luka. "Did you hear that?"

"Hear what?"

The faint banging picks back up, and we both take off toward the sound.

"Is he stuck down there?" I say more to myself than to Luka as I rush down the hallway to the safe room, where I find the bunker door clamped shut.

Bang. Bang. Bang.

"Leo?" I say as I try to pull the rusted metal latch, but it doesn't budge.

"Ivy! Ivy, baby, is that you?" Leo's muffled voice says from the other side of the door.

Luka jumps in beside me, and we strain to pull the door open, but even with both of us, it still doesn't budge.

"Yes, it's me!" I glance around the small room. There are no holes to give us sunlight, and it takes a minute for my eyes to adjust to the darkness. "Don't worry; we're going to get you out of there. Just hang tight, okay?"

"Ivy, I'm so sorry. I'm sorry I ruined your plans for today. I know how hard you worked, and I just wanted you to have your list before you left ..."

Luka gives me a confused look, but doesn't say anything, just keeps pulling at the latch.

"Don't apologize. This is the sweetest thing anyone's ever done for me, and you didn't ruin anything ..." I grab a shard of metal from the corner and carry it over to the latch. "Maybe we can pry it open with this?"

Luka shrugs for me to try, and I shove the thin metal in the crack, but it just bends as soon as I put my weight on it.

"The door's stuck. Do you think you can push it from the inside?" I call out.

"Yeah, I'll try."

I move back to the latch and brace myself just as Jett bursts through the door, looking wild and like he's ready to fight someone or something—I'm not entirely sure.

"Good, you're here. Come help us with the latch," Luka says, and Jett immediately stalks over to help, not questioning a thing.

"On three," I say loud enough for Leo to hear me as we all brace ourselves.

"One. Two. Three."

We yank the latch, using all our strength. The metal door lifts, creaking a screech of protest, and the heavy door crashes to the ground with a loud thud. Dust clouds fog the air around us, making us all cough to catch our breath, and then Leo's pulling me into him, pressing me against his big chest and holding me so tight that it knocks the air from my lungs.

"Fuck, baby girl, I've never been so happy to see you." His lips crash over mine as he kisses me like I'm his only source of air and he's suffocating.

I wrap my arms around his neck and then pull my legs around his waist, forgetting all about my open wound because the rush of adrenaline and relief that he's okay and he's here are all that matters.

"Ivy, baby, please forgive me. I'm so fucking sorry." He wipes my matted hair from my face and swipes a thumb over my tear-streaked cheek. "I'm so happy to see you. I started to think I wouldn't be able to say goodbye—"

I shake my head. "Leo, listen, about that ..."

"What time is it?" He checks the time on his phone and lets out a sigh of relief. "Fuck, I really thought I'd screwed everything up, but you still have time to make it if we leave now." He grabs my hand and starts walking toward the doorway.

I should be relieved because he's right; I do have time. If we leave right now, I could still make it. Sure, I wouldn't have any of my things, but it wouldn't be hard for him to ship them to me, and it's not like I don't have money to buy new clothes in the meantime ... but what about Fern's ashes? They're with the rest of my things in the back of Leo's car.

If only I'd been willing to let her go the other night, none of this would be happening. If I hadn't been such a coward, maybe I wouldn't have dropped the list, Leo wouldn't have felt like he needed to sneak away to look for it, the festival events wouldn't be running behind schedule, and everything would've gone according to plan.

Who am I kidding? Isn't this exactly the type of thing that always happens when I'm in charge? Isn't this exactly what I've been trying to avoid by following my sister's list? I can't help but wonder if there's a hidden message in all the chaos.

Leo's right; I could leave right now and be there on time to board my flight ... but the thought of leaving so abruptly feels like my heart's being ripped in two. I'm not ready to say goodbye—and not just to Leo, but to this town. I feel like I have unfinished business, and I'm torn between following my sister's plan and sticking around to finish, to finally follow through on something for the first time in my life.

I chew on my lip and shake my head, pulling my hand free from Leo's grip. "We have to go back to the festival—"

"Baby, we don't have time. It's going to take an hour to get to the airport as it is, and you still need to account for security—"

"I've got Guy stalling right now, and the whole ending ceremony depends on you being there."

He shakes his head. "There's nothing more important right now than making sure you catch that flight. Ivy, I can't let you do this, not for me. I couldn't live with myself if I messed this opportunity up for you."

I cross my arms over my chest. "I can't leave my sister's ashes. We'll deal with this later, but right now, we need to hurry, or all of this will be for nothing."

He purses his lips because there's no way he can argue against that.

"Do you two need a minute of privacy or ..." Luka interrupts.

We both look over. I forgot they were here. Poor Leo looks so startled that I truly don't think he even noticed his brothers before he kissed me.

He looks back at me with confusion on his face, and I shrug.

"I might have asked your brothers for help. Hope you don't mind."

"Well, now that we know you're safe, I think I'll head back," Jett says, pulling out his keys from his pocket.

Leo opens his mouth to respond, but then his eyes go wide, and he's dropping to his knees in front of me to get a better look at my wound. "Jesus Christ, Ivy, what happened to your leg?"

"It's not as bad as it looks." I try to pull him up, but he doesn't budge as he examines the cut.

"This is going to need stitches. We need to clean this up, so it doesn't get infected."

I grab his face between my hands. "Leo, I'm fine, really. It's just a cut."

His eyes search mine, and he finally nods. "Okay. Well, if you insist on going back, then we're stopping at the medical tent first thing. I don't want to hear any arguments."

"Okay," I say sheepishly, feeling so mixed up about everything and hoping I'm making the right decision.

Leo looks up at Luka. "Can I ask you for one more favor, little brother?"

Luka shakes his head. "Don't even think about it—"

"I'll owe you one. Big time," he says, holding out his hands.

Luka pauses, staring at him like he's considering, then pulls his keys from his pocket with a sigh. "Fine, but you'd better not put a single scratch on her, or I'll never offer to help you out ever again."

Leo catches the keys and dangles them in front of me. "All right, let's get to that parade."

CHAPTER THIRTY-SEVEN

Leo

"Thanks again, Dr. Stone."

Ivy put up a good fight, assuring me she was fine, that this could wait, that we didn't have time to stop first, but I wouldn't budge on this. I don't consider myself to be a squeamish person, but seeing her covered in blood like that really did a number on me.

Luckily, Dr. Stone was already waiting with all the supplies to give her stitches, and it saved us hours of sitting in the emergency room. It's one of the many reasons I love this town—everyone's always willing to go the extra mile to help one another.

Maybe Ivy missing her flight was inevitable whether we came back or not, but it didn't stop me from trying to think of every solution possible the whole ride over. I begged her to let me try to fix this—well, as best as I could, talking through a motorcycle helmet.

I offered to swing her by and grab her bags and her sister's ashes so we could at least attempt to make her flight. I even suggested calling in a favor at the airport, maybe making a donation if they agreed to stall the flight to buy us time to get there, but Ivy wouldn't hear of it.

If I didn't know better, I'd think this was another way for her to avoid having to deal with telling her sister goodbye ... or maybe telling me goodbye. But who am I to force her to leave when she doesn't feel ready? Fuck, of course I can't stand the idea of telling her goodbye, but I can't let her give up on her dreams for me either. This entire situation is a mess, and it's all my fault for disappearing on her today.

I don't know what's going through that head of hers. All I know is, she chose to come back to the festival over following the list, and that has to mean *something*. Besides, I'm relieved that I still get to surprise her.

"Of course. Anything for my godson and this special lady." He shakes my hand, giving me a curious look, though he doesn't ask how she injured herself. "Make sure to keep it clean. You can stop by my office in about two weeks, and we can remove those stitches."

"I'll take good care of her, Doc. She won't have to lift a finger," I say, wrapping an arm around her.

"I have no doubt, son."

"Okay, I'm fine. Can we go now? You're sort of the main event, you know. I don't know how much longer Guy can stall everyone," Ivy says, snapping back into planner mode as if the events over the last few hours never happened.

I wrap my hand in hers, wanting to savor every last moment I have left. "Don't worry, baby; we're not going to miss it. Guy and Luka are on it. Jett texted me after he dropped him off. Everyone's in position, and I'm sure everyone will be more than entertained while they wait," I assure her as we make our way to the middle of the parade.

I can see the giant red throne of my dad's float, and I realize they aren't moving. So, I guess whatever Guy's doing to stall is working.

We weave our way through the crowd of people until we finally make it to my dad's float. His face flashes a look of relief when he sees me as he waves and smiles to everyone.

Ivy tries to sneak inside through the hidden door, but I catch her arm, shaking my head.

"Stay with me. Who cares about the plan? I need you by my side."

She nods, standing there awkwardly beside me as my mother hugs her in greeting, whispering something in her ear that makes her relax.

Then, she hugs me, wrapping a cape around my back as she hisses in my ear, "Where the hell have you been? Your father and I have been worried sick ever since we heard you were missing."

"Sorry about that. I'll fill you in later. How's everything going?"

The corner of her lip curls into a grin. "See for yourself. I think they're almost finished."

I follow her eyes as I see Guy—at least I think it's Guy—draped in a dark, loose-fitting dress, wearing a long, dark-haired wig as he falls to his knees, begging for his life.

He's on his own float, but it's basically just a flat trailer bed that they must've added right before my dad's so he could stall. That's actually really smart. It almost looks like it was always supposed to be part of the parade.

Smoke fills the air around him, and he tries to fight back a cough, but eventually gives in.

"Is that a fog machine? Are they reenacting the—"

"Shh ... this is the best part," my mother says.

I glance at Ivy, who appears to be equally confused.

"Don't ask me," she says.

Suddenly, there's a large boom, and someone dressed in a Phantom costume, bobblehead and all, drops in front of him.

"How the hell did they have time to get ahold of the high school mascot costume?"

"Would you zip it? This is a beautiful moment your brothers are creating," my mother hisses under her breath, confirming the other character to be none other than Luka.

Jeez, where do these two come up with this shit? It's almost terrifying how good they are. It makes me wonder how much time they spent practicing this in their free time.

We watch as my brothers captivate the crowd in their reenactment of the Phantom's first appearance. Luka even goes as far as placing his foot over Guy's throat as he delivers the Phantom's infamous warning.

The crowd falls silent as Guy writhes beneath him in fear. Then, another cloud of smoke appears, and suddenly, Luka's gone.

·Everyone erupts in applause as Guy and Luka return, both bowing and waving as the high school marching band plays the fight song behind them.

Holy shit. Consider me impressed.

After the song ends, my mother turns on her mic, thanking my brothers for their epic performance that will undoubtedly become a permanent addition to all future festivals.

"Now, I'd like to give my husband an opportunity to say a few words." She passes the mic to my dad, who moves from his throne at the top of the float down to the pavilion beside us.

"Thank you, Mary. You know, when I started Kingsley Industries, I had one goal. To make the world a better place. I know; I know. That's a lofty goal indeed, but when I look around this town, it is clear that's exactly what we've done here.

"None of it would have been possible without the people of this wonderful community. I don't know that our business could've thrived anywhere else because I might have had the idea, but you all created the spirit and energy that kept us going.

"And from that little seed of an idea, all of this was born." He spans his arms wide. "I've devoted the last twenty-five years of my life to this company, and it's going to be a hard adjustment to step away from it." He turns to face my mother, who looks so proud. "But that's the way life should be. We get to have something for a season, and when that season is over, we have to let it go. It's like raising children in a lot of ways—you spend all this time molding them and guiding them, but at the end of the day, they get to go out there and be their own people. All you can do is be there for them, cheer them on, and hope that you've prepared them as best as you could.

"It's why our work is important. Because it impacts those around us and creates opportunities for those who maybe wouldn't have them otherwise. Our identity as an individual, at the core of who we are, is so much bigger than any title we can earn.

"So, as it comes time to name my successor, there was always only one choice about who it could be, someone who's proven to be trustworthy and who's committed to keeping our mission alive and making the world a healthier, cleaner, better place."

He places a hand on my shoulder, giving me a little nod as he looks at me with so much pride. "So, without further ado, I'd like to pass the baton over to my son, Leo Kingsley."

He removes the gaudy plastic crown from his head and places it on mine as everyone around us applauds and cheers.

But I'm not looking at any of them because my eyes are trained on Ivy, who's trying to mask her own tears as she stands beside my mother. None of this would have been possible without her, and I owe her everything for helping me to finally let go of my armor of guilt.

"Thanks, Dad. This means so much to me. I've spent my whole life working toward this goal, and you have no idea how amazing it feels to be given this responsibility. I do not take it lightly.

"I'd like to thank you all for coming out to celebrate the one hundredth anniversary of our town's infamous Phantom sighting. We love putting this festival together each year to celebrate our town's history, and you might have noticed this year's festival has been the best one yet ..."

I pause as I wait for the crowd's applause to calm down and gesture for Ivy to come closer.

"None of this would have been possible without this incredible woman standing beside me, the woman who's captured all of our hearts from the moment she arrived." I check my watch. "She's supposed to be boarding a flight to go halfway across the world right now, but instead, she chose to come back here to make sure everything went according to plan, which just goes to show the level of dedication she has and the effort she put in to make this festival so spectacular. Which is why we wanted to give you a token of our appreciation ..."

Her eyes go wide, and she looks around trying to see what I'm talking about.

"Leo ... what is this?" she whispers under her breath.

I take her hand in mine as I lead her off the float, lifting her down and placing her gently on the ground. I lead her over to the Phantom statue that stands in the center of the town square, to where a tarp is draped to cover something on the other side.

I turn to face her. "All of this might have started out as a fake plan to convince everyone I was a changed man ... but the way I feel about you is anything but *fake*."

"You've not only stolen my heart, but you have everyone in this town rooting for you too. We know you've got a big future ahead of you, and you're only at the beginning of your journey to find yourself."

I grab the corner of the tarp, pausing as I let my words sink in. Her eyes well with tears as she looks at the familiar faces around her.

Big Dan stands behind her, his arm wrapped around his wife, Susan, who Ivy helped him surprise for their anniversary on her first day here.

Miss Scarlett wipes her eyes with a tissue, her nose red and swollen from crying.

My family's all gathered together, even Jett, standing by in support, and I even catch sight of Ricky and Janice, who've been inseparable since that wild company trivia night. She's touched so many lives in her short time here, and I don't think she even realizes it.

I pull the tarp away, revealing a shiny, new bench that sits just in front of the Phantom. "You always have a place here in Ashford Falls to call home."

Ivy gasps, her hands covering her mouth as she takes a step closer to get a better look. Her fingers trail over the inscription, and she looks back at me with tear-filled eyes.

It reads, *In loving memory of Fern Ophelia Lane.*

"Leo ... I can't believe you did this. This is too much. It's ... it's ..."

I take a step toward her. "It wasn't just me; we all did this. We took a town vote, and it was unanimous. We wanted to honor your sister and give you a home base you could always come back to. I know you're young, and you've still got things you need to do to find yourself, but you'll always have a home here. You breathed a new life into this town, and we wanted to show you how much you're going to be missed."

She shakes her head. "Thank you. You have no idea how much this means to me ..." Her words trail off as she wipes her tears with the back of her hand.

"Oh, I almost forgot." I stick my hand in my pocket and pull out the worn, small, folded piece of paper. "I found this underneath one of the cots down in the bunker. It must've fallen out of your pocket when we were down there."

She slowly takes the fragile list as a look of relief washes over her face, but then her eyes drop, and I can see the slight quiver in her lip.

I tilt her chin up. "Hey, baby girl, don't worry. I promise we're going to figure it out. I'll have you on the first flight out in the morning. I promise you're not going to miss your first day even if it means I have to buy a commercial airline and schedule the flight myself. I'll do whatever it takes to get you there—that is a promise."

She bites her lip and sighs as tears fill her eyes. I swipe a fallen tear from her cheek with my thumb, and it kills me to see her so emotional, but I stay quiet and give her time to compose her thoughts.

"It's not that," she says through sniffles. "It's just ... a lot ... and I feel like I'm being torn between two really good things. And I don't know what to do because my heart wants both of them ... and then I feel guilty for even questioning my sister's list when she's the reason for all of this." She opens her arms wide, then wipes her tears with the back of her hand. "I'm so confused, and I don't feel ready, and that list is just another reminder that there *is* a choice to be made."

She sniffles. Miss Scarlett offers her a tissue with a gentle pat on the shoulder, and then she's gone just as quickly as she appeared.

Ivy blows her nose and laughs because it's exactly like Miss Scarlett to eavesdrop just enough to be helpful before leaving to give us privacy.

"You know I'm here for you, right? I'm here to support you however you need it. I'm so fucking proud of you."

She nods, dabbing away the last of her tears. "I know."

I nudge her with my arm. "Why don't we go home so you can get some rest, and then I'll help you figure this out? We still have a little time, and there's nothing we can do about it tonight. Let me draw you a bubble bath and make some calls."

"What about all of this? We still need to clean things up.

There's so much that needs to be done. I don't want to leave all this work for everyone else—"

Miss Scarlett pops out of nowhere, placing a hand on Ivy's shoulder. "Honey, we've got it. Please, for the love of God, listen to this seasoned woman's advice. When a handsome man offers to draw you a bubble bath and fawn over you, you take it." She whistles with her fingers, commanding everyone's attention. "All right, everyone, you know the drill. Let's get this cleaned up. We don't want to be here all night."

Without missing a beat, everyone jumps into action—breaking down tables, offering to pack up supplies. No arguing, just pitching in to help. The sight warms my heart. It's not that I ever doubted they'd pull through to help—hell, I've seen this modeled for me my whole life—but it still never gets old.

I tug Ivy's hand and pull her toward me. "See, there's nothing to worry about. Let me take care of you for one more night."

"Okay," she says, sounding so meek and defeated and nothing like the spunky firecracker I've grown to love.

Looks like I've got my work cut out for me tonight.

CHAPTER THIRTY-EIGHT

Leo

"There you go, baby. Why don't you soak in here and I'll go make some calls?" I turn around to find her standing there, completely naked, those big eyes staring right through me, and the sight nearly knocks me down.

She steps into the tub, slowly lowering herself, and she's already scooting forward to make room for me. I don't hesitate before sliding in behind her, sighing as the hot, sudsy water laps up around me, and my skin slowly adjusts to the temperature. My aching muscles relax as the stress of the day melts away, and for a moment, nothing else exists.

Ivy leans against my chest and lets out a little sigh, and I have a feeling she's thinking the same thing. Good. She deserves to relax after the stressful day she had. I've got all night to figure out a game plan, but right now, I've got her naked in my arms, and I'd be a fool to waste this moment.

I squirt some soap on a loofah and massage her shoulders, stealing touches of her soft skin as I wash my way down her body. She moans, tilting her head to the side to give me better access, and by the time I make it to her legs, I can't keep my composure any longer. I toss the loofah to the side and trace my fingertips over her delicate curves.

Fuck, I'm going to miss this.

She lets out an exhale as she wiggles her ass against me and parts her thighs to give me more access. My cock grows impossibly harder as I brush my fingers along her slick center, feeling how wet she is, how responsive her body is to my touch.

I slide a thumb over her clit, and she sucks in a gasp, her perky tits bouncing above the bubbles as she writhes around, clearly needing this release just as badly as I do. I squeeze one of her breasts in my palm as I tease her tight entrance.

"Fuck, baby girl, you're already so wet," I whisper as I kiss her neck, loving how her slick body feels, rubbing against my cock.

We're both so desperate for a release.

I slide two fingers inside of her tight pussy as her slick, soapy body wiggles against me, and I play with her nipple. She lets out the sexiest little mewl of pleasure as her head falls back on my shoulder and spreads her legs wider. I feel her muscles start to tense, and I know she's close, so I keep my pace, deepening my strokes as I fuck her with my fingers.

"Oh God. Yes. Yes, Leo. I'm … I'm …"

"Come for me, baby girl. Come all over my fingers like Daddy's good little slut," I whisper as I kiss and suck her neck, knowing she'll be wearing my marks tomorrow.

Her pussy spasms around my fingers as she squirms and moans, and I drink in the view of her gorgeous body that fits so perfectly around my own. It's almost too much to bear, and my cock strains, painfully erect just from the sight, from knowing I'm the reason for her flushed cheeks and her racing heart that's beating in rhythm with my own.

I've never felt so alive, so connected to another person, and all I want is to bury myself so deep inside her that our souls intertwine so I can feel her with me, no matter how many miles separate us. I can't stand the thought of her leaving, but I wouldn't be able to live with myself if she gave up her dream for me either. I love her so fucking much that I'd rather lose her than see her choose me over herself. She's spent her whole life putting everyone's emotional needs and happiness above her own. It's time for Ivy to follow her heart … even if it means breaking mine.

"I need to be inside you," I grunt.

I scoop her up and wrap a towel around her dripping body before carrying her to the bed.

Goose bumps erupt over her skin as I lay her down on the cool sheets of my bed. I slide my palm over her hard nipples, admiring my view as I look down at her, trying to memorize her every curve and freckle. Her bare pussy looks so fucking beautiful, and my mouth waters to taste her, but the thoughts going through my head have me so turned on that I'm afraid I won't last much longer.

"Fuck, baby, your pussy is so pretty."

I slide my palm over her mound, and she flinches from my slight touch as I line my cock up with her entrance.

I grab her hips, pulling her closer to me, and thrust myself inside her in one swift movement, both of us gasping for breath as I drive my cock inside her tight heat.

"Fuck," I groan, using one hand to cup her tit. I press my

other to hold her hip in place as I find that perfect angle that makes her toes curl.

Usually, I ease her into it, but not tonight. Tonight, we're needy and desperate. Tonight, I don't have the strength to hold myself back. Tonight, I need to take just as much as I give because this might be my last chance to hold the other half of my soul.

I lose myself in her, intertwining my fingers in hers as our bodies say everything our words can't.

Goodbye.

I love you.

Please don't leave me.

I take my time, drawing out every touch, every stroke as I keep my eyes trained on hers, swallowing her whimpers of pleasure with my kisses as we both fall apart. Again and again.

We give each other everything we have to give, riding the currents of pleasure until we collapse in the twisted sheets in a sweaty heap of tangled limbs. I pass Ivy a bottle of water from my side table before grabbing a wet washcloth to clean her up. She doesn't fight me when I wrap her in a soft white robe or when I insist on helping her brush out her tangled hair before tucking her into bed beside me.

I think we both needed this night.

I click off the lamp and hold her, eyes wide open as I stare up at the ceiling. It doesn't take long before her breathing grows heavy, and she's fast asleep, looking so goddamn beautiful, like a fallen angel. My naughty, bratty angel sent to unravel me from the tangled shield of guilt I kept woven around myself. In just thirty days, this devastatingly perfect woman has changed my whole damn life.

The thought of losing her outweighs any fear I've ever had. Could I give it all up if it meant I wouldn't have to say goodbye?

In a heartbeat.

Suddenly, an idea pops into my mind, and before I know what I'm doing, I'm sliding out of bed, and making my way upstairs to my office.

Lucky for me, Roman answers on the first ring.

CHAPTER THIRTY-NINE

Ivy

"Good morning. I've got your coffee here, just the way you like it," Leo says as he places my favorite coffee mug on the side table before ruffling my hair.

A small smile pulls at my lips because I love how gentle he is with me in the mornings, how he's so nurturing with the way he wakes me up.

He walks to the windows, drawing the curtains open. Warm rays of sunshine streak through the room, and the sun peeks between the mountains in the distance. It's a view that should be on a postcard, and I feel so lucky to be one of the few people who can say they've seen it in person. Leo disappears into the bathroom, and I hear the faucet turn on as he brushes his teeth and shaves.

I reach my arms over my head and stretch my aching muscles, feeling lighter than I have in weeks despite the unease that's still coiling in my stomach over what to do. Usually, I'm not one to stress because I know things have a way of working out, but this feels different somehow, like the stakes are so much higher and I don't want to make the wrong choice.

My mind was racing nonstop last night, and I knew there'd be no way I could fall asleep, but then Leo found a way to take my mind off it. It's like he knows the inner workings of my mind better than I do, and he gave me the best distraction anyone could ask for. By the time he was through with me, I was so sated, so exhausted, that the only thing I could do was sleep. It was exactly what I needed and everything I'm going to miss.

Last night, I let my heavy eyelids drift closed, and the next thing I knew, I was sixteen years old, sitting with my sister in my childhood bedroom.

I touch my cheek, remembering the dream. It was so realistic. She was sitting across from me, holding my hands, and I could feel her calm, reassuring presence. She looked exactly the way I remember... before she got sick. I told her all about my adventures in Ashford Falls, how I managed to check nearly everything off her list. I told her about Leo and how strong my feelings for him had grown. We laughed as she teased me, prying for all the details, and I told her *everything*. I held nothing back as her eyes widened and her cheeks burned in embarrassment. This was how I'd always imagined it would be between us. We'd grow older, and we'd share our lives—the good, the bad, and everything in between. We'd keep no secrets because we always knew when the other was lying anyway.

And when I was finished, she smiled at me and told me how proud she was to see me living my life and that I deserved to be happy. She said that she'd always be there, watching over my life like it was her favorite soap opera, and to make sure I didn't let it get too boring, or she'd be forced to cause chaos for her own entertainment. It's exactly something she'd say, and for some reason, I believe it.

I replay the last words she spoke to me as I was hugging her goodbye. *"I have to go now, Ivy, but I want you to know that I'm ready, and I think you finally are too."*

Then, she just disappeared, and I woke up.

Leaning against the headboard, I let out a sigh and slurp my hot coffee that's perfectly sweetened, just as Leo walks in from the bathroom, freshly shaven. He's dressed in a black T-shirt that hugs his chest and khaki shorts that show off his incredible thighs, and the sight of him has my mouth watering.

I catch a whiff of his aftershave as he approaches, his lips twitching to hold back a smile. I haven't seen myself, but I'd be willing to bet I've got some wicked bedhead going on after how hard I slept last night.

"I'm going to finish up a few things in my office. I went ahead and laid out some comfy clothes for you, and I've already got your bags packed and loaded in the trunk of my car." He bends down to kiss the top of my head, his hand cradling the back of my neck as he says, "I had to pull a few strings, but I was able to get you on the next flight out to Romania. We'll need to leave no later than noon to get through security on time."

My heart starts to race as a fresh wave of anxiety rips through me. I glance at the clock and let out a sigh of relief, realizing we still have time. "Do you think we could leave in about an hour? There's something I need to do before I go."

He nods, pursing his lips. "Just say the word."

I sink back down in the bed as I watch him disappear through the doorway, holding on to my sister's message like a lifeline.

What if I'm making the wrong choice?

Ferny, please tell me what I should do.

*   *   *

"Are you sure about this?" Leo's green eyes stare back at me, filled with worry and concern as he passes me the urn.

We're standing in front of the biggest of the seven waterfalls as the sound of crashing water fills the otherwise silent space between us. There's no heaviness this time, and I feel a sense of calm and safety that I know is from Leo.

I give him a silent nod as a sense of peace washes over me, and I know without a shadow of a doubt that this is what she would've wanted because she told me last night. It was so real, and there isn't a cell in my body that doesn't believe it was really her, that someway, somehow, she managed to visit me. My sister defied space and time just to reassure me that we were both finally ready ... and now that I know she's capable of *that*, she'd better know I expect her to do it again.

I hold the small urn against my chest, the one I've carried around with me everywhere I've moved for the last five years, pressing it firmly against my heart with only the denim of my overalls and my sister's list between.

I think back to the little girl I talked to the morning of the festival, remembering what she told me and how I could still talk to my sister.

Closing my eyes, I take a deep breath, holding it for a few seconds as I cross my fingers over my heart. I think of my sister's smiling face, her gray eyes, and her dark humor as I tell her how much I love her, and in that moment, it feels like she's right next to me.

I finally let myself exhale, feeling my shoulders sag in relief, and when I open my eyes, all the pain dulls. It's still there—I don't think it's possible for it ever not to be—but rather than emptiness, I feel more nostalgic. It's like I'm remembering the best of times with fondness, of someone who's lived a full life and doesn't have a single regret.

It feels like peace.

"I love you, Ferny, and I'm so grateful for this wild list you dreamed up that's led me to all these incredible adventures. I get it now, why you made the list and why you insisted I complete it without you. You wanted to push me out of my comfort zone, and you knew I needed something to help me process my grief. You didn't want me to fall complacent and settle like our parents, and you didn't want me to stop living my life just because I didn't have you by my side, calling the shots."

I laugh and wipe a tear from my eye as Leo stands beside me, my strong, dependable rock.

"I miss you so damn much. There's not a day that goes by that I don't think about you, and I used to think that meant I was doing it wrong, that I was grieving wrong. I ran from the pain of missing you and filled my life with distraction after distraction just to keep some of the grief at bay.

"But now, I realize, grief isn't something you can run from ... it always catches you eventually. I thought I could ignore the pain, and it'd fade like an old scar over time, but the more I tried, the more painful it was to remember you. Then, I dived headfirst into your list and thought that was the way to the other side of my grief.

"I thought if I could just do all the things you wanted to do, then maybe I'd keep your memory alive and feel closer to you at the same time. And I did for a while. I tried things I never would've done on my own, traveled places I wouldn't have known to look for, and met some pretty amazing people along the way."

I look at Leo, who looks at me with an intensity that borders obsessive, and my heart does a little somersault in my chest because I feel the same way about him. It feels like a dream come true, a dream I never even knew I had.

"Thank you for pushing me out of my comfort zone, Ferny. Thank you for giving me a road map to get started. Thank you for always taking care of me and looking out for me—and I know you still do because you led me here."

I open the urn and hold it out over the water. "Goodbye, twin sister. I love you so much, and I promise to always live a life that makes you proud."

As I pour the ashes into the water, I expect the familiar ache of sadness to knock me off my feet, but instead I'm filled with a relief I've never known. Warmth spreads through me like a balm on a wound, soothing the cracks and holes in my broken heart.

Leo squeezes my shoulder. "I'm proud of you, Ivy, and I know Fern is too. I hope you're proud of yourself for how far you've come."

Wiping the fresh tears from my cheeks that I didn't even realize had fallen, I nod. "I really am."

I pull the list from the pocket of my overalls and unfold it, staring down at the final box left unchecked.

Visit Dracula's Castle in Transylvania.

I've already gotten my first assignment as a groundskeeping assistant, which is probably a nice way of saying I'll be taking out the garbage and picking up dog turds. I signed a contract ... and I'm not sure how I'd go about getting out of it.

I bite my lip, but before I can say anything, Leo wraps an arm around me, pulling me into a hug. He kisses my forehead as he strokes his hand down my back.

"Come on. We've got an hour-long drive to the airport, and I don't want to get stuck in traffic."

"Yeah ... okay." I nod as I take his hand and let him lead me through the forest and back to the car.

I'm silent the whole way as I gnaw on my cheek, second-guessing everything I thought I'd decided this morning. When I glance at Leo, I see him tapping his fingers to the beat of the music on the steering wheel, looking as carefree as I've ever seen him.

Is he not sad about me leaving? Did I misread him last night? Will he even miss me at all, or does he know he'll be too busy in his new CEO role?

The questions weigh heavy on my tongue, but the more I watch him sing along to Taylor Swift's "Out of the Woods"— from the playlist I made him—the more I realize that maybe all this time, I was falling in love all on my own.

I think of my sister and the list that weighs heavy in my pocket. This was always the plan, right? Who was I to think I could veer off course?

Tears burn behind my eyes as the realization finally sinks in, and a lump tightens in my throat, making it hard to breathe. Leo pulls into the airport parking lot rather than going through the drop-off line.

"You don't have to stay. I'm more than capable of checking myself in," I say, pulling the latch of the door handle the very moment he puts the car in park.

"Ivy, what are you—" Leo's words are interrupted as I jump out of the car, rushing to the trunk to grab my things.

Maybe he isn't upset about saying goodbye, but I don't think I can look him in the eyes right now without crying, and the last thing I want is for him to take pity on the twenty-two-year-old who caught feelings when he'd made it abundantly clear what his motives were.

I feel like such an idiot. Of course he'd follow the plan without question. It's the only reason either of us was helping each other, and it's not like I ever told him I had second thoughts.

I tap my foot as I impatiently wait for him to pop the trunk, holding back the stinging tears.

He walks to stand beside me, placing a palm over mine for just a moment before I snatch my hand away.

"Leo, don't. Just ... just open the trunk and let me get my stuff. Let's not drag this out any longer than we need to ..."

I can feel his gaze on me as he stands there, probably trying to decipher my closed-off body language and feeling confused because this is what I've been talking about ever since we met.

"Ivy ... I want you to know -"

"Just open the trunk, Leo," I bite out, my tear-filled eyes looking up to meet his, where he gives me a look of utter confusion.

He reaches for me, but I take a step back, shaking my

head, feeling so stupid and heartbroken with only myself to blame.

His lips roll together, and if I didn't know better, I swear I'd think he was trying to hold back a smile.

Great, so he agrees that I am being ridiculous. Fantastic. I suppose it helps to know this was one-sided, that I've been misreading his signals for weeks. At least by tonight, I'll be on the other side of the world, and I can pretend this never happened. Hell, maybe I'll move there permanently, and then I'll never have to worry about seeing him ever again or hearing his name or anything that reminds me of Ashford Falls.

He clicks a button, and the trunk pops open, revealing not just one, but two large suitcases. I look at him in confusion as the tiniest spark of hope flutters in my chest.

This time, his lips pull into a full-on grin, and his eyes crinkle at the corners. He takes a step, closing the distance between us, and he tilts my chin and brushes my hair from my face. "If you thought for one second that I'd let you move halfway across the world without me, then you're even crazier than I thought, baby girl."

I shake my head. "What? No. Leo, what are you saying? You can't come with me. You're the CEO now. I can't let you give that up for me. It's everything you've always wanted ..."

He runs his thumb over my trembling lip as he stares down at me. "You, Ivy Lane, are everything I've ever wanted. I just didn't know it until I found you wandering around in those woods."

"You can't. I can't let you give this up for me—"

"Ivy, baby, I'm not giving anything up. I don't have to."

My brows furrow. "I don't understand."

"Someone once told me that things aren't always black and white; sometimes, the solution is in the in-between. So, last night, after you fell asleep, I called my brother and offered him a new job. Roman agreed to oversee the US production while I focus on growing our international presence ... starting in Romania." He touches his finger to the tip of my nose, wiping a tear away.

I shake my head. "What? How? Are you serious right now? But I thought you'd want to be involved in everything ... to make sure things are done to your standard ..."

He shrugs. "That was the old me. The new Leo realizes that systems work more efficiently when there's a diverse group sharing the responsibility, and we've built a team of dependable people. I can't do it all on my own, and I don't want to."

"Oh my God, so this is real? This is really happening?"

He pulls out his phone to show me the boarding passes—two one-way first-class tickets to Romania. "I'm coming with you, and I'll fly back and forth when I need to, but there's nothing that could keep me away, and I couldn't dream of asking you to give up this adventure for me.

"I love you, Ivy, and I'm in this. You lead the way, and I will move mountains to make sure I'm standing right beside you—that is, as long as you *want* me there ..."

I don't wait for him to finish before I'm jumping in his arms, wrapping my legs around his waist. "Thank God, because I love you too. I was so afraid it was just me."

I kiss him so deeply that everything around us falls away, and it's just the two of us. He grips my ass, tightening his hold on me, and I can feel his enthusiasm growing more and more intense. I'm seconds away from climbing back into that car and letting him give me a proper apology for scaring me like that, but then he pulls away, breaking our kiss.

"It wasn't just you. I've been in love with you ever since that night you had that asthma attack and you told me about your sister's list. I was so scared, and I knew right then and there that I'd stop at nothing to help you check every single box. I was a goner long before I let myself admit it, but I didn't want to impact your decision to leave. I didn't want you to give this up for me. I only wish I'd thought of this plan earlier, so I didn't have to suffer as the days ticked by way too damn fast."

I press my forehead to his, finally feeling the knot in my stomach disappear as the formerly sunny sky grows darker and rain clouds fill the sky around us.

Leo carefully sets me down, grabbing both suitcases from his trunk. He nods his head toward the terminal. "Come on, baby girl. Let's go check off that last box."

He doesn't have to tell me twice as I skip a step to keep up with his quick pace, not even trying to take my bag because I know he won't let me carry it anyway.

"And then what will I do after I finish the list? How am I supposed to know what happens next?"

He pauses his steps and turns to look at me. "Then, we'll make a new one, filled with all the things we want to do together. We'll write our own dreams, and I will follow you to the ends of the earth to make sure you get to experience every single one." He quirks a brow. "How does that sound?"

"Perfect."

EPILOGUE

Leo

Three Years Later

I trace my thumb over the scar on her leg that's almost identical to mine, the scar that, thanks to Ivy, I've now grown to love.

I don't know why I'm so anxious. This night isn't about me; it's all Ivy.

She looks so fucking gorgeous tonight. She's wearing a floor-length fitted red gown with a deep slit that reveals her shapely legs... which is why I'm struggling to keep my hands to myself.

Fuck, this woman is incredible, and with every day that passes, I find myself falling more and more in love with her. I've never met someone with so much spunk, like her soul is a fragment of the actual sun. It's an addictive, magnetic energy that warms even the coldest hearts, and no one can resist her charm.

It's why she's being recognized tonight as the youngest recipient of *Glint Magazine's* 30 Under 30 Most Impactful Entrepreneurs award, and I don't think anyone who knows her is the least bit surprised.

It turns out, Ivy has quite the knack for planning and organizing events despite her chaotic mannerisms and impulsivity—or maybe *because* of it. It's like she sees every possibility where most people can only see a few. She isn't afraid to dream big or take chances. She isn't afraid of looking dumb or failing for that matter, and she certainly isn't afraid to roll up her sleeves and take on the job that everyone else thinks they're too good to do.

I fell in love with her all over again, watching her grow into herself in Romania. My headstrong, hardworking girl started out at the bottom—she was literally the designated dog-shit cleaner—and despite my begging, she refused to let me make a call to get her a better placement. She insisted she needed to do her time and learn everything she could. She worked every entry-level position she was assigned with a sense of pride and respect and inspired everyone around her to do the same.

After she fulfilled her one-year contract in Romania, we moved back to the states, and I'm happy to say we now both call Ashford Falls home. I paid off her mother's medical bills, and—with Ivy's permission—had her transferred to the next town over, to the finest inpatient living facility in the state. Their relationship is still pretty rocky, but the time and space Ivy's had to chase her dreams has helped relieve some of the tension between them.

Now her dad's a whole other story.

As soon as word got out to the media about our whirlwind relationship, Mr. Lane didn't hesitate to reach out... or should I say, hold his *hand* out... I stood by my strong, heart-of-gold girlfriend when she declined his every request to reach her, and I supported her when she ultimately told him not to contact her anymore. I had to refrain from the urge to tell him that *I'm* her daddy now... There are some people who deserve our forgiveness, and some that don't. I'm proud of Ivy for respecting herself and knowing when to draw those boundaries.

It's why she's here tonight, why she's been honored with such a prestigious award, and only one of the countless things I love about her.

Her ability to connect with everyone she meets with curiosity and a desire to really see them is her secret weapon —that and her dedication to doing a good job. It's as if she has the Midas touch, transforming every project she's worked on into gold, with her warmth and showstopping smile.

It only took six months before she was promoted to middle management, and she just kept moving up from there. By the time her contract was up, she had permanent job offers from four different tourism companies, just from word of mouth alone.

But as much as she loved the tourism industry, her heart was in event planning, and she finally felt ready to start her own event planning company with a focus in eco-friendly and sustainable materials. We even collaborated and are set to carry her brand's one hundred percent compostable party supplies in a few of our larger stores next year. It's something that's never been done, and she's filling a hole in the market that nobody realized existed.

She's a trailblazer with a heart of gold, and I still can't believe I get to call her mine.

I shift in my seat as a bead of sweat drips down my temple, feeling a fresh wave of nerves like a flock of pigeons in my stomach.

Ivy places a calming hand on my thigh to still my shaking. "How is it that you're more nervous than I am? Do you want to sneak off to the restroom for a quickie? Because you know I chose this wrinkle resistant dress for that very reason."

I suck in a hiss as her hand brushes over my balls, and I quickly swat her away. "Jesus, woman, we don't have time for your games. I wouldn't be able to live with myself if we missed the award entirely because we were fucking in the bathroom."

She bites her plump, red-stained lip as her eyes drift down my chest before moving her hand back to my now fully erect cock. What can I say? I've been fighting the urge to pull her away and do just that all fucking night, which makes me feel like an asshole for being so distracted. But that sliver of mesh between her tits has been taunting me, along with the way I'm so fucking tempted to slide my hand beneath the silky fabric ... to slide my tongue along her collarbone, to hike up her gown and fuck her until she's a whimpering mess, just to test how wrinkle resistant her dress really is ...

I close my eyes as her soft touch caresses over my cock beneath the table, and it's as if she knows exactly how to calm my nerves. My family fills in the seats beside us, all turned to face the stage as someone goes on about another award. It really is an incredible experience that I should be paying attention to, but when my girl strokes me like the fucking brat she is, I can hardly keep myself from losing it right there.

Ivy's soft strokes grow deeper, her fingertips alternating to caress my sensitive head and cup my balls. I try to mask a moan with a cough, and my stomach tenses, the threat of my release dangerously close.

"Baby, stop. Fuck, you're so good at that." I try to swat her hand away, but it only seems to encourage her more.

I've never been more thankful to be sitting in the corner in a dark ballroom as everyone's attention is trained on the ceremony.

I grit my teeth as I try to muster the strength to brush her off, but it's like my arms have gone completely weak, and I'm moving in slow motion, like when you try to fight someone in a dream.

"What's wrong, Daddy? You seem distracted. Aren't you enjoying the ceremony?" she whispers as she quickens her pace, masterfully jacking me off beneath the table, and, fuck, it's hot.

I can't help but wonder how long she's been planning this payback. Knowing Ivy, it was probably the moment I did this very same thing to torment her. It's just like my little brat to play the long game.

"Thank you all so much for joining us tonight and helping us honor these incredible world changers. We have one final award to give, as there's been one standout duo who's transformed the party industry as we know it, which has trickled down to an entire movement that is only just beginning."

My eyes roll back in my head, and I clench my jaw, trying

like hell to hold on to the last bit of resolve I can muster. I can't give her a reaction; I can't let her see me struggling.

"Ivy," I growl under my breath. It was intended as a threat, but thanks to her talented hand, it comes out more like a plea.

"With their partnership, they've started a fresh brand of sustainable party planning supplies and merged their companies in a way that is creative, innovative, and sustainable, and we at *Glint Magazine* couldn't let the night pass without paying tribute for their efforts."

What? she mouths, feigning innocence as she dips her finger over my balls, brushing my taint.

My head falls back as I stare up at the ceiling, my impending release only moments away. Fuck, I can't hold off any longer, and I can't fight the images flooding my memory. I have entirely too much material to work with. I try to push down the images of Ivy's naked body, strapped down as I taunt and tease her, punishing her just the way she likes. Fuck, I can't stop thinking of all the things I'm going to do to her as soon as I get her home, how I'm going to torture her so damn good ...

Ivy bites her lip playfully and gives me a wink, then leans in and whispers, "I want to climb underneath this table and suck you off with my mouth... until my lipstick is smeared all over my face and my eyes are watering from gagging on your massive cock."

Holy fuck. That'll do it.

I swallow a gulp just as she gives me one last stroke, the image she just painted pushing me right over the edge. There's no holding myself back. My ears ring, and my vision goes blurry as I come in an explosive rush, and liquid heat shoots into my boxer briefs and down my leg.

Ivy sits back with a satisfied smirk, looking so damn proud of herself, as everyone around us is distracted by the man speaking onstage, and I take a deep inhale to calm my racing heart.

"So, without further ado, I'd like to present the first Glint Innovation and Excellence Award to none other than Ivy Lane and Leo Kingsley!"

Ivy's spine goes rigid, and her look of shock is quickly replaced with delight. It takes me several moments to register what I heard.

My parents both cheer in surprise, taking turns to hug her, as my brothers clap and smile, whispering their congratulations.

"What are you waiting on, Leo? Get up there and get your award!" my mom says.

My head snaps to Ivy, who looks equal parts worried and proud.

Fucking hell, this brat is going to pay for this stunt. She won't be able to walk for a week after I get through with her.

She tries to bite back her smile as she holds out her hand. "Come on, Daddy. Let's go accept our award."

I let out a grunt as I shrug on my suit jacket. Taking her small hand in mine, I try my best to look unaffected despite the warm jizz that's now dripping down my thigh. I've never been so thankful to be wearing black ... or for dim lighting.

The hard ring case I've been carrying around for weeks shifts inside my pocket. I've been waiting for the perfect moment to ask her to marry me, but somehow, it's never exactly right, and Ivy deserves the *perfect* proposal. I thought it'd be tonight at the ceremony, but now, I'm not so sure ...

I take her hand, carefully leading her up the stairs to accept our surprise award. Ivy makes a little speech that's absolutely perfect, and I tag on a few thank-yous of my own as cameras flash. The weight of the moment finally hits me. All of this is only the beginning, and I can hardly contain my excitement for the future.

This woman has completely infiltrated my life in all the best ways, and I will spend the rest of my life trying to keep up with her.

My plans for the evening might have taken a turn in ways I never expected, but I guess I shouldn't be surprised.

Only Ivy could manage to get a thirty-eight-year-old grump on stage in front of hundreds of people to accept an award ... with warm jizz dripping down his leg ...

See what I mean? The woman can do anything...

She flashes me a knowing, devilish grin as she holds up our award. And then, I know exactly how I'll do it.

I think we're both going to thoroughly enjoy her *punishment* tonight...

Want to find out how Leo proposes? Sign up for my newsletter to get a Bonus Epilogue:

BE A BOOK BABE

Do you want to be my friend?

Join my reader group: Jeré Anthony's Bantering Book Babes Where it feels like an grown-up slumber party every day.

We discuss books/reading, I tell my embarrassing moments–that happen all too often, and those hilarious inappropriate stories that only women will understand. Plus Giveaways!

It's a place for positive vibes + laughter + community and all the book talk!

So if you love my books and that sounds like you jam, come join us!

ACKNOWLEDGMENTS

Every now and then, a story comes along that changes you. It changes the essence of who you are, challenges you to see yourself if ways you've been to afraid to accept, and demands authenticity even when you're afraid no one will like it.

Don't Call Me Daddy was that story for me and as painful as this process was, I am forever grateful to have been presented with the challenge.

I tried to like hell to write this story about six different ways, tried to force my process to make sense on paper, tried to fit this idea in a more conventional box... but in the end, fighting against it was too exhausting. So I finally gave up and surrendered to what my intuition had been telling me the whole time.

And I'm so happy I did.

It's not easy being an ADHD writer (who leans toward a Four on the enneagram) because I want everything to *feel* special, unique, and true.

Writing this book broke me. There were so many speed bumps I hit along the way–some so big that I thought they'd surely take me out for good. I questioned everything from my ability, to the story itself. Truth be told, my ego was destroyed.

But then, something incredible happened.

As I looked at myself in all the broken pieces at my feet, I was able to select to pieces I wanted to keep, and I began to rebuild not only the fragmented story, but the real me.

Through the pain, doubt, and tears, I was able to identify the most ideal version of myself, and I began the process of *becoming* her.

Of course, I wouldn't have been able to do that without the help of some pretty incredible people.

To my friend, Julie Olivia... Girl, you have no idea how much your support has helped me over the last year. Thank you so much for always being there for me, for cheering me on every step of the way, and all the brainstorming sessions early on. I know I wouldn't have had the courage to write Bart's birthday party without your stamp of approval or the wet t-shirt contest scene. I owe you big.

To my friend, Natalie Ferrington... Thanks for still being my friend after listening to me whine and complain for the last year. It couldn't have been easy and you deserve an award for your patience. And thanks for the countless Marco Polo sessions, helping me plot this story and giving me the courage to tell it so authentically. You inspire me to be myself and to enjoy the little moments in-between the milestones.

Becca Mysoor, thank you so much for helping me organize this idea and helping me see the big picture. I know this series is going to flow so much better because of your help!

To my amazing beta readers: Vera-Michele, Hannah Kroenert, Carleigh Shaw, Tiffany Noriega, Marielli Prestes Bittencourt, Amanda Dzura, Briana Jacobus, Ashly Wickham, Karrie Valentin.

You ladies showed up for me and made this story pure magic with your suggested changes. Seriously, you have no idea how privileged I feel to have amazing readers who not only support me, but spend their free time reading an unpolished story and sharing ideas of ways to improve it. Your support is everything and I have no doubt this story is stronger because of your suggestions!

Shoutout to my therapist, Jason, who's been there every step of the way in my author journey. Your support and patience has been integral to my ever-growing quest toward self love. Just look at how far we've come.

And lastly, to my incredible, amazing, supportive husband, Stephen, who's been there to fill whatever gaps our family needs. You're the reason for my daddy kink and the real MVP here. I love how you know exactly how to love me. I wouldn't be here without you picking up my slack, or your countless hours spent alpha reading and reassuring me that this story was good. You are a saint and I fall more in love with you every single day.

ABOUT THE AUTHOR

 Jeré Anthony (pronounced like hooray with a J) writes steamy, swoony, and hilarious romantic comedies with depth.

She is a mental health advocate, a lifelong anxiety warrior, and is ADHD AF. Her quirks bleed out into her stories making for an exciting group of characters. Because of her undiagnosed ADHD, growing up she always felt different from everyone around her. Now she strives to create stories that give readers an escape from reality while also helping them feel seen.

She loves a strong cup of coffee and thinks beer + buffalo wings are a delicacy that is unmatched.

Jeré currently lives in NW Arkansas with her husband, three children, dog, and two cats. When she's not writing, you can find her reading, driving her kids all over for travel soccer games, watching cat videos on her phone, or trying to convince her husband to go on another family adventure somewhere new.

. . .

Connect with Jeré:

Join my Facebook Reader Group: https://www.facebook.com/groups/616896780151111

NEWSLETTER: https://mailchi.mp/87e346b13331/jere-anthonynewsletter

INSTAGRAM: @author_jere_anthony

TIKTOK: @author_jere_anthony

WEBSITE: JereAnthony.com

Sign up for my newsletter to stay up to date with future releases, sales, and freebies

Made in United States
Troutdale, OR
07/24/2024

21509937R00284